miller
schotte

LOVE CHANGES EVERYTHING

She longed for love...

Fourteen-year-old Trixie Jackson hopes she has a future to look forward to, but when she is sacked from the local factory she is forced to work as a housekeeper for one of her father's friends – a man she instinctively dislikes. Kept under lock and key, her life soon becomes a living hell, but in her haste to escape she injures herself and ends up in hospital. When her mother is involved in a tragic accident and dies, Trixie and her sister Cilla are left at the mercy of her bullying father, who loses no time in bringing his mistress Daisy into the house...

LOVE CHANGES
EVERYTHING

Love Changes Everything

by

Rosie Harris

Magna Large Print Books
Long Preston, North Yorkshire,
BD23 4ND, England.

British Library Cataloguing in Publication Data.

Harris, Rosie
    Love changes everything.

    A catalogue record of this book is
    available from the British Library

    ISBN   978-0-7505-3160-3

First published in Great Britain in 2009 by Arrow Books

Copyright © Rosie Harris 2009

Cover illustration © Rod Ashford

Rosie Harris has asserted her right to be identified as the author of this work in accordance with the Copyright, Designs and Patents Act, 1988

Published in Large Print 2010 by arrangement with
Arrow Books,
one of the publishers in The Random House Group Ltd.

Magna Large Print is an imprint of Library Magna Books Ltd.

Printed and bound in Great Britain by
T.J. (International) Ltd., Cornwall, PL28 8RW

For my sons
Roger Mackenzie Harris
and Keith Mackenzie Harris
who do so much for me and are
always there when I need them

Acknowledgements

Many thanks to my excellent editor Georgina Hawtrey-Woore and all the team at Random House and to my agent Caroline Sheldon for all their wonderful support.

Chapter One

Liverpool, 1920

'I keep telling you that I don't want to work in a factory.' Fourteen-year-old Trixie Jackson stuck out her chin defiantly as she faced her irate father. Tall and slim with straight brown hair framing her oval face and expressive dark eyes, she took after Sam Jackson in looks.

'Think yourself bloody lucky that you have a job to go to, you stupid Judy,' Sam Jackson snapped, glowering at his eldest daughter. 'It's taken me weeks of grovelling to fix this up for you with the foreman so don't you damn well let me down. You'll go there, my girl, and what's more, you'll like it; now is that understood!'

'You're not listening, Dad, I don't want to work there, or in any other factory if it comes to that; not unless it's in the office. I've worked hard at school and I'm good at sums and I got top marks for neatness and I want–'

'What you want and what you end up getting in this life are two different things and the sooner you realise that the better. I

13

never wanted you or your stupid halfwit of a sister, or to be living in a squalid dump like this place, but that's what I've ended up with.'

'And whose fault is it that Cilla is like she is?' Trixie accused him, looking across the room to where her younger sister was sitting on the floor hugging a doll.

As her father's open hand caught her in a stinging blow across the side of her face Trixie staggered back, crashing against the corner of the wooden table and clutching at one of the rickety wooden chairs to save herself from falling. Her dark eyes narrowed with loathing as she wiped a trickle of blood from the corner of her mouth. 'I hate you! One of these days I'll call the cops when you hit me or Mum and I'll report you,' she choked shakily, pushing her shoulder-length hair away from her face.

'Factory gate, seven o'clock sharp tomorrow morning,' he commanded, ignoring her threat, 'and think yourself lucky that you've got a job to go to. With all the blokes that have come back from the war unable to find jobs there're plenty of willing workers in Liverpool ready to jump into your shoes, remember.'

Turning away he pulled his greasy tweed cap out of the pocket of his brown jacket and rammed it squarely on his thick crop of dark hair. 'When your mother gets back from her charring tell her I've gone for a bevvy,' he ordered as he made for the door.

Trixie didn't answer till after it had slammed behind him. Then her lips curled in a sneer.

'Miserable sod,' she hissed. 'Hope you drop down dead.'

It was an idle threat and she knew it. Her father was only forty and in the prime of life. He was a tall, handsome-looking man with broad shoulders, sharp dark eyes, strong features and thick dark brown hair. He was fighting fit in every respect and a picture of robust health since he always made sure he received the largest portion of whatever his wife Maggie managed to put on the table each day.

If anyone was likely to drop down dead it was far more likely to be her mother, Trixie thought sadly.

Maggie Jackson was overworked, undernourished and as skinny as a wild rabbit. She'd once been fresh-faced and pretty but now there were dark shadows under her grey eyes and her once gleaming hair was now lank and stringy.

She was so browbeaten that she cringed if anyone raised their voice, as if she were expecting a blow to follow. Often, though, blows came without a word being spoken, especially when Sam Jackson had imbibed more beer than was good for him.

Maggie always claimed that being on the receiving end of one of his vicious drunken blows when she'd been six months' pregnant had been the underlying cause of poor little Cilla's state of health. The resultant premature birth had left Maggie very weak and the baby fighting for her life. They'd both survived, but although she was now five years old and should have been ready to start school, Cilla was still more like a two-year-old both physically and mentally. She spent most of the day in her high-sided cot or tied into her high chair till Trixie came home from school.

Sam Jackson had been shocked when he'd first seen Cilla. He seemed to instinctively hate the child. He claimed that Cilla's arrival had brought nothing but misfortune on his head. Up till then he'd had very few serious problems in his life. He'd grown up in Anfield and when he'd left school he'd gone to work at the local abattoir. At first he'd been sweeping up, scrubbing down, spreading clean sawdust and a hundred and one other menial tasks. He'd stuck at it, though, enjoying the company of the older men who worked there and convinced that one day in the near future he'd become as experienced a slaughter man as most of them were.

For the moment, though, he'd been content with his life as it was. He had money in his pocket after he'd paid his mum and dad for his keep, and he was able to enjoy himself. He was popular, he had plenty of friends; girls queued up to go out with him. He liked a drink and was always ready to gamble a few bob on the dogs or horses and he was considered by one and all to be good company.

Things had changed slightly, but only for the better, when he'd met Maggie Wilson, a curvaceous girl with auburn hair who was a few years younger than him. She'd fallen for him at their first meeting and thought him the most handsome, wonderful person in the world. When she became his steady girlfriend, he was the envy of all his mates because she was by far the prettiest girl around.

Maggie had been well brought up, though, and kept him at arm's length, which made him all the more eager and he couldn't wait to get married. His boss told him he could have the one-up, one-down cottage attached to the abattoir if he was prepared to act as caretaker. It was the perfect love nest; he'd no rent to pay so he was able to go on enjoying himself, even though he had a wife to support.

They'd married on a bright sunny day in June 1905; Maggie had looked a dream of loveliness in her white dress and flowing veil. The future had seemed so bright; till one thing after another started to alter.

The first change had come a few months later when Maggie's parents had decided to emigrate to Australia to join Maggie's brother Stephen who was already living over there and had a young family. They tried to persuade Sam and Maggie to go with them but Sam was settled and enjoying his life in Liverpool too much to agree to doing anything like that. He made the excuse that since Maggie was expecting their first baby he didn't think it was the right time for such an upheaval.

Trixie was born a month later and after that Maggie's life was centred around looking after the baby. Sam craved company and began to spend more and more of his spare time at the pub with his cronies. Both he and Maggie accepted that this was normal now that they were married and, in their own way, each of them was more or less content with the way things were turning out.

Trixie had just started school when Sam's mum died suddenly in October 1911. None of them had known that she had a bad heart so it came as a great shock when she collapsed while out shopping, was rushed to hospital and died the same day. The following year Sam's father, who was unhappy on his own, decided to leave Anfield and move to Rochdale to live with his widowed sister.

Gradually they'd lost touch because other more startling developments were taking over their lives. There was talk of war and when it finally broke out Sam was one of the first to volunteer. He'd begun to find that married life with a young child had become somewhat humdrum. Maggie had changed; she was no longer the sparkling twenty-year-old he'd courted and married. After several miscarriages she was frustrated knowing that Sam wanted a son and that he was angry and disappointed because she was failing to give him one.

No sooner had Sam gone into the army than his boss at the abattoir informed Maggie that she would have to vacate the two-roomed house that had been their home ever since they were married. With Sam no longer there to act as caretaker someone else would have to take on the job and he needed the accommodation for them.

On her own, with no money saved and expecting a second baby within a few months, Maggie didn't find it easy to find somewhere else to live. She had ended up renting the upper rooms of a house off Scotland Road, one of the poorest areas in the whole of Liverpool.

When Sam came home on his first leave a couple of months later he was mortified to discover where she was living and even more taken aback when she told him she was six months' pregnant.

On the last night of his leave, after a night out drinking, he'd even refused to believe that it was his child she was carrying. He'd given vent to his anger and frustration by giving her such a severe beating that when he'd finished Maggie was unconscious and had to be rushed off to hospital. It was left to the neighbours to take care of Trixie till Maggie was well enough to come home again.

Cilla was almost three when Sam returned home at the end of the war and saw her for the first time. His first impression was her pretty round face, auburn curls and huge grey eyes.

Then, when he'd become aware of Cilla's disabilities, he'd been appalled and had refused to have anything at all to do with her. He couldn't even bring himself to hold her hand when she attempted to stand or walk. Whenever she had one of her crying fits he'd retreat to the nearest pub.

Maggie treated Cilla as if she was still a helpless baby, but Trixie refused to accept that she was backward and always talked to her as though to someone of her own age. Cilla would listen, her big grey eyes fixed on her sister's face so intently that Trixie was convinced she understood every word she said.

Trixie also encouraged her to walk and

play. No matter how great a hurry she was in she would hold Cilla's hand and let her toddle along at her side, instead of sweeping her up into her arms like a bundle of washing like Maggie usually did.

When Sam Jackson had come out of the army and was told that his job at the abattoir had been given to someone else, he'd been bitter and disillusioned.

Maggie had found it was quite difficult to manage on her army allowance while Sam was a soldier but at least it had been regular and, with careful budgeting, she'd managed to keep out of debt. Now, though, she never knew how much housekeeping money she'd have from week to week. Sam claimed that it was because he never knew how much there would be in his wage packet; it all depended on whether he managed to get taken on or not.

Maggie suspected that it depended on whether he was sober enough to get out of bed early enough to be on the dockside in time to be selected by the ganger.

About a month after he'd been demobbed, she was finding it impossible to manage and asked him for more money because Cilla needed so many special things and Trixie was growing so rapidly that she needed new clothes; Sam laughed contemptuously. He told her bluntly that if she wanted more than he gave her she'd have to get off her ckside and earn it.

Cleaning offices first thing in the morning and again in the evening had been the only sort of work she could find that fitted in with twelve-year-old Trixie being there to look after Cilla. As it was, it meant that Trixie had to leave for school in the morning before Maggie returned home from work and in the afternoons Maggie sometimes had to leave home before Trixie came in from school.

Now that Trixie had just left school, her father's insistence that she should take a job at the biscuit factory in Dryden Street where she would be starting at seven in the morning worried Trixie. It would mean Cilla would be on her own much longer each morning because her mother didn't get home from her charring job till around nine o'clock. That was unless her mother gave up her charring now that there was more money coming in. But would she? Would her father let her? Once I'm working he'll probably give her even less housekeeping money than he does now, Trixie thought resentfully.

There were times when she thought that they might have been happier if her father had never come home from the war. Why should a hardhearted, bad man like him still be alive when so many good, kind men had died?

Trixie felt wicked when these thoughts came into her head but she couldn't help

22

wishing that he would behave as a husband and father should do.

Leaving Cilla on her own meant that for her own safety she had to be tied either into her cot or into her high chair. In the morning she was usually still asleep and Maggie told Trixie to simply fix a blanket over the cot to stop her climbing out and that it would be all right because she'd be home before Cilla woke up. Often, though, Maggie came home to find Cilla not only awake, but screaming so loudly that she could be heard out in the street and both Maggie and Trixie worried in case one of the neighbours reported them for neglecting the child.

At first it had been much the same in the afternoon. When Maggie tied Cilla into her high chair she screamed and cried. Maggie hated leaving her on her own, even though she knew it would only be ten or twenty minutes before Trixie was home.

Gradually, however, Cilla became used to the routine and more or less accepted it. Maggie always gave her a rusk or a biscuit before she left and this seemed to pacify her.

Even if he was off work, Sam refused to look after Cilla, even for a few minutes. He still resented her presence and couldn't bear to touch her. He never kissed or cuddled her or even took her on his knee.

Sometimes Maggie caught him looking at Cilla from over the top of his newspaper and she wondered what he was thinking. Several times she had tried to talk to him about Cilla, hoping to enlist his help with her, but he either immersed himself in the newspaper and refused to listen or he stalked off to the pub.

When this happened he usually returned home so drunk that he had a hangover the next morning and was incapable of going to work. As a result he handed over even less housekeeping money than usual at the end of the week so that Maggie eventually avoided even mentioning Cilla's name.

Knowing how quick Sam was to use his fists if anything upset him she also made sure that she kept Cilla out of his way as much as possible. She was always afraid that Cilla's crying might spark off some sort of reaction but, fortunately, he always seemed to ignore it, even though her high-pitched wail was almost unbearable.

The only one who was always willing to look after Cilla was Trixie. She never seemed to lose her patience with her and was always prepared to bath, feed and play with her. As a result, as the months passed, it did seem that Cilla was slowly making some progress. Even though she was now five and could stand and walk on her own, it seemed unlikely that she could go to school. She would never been be able to understand what was going on around her or take part in normal play or lessons with the other children.

Trixie was concerned that once she started work she would have less time to look after Cilla and that as a result Cilla mightn't keep up the progress she seemed to be making.

'You must make time to play with her and talk to her more, Mum,' Trixie told her when she voiced this worry aloud. 'She understands a lot more than you think.'

'I haven't the same energy as you have to do that,' Maggie sighed. 'I have all the cleaning, washing and ironing to do as well as the cooking and shopping.'

'I know that, but talk to her while you are preparing the vegetables and cooking. Don't just sit her in her high chair with a biscuit while you are dusting and cleaning; give her a duster and let her help you. Let her walk to the shops...'

'Don't talk daft. She's tired out by the time we get there and then she wants to be carried and I can't carry her and all the shopping as well.'

'You don't have to. Take the pram, but let her walk till she gets tired and then you can put her and the shopping in the pram, the same as you do now.'

'You make it sound so easy, but when I pick her up to put her back into her pram she kicks and screams and makes such a fuss that everyone stops to look.'

'She won't make a fuss if you tell her

you're going to do it because you know she's tired. It's because you simply pick her up and dump her in the pram without a word that she struggles and tries to resist. Remember the hullabaloo she used to make when you went out and left her on her own in the afternoons, but now she accepts it. It takes her a while to get used to any changes and you have to tell her why you're doing them and then she stops protesting.'

'She does for you,' Maggie sighed. 'You're more a mother to her than I am because you have more time and a lot more patience and never try and rush her.'

'I tell you what, let's go out shopping together on Saturday morning,' Trixie suggested. 'We'll let Cilla walk to the shops and then I'll explain to her that you're going to pop her into the pram once we've done the shopping so that she knows that's what we both want. I'm sure she won't cry. I think the secret is to talk to her all the time and to keep telling her what you are going to do.'

'Perhaps you're right, I tend to think she doesn't understand and I don't talk to her half as much as you do. The trouble is she's going to have to be on her own a lot more once you start work.'

'Then before you go off to work tell her that's what's happening. Explain to her that she has to be strapped into her chair so that she won't come to any harm and tell her that I'll be home in no time at all. Perhaps if I can teach her how to tell the time you can show her where the hands will have to be before I come home.'

'It still means leaving her on her own,' Maggie said worriedly. 'She's grown quite a bit lately and is so much stronger than she used to be. I'm afraid that she's going to struggle to get out of her high chair and tip it over and fall and hurt herself and there'll be no one here to help her.'

'Perhaps you should pack up your cleaning jobs and stay home and look after her. Don't forget you'll have my wages and I'll be working a full week now I've left school, not just a few hours each day.'

Chapter Two

It was not yet eight o'clock, on a sultry Monday morning in late July, with the promise of unbearable heat to come later in the day. Maggie Jackson could hear Cilla screaming the minute she turned into Virgil Street.

She'd skimped on her work that morning in order to get home as soon as possible. Trixie had left school the previous Friday and had started work that morning so she knew Cilla would be playing up.

Although the biscuit factory in Dryden Street was only a few minutes away from their home, Maggie knew that on her first day Trixie would have left over an hour ago because she was due to clock on at seven.

That meant Cilla would have been on her own ever since Trixie had left and so she was probably hungry and thirsty and wondering why no one was picking her up. Even if Sam was still there he would ignore her.

Maggie thought again about Trixie's suggestion that the time had come for her to give up her charring to stay at home and look after Cilla. So far she hadn't plucked up the courage to find out what Sam thought about that.

'You ought to tell him that's what you're going to do, not ask him,' Trixie had told her. 'If you ask him he's bound to say it's impossible. You need to do it right away before I get my first wage packet and he has the excuse to give you less housekeeping money.'

Maggie knew that what Trixie said was right, but she lacked Trixie's courage when it came to facing up to Sam. She knew she ought to be the one who put him in his place, not leave it to Trixie. She sometimes wondered what would happen when Trixie left home but consoled herself that as Trixie was only fourteen that was years away.

Ever since the day war had broken out in 1914 and Sam had gone into the army he'd been a changed character; so much so that she was sometimes afraid of him, especially when he'd been out drinking.

She'd never forget the first time he'd come home on leave; he'd been like a stranger he'd been so hard and brusque. When she'd told him why they'd been turned out of their little home he'd told her she should have stood up to the boss at the abattoir and refused to move out.

He became even angrier when she told him that she was pregnant.

She hadn't seen him again till he'd been demobbed and then when he came home and discovered that the new baby was retarded he'd blamed her. He'd been unable to accept Cilla's condition; the situation had incensed him and turned him into a complete bully.

He'd always liked his beer, but in the early days of their marriage it had made him merry. These days it made him moody and aggressive and she had plenty of bruises to prove it. Come to that, so had Trixie, although mercifully in her case it was usually nothing more serious than a cuff across her head with the back of his hand or a slap across her face.

This was the only time that Maggie was thankful that he never touched little Cilla no matter how boozed up he might be. Sometimes she wished he would take some notice of her, sit her on his knee or even take her by the hand and help her walk down the road. Instead he ignored her completely, as if she didn't exist.

As she expected Maggie found that Cilla was still in her cot and that there was a sheet fastened over the four corners of it to prevent her from climbing out. Cilla was scarlet in the face from screaming, her cheeks streaked with tears and her bedding was in a tangled heap as she'd struggled to get free.

Maggie picked her up and hugged her, crooning to her to try and calm her. Then, holding Cilla in one arm and hoping that her gulping sobs would subside, she prepared some breakfast for her. She warmed up some milk and poured it on to a basin of broken-up scraps of bread sprinkled with sugar to make a dish of pobs, knowing it was Cilla's favourite.

As she sat spoon-feeding Cilla she looked round the shabby room in despair. How had she been reduced to living like this? she wondered dejectedly. Not for the first time she felt full of guilt; suspecting that perhaps Sam was right and that it was partly her own fault because she always accepted whatever fate dished out instead of fighting back.

Even though she'd vowed that she would continue to practise her faith after she was married, Sam had soon talked her out of it. He'd derided her for getting up to go to early morning Mass, especially on a cold winter morning when she could stay cuddled up to him in a nice warm bed.

She'd been an only child, brought up in a respectable area in Anfield, in a comfortable furnished house where everything shone from all the polishing and cleaning her mother did. She was so house-proud that they even had to take their shoes off as they came in the door and the only time they used the front door was if visitors came.

Her mother had a strict routine, and each day was allocated for special jobs: spring cleaning was a momentous event and every carpet and rug was taken up, hung over the clothes line and beaten; the heavy winter curtains were taken down before Easter and crisp summer ones hung in their place; the antimacassars that protected the arms and backs of the plush green armchairs and sofa were taken off and replaced by linen ones.

Her parents had been exacting but she'd never gone short of anything. They'd lived an orderly life; regular meal times and bed times. They'd been very devout Catholics so it was always fish on Fridays and High Mass on Sunday.

It had been a tremendous disappointment to her parents when she'd said she wanted to marry Sam Jackson.

'He's not suitable, luv; for one thing he's not a Catholic,' her mother had pointed out in a shocked voice.

'I know that, but I'll never love anyone like I love him,' she'd insisted.

They'd finally agreed she could bring him home so that they could meet him. They'd done their best to persuade Sam to convert, but he'd laughed at the idea. Father O'Connor had been reluctant to marry them and had tried his best to make her change her mind by saying that they would need a special dispensation in order for her to marry Sam if he refused to embrace the faith.

Sam had remained stubborn, even suggesting that they should elope if the opposition to their being married continued. It had caused a serious rift with her parents when they married in a register office, one which she bitterly regretted especially when not long after she and Sam were married her parents had gone to live in Australia.

When Trixie was born Sam objected to having her baptised or christened so she kept putting it off, partly because she no longer bothered to go to church at all any more herself. At one time she used to say her prayers morning and night like she'd been brought up to do but the demands of family life took over and she stopped doing even that.

It was only when something went wrong, she reflected, that she offered up a prayer to the Virgin Mary, or called on one of the saints to intercede on her behalf. When nothing happened as a result of her prayers she resigned herself to the fact that she'd deserted God and now he and his angels were turning their back on her.

When Trixie was old enough to start school Maggie made a futile attempt to send her to a Catholic school but had ended up sending her to the one nearest where they lived. Sam had pointed out she wouldn't understand what was going on and if there were nuns teaching them then she'd probably be frightened to death by the sight of them in their long black habits and white wimples.

Maggie often wondered if it was because of all this that so much had gone wrong in her life, but, even so, she couldn't bring herself to admit it openly. Instead she always crossed the road to avoid any contact with priests or nuns in case they recognised her as a lapsed Catholic and tried to save her.

One of her mother's sayings had been 'You've made your bed so now you must lie on it' and she was trying to do exactly that. She knew she couldn't turn the clock back, much as she'd like to; she had to make the best of what she'd got but it would be so much easier if Sam would help.

Cilla's piercing scream for attention roused Sam Jackson from a deep sleep to the harsh realities of a new day. The bed beside him was cold which meant that Maggie must have left for her charring job some time ago.

He pulled the covers up over his head, trying to shut out the sound of Cilla's screams but they were so piercing that all it did was muffle them.

He reached for his packet of cigarettes, lighted one and then squinted at the cheap tin alarm clock beside their bed. When he saw that it was almost eight o'clock he suddenly remembered that not only was it a Monday morning but that Trixie was starting work today at the biscuit factory.

He bellowed out her name and when there was no answer he threw back the bedclothes and padded across the room, pulled aside the curtain that separated the half of the room that Trixie shared with Cilla from his and Maggie's bed, just to make sure she wasn't still there.

When he saw that her bed was empty he gave a grunt of relief. From the cheeky insolence she'd shown when he'd told her about the job he'd fixed up for her he'd half expected her to defy him.

For a brief moment, as she sensed his presence, Cilla stopped screaming. Then, when he took no notice of her, didn't even speak to her, she began screaming again and shaking the bars of her cot in a vain attempt to either get out or attract attention.

It was stiflingly hot in their top-floor rooms and he felt a twinge of guilt as he hurriedly dressed and left without even stopping to see if Cilla was all right or not.

He was late already, he told himself. If he didn't get down to the Pier Head right away then there'd be no chance at all of him being picked for a day's work. Not that it mattered, he thought smugly, since Trixie would be bringing home a wage packet at the end of each week from now on.

The prospect of not having to dib up as much housekeeping in future cheered him. By the time he reached the dockside he was whistling and calling out greetings as he joined the crowd of men all hoping for a day's work. He didn't even feel any animosity to those who'd already been taken on by a ganger and been allocated work on one of the ships.

It was going to be swelteringly hot by midday and he'd be more than happy to spend it sitting inside a pub and downing a cool beer rather than slaving in the glaring sun on the deck of a ship or on the wharf itself.

Sam considered work to be overrated. He'd been disillusioned from the day he'd found out that he'd not only lost his job, but also his home. He felt as though he'd been kicked in the face and from that moment on everything had gone downhill.

Life in the army had been grim; there'd

been none of the glamour or excitement that he'd expected. Once he'd finished his basic training and been home on embarkation leave that was it; he hadn't seen England again throughout the entire war.

They'd been in grave danger from the enemy on so many occasions that he knew he should have felt thankful to come through it all unscathed; a great many of his comrades in the trenches hadn't done so.

His years working at the abattoir had stood him in good stead in that he could face any amount of blood and gore without turning a hair. While many alongside him were shocked out of their senses and spewing their guts up at the sight of the carnage all around them it had no effect at all on him. To him it made no difference if it was a man or a pig bleeding to death.

When the rats began attacking the dead bodies, he didn't shudder or squirm away from them but lashed out with his bayonet or even his boot and killed them.

The only thing he did object to was the brutal treatment that was dished out to those who suffered from shell-shock. Tying them up to a gun carriage right in the line of fire to harden them up was more of a punishment than a cure and many of them had ended up completely deranged.

What had alarmed him far more was coming home to find he was living in a slum and that he now had two kids to bring up. He'd never forget the first time he'd seen Cilla. She'd been like a little doll with the face of an angel. She had her mother's auburn hair and huge grey eyes, so it had been a tremendous blow to discover how sickly and backward she was and to realise that he'd probably have to support her for the rest of his life.

He was also disturbed by the change in Maggie. It was hard to believe that she'd once been the prettiest girl in Anfield and that he'd been the envy of all his mates. Even though she was only in her mid-thirties her once glossy auburn hair was bedraggled and her skin sallow. She no longer took any interest in what she was wearing and she looked middle-aged and dowdy.

Finding that someone had stepped into his shoes and he had no job was a further blow. After a few abortive efforts he'd given up hope of ever becoming the skilled slaughter man he'd hoped to be and resorted to labouring.

Feeling bitter and resentful he decided that as long as he had enough money for smokes and beer and a bit left over for the dogs or gee-gees he'd try not to think any further ahead.

When, a couple of weeks after he started work, Maggie had started bleating about needing more money than he was prepared to give her because their youngest was sickly and needed special foods he'd told her to get off her backside and go and earn it. To his surprise she'd done just that.

At first he'd felt ashamed at the thought of his wife going out charring but time soon dulled his conscience. The kid was her responsibility and if she didn't want to put Cilla in a home then she'd have to help earn the money to bring her up and the sooner she realised it the better.

It was the same with Trixie. He knew she'd had high hopes of working in an office but to hell with that. She'd be getting a mere pittance for the first couple of years and then by the time she'd worked up to earning a decent wage she'd up and marry some bloke and so he'd never benefit from all the money he'd spent on feeding her and clothing her and putting a roof over her head.

Persuading Fred Linacre to give her a job in the biscuit factory provided a much better prospect. It was right on the doorstep so she'd have no fares to pay. She'd be wearing an overall so there was no need to dress up to go to work. He'd let her keep a few bob for herself each week. Enough to buy a few clothes or whatever it was young girls spent their ackers on and the rest he'd divide between his own pocket and the house-keeping.

He couldn't be fairer than that, he told

himself and, given time, she'd see the sense of it and thank him. She didn't need a career or a job with prospects, not like she'd have done if she'd been a boy; she wasn't going to have to be a breadwinner for the rest of her life.

She was pretty enough when she wasn't on her high horse or had a face like a fiddle because she couldn't get her own way. As long as she found herself a bloke who had a steady job she'd end up all right. He'd bet any money you liked that in a few years' time she'd be married with a couple of brats of her own.

The thought that he would then be a grandfather sent a shudder through him. He should never have got married; family life didn't suit him. For all the home comforts he was getting he might as well be on his own; in fact, he might even be better off, he told himself. At least he wouldn't have to account for every penny he earned, or be expected to turn any of it over.

He was still ruminating on what a sorry hand fate had dealt him when someone called out his name and he found himself being signed up to help unload a cargo of cotton from a ship that was moored alongside.

For a moment, because he knew the job would be hard and tiring, he toyed with the idea of refusing, saying he didn't want the work. Then common sense prevailed. Turn down a shout, he reminded himself, and you might never get another.

Chapter Three

Trixie Jackson was nervous; it was her very first day at work and she felt more scared than she had ever been in her life. Her heart was thumping away nineteen to the dozen and her entire body was shaking as she went in through the gates of the biscuit factory and followed the rest of the crowd of women and girls towards the entrance.

Even though she didn't want to work there or in a factory of any kind, her first day at work was still a milestone. She hadn't even been able to have a paper round because of looking after Cilla so she'd be earning money for the very first time in her life.

She'd been thinking about this for weeks and day-dreaming about going to the pictures with friends from school and all the dozens of things she wanted to buy. Not only clothes for herself, but lots of nice things for Cilla as well.

When she'd talked about it to her mum, though, Maggie had warned her not to make too many plans because her dad would expect her to hand over her unopened pay packet to him.

'I don't want to do that; I'm looking forward to opening it myself. Why can't I hand over what I have to give you and keep the rest and spend it whatever way I wish?'

'Your dad won't agree to that, luv,' her mother sighed, shaking her head. 'Don't worry about it,' she went on quickly when she saw Trixie's shoulders sag, 'I'll make sure that he gives you back some pocket money.'

'Yes, and knowing him, he'll trouser half the rest before he hands any over to you for housekeeping,' Trixie said in a disparaging voice. 'Either that, or he'll give you less himself.'

'You're probably right,' Maggie sighed, 'but we'll have to wait and see. Make sure you don't say anything that might get his back up when you hand him your pay packet,' she warned. 'Go along with his wishes for the time being and I'll help you to sort it all out later if we have to.'

Trixie knew her mum was right and even though it wasn't what she wanted to do, any more than going to work in a factory was the sort of job she dreamed of doing, she realised that it made sense and promised to do as she advised.

Far more worrying was actually going to work for the first time. She knew she'd have to wear some sort of overall, but nevertheless she made sure that her hair was well brushed and gleaming because she was anxious to make a good impression on her first day.

Her Mum had shaken her awake before she left the house at half past six that morning, reminding her that she had to be at the factory by seven o'clock.

'Don't forget, I've washed and ironed your blouse and skirt ready for you and left them to air on the clothes horse in front of the fire,' she said.

'Whatever you do don't go making a noise and waking your dad up. He had a skinful last night so he won't be in the best of moods,' she cautioned. 'Before you leave make sure the cover is on Cilla's cot so that she can't get out because I won't be home till gone nine and she's bound to be awake long before then.'

'Are you sure I shouldn't call Dad? He ought to be at the dockside before eight o'clock!'

'Yes, I know that,' her mother sighed, 'but he may decide to have a lie in instead of going to work today. It depends on how he feels. If he does wake up before you leave then make him a cup of tea but don't mention going to work or anything else that might upset him. Do you understand?'

'Yes, Mum, don't worry I won't have time

to start an argument with him. I want to get to work on time myself.'

'You'll be fine, luv!' Maggie gave her a reassuring kiss. 'Work's not all that different from going to school; mind you, do as you're told and don't answer back.'

To Trixie's relief her dad had still been snoring his head off when she was dressed and ready to leave so she'd checked that Cilla was all right and then crept out as quietly as possible.

The factory was only a few hundred yards away and Trixie knew she could have made it in five minutes but she wanted to be there in good time.

Her dad had told her to ask for Fred Linacre the foreman who was one of his drinking mates. He'd also told her over and over again to remember that she was lucky to get taken on since she had no experience and there were ten people after every job in Liverpool.

Fred Linacre was a wiry, sharp-faced man who wore pebble glasses perched on his beak-like nose. He was standing just inside the entrance and although it was over five minutes before seven o'clock, he tapped ominously on his watch as she made herself known to him.

Trixie was not the only new girl starting work there on that Monday morning. The other newcomer was Ivy O'Malley, a small

43

dark haired girl with vivid blue eyes who was a few years older than Trixie.

Fred Linacre ordered one of the charge-hands, Dora Porter, a worried-looking, plain-faced girl in her late twenties, to show them where they were to hang their coats and to find them some overalls so that they could take their places on the assembly line and not waste any more time.

Dora hurried them through to a small room at the back of the building and told them to hang up their coats on one of the pegs. All of them were already in use so Trixie put hers on top of someone else's and hoped they wouldn't mind. Dora handed them both a long white coat-style apron and a white cotton mob cap to cover their heads with. Then, very fussily, she made sure that every strand of hair was tucked inside the cap, checked that their hands were clean, and then hurried them back on to the factory floor.

Under the watchful eye of Fred Linacre, who was strutting up and down like a sergeant major, Dora pointed out where they were to sit. The twenty other girls and women who were already busily working looked them up and down critically as they took their places and Dora instructed them about what they had to do.

Trixie found working at the biscuit factory was even worse than she had thought it

44

would be. She would have given anything to be back at school, sitting in a classroom with her head buried in a book or absorbed in writing or even doing arithmetic. She could make sense of all that because it had a purpose; it was not only interesting but was also exciting, not like the task she was doing now that seemed to lead nowhere.

Each of the women on the assembly line had her own part to perform as the biscuits in various stages of production passed in front of them. Ivy had worked in a factory before; it had been a canning factory but the methods used were fairly similar, so she had no difficulty in understanding what she had to do.

Trixie's fingers were nowhere near as nimble or accustomed to performing the tasks expected of her and so she found it difficult to keep up with the others. The others worked automatically and although they weren't supposed to talk they communicated in whispers when Fred wasn't looking their way, knowing that he wouldn't hear them over the noise of the machinery and the general hubbub as boxes and tins were stacked up or moved around.

As the morning wore on she found performing the same repetitive task was increasingly monotonous. She was also aware that Fred Linacre seemed to take a special interest in what she was doing and that he

45

was highly critical when she failed to do it right.

Over the next few days Fred not only made sure that Dora constantly changed Trixie's jobs on the assembly line, but he also seemed to expect her to work twice as hard as the other girls. It was as if he'd taken a personal dislike to her and she had no idea why.

What really upset her, though, was the way he constantly taunted her whenever she made the slightest mistake, telling her that Ivy had no problems doing whatever was asked of her.

'I thought your dad told me that you were the brightest girl in your class at school,' he would comment in a loud voice so that everyone could hear. 'If there's a grain of truth in that then I can't understand why you're are so slow picking things up or why you're so clumsy.'

If she failed to put right whatever it was she'd done wrong or to do it to his satisfaction he would ridicule her even more and sometimes order her to climb down from her stool and find a brush and sweep the floor.

'You won't be able to make too many mistakes doing a job like that,' he'd smirk and look round expectantly waiting for the rest of the girls to laugh.

Fred Linacre would stand there, hands

deep in his white overall jacket, watching every move Trixie made as she swept the floor, pointing with his toe if she missed a few crumbs, or a scrap of wrapping paper.

She tried hard not to let it worry her, but she felt mortified. She'd dreamed about leaving school and going to work at one of the shipping offices in Old Hall Street. She wouldn't have minded what she did; filing, copying things into ledgers, or even running messages and making the tea.

She'd planned that she would go to evening school and learn shorthand and typing and one day in the future she'd be promoted to the typing pool. Later on, once her shorthand was so proficient that she could take down letters that were dictated to her and type them back word perfect, she might even become a secretary to one of the managers or even one of the directors.

By then she'd be earning such good money that she'd be able to afford to move out of the miserable hovel in Virgil Street with her mum and Cilla to somewhere clean and respectable; perhaps even over to Wallasey.

She'd be able to afford to pay someone to teach Cilla to read and write because she was quite sure that, given the right encouragement, Cilla could do those things as well as other children did.

Sometimes Cilla had such an intelligent

look in her great big grey eyes. It was only a question of finding the right person to unlock her little mind and encourage her to make the effort to learn such things.

There were times when she wished she was a Roman Catholic like her mum so that she could ask the Virgin Mary, or one of the saints, to help her. A couple of times she'd crept into one of their churches and lit a candle in Cilla's name and she was sure that for several days afterwards Cilla had shown signs of improvement.

She'd told her mother about what she'd done, but her father had overheard and flown into a rage and forbidden her to ever do such a thing again.

'We don't want any of that bloody popish nonsense,' he'd told her angrily. 'We're not Micks or Paddies, so don't let me catch you going near any of their places ever again.'

Her father had been so incensed about what she'd done that she'd not dared to even risk doing it ever again, but it made her all the more convinced that there was something in it after all.

'Listen to what he says,' her mother warned. 'He'll beat the living daylights out of you if he ever finds out you've been near a church again.'

'But why, Mum? What does it matter to him if it can do Cilla some good?'

'Your dad's against the Irish Catholics and

all they stand for, as well as any other form of religion, and that's all there is to it,' Maggie told her. 'Mind you, he'll be in the thick of the fray on Orangemen's Day so mind you keep clear of him when they parade through the city because the very sight of them puts him in a real fighting mood. A few drinks and his fists are flying and you know only too well what the consequences can be.'

As Trixie recalled how she'd had to bathe her mother's black eye that had been the result of her mentioning that she was thinking of giving up her charring jobs now that Trixie was working, she nodded in agreement.

It made Trixie all the more determined that one day she'd realise her dream to earn good money and then she'd take Cilla and her mother somewhere else to live; somewhere right away from Liverpool where the three of them could feel safe and be free from her father's bullying.

In the meantime, Trixie decided she'd try and make the best of her job at the factory. A couple of the older women on the assembly line tried to boost her confidence by telling her to take no notice of what Fred said.

'He's a crusty old bachelor, that's why he's grumpy so much of the time.'

'That's right! He's only picking on yer

because you're a pretty little thing. Let him touch you up or even give you a kiss now and again and you'll find he's like a lump of putty in your hands.'

'S'right,' another cackled. 'Let him have his way and you might even get a pay rise.' She raised her thick grey eyebrows and laughed raucously.

'Yeah, if you let him get his leg over he'll make you forewoman. How do you think that po-faced Dora got where she is and was made a chargehand?'

Trixie shuddered at their crude jokes. She couldn't even bear it when Fred stood close to her, let alone let him fondle her. Even the feel of his hot breath fanning her neck made her want to scream.

The only one who seemed to understand her dilemma was Ivy. Small and quiet she seemed to melt into the background most of the time. She was deft with her hands, and had no problem in mastering whatever job she was given.

'I left my job at the canning factory because the chargehand was a chap like Fred Linacre,' she confided in Trixie at the end of the first week as they were taking off their overalls ready to leave. 'He picked on me from day one,' she added.

'I really do try to do my best, surely he must realise that,' Trixie sighed as she took her coat off the hook and put it on.

'That's got nothing to do with it,' Ivy laughed. 'It's because you cringe whenever he stands near you or try to move away,' she explained.

'I can't help it! It's horrible when he's so close that I can feel him breathing down my neck.' Trixie shuddered and turned up her coat collar.

'Don't I know it? This chap I've been telling you about was the same. He was always making advances to the youngest and prettiest girls there and, like Fred, he had his favourites. If you didn't mind him giving you the odd sly squeeze or letting him kiss and cuddle you, then you couldn't go wrong. The work could pile up in front of you and he'd simply stop the belt and make one of the others help you clear your pile. In my case, he'd stop the belt but make a scene and tell everyone that it was because I couldn't keep up and that it was costing them money because they'd lose their bonus.'

'So you weren't one of his favourites?' Trixie said dryly.

'I felt the same way about him as you do about Fred Linacre,' Ivy told her as she pulled on her hat.

'So what happened? Did you simply hand in your notice, or did you get the sack?'

'I stood up to him. One day when he put his arm around me and squeezed me tight up against him, I swung round and slapped him across the face.'

'Oh, Ivy!' Trixie stared at her with a mixture of horror and admiration on her face.

'It was what all the rest of the women had said time and again they wanted to do when he got fresh with them,' she laughed.

'So did a big cheer go up?'

'No, everyone looked pleased, but not one of them took my part or spoke up for me when he ordered me to leave there and then,' Ivy said, her voice tinged with bitterness. 'They were all afraid of getting into trouble and losing their jobs.'

Trixie's eyes widened. 'So what happened?'

'I was dismissed on the spot; even though he was the one who was in the wrong.'

'Couldn't you have appealed to his boss or someone?'

'What good would that have done? He was a nasty piece of work; he'd have twisted things around so that I would be the one in the wrong and it would be his word against mine and I'd have been given the sack anyway.'

'It's exactly what I'd like to do to Fred Linacre when he comes near me but I wouldn't dare because he drinks at the same pub as my dad. If I got the sack I'd get a leathering from my dad as well,' she added ruefully.

They looked at each other in dismay then Trixie started laughing and, after a moment,

Ivy joined in. They laughed so much that tears were streaming down their faces by the time they reached the factory gates.

'You've cheered me up,' Trixie told her when they said goodbye to each other on the corner of Scotland Road. 'I was so miserable that I didn't know how I was ever going to make myself come back again on Monday morning. Talking to you has changed all that.'

'Good. Remember, it's always "them" and "us" so perhaps the two of us should stick together from now on,' Ivy suggested.

'And make sure we don't let "them" get us down,' Trixie agreed fervently.

'See you Monday morning, then, bright and early,' Ivy grinned as she crossed the road and headed for the maze of streets on the far side of Scotland Road.

Chapter Four

At first Trixie found it very hard to get used to working at the biscuit factory. She knew that without Ivy's support and encouragement she would never have managed to endure the long day or survive Fred's constant nagging and taunting which made her so nervous that she ended up making even more mistakes.

There were so many different jobs to be learned because the factory made such a wide variety of biscuits. Some days it was straightforward enough when they were making the plainer biscuits like Marie, Shortbread, Gingers, Arrowroot or even Garibaldi. With these they merely had to check that the finished biscuits were all intact and the right shape before they were carefully stacked into the big square tins at the end of the line ready to be taken to grocery shops all over the Liverpool area.

At other times, when they had to add a filling or decorate the biscuits as they passed by, it was far more complicated. One girl would put on a blob of white icing, and the next would top it with a dot of bright red or some other colour. Or they would have to add a layer of custard cream or jam as a filling and then the next girl would add a biscuit on top, like a sandwich.

The worst job was when they had to smear the cream filling over a very thin wafer biscuit which would then be topped with another wafer and so on till it was three or four layers deep.

In time, though, she found she was actually begin to enjoy the variety of her work. She also learned to more or less ignore Fred's constant sarcastic remarks. She knew that the moment she and Ivy were on their own they'd have a good laugh about what he'd said or done to try and humiliate her and how she'd reacted.

It had become almost a game with them. When they met up each morning before they started work they'd try and work out how Fred would try to victimise Trixie before the day was out.

She and Ivy had become such good friends that after a few weeks they shared confidences about most things, including talking quite a lot about their respective families.

Trixie knew that Ivy's mother was a widow and that Ivy's father had been killed right at the beginning of the war. She also knew that Ivy had an older brother, Jake, and a sister called Hazel.

'Hazel has already left home and Jake's three years older than me and he works over at Camell Laird's shipyard in Birkenhead,' Ivy confided. 'We both give up practically all our wages to help Mum make ends meet, but with the price of everything going up we're still on the bread-line. It will be easier when Jake finishes his apprenticeship and starts earning a man's wage.'

'Why doesn't your mum go out to work till then?' Trixie asked in surprise.

'She did till about a year ago, but she was in a terrible accident when she was crossing the road in Lord Street with my youngest sister Nelly.'

'What happened?'

'They were knocked down by a tram,' Ivy told her. She shook her head sadly. 'Our Nelly was so badly injured that she never recovered and died in hospital about a month later.'

'Was your mum hurt?'

'Yes! Mum's left arm was broken and some of the nerves in it were damaged so that she's almost lost the use of it. She can't carry anything and has difficulty picking up anything heavier than a plate with her left hand. It was because of that she lost her job. She hasn't been able to get another one since.' She sighed. 'She was an Alteration Hand at Hendersons so now she does dressmaking and alterations at home, but it's not like a regular job.'

'My mum goes out charring and it means my younger sister is on her own from when I leave for work till she gets in just after nine, and then again in the evening from when Mum goes out around four o'clock till I get in after five,' Trixie confided in return.

'She wanted to give up her job now that I've started work but my dad wouldn't let her, so she's not done so. I don't think she can go on working for much longer, though, because of leaving Cilla on her own,' she added.

'Why's that? Isn't your sister old enough to take care of herself after school or is she ill or something?'

Trixie hesitated. She liked Ivy and she didn't want to lose her as a friend but she knew a lot of people didn't like the idea of being around anyone they considered to be barmy. She didn't think that Ivy would be like that but she wasn't sure.

'Well, tell me,' Ivy insisted, looking at her curiously as she waited for her answer.

Trixie took a deep breath and decided that Ivy's reaction when she told her the truth about Cilla would be the real test of whether their friendship was going to last.

'She's five...'

'So what's the problem? At that age she should be able to get herself dressed and ready for school in the morning and she can play out with the other kids for an hour when she comes home at night till you get in.'

'She doesn't go to school.' Trixie bit her lip, then said in a rush, 'Cilla doesn't go to school because she's different; she's sort of a bit backward.'

'Are you saying that she isn't quite right in the head?' Ivy asked, her blue eyes sharp as she stared at Trixie.

Trixie shot her a sideways glance, not sure what she might be thinking. Then when she saw the concern on her friend's face, she relaxed. As they walked through the gates into the factory she did her best to explain all about Cilla in the few minutes they had while they changed into their white overalls.

'Poor little mite,' Ivy murmured sympathetically. 'Is that why you said you didn't want to go to the pictures with me when I suggested it last night?'

Trixie nodded. 'Any spare time I have after work I spend helping my mum or looking after Cilla. She loves me taking her out or playing with her,' she said, smiling.

'I can understand that. I wish you'd told me. I didn't know what to think. I thought perhaps you were ashamed to be seen out with me because my clothes are second-hand and I look so scruffy,' Ivy grinned as they put on their mob caps and fastened up their overalls ready to start the day's work.

They looked at each other and laughed, knowing that under the white overalls both of them were dressed in cheap bargains they'd managed to find in Paddy's Market.

'Tell you what,' Ivy suggested before they separated to take their seats on the assembly line, 'since it's Saturday and we finish work at midday, why don't I come with you when you take your Cilla to the park or wherever you're thinking of going this afternoon?'

'That would be wonderful; I'd love that,' Trixie agreed enthusiastically.

From then on, spending Saturday and Sunday afternoons together and taking Cilla out somewhere became their regular routine. Ivy liked Cilla from the first moment she saw her and, to Trixie's relief, treated her as though she was perfectly normal.

Trixie enjoyed having someone to share her outings with and who didn't object to Cilla being with them because it meant she was able to do so much more. She was no longer restricted to walking to St John's Gardens or down to the Pier Head. When the weather was good, with Ivy there to help her, they'd even be able to take the ferry boat over to New Brighton or perhaps a bus to Southport or anywhere else they fancied visiting.

With so much extra attention Cilla seemed to improve in leaps and bounds. When Ivy was with them and there was someone on each side to hold her hands she walked more and more. She liked nothing better than to be allowed out of her pram and to be trotting along between them, squealing with delight when they swung her up in her air, or helped her jump over cracks in the pavement.

'I think she would enjoy our outings even more if we took her out in a pushchair rather than in this thing,' Ivy mused as Cilla struggled when they had to put her back in her big pram even though she was too tired to walk any more.

'I'm sure she would but we can't afford one, not even a second-hand one,' Trixie sighed.

'My mum's still got the pushchair she used for my kid sister so perhaps we should use that,' Ivy said thoughtfully. 'She's only hung on to it because of her bad arm so that when she buys heavy things like potatoes she can wheel them home from the shops rather than try to carry them.'

'That would be great if your mum wouldn't mind us borrowing it,' Trixie agreed.

'It would make things a lot easier, especially when we want to go on a tram or bus; in fact, if we use that we'll be able to go wherever we want,' Ivy pointed out.

'As long as we have a penny for the fare, you mean, don't you?' Trixie laughed. 'And, as I said, as long as your mum doesn't mind us using it.'

'I'm sure she'll agree,' Ivy assured her. 'Once she meets Cilla she'll probably suggest it herself.'

Saturday turned out to be so grey, dismal and cold that when they finished work at midday, Ivy thought that it would be a good idea for Trixie to bring her little sister round to meet her mother rather than go out anywhere.

'I'm to bring Cilla round to your place, then?' Trixie asked as they left the factory. 'Are you sure your mum won't mind?'

'Of course she won't mind; why should she? She's always saying she wants to meet you.'

'Well, with your little sister dying and you saying that she would have been about the same age as Cilla, I thought it might bring it all back and upset your mum.'

Ivy's eyes clouded but she shook her head. 'Don't be daft! She'll love seeing her. Do you want me to come and meet you?'

'Well.' Trixie hesitated for a moment. She had to admit she did feel nervous about meeting Mrs O'Malley for the first time, though she wasn't quite sure why. 'Walk to the corner of your street and wait for me there unless it's raining,' she suggested.

'Right. If it is, then I'll be waiting on the doorstep for you, how's that!'

'I'll be there about three,' Trixie promised.

Ella O'Malley was a motherly little roly-poly woman with brown hair, hazel eyes, plump cheeks, a kindly smile and an easy, friendly manner.

'Ivy's talked about you so much that it's as if I've known you for ever,' she greeted Trixie. 'Come along in and make yourself at home. I've got the kettle on. And whose little girl are you?' she asked, patting Cilla's curly hair and smiling kindly at her.

When Cilla simply stared at Mrs O'Malley and didn't say a word Trixie explained that Cilla didn't talk very much and that she was inclined to be shy with strangers.

Ella nodded understandingly. 'An, she'll come round given time,' she said philosophically. 'She's never seen me in her life before so why should she want to talk to me? Better that way than talking to every stranger who speaks to her.'

'It's a little bit more than mere shyness,' Trixie said rather hesitantly. Then, before she knew what was happening, she found herself telling Ella O'Malley all about Cilla and wondering why Ivy hadn't already done so.

Ella nodded her head from time to time sympathetically but said very little. Nevertheless, she seemed to be a little taken aback when Trixie told her that Cilla was five years old.

'Sure and it's hard to believe that such an angelic-looking little girl is retarded,' she said sadly. 'You come with me, chooks, and I'll find you a nice biscuit.' She held out her hand to Cilla.

Cilla hesitated for a moment, but Ella waited patiently till Cilla walked over to her, then she led her into the kitchen, talking to her all the time.

When she was sure that Cilla was contentedly enjoying a biscuit and a cup of milk, Ella brought in tea for the rest of them and began asking Trixie more and more questions about her sister.

'My Nelly was four when she died,' she said dreamily. 'I remember her so well when she was a little toddler. I still can't believe I'll never see her again. She had a mop of curly hair just like your Cilla, only it was dark like Ivy's. Our Hazel is the only one who takes after me and has brown hair. Jake and Ivy are dark like our Nelly was; they take after their dad's side of the family. He ran away from his home in Ireland when he was fourteen and went to sea and stayed over here the first time he came ashore because...'

She'd obviously being going to say much more but they were interrupted by Jake arriving home from work. Although much taller than Ivy he had the same jet-black hair. As he shook hands with her and his gaze held hers, Trixie felt quite mesmerised by the vividness of his blue eyes.

It was the first time Trixie had met him and she liked him right away. He had the same friendly manner as his mother and she felt at ease talking to him.

He greeted Cilla by picking her up and holding her high in the air so that her head was almost touching the ceiling. Trixie thought Cilla would be frightened, but to her surprise she gave a happy laugh as if she was thoroughly enjoying it. When Jake put her back down on the floor again she clung on to him and insisted on sitting on his knee while he drank the cup of tea his mother had poured out for him.

Ivy took advantage of the convivial atmosphere to ask her mother about them borrowing the pushchair to take Cilla out.

'Of course you can use it! It will need a good clean and polish up, though. When do you want it?'

'We thought of taking her out in it tomorrow afternoon if it's a nice day,' Ivy told her.

'Then I'll get on and do it the minute we've finished our cuppa,' Ella promised. 'It's got a bit of a squeak,' she warned them. 'Do you think you can do anything about that, Jake?'

'I'll have a look at it. Probably all it needs is a spot of oil on the wheels or the brakes to sort it out.'

'Well, you'd better get on and do that first,' his mother told him. 'I don't want you getting oily finger marks all over it after I've finished putting a shine on it. While you're doing that I'll go upstairs and see if I have a nice little cushion to put in it for her, and I'm sure I've still got a warm blanket to put round her legs tucked away somewhere.'

'There you are, I told you she'd be happy to let us use it.' Ivy smiled after her mother went out of the room to search upstairs for the things she'd promised them.

'I'd better go and do my bit, then.' Jake grinned as he passed Cilla back to Trixie and went out whistling.

'It's awfully good of your mum and Jake to take so much trouble,' Trixie told Ivy when they were on their own. 'It means so much

64

to me that they both really seemed to take to Cilla and were happy to have her around.'

'Why shouldn't they be? Cilla's a lovely little girl and she's always as good as gold when we take her out.'

'I know, but because she's so slow and is a bit backward and doesn't walk very well, a lot of people treat her as if she is some sort of freak. There's an awful lot who don't want to have anything to do with her.'

Ivy shook her head as if she couldn't understand it. 'They're dafter than her, then. In fact,' she corrected herself quickly, 'I wouldn't say she was daft at all, and if you hadn't mentioned it then I'd probably never have noticed.'

'I hope my bringing her round to your place hasn't brought back too many sad memories for your mum,' Trixie murmured.

'I think Mum enjoyed seeing her and I could tell that Jake did. I think he misses Nelly more than I do. Being the eldest he was the one left in charge while Mum was at work. I used to get fed up of playing with Nelly and start reading a comic or something but he never did; he'd amuse her for hours. Jake was always the one who comforted her if she fell over and hurt herself or if she wasn't feeling well.'

'It must have been wonderful having a brother to share things with,' Trixie said dreamily.

'I had a brother but no dad; you had a dad,' Ivy reminded her.

'Your brother is so nice and understanding that I can't help wishing it had been the other way round,' Trixie said wistfully.

Chapter Five

The first time Trixie and Ivy took Cilla out in the pushchair she was so scared that even though she was safely strapped in she clutched hold of the sides and whimpered as if she was afraid of falling out of it.

'Why don't you walk by her side and hold her hand and I'll push it,' Ivy suggested.

It only took one more outing for her to get used to the pushchair and after that Cilla hated being in her big pram so they only used it if it was raining, although Maggie still had to use it, of course, if she took her out when Trixie was at work.

Cilla loved seeing Ella and Jake and their regular visits on Saturday and Sunday afternoons to collect the pushchair became one of the highlights of her week.

Ella was very patient with her and encouraged her to talk; she knew a variety of little rhyming ditties, as well as all the usual nursery rhymes, and she would repeat them over and over, quietly waiting for Cilla to say the words after her.

Whenever Jake was there and joined in as well Cilla's face would light up and her grey eyes would shine with enthusiasm the moment he and Ella started chanting one of the little verses along with her. As soon as she was singing away with them they would stop and wait to see if she could remember all the words on her own. She usually managed to do so and when she'd finished both Jake and Ella would clap their hands, praising her and telling her what a clever girl she was.

When she was at home Cilla would sit repeating the rhymes and verses over and over again and having something to occupy her mind meant that she was less fractious.

Being able to entertain herself meant she rarely screamed for attention any longer.

In the afternoons, when she was strapped into her high chair, Maggie would give her a big wooden spoon before she left home so that she could bang on the table attached to her high chair in time to the song she was singing.

However, if Sam returned home before Trixie, the first thing he'd do would be to grab the spoon away from her which usually resulted in Cilla bursting into tears and she'd still be sobbing when Trixie arrived home.

Trixie tried to reason with him. 'If you took

more notice of Cilla and picked her up when you came in, or even talked to her, Dad, then she'd stop her singing and making such a noise with the spoon,' she pointed out.

Sam rarely answered or took any notice, but if he was in a particularly bad mood it often resulted in Trixie getting a backhander across the mouth unless she was quick enough to move out of his reach.

'It's a complete waste of time you trying to get your dad to take any notice of Cilla,' her mother warned her, 'so stop trying. As long as you pick her up and see to her as soon as you get in she won't come to much harm.'

Although neither Trixie nor Ivy had more than a few pence pocket money each week after handing over the bulk of their pay-packets, they made the most of it by going somewhere different with Cilla every weekend.

'We won't want to do this very often when the weather starts getting colder,' Trixie laughed as, on the last Saturday in September, they squared up to the brisk early autumn breeze that whipped the grey Mersey to a foaming froth as they boarded *The Royal Daffodil* to go across to New Brighton.

'Why not? The fresh air is so lovely and bracing that it will do us both good after being shut up in that horrible factory all week! A good sharp walk along the promenade when we get off the boat on the other side will get rid of all our cobwebs.'

'As long as we don't all get blown away!' Trixie laughed. 'It's a good job Cilla is in the pushchair because I don't think she'd be able to stand up to this wind if she had to walk.'

As they left the ferry boat at New Brighton and made their way along the Ham and Egg Parade and carried on walking towards the far end of the promenade, which was usually less crowded with day tippers, their talk inevitably turned to what had gone on at the factory the previous week.

The way Fred Linacre continued to pick on Trixie was always the main topic of their conversation.

'He's always telling Dora to move me to another place on the assembly line and making out that I'm not doing the job properly,' Trixie moaned.

'I know,' Ivy commiserated, 'but even though I've tried to get some of the other women to protest along with me about the way he treats you, and to take your side, none of them will risk doing it in case they lose their jobs.'

'I can understand that,' Trixie agreed. 'The one thing that worries me is that one of these days he'll sack me and then there will be all hell to pay when my father finds out.'

'Not if you tell him about the way Fred

picks on you and finds fault with everything you do all the time.'

'It won't make any difference what I say because he'll believe whatever yarn Fred spins him and you can bet your boots he'll make out it's something I've done wrong,' Trixie told her as they stopped to buy some ice cream cornets.

'I was telling Jake about it,' Ivy told her as she waited while Trixie tied a bib around Cilla and helped her hold her cornet. 'He said that if we belonged to a Trade Union, then Fred wouldn't be able to pick on you like he does. You'd be able to report it and if you could prove he was picking on you for no reason at all, then the Union would support you in your fight and take it up with the bosses on your behalf. If they weren't able to get them to agree to sort it out then they'd call a strike and everyone would stop work till it was dealt with by an arbitrator.'

'Really?' Trixie's eyes widened.

'Yes,' Ivy laughed, 'and Jake also said that the bosses at the factory would be so angry that they'd sack the lot of us if we tried to do anything like that so the best thing we could do would be to find ourselves another job.'

'If I could find another job away from Fred Linacre I'd take it tomorrow,' Trixie agreed as they began to walk on again. 'There's not much chance of that happening, though, because, as my dad is forever telling me when he's laying down the law, here in Liverpool there's a dozen after every job that comes vacant.'

'Yes,' Ivy sighed. 'I suppose the only thing we can do is put up with Fred Linacre and ignore the way he rants and raves as much as we can.'

'At least we get a bag of broken biscuits to bring home at the end of the week.'

'True and that was something that didn't happen at the tin-can factory,' Ivy agreed with a grin.

'And we always have something to talk about when we go out together,' Trixie added.

'What we can't change we have to put up with, I suppose.' Ivy shrugged. 'Anyway, let's get the next boat back and talk about something else; something much more exciting.'

Trixie looked puzzled. 'Like what?'

'Like going dancing? Do you think that you can get your mum to put Cilla to bed and so on so that we can do that?' Ivy asked quickly.

'Of course she will, but I can't dance.'

'Rubbish. Anybody can dance. Once you hear the music then your feet will know what to do.'

'Yours might, because you're Irish,' Trixie laughed. 'Are you going to teach me?'

'There's no time because it's next Satur-

71

day. Don't worry about it, though, because Jake will be your partner and he's a smashing dancer and he'll teach you in no time.'

'Jake?' Trixie's face lit up. 'You mean he's coming with us?'

'My mum wouldn't let me go to a dance on my own, even though I'm seventeen,' Ivy laughed. 'This is special. There's a group of us all going together: Jake, his best friend Andrew, Sid, another boy they knew at school, and Sid's sister Katy; it's her twenty-first birthday.'

'It sounds as though it will be good fun, but I've never been to a dance so I've nothing to wear.'

'None of my things will fit you,' Ivy frowned, 'hasn't your mum got a dress you can borrow?'

Trixie shook her head. 'I shouldn't think she's ever been to a dance in her life either.'

'Hazel's party dress would fit you,' Ivy said thoughtfully. 'Mum made one for her and one for me just before Hazel left home. In one of her rash moments she'd bought these two dresses from an old clothes stall in Paddy's Market because they were so lovely. She altered them to fit us but we hardly ever wear them because they looked so posh.'

'Won't your sister mind me borrowing it? It seems a bit of a cheek since she's never even met me.'

'Our Hazel isn't likely to mind; she left it

behind when she left home and now she's married and living in Canada,' Ivy laughed. 'Don't worry, I'll ask my mum first,' she promised when she saw Trixie looking indecisive.

'You get all ready except for putting on your dress and then come round to our place and I'll help you to put it on and make sure it looks all right on you,' Ivy told her.

It all sounded so wonderful and the thought of dancing with Jake so exciting that Trixie couldn't wait to get home and ask her mother if it was all right for her to go with them.

'You'd better wait and see if this dress that Ivy is lending you fits you before you make up your mind,' her mother cautioned. 'If it doesn't, then there's nothing else you can wear.'

The dress, which was sleeveless, was in green taffeta with a pattern of white spots on it and had a round neckline and reached to her mid-calf. Much to Trixie's delight it fitted her better than any of her own clothes did and made her feel very grown-up.

Ivy's dress was also sleeveless and in blue crêpe-de-Chine, the same colour as her eyes, and the neckline was edged with a lighter blue grosgrain ribbon.

'You both look lovely,' Ella told them. 'Now promise you will stay together,' she said anxiously.

The evening was a revelation to Trixie. The lights, the music, so much noise and so many people made her head whirl. As she looked at all the pretty dresses and smartly dressed men she was able to feel that she was as well dressed as any of them and felt grateful to Ivy for all her help.

She made sure she stayed close to Ivy and Jake and their friends. As Ivy had said, Jake was an excellent dancer and she watched enviously as he whirled first Ivy and then Katy around the floor. When they played a waltz and he suggested that she should dance with him she felt herself stiffen with fright and she knew she was like a board as they took to the floor.

After a few minutes, though, once she became accustomed to the pressure of his arm around her waist, she was able to relax. As she listened to his voice quietly telling her what to do she found herself moving in accord with him and the music and knew the thrill of being able to dance.

From then on she really began to enjoy herself and to join in their fun and laughter when they took a break and sat drinking their beers and fruit juices.

When she went on to the floor with Andrew and later with Sid, she managed to get round without stumbling, but it had none of the magic that she'd experienced when dancing with Jake.

She wasn't sure whether this was because they weren't nearly such good dancers or because she didn't know them very well. Sid was pompous and talked rather loudly but Andrew was so tall and handsome that although she felt nervous, being in his arms was far more exciting than dancing with Jake.

It was after midnight when she reached home, tired but so keyed up with excitement that she was sure she wouldn't be able to sleep for thinking about the wonderful time she'd had.

She crept in as quietly as she possibly could after they left her on the doorstep and she was surprised to find that her mother was still up and waiting for her.

'I've had a wonderful time, a night I'll never forget,' she breathed happily as her mother came out into the hallway. 'You shouldn't have waited up, though–'

Maggie placed a finger to her lips and indicated with her head towards the living room. Before Trixie could work out what she was trying to tell her she heard her father shouting at her to get in there right away as he had something to say to her.

'What have I always tried to drum into that thick skull of yours ever since you were a nipper?' he bellowed angrily as she went into the room.

She smiled at him uncertainly, not sure what he was getting at although she could see from his face that he was in a towering rage about something.

'It's after midnight and you've been out gallivanting all bloody night,' he exploded when she stood there looking from him to her mother in bewilderment.

Her face hardened. 'I've been to a dance with one of the girls from work and we went with her brother and some of his friends. I asked Mum if it was all right.'

'I bloody well know all that and I also know that she's one of the O'Malleys from Horatio Street and that they're Irish Cat'lics! You've been out with the buggers after all that I've told you about steering clear of that slummy popish lot.'

'I've been to a dance, not to church,' she protested.

'Bloody Micks! Come over here and snaffle up all the decent jobs. I've told you time and again I want none of you to have anything to do with them and yet you don't take a blind bit of notice of what I say,' he thundered.

'You don't ask people what their race or religion is when you meet them,' Trixie defended. 'They're not slummy, and the friends with them weren't slummy either. Andrew Bacon works in a bank,' she added triumphantly.

'Keep well away from the whole bloody lot of them in future and let's have less lip or you'll feel my strap across your backside the next time you answer me back,' Sam told her furiously.

'I work with Ivy, so I can't ignore her,' Trixie protested. 'Anyway, she's my friend–'

'Troublemakers, the pair of you, from what I've heard,' he sneered. 'Steer clear of her in the future. Understand? Now get yourself to bed and don't let me find that she's set foot over this doorstep ever again.'

Chapter Six

Trixie had been working at the biscuit factory for just over two years when Fred Linacre announced the Christmas savings scheme.

'My dad will be hopping mad when he opens my pay packet and finds that it's sixpence short. He won't believe me when I say it's been deducted out of it because they're saving it up for us for Christmas,' Trixie commented when she and Ivy met up the following Saturday.

Since the night of the dance they were very careful not to meet in Virgil Street or Horatio Street just in case Sam Jackson spotted them.

It had taken Trixie every ounce of will power to explain the situation to Ivy because she'd been afraid it would be the end of their friendship and sharing things together.

Ivy had taken it in good part and merely shrugged. 'It doesn't bother me what he thinks about Catholics,' she said indifferently, 'we can still be friends.'

'My mum says if we're careful not to let him see us together he may forget about it, given time,' Trixie said hopefully. 'He'll probably be more concerned about me being sixpence short,' she giggled.

'My mum won't too happy about being sixpence short either,' Ivy agreed, 'because she says every penny counts. Still, I suppose it mightn't be such a bad thing. We never manage to save up for Christmas so someone else doing it for us means that at least there'll be a couple of bob to spend on luxuries.'

'It's only September; Christmas seems such a long way off that I don't want to think about it, certainly not start saving up for it,' Trixie sighed.

'It will be Christmas Day in exactly fifteen weeks' time,' Ivy told her.

Trixie stopped in the middle of the pavement and stared at her in surprise. 'You mean that you've worked it out, then?'

'Of course I have; I want to know how much there's going to be to spend, don't I?'

'And how much will it be?'

'I would have thought that since you were the brightest girl in your class and supposed to be good at sums you'd be the one who knew the answer to that,' Ivy teased, imitating Fred Linacre's way of taunting Trixie.

They both laughed. 'It will be seven shillings and sixpence,' Trixie said.

'Not really a fortune, is it?' Ivy said pulling a face. 'Still, it's better than nothing, I suppose. Fred did say that we could put in as much as we liked extra each week if we wanted to do so.'

'Not me, not out of the few pence pocket money my dad gives me back,' Trixie affirmed. 'It's hard enough as it is making that go as far I want it to, and I know what he'd say if I asked him for more to put away for Christmas.'

'I don't suppose I'll be able to afford to save any extra, either,' Ivy agreed as they stopped so that Trixie could tuck the blanket in around Cilla's legs. 'Anyway, I'm not sure I want to trust Fred with my hard-earned money.'

'Why's that, do you think he might go off on the razzle and spend it all?' Trixie giggled as she straightened up. 'Anyway, he won't be the one looking after it, will he? He said that they were going to appoint someone as treasurer, so whether we decide to give up our weekend outings or not so that we can save more for Christmas will depend on who that is,' Trixie mused.

'Yes, I suppose it will,' Ivy agreed solemnly. The two girls looked at each other and giggled. 'We're talking as if we have a fortune to invest,' Ivy said.

'If we had a fortune then we wouldn't need to save up for Christmas or for anything else. Just think what it would be like to have so much money that you could buy anything you wanted any time you liked,' Trixie exclaimed dramatically.

'I wonder who will be treasurer though, and whether it will be someone we can trust,' Ivy pondered. 'There're twenty of us on our line who're being forced to save, which means that by Christmas there will be at least seven pounds in the kitty, probably a great deal more because some of the older women reckoned they'd be putting in at least another shilling a week. If they do, then there could be over ten pounds and think what a nice little haul that could be for the treasurer if she decided to scarper with it!'

'It mightn't be a she; it might be Fred himself when he works out how much money will be involved,' Trixie pointed out as they waited to cross the road. 'If it is Fred, then I certainly wouldn't trust him to look after it,' she added indignantly.

'Mind you, he's probably the best person

of all to do so,' Ivy said thoughtfully. 'He's hardly likely to risk losing his job for the sake of a few bob, now is he? As Foreman he probably earns twice as much each week as we do, even if our wages were put together.'

'Or even more. He goes drinking every night of the week. I know because that's how my dad got friendly with him; they go to the same boozer.'

'Heavens, does your dad go drinking every night?' Ivy asked in surprise.

Trixie nodded glumly. 'That's his hobby, going for a bevvy. It's where most of our money goes and it's why my mum has to go out to work.'

'I don't think I ever want to get married,' Ivy admitted with a deep sigh. 'Something always seems to go wrong and it's more trouble than it's worth.'

'What about if you fall in love with someone, won't you want to get married then?'

'I'll make sure I don't. Once you're married and have got kids, the husband always seems to start drinking. Or else he beats his wife up, or does both!'

They looked at each other and laughed.

'It makes you wonder why our mums make such a fuss about saving up to have a good time at Christmas,' Ivy said philosophically, 'when the rest of the year they're fighting like cat and dog or going short of things they really need.'

'Come on, for the moment let's enjoy a lovely big cornet and put off thinking about Christmas till we have to,' Trixie laughed as she bumped Cilla's pushchair down from the pavement so that they could cross over the road to where an ice cream van was stopped.

When they went into work the following Monday morning they found that chatter was all about the savings fund and who was going to be treasurer. Mid-morning, when Fred called for silence because he said he had an announcement to make, all of them waited expectantly to hear what he had to say.

'I've talked to the management about these Christmas savings,' he told them pompously, 'and as a result of my recommendation it's been agreed that Trixie Jackson will be appointed treasurer. That means she'll be the one who will be looking after all your savings from now till the middle of December.'

For a moment there was a stunned silence, then came an outburst as voices were raised in disapproval. Everyone, it seemed, was questioning the decision.

'Trixie Jackson! She's only a kid!'

'She hasn't been here five minutes.'

'She's not old enough to look after our money.'

'Bloody nonsense, picking a kid like her; if it's got to be one of the women, then we want someone older and more responsible to take charge of it.'

'That's right! Someone we know and trust.'

Fred held up his hand for silence and waited till the turmoil died down. 'Trixie Jackson was the brightest girl in her class at school, I know that for a fact, because her father tells me often enough,' he announced solemnly, looking round the circle of faces as if challenging anyone to dispute it.

'Your money'll be safe with her,' he went on, 'she's got good, clear handwriting, so we know she can write it all down, and she's good at sums, so she'll keep the records properly. Now, if any of you want to add more than the sixpence a week that will be deducted from your wage packet, give it to her and make sure that she writes it down against your name in this ledger,' he told them, waving a thin dark green book in front of them.

'Any time you want to look at it and check for yourself that she's doing a proper job of keeping the records, you've only to ask her to let you see the ledger,' he added as there was a low muttering all around him.

'So where are you going to keep all this money of ours, then, Trixie Jackson? Will it be in your sock or under your bed?' one of the women questioned, raising a noisy laugh from some of the others.

'I haven't even said that I will look after the money for you; no one's asked me if I want to do it or not,' Trixie protested in a small, scared voice.

The thought of acting as treasurer frightened the life out of her. She knew how much it mattered to the women involved that the money was safe and she could understand them thinking she was far too young and inexperienced to take on such a big responsibility She couldn't understand what Fred was thinking to put her name forward to do it.

'No one asks you what job you want to do on the assembly line when you come to work here,' one of the other women chimed in. 'You do as you're told; we all do, from day one. Fred's told you that you're going to be treasurer and look after the Christmas money, so that's that.'

'Right, well, now that's all settled, will all of you get back to work,' Fred ordered smugly. 'You've wasted enough time today with all your chattering; if you're not careful, you'll all be finding you've another stoppage for wasting working time when you get your pay at the end of the week.'

Although they all obeyed Fred and busied themselves with their appointed task, there was a definite air of unrest for the rest of the morning. Many of the women were grumbling, whispering their views to the women

next to them, who then passed the comments along the line. There was no doubt
about it that no one approved of Trixie being
put in charge of their savings.

Trixie agreed with them wholeheartedly.
She didn't want the job even though she
wasn't sure about what was involved; the very
thought of the responsibility, she was being
asked to shoulder made her feel depressed
and the remarks she overheard from the
women made her feel very uneasy.

She desperately wanted to talk to Ivy about
it and see if she could think of a way for her
to refuse to do it without getting Fred's back
up. Whatever happened she knew she
mustn't do that in case she jeopardised her
job; her father would kill her if she got the
sack.

When she had mentioned to her mother
the fact that Fred had said that there was
going to be a deduction from their wage
packets each week Maggie had looked dismayed.

'Don't mention anything about it to your
father, not till you're quite sure it's going to
happen,' she cautioned. 'You never know, he
may have been just sounding you all out to
see if everyone was in favour of the idea.'

'A lot of them aren't,' Trixie admitted.
'Some of the women seemed to be dead
against the idea.'

'That's because they probably need every

halfpenny they earn for something or other to keep their family going.' She sighed. 'Why else would they be working in a place like that if they didn't need the money?'

'No, you're probably right, mum. Some of them are probably no better off than we are.'

'A lot worse off, in all probability,' her mother agreed. 'Most things, from coal to bread, seem to be going up in price; everything, that is, except wages.'

Now, Trixie reflected, she was not only going to have to tell her mum that there definitely would be a deduction, but also break the news that she was going to be the one looking after all the money.

Her mother looked as concerned as she was. 'It's not right, expecting a young girl like you to be accountable for other people's money. One of the clerks from the office should be responsible for that sort of thing, not someone on the assembly line. I wonder how Fred Linacre can manage to get away with such an idea.'

'I'm wondering what Dad is going to say. I suppose I ought to tell him before that Fred does, otherwise he'll think I've been holding out on him.'

'The best thing to do is to wait till he comes in from the pub tonight. He should be in a good mood by then, and if you tell him about it while he's eating his supper, you can go straight off to bed so there won't be time for any arguments,' Maggie advised. 'I still think you're far too young to have a burden like this placed on your shoulders and I can't understand what this Fred is thinking about,' her mother said over and over again.

'Oh, I know what he's up to,' Trixie told her bitterly. 'He's hoping I'll make a mess of the whole thing and then he'll have something else to taunt me about.'

'I don't understand why he's taken against you like this in the first place. It's all very strange because your dad claimed that he was a good friend of his.'

When Sam walked in the door just after ten o'clock that night his first words stunned them both. 'What's this I hear about you from Fred Linacre, then?' he demanded. 'He tells me that everyone is putting sixpence a week away for Christmas and that you're the one in charge of all the money?'

'Yes, Dad, that's right. I've waited up so that I could tell you about it.'

'Right fool I looked when he spouted it out and I didn't know a damn thing about it.' He grabbed hold of Trixie by the shoulder and shook her hard. 'Why the hell didn't you tell me about what was going on?'

'I was going to do so if you gave me a chance,' she retaliated, her eyes filling with tears of pain. 'Why do you think I've waited

87

up till now?'

'Don't you answer me back, my girl!' Sam thundered. 'You might be able to cheek Fred, but don't you give me any of your lip here at home, not with me, at any rate, or you'll find the back of my hand across your face.'

'For heaven's sake, Sam, stop shouting at the girl. She only knew today about what was happening and, as she's just told you, she's stayed up so that she could tell you all about it the minute she saw you,' Maggie protested.

'You get into the kitchen and make my supper and keep out of this. I'm talking to her, not to you.'

'Your supper's ready, I'll bring it in right away. Do you want some pickle on your bread and cheese, Sam?' Maggie asked quietly, hoping to divert some of his anger away from Trixie.

'Haven't you any bloody meat?' he demanded angrily. 'How do you expect a man to do a labouring job on bread and cheese?'

'It's what you usually have for your supper and there's nothing else,' she told him mildly.

'Spent it all on fancy foods for that snivelling little brat, I suppose,' he roared as Cilla, disturbed by all the noise, began crying. 'About time you stopped pandering to her and packed her off to school like any other kid of her age.'

Trixie pulled away from her father's grip and made for the door. 'I'll go and see to her,' she offered.

'Come back here, I'm talking to you,' her father demanded. Reaching out he grabbed her hair, pulling on it so hard that she screamed with pain. 'Now then, spit it out, what's all this bloody nonsense about you being trusted with the money the other women at the factory are saving up for Christmas?'

He listened in silence, apart from the occasional drunken belch, as Trixie did her best to explain about the savings scheme and that she would be responsible for looking after the money that the women on the assembly line had deducted from their wage packet each week.

'Bloody silly idea, if you ask me,' he muttered when she'd finished. 'Especially letting a kid like you look after it.' He looked thoughtful for a moment, then a gleam came into his sharp eyes. 'You'd best hand it over to me each week and I'll take care of it till you have to pay it back to them in December.'

Trixie looked worried and bit her lip. That was the last thing she wanted to do. She was pretty sure that if she handed it over to him then he'd be straight down to the boozer spending it. He'd be showing off and paying for pints for anyone in the bar who would raise a glass with him.

For a fleeting moment she wondered if this was what Fred Linacre had had in mind when he decided to make her treasurer. If he knew her dad as well as he was supposed to, then perhaps he was deliberately doing it to needle him and get her into trouble, though she couldn't understand why.

She squared her shoulders and was about to say that whatever happened it was the last thing she'd do when she saw her mother looking at her and shaking her head, an anxious look on her face.

'I'll have to think about that and see what Fred Linacre thinks of the idea,' she hedged.

'What's it bloody well got to do with him? Stand on your own two feet, my girl, that's what he expects. That's why he's given you this job. He's testing you.'

Trixie didn't know what to say. She had no intention of trusting her father with the savings money, but she didn't know how to tell him that, or, for that matter, what she was going to do with it. If she brought it home, then no matter how carefully she hid it away, he'd be bound to find it. Yet what else could she do with it? she asked herself. She couldn't leave it lying around at work and she didn't think that Fred Linacre would be prepared to look after it for her.

It was a problem that kept Trixie awake most of the night. By morning she still hadn't thought of a solution and on the way to work she asked Ivy what she would do in her shoes or if she could think of any way of getting out of it.

'I don't think you can, not without upsetting Fred.'

'I suppose I'll have to do it even though hardly any of the women seem to want me to be the one looking after their dosh,' Trixie said gloomily. 'It's where I'm going to keep it that worries me, so if you get any bright ideas then let me know.'

'Tell you what, when you bring Cilla round on Saturday to see my mum, why don't you ask her?' Ivy suggested as they parted outside the factory gates.

'Why don't you ask her then she'll have time to think about it and I'll keep my fingers crossed that she'll come up with a solution, because I'm worried silly about it,' Trixie called after her.

Chapter Seven

'Don't forget when you bring Cilla round this afternoon to ask my mum what she thinks you should do with the money,' Ivy reminded Trixie as they left the factory on Saturday at midday. 'By the way, what have you done with it in the meantime?'

'Tied it up in my hanky and put it down the front of my blouse,' Trixie told her, patting her chest.

'So what are you going to tell your dad if he asks you where it is?'

'I'm hoping to be out of the house and on my way to see you before he gets home.' Trixie grinned.

She would have managed it, she reflected later, if she hadn't stopped to change into a clean blouse.

'Well, come on then, girl, where's all the money that Fred handed over to you for safe keeping?' her dad greeted her as she came out of the bedroom.

For a moment she was too taken aback to answer. She'd been thinking about it, ever since Fred Linacre had handed her the pile of sixpences and warned her to 'guard them with her life'.

92

She knew he was being sarcastic but his words had left her shaking. It was such a responsibility. Ten shillings was quite a bit more than she received in wages each week and she couldn't help thinking about all the wonderful things that she could buy with it if it had been hers to keep.

Out of the corner of her eye Trixie saw that her mother had come into the room carrying Cilla dressed ready to go out. She hoped she wouldn't try to interfere because she was sure it would make things worse.

She'd thought of saying that Fred had it but that was rather risky as her dad was cunning enough to ask Fred and if he found out she'd been lying then he'd belt her, there was no doubt about that, and Fred would also know that she told lies.

When she'd changed blouses she'd made sure it was still safely stored there and now, as she faced her dad, she was scared in case his sharp eyes could see the bulge it was making.

'I'm in a hurry, I promised to meet a friend at three o'clock,' she prevaricated as she reached towards the clothes horse for the piece of old sheeting that they used to cover the faded mattress in the pram. She'd washed it out the night before. She'd intended to iron it but it was too late for that now, and if she stretched it really tight over the mattress she hoped that would get rid of the creases.

'Stop fiddling about and listen when I'm talking to you,' her father growled, snatching the piece of cloth out of her hands. His face was thunderous and she backed away from the overpowering smell of beer and cigarettes that enveloped her as he spoke. 'Where's the bloody money? I told you I'd look after it!'

'I know you did, Dad, but I think Fred expected me to do it myself,' she said quietly. 'Like you said when I told you about it, he's probably testing me out to see if I can do it, and for your sake, I don't want to let him down.'

Sam Jackson's eyes narrowed. 'You taking the bloody mickey, my girl?'

'It is what you said, Sam,' Maggie Jackson said quickly. 'Give her a chance to see if she can do it, then if she can't, I'm sure she'll ask you for help. That's right, isn't it, luv?'

'Yes, Mum, that's right,' Trixie agreed, taking a deep breath, crossing her fingers and silently praying that her father would accept what her mum had said.

There was an ominous silence. Sam Jackson slumped down into his armchair obviously too drunk to think clearly. He was still holding the piece of sheeting in his hand and she decided she daren't risk asking him for it or taking if off him so she quickly turned the mattress over, hoping that the

94

underside might be less grubby, and strapped Cilla in. She didn't stop to put on her own hat and coat but slung them over the handle of the pram as she bumped it over the doorstep and fled down the street before he could speak again.

She knew she would have to face him when she came home but perhaps by then, she thought hopefully, she might have some sort of solution, although whether he would go along with it was another matter. Whatever happened, she was determined not to let him get his hands on the money.

Ella and Ivy were waiting for them and Ella's face lit up the moment she saw Cilla. 'Come along, then, leave the pram here in the passageway and I'll take the little darlin' into the living room,' she greeted her eagerly. 'Come along in and sit yourself down; I've a cup of tea all ready to be poured,' she added with a warm, friendly smile.

The minute Trixie unstrapped Cilla and lifted her out of the pram she'd held out her hand to Ella and toddled off into the living room alongside her with the utmost confidence, not even looking over her shoulder to see if Trixie was following them.

Ella had already spread a blanket on the floor for Cilla to sit on while she drank the mug of milk and ate the two biscuits she had waiting for her.

'Don't you worry about her,' she told Trixie, 'you sit back and enjoy your cuppa. If she does make any crumbs or spill her milk it won't matter a jot.'

Trixie relaxed as she always did when she came to the O'Malleys' and looked round the room appreciatively. It was not only bigger but, even though everything in it was a trifle shabby, it was also far better furnished than their place in Virgil Street.

There was an armchair on either side of the fireplace as well as a sofa pushed up against the far wall. In the centre of the room was a square table covered with a red chenille cloth and a white runner on top of that with a heavy ornamental statue placed in the centre of it.

On the mantelpiece were several photographs: one was of a heavily built man, whom she assumed was Mr O'Malley, holding a tiny baby in his arms, and then there were several others of the child at different ages. The last one, in a very ornate frame, had been taken when the little girl looked to be about four years old and remembering what Ivy had told her, she assumed it was just before the accident had happened.

'Yes, she was a little beauty wasn't she?' Mrs O'Malley sighed as she saw Trixie's gaze resting on the photograph. 'She was a little angel, just like this one!'

Quickly she looked away, dabbing at her

eyes with a handkerchief and shaking her head as if to dispel her thoughts before getting up and going out of the room.

'Oh dear, I didn't mean to upset her,' Trixie apologised.

'You haven't! Don't worry about it; she often has a little weep. I think it does her good. She'll be back in a minute and she'll be smiling and as bright as ever.'

When Ella returned a couple of minutes later she was carrying a box containing a wooden jigsaw which she tipped out on to the floor alongside Cilla.

Cilla picked up first one and then another of the brightly painted pieces and looked at them intently.

'Shall I show you how the pieces fit together, me darlin', and make a lovely little picture?' Ella said, getting down on her knees alongside Cilla.

Cilla looked at her wide eyed, then nodded and handed the pieces she was holding over to Ella.

Trixie watched in silence as Ella took them and, after fitting two or three of them together, put another piece into Cilla's little hand and gently guided it so that she fitted it to one of the pieces that was already in place. Almost immediately it became clear that it was going to be the picture of a horse and Cilla clapped her hands in delight and grabbed hold of another piece to add it to the puzzle.

'No, my little luv, it doesn't go there,' Ella told her and once again she took hold of the child's hand and guided it to show her where the piece fitted in.

When the picture was complete, Cilla stood up and danced around excitedly, grabbing hold of Trixie's hand and pulling her towards the floor.

'That was very clever, shall we do it all over again?' Trixie suggested, leaning over and breaking up the picture and shuffling the pieces.

For a moment Cilla looked bewildered, her eyes filled with tears as she clenched her fist and her lower lip stuck out as if she was going to throw a tantrum. Then, as Trixie began putting one piece after another together, she pushed her sister to one side and took over, trying to complete the puzzle herself.

'It's the only way she'll learn,' Trixie said half apologetically to Ella.

Ella smiled non-commitally. 'She's bright enough, I can see that. She takes a lot of understanding, though, and that must be quite a problem for you,' she added as she struggled to her feet and sat down on a chair.

'It's not Trixie's only problem,' Ivy butted in quickly. 'I told you about the Christmas savings scheme and that Trixie has to look after all the money each week. That's an even bigger problem for her at the moment.'

Ella nodded understandingly. 'Sure, and it would bother me to be lumbered with someone else's money. Apart from being tempted to spend it, I'd be scared witless in case I lost any of it, so I would. Can't you ask your mum or dad to look after it for you?'

'No, I'm afraid to let my dad have it in case he spends it on booze,' Trixie confessed, red-faced with embarrassment.

'Aah! A drinking man, is he? Well, then, he's not to be trusted with it, that's for sure.'

'He'd be bound to find it if I kept it at home, or if I gave it to my mum to look after.'

'So you're looking for a safe place for it, are you?' She pursed her lips thoughtfully as she took the cup of tea Ivy handed to her. 'I know what I would do.'

'Go on, Mrs O'Malley, please tell me,' Trixie pressed, looking at her hopefully.

'I'd put it in a bank, of course, then no one but you could touch it,' Ella said as she sipped her tea.

'I haven't got a bank account, though, and I can't see any bank being interested in a few shillings each week.'

'Don't you believe it. They like to encourage people to put their money with them. They use it, of course, but it's quite safe,' she went on quickly as she saw Trixie frown. 'You can draw it out again any time you wish to do so.'

'Do you put your money in a bank?' Trixie asked, her voice a mixture of awe and surprise.

'No, no, me darlin', of course I don't, but that's because I haven't any spare to put in there. If I did have a few shillings left at the end of the week then I most certainly would, though. Safest place in the world to keep it,' she added.

'I've never even been inside a bank, so which one do you think I ought to go to?' Trixie asked.

'Well, now, I don't know much about them either, but you've met that school friend of Jake's who works in a bank, so he could tell you what to do. He's been there three years now and he's working himself up the ladder.' She drained her cup and handed it back to Ivy. 'He's what they call a teller, that means he works on the counter and when you pay money in he takes it off you, counts it and gives you a receipt. Other fellas much higher up than him look after it after that and they invest it or lend it out again and charge people for the privilege of borrowing it and all that sort of thing.'

'It all sounds very complicated,' Trixie sighed, 'but it seems like a good idea if you think it would be safe with him. Which bank does he work at?'

'Martin's Bank. They've got several branches not only in Liverpool and all around Merseyside but also in the rest of the country as well.'

'The trouble is I can't get along there, not while I'm working. They close before I finish work each day.'

'They don't close till one o'clock on a Saturday and you finish at twelve, Trixie. If you went straight there you'd manage to catch them open,' Ivy pointed out.

'Would they be willing to open an account so near to shutting?' Trixie frowned.

'I'm sure they would if you had everything they needed to know all written down and ready for them. I tell you what, chook, I'll ask Jake to ask Andrew. Jake can also tell him that you'll be dropping by next Saturday and so he'll know all about it and be expecting you.'

'That sounds like a good idea, Trixie. I'll come with you, if you like,' Ivy volunteered. 'I can make sure you see Andrew and not someone else so then there won't be any problem at all.'

'It all sounds wonderful,' Trixie said gratefully. 'Thank you very much, Mrs O'Malley.'

She felt elated by Mrs O'Malleys' suggestion, not only because it would set her mind at rest about the money but also since it would mean she would be meeting Andrew Bacon again and she'd thought about him a lot since the dance.

'Right, then; now we've got all that settled

and out of the way, what about another cuppa? You two girls can make it while I play with little Cilla. I've brought one of Nelly's dolls down and she hasn't even seen it yet, but I'm sure she'll enjoy playing with it, won't she, the little darling?'

Chapter Eight

The idea of opening a bank account filled Trixie's thoughts for the rest of the week. She looked forward to Saturday not only because it would mean the money would be in a safe place somewhere where her father couldn't get his hands on it, as he seemed determined to do, but also because it meant she would see Andrew again without Jake or Ivy being there at the same time.

She'd only seen Andrew twice since the dance and each time he'd been with Jake and they were going off out together so they'd not had time to talk, but she'd not been able to put him out of her mind. On both occasions she'd been impressed by how handsome he was and how charmingly courteous his manner was in contrast to Jake's, with his big grin and brotherly hugs.

She'd hoped that perhaps she and Ivy might be invited to another dance with Jake and Andrew but it had never happened. She frequently relived that wonderful night and the memory of being in Andrew's arms as they moved around the floor in time to the music.

She'd never realised how magical dancing could be till the moment Jake had taken her on to the dance floor and shown her what to do. She wished that she and Ivy could afford to go dancing sometimes, although she didn't think it would be the same unless Andrew was there as well.

When they'd told Jake about her wanting to open a bank account and he'd said he'd tell Andrew, she'd looked forward to meeting him again. She hoped, though, that it would be at Jake's house because she knew she'd feel uncomfortable if Andrew saw how shabby her home was. Instead, it seemed Jake had been able to tell him all he needed to know.

She knew she should feel grateful because at least it meant the money would be safe, but she couldn't help feeling disappointed and once again wished that she'd never heard about the Christmas savings idea.

When she told her mother about what she was intending to do Maggie looked doubtful. 'I don't think your father will let you do that,' she remonstrated.

'He can't stop me,' Trixie protested.

'Don't be too sure about that. You probably have to be twenty-one before you can open your own bank account; well, eighteen, anyway, and then only with your parents' consent.'

'That's wrong, I'm sure,' Trixie protested. 'What about heiresses and people like that; where do they keep their money?'

'Well, their parents look after it for them till they come of age, I suppose.'

'What if their parents are dead?' Trixie added as she picked Cilla up and cuddled her.

'Well, then their guardian would do it. Anyway,' she muttered rather crossly, 'why bother talking about what people like that do? You're never likely to be an heiress.'

'No, I know that,' Trixie said bitterly, looking round their shabby room. 'I do have some money to look after, though, and since it's not mine, then putting it into a bank where it will be safe seems to be the most sensible thing to do.'

'Sensible, maybe, but I'm not sure what your father is going to say when he hears what you're planning to do. I'm pretty certain he won't be very pleased.'

Sam Jackson wasn't. He took it as a slur on his character, although he didn't openly admit such a thing. He'd tried all week to find out where Trixie had hidden the money because he was sure it was somewhere in the house. After all, he asked himself, where else could she stash it? Not unless she'd asked Fred Linacre to look after it, and from the smug looks Fred was giving him he did wonder if she'd left it in his safe keeping.

He'd even thought of belting the truth out of her, even though Maggie would stick her oar in and try to defend Trixie and say the girl had done nothing to deserve a hiding. He supposed that was true up to a point, although a chit of a girl defying her father was a crime in his eyes.

He was determined to get to the bottom of it, though, for his own peace of mind. After all, it was his duty as a father to do so.

When Trixie came home the following Saturday and with a beaming smile announced that she'd opened a bank account, Sam could hardly believe his ears.

'You've done what?' he bellowed.

'I've opened a bank account so that I have somewhere safe to keep the money I have to look after,' she told him defiantly, throwing back her head and looking him square in the face.

'Oh, you have, have you? You do know it won't be legal because you're too young?'

Trixie shook her head. 'No, I checked it all out with the bank clerk and made quite sure about that. It's all safe and above board. What's most important of all,' she added with a cheeky grin, 'no one but me can get at it.'

His hand went out and caught Trixie across the mouth before he could stop himself. Then, with her scream of pain ringing in his ears, he rammed his cap on his head and slammed out of the house without another word. His own head was thumping as he went straight down to the pub to look for Fred Linacre.

'You should know better than to cheek your dad like that, luv,' Maggie sighed as she bathed the gash at the side of Trixie's mouth. 'You know how quick he is with his backhanders. You should have told him about what you were going to do with the money before you went ahead and did it.'

'If I'd told him he would have tried to stop me, or even forbidden me to do it,' Trixie said sulkily, wincing with pain and pushing her mother's hand away from her lip.

'Well, luv, banks aren't really for the likes of us. I don't know how you managed to open an account anyway. I don't think that any of us have ever been inside a bank in our lives. Which bank did you go to?'

'Martin's Bank. Andrew, a friend of Ivy's brother, works there. I met him when I went to that dance with Ivy ages ago. Jake told Andrew about the Christmas savings and I went into the bank when I finished work last Saturday He had everything set up and ready. All I had to do was check that he'd filled in my name and all that correctly, but it was quite easy.' Her eyes misted dreamily. 'He's a really nice chap, Mum. He's got thick fair hair and a really lovely smile. He's tall and he looks ever so smart in his dark pin-stripe suit, white shirt and blue-and-white tie.'

'Was your trip to the bank simply to make sure the money was in safe keeping or was it so that you could meet this young man again?' Maggie asked dryly.

'Mum! What a question to ask! Of course it was so that I would know the money was safe. It was nice meeting him again, though,' she added with a little smile.

'Don't let your dad hear you rhapsodising over him or it will be more than a backhander he'll be dishing out. He won't stand for you messing about with boys, not at your age. No good can come of it, you know that. Anyway, he doesn't seem to be the sort of boy you should be interested in.'

Trixie looked puzzled. 'Why ever not, Mum?'

'If he works in a bank, then he probably comes from a posh home over Wallasey way, or somewhere like that; not from around Scotland Road.'

'Mum, he's a friend of Ivy's brother, they went to school together. He probably lives in the next road to them, or perhaps even in Virgil Street,' she added with a grin.

'That will do. Forget about him and whatever you do don't mention his name to your dad or he'll be down at Martin's Bank and demanding to know what he's up to. In fact,' she added thoughtfully, 'it might be a good idea if you don't tell your dad which bank you've put the money in.'

Although she'd agreed with everything her mum said, Trixie couldn't stop herself thinking about Andrew Bacon. He was so different from any of the boys she'd known at school. He looked so clean and handsome and he was so polite and well spoken.

When she'd mentioned this to her mum, Maggie had laughed. 'You'd probably find he was quite different when he wasn't all dolled up for work,' she'd warned.

'I don't know about that. He looked very smart when we went to the dance. So did Jake, Ivy's brother,' she added with a smile, 'and usually he's in greasy overalls when he comes in from work.'

'Forget about him as well,' her mother warned. 'As I've just told you, if your dad finds out that you are larking about with boys then he'll tan the hide off you.'

Nevertheless, Trixie found herself constantly thinking of Andrew Bacon. Every time her dad asked probing questions about the money, Andrew's handsome face came into her mind and with it a lovely warm feeling knowing that the money was completely safe because he was looking after it for her.

Fred Linacre had raised his eyebrows in a supercilious manner when he'd questioned her about the safe keeping of the money and she'd told him that she was banking it each week. The other women on the assembly line had also seemed rather surprised at such audaciousness.

'Not just a pretty face, then; got yer 'ead screwed on as well, have yer!' one of them remarked.

'I suppose you keep all yer money in a bank then, do you?' another jibed.

'Fancy you're better than us now just because you've got a bank account, do you?'

'No,' Trixie told them quietly, 'but since the Christmas money isn't my money, I was determined to make sure that it was in a safe place so that none of you would have to worry about it.'

After that they began to treat her with grudging respect and a lot more consideration. They often took her side when Fred started ridiculing something she'd done wrong.

'Give the girl a chance, Fred, she can't be a genius at everything and she certainly knows her onions when it comes to minding our Christmas money.'

'Making a better job of it than you'd have done,' another woman told him. 'At least we know where it is.'

Trixie and Ivy laughed about it all as they

sauntered down Cazneau Street on their way home, chatting about what had gone on that day before they parted.

Their friendship was as strong as ever despite her father's vehement dislike of the Irish. Now that the weather was often wet and cold at the weekends Trixie usually took Cilla round to the O'Malleys' where Ella was always pleased to see them and to have the chance of playing with Cilla.

Trixie would have liked to have invited Ella and Ivy to her home but when she had suggested it Maggie had demurred. 'I don't think your dad would stand for it. You know he warned you never to bring Ivy over the doorstep again. If he walked in and found the O'Malleys sitting here drinking tea and chatting he'd be bound to turn nasty and perhaps order them out. You know what he's like, especially when he's had a skinful.'

'Well, perhaps you could come round to their place one day. Mrs O'Malley has said she'd like to meet you and I'm sure you'd like her. Cilla loves her and she's ever so good with her. She even lets her play with all the toys that used to belong to her own little girl who died when she was about Cilla's age.'

Maggie smiled and nodded, but refused to commit herself to any arrangement. Trixie wasn't sure whether it was because she didn't want to meet Ella or whether she was waiting for a proper invitation.

As Christmas 1922 approached the talk on the assembly line was all about how the women were going to spend their savings. Over and over again they asked Trixie if they could take a look at 'the book' just to make sure they'd saved up as much as they hoped they had.

'Discuss it in your break time and stop talking about it when you should be working or I'll confiscate the whole damn lot,' Fred warned them.

'You'd have a job seeing as how you can't get your bleeding mitts on it,' one woman told him.

'You'd probably have boozed it all away by now if you'd been the one looking after it,' another laughed.

'Or else you'd have put it on a three-legged horse,' another woman chortled.

It was finally agreed that as Christmas Day would be on a Monday then they ought to have their pay out on the Friday or Saturday before in order to have an opportunity to do their shopping in time for Christmas.

'If you go to the bank on the Friday then you can give it to us on Saturday morning,' Dora Porter told her.

'I can't do that,' Trixie said quickly. 'The bank closes before we finish work at night. In fact, I can't get to the bank till after we finish here on Saturday morning so you'll all have to hang around till I collect it and come back with it.'

There was an immediate chorus of disapproval.

'That's no bloody good!'

'We need our money to do our shopping as soon as we finish work!'

'I can't hang around here waiting while you traipse off to the bank on Saturday.'

'By the time you get back and share it out half the day will be gone.'

The women were getting more and more heated and annoyed, so Dora suggested that, if they were all in agreement, she'd ask Fred if Trixie could be allowed time off to go along to the bank and collect the money sometime during the morning on Saturday.

'That sounds all right, but how do we know they'll have that much there in the bank to pay her out?'

'Don't talk so daft,' Dora told her contemptuously. 'The amount of money you lot have saved up is chicken feed to what they keep in the bank.'

'Dora's right,' Trixie confirmed. 'Anyway, I'll let them know that I'll be going in Saturday morning to collect it so the teller will have it all ready for me.'

'Then make sure you tell him you want it all to be in shillings and sixpences and not in bloody great notes, so that you can share it out properly,' one of the women shouted.

'Leave it with me. It will all be fine,' Trixie promised.

When she next took their money in to the bank she explained all of this to Andrew and asked if he could have it ready for her when she came in the Saturday before Christmas because she would only be given a few minutes' time off to collect it.

'Would you like me to put it all up in separate envelopes and write the women's names on each one so that all you have to do is hand it out?' he asked.

'That would be wonderful,' Trixie smiled gratefully, 'but won't that be an awful lot of trouble for you?'

'Well, let's say I wouldn't do it for everybody,' he joked, 'but for a special customer like you it will be a pleasure.'

'I'd be really grateful if you could do that,' she admitted, blushing furiously. Secretly she'd been worrying about collecting it and making sure that each woman received the right amount. If she was flustered, as she knew she would be, then it would be easy to make a mistake.

'You have kept a list showing how much money each person has been giving you every week?'

'Yes, of course I have.'

'Then, if you let me have it,' Andrew went on, 'I'll put the exact money in each envelope. All you'll have to do is to come into the bank, collect the envelopes, and then hand them out.'

'I haven't got the list on me but I could let you have it later in the week.'

'Right, well, if you give it to Ivy and tell her to ask Jake to give it to me, that will be fine,' he told her smiling.

'Yes, that sounds a very sensible idea,' she said quickly, hoping he didn't think she was suggesting that they should meet up one evening.

Andrew nodded gravely. 'If you can do that I'll see you in here next Saturday morning. That will be the twenty-third of December,' he added, jotting it all down on a notepad. 'Can you come over about eleven o'clock?'

She nodded. 'Of course!'

As she walked out into the street Trixie felt as if a load had been lifted from her shoulders. If she was collecting the money straight from the bank and taking it back to work, then her dad couldn't get his hands on it. What was more, she wouldn't have to sort it all out herself. She had been dreading doing that, knowing that if she made a mistake Fred would start taunting her.

Soon, very soon, she thought with relief, the onus of looking after other people's money would be over. She would make sure she never took on anything like that again.

The only part of the arrangements she didn't like was that she'd have no excuse to go into the bank again after Saturday, which meant she might never have the chance to really get to know Andrew Bacon and, she had to admit, she really did like him.

Chapter Nine

Trixie felt a warm glow of happiness as she dashed home with her pay packet and her envelope containing her Christmas savings. Andrew had kept his word and had the savings divided up into the right amounts and all in twenty neat little brown envelopes with the name on the outside.

The women had all been delighted and even Fred Linacre had been impressed by the businesslike way she'd handled things.

'Perhaps your old man was right after all and you really were the brightest girl in your class,' he commented.

He had said it so many times that Trixie usually turned a deaf ear to it but this time there was genuine admiration in his voice, not the usual taunting sneer.

She'd rushed home to tell her mum how well everything had gone and also to share with her the money she'd saved.

As she ripped open the brown envelope and shook the money out on to the table she felt a massive hand clamp round the back of her neck, forcing her head down so that she banged her nose on the table with such force that it brought tears to her eyes.

'What have I told you about opening your bloody pay packet! You hand it over to me and I'll dole out what's inside it.'

'Hold on, Sam, she hasn't touched her wages, this is the Christmas money.'

'That's mine, too!' Sam Jackson released his hold on his daughter's neck and his hand shot out and grabbed at the seven shillings on the table.

'No, it's not!' Furiously, her eyes full of tears, Trixie tried to snatch it back. The answering blow sent her sprawling on to the floor.

'It's mine by rights,' her father snarled. 'If it hadn't been docked out of your pay packet each week then I'd have received it each week. As it is it's now in a lump sum,' he added as he shovelled it into his trouser pocket.

'It's mine and I want it so that I can buy a present for Cilla and then share the rest with Mum so that we can have some extras for Christmas,' Trixie defended as she pulled herself up from the floor and held on to the edge of the table to support herself.

'One more word from you and you won't

even be here to see Christmas.'

'Chuck me out into the street would you?' she snuffled defiantly, ignoring her mother's warning gestures. 'That'll give the neighbours something to gossip about.'

Sam's eyes narrowed. 'No, but I've something else planned for you my girl, just wait till after Christmas,' he added ominously.

Although she tried not to let her father's veiled threats spoil things over Christmas, it did put a dampener on things. She questioned her mother about it so often that in the end even Maggie became worried and told her rather sharply not to mention it again.

'Enjoy what we've got and stop fretting about the future,' she admonished. 'Your dad probably only said that to scare you because he was so angry with you.'

To please her mother Trixie did try to forget his threat but it wasn't easy. He kept giving her strange glances. She was glad when she could escape from Virgil Street to go shopping with Ivy.

It was something they'd both been looking forward to doing that Saturday afternoon; Maggie had promised to look after Cilla and they planned to buy presents for their families and make sure they didn't spend their money on anything else.

Scotland Road was packed with people all looking for bargains and they had so little money to spend, that it was very frustrating as well as exciting.

'What are you looking for, Ivy?' Trixie asked as they paused in front of the different windows, most of which were brightly decorated as well as packed with all sorts of tempting items.

'Presents for my mum and Jake. They will probably both be something they can wear. Not too practical, though, but the sort of thing they'd like to buy for themselves if they could spare the money. Mum hardly ever spends anything on herself yet she loves pretty things. I'm hoping to get her a really nice warm scarf; one that's as big as a shawl, almost, so that she can pop it on around her shoulders when she nips to the corner shop. The one she uses now is so old that even the darns in it have been darned again.'

'And your brother?'

'I'll probably buy him a new tie. He likes to look smart when he gets dressed up to go out in the evening. His friend Andrew – you know, the chap you met in the bank – is always dressed up to the nines and I know Jake tries to keep up with him.'

Trixie felt the colour flooding into her face at the mention of Andrew's name. She wished she knew him well enough to buy him a present to thank him for all the help he'd given her with the Christmas money, but it was completely out of the question since she didn't have the money to spare.

Trixie wanted to get something special for Cilla and, knowing how much she enjoyed playing with the dolls that had been Nelly's when she went to the O'Malleys', that was what she intended to buy for her.

'Why buy that when she can play with them round at my place?' Ivy asked her. 'Why not get her something different?'

'I want to get her a doll that she could cuddle in bed when she goes to sleep at night.'

'Most dolls aren't very cuddly, not unless you buy her a rag doll, and I don't think she will like that after playing with Nelly's because they have real porcelain faces and eyes that open and shut.'

'Yes, you're right,' Trixie admitted as they looked at the ones on display, 'so what do you suggest instead?'

'Why not get her a teddy bear?'

'I think she's too old for one of those,' Trixie argued.

'Then what about a furry animal, like a dog or something?'

Trixie stopped in her tracks and clapped her hands excitedly. 'I know, I'll get her a Bonzo; you know, that little dog that's got those big ears, one black and one white.'

'And spots and big blue eyes,' Ivy added. 'She'd love one of those and they're quite cuddly.'

'I might have a job finding one,' Trixie sighed.

'That's rubbish! Bonzo is ever so popular, there's even a Bonzo comic.'

'Well, we can look. Where shall we start, then? Shall we go to Paddy's Market?'

'That's probably the best place,' Ivy agreed as they hurried up Great Homer Street. 'How much do you want to spend?'

'I've only got three shillings and sixpence and I want to buy something for Mum out of that as well.'

'What about your dad?'

Trixie made a face. 'I wouldn't even buy him a wet *Echo*, the miserable old devil. Do you know, he nearly gave me a hiding because I'd dared to open the envelope with my savings money in it instead of handing it over to him. He tried to grab at it and said it was his by right because it was part of my wages, only my mum stood up to him and insisted that it was mine to do as I liked with.'

'Come on, then, let's start looking,' Ivy told her. 'We'll see if we can find a Bonzo first and then you'll know how much you've got left to spend on your mum's present.'

'As we go round I can still keep an eye open to see if there is anything I think she'd like.'

'You haven't said what you're looking for, would it be something to wear?'

'I don't think I can afford anything like that. I thought perhaps a pretty cup and saucer that she can drink her tea out of when she's there on her own.'

'Mm! She'll probably put it on a shelf or on the mantelpiece where she can look at it and admire it, but she'll be afraid to use it in case it gets broken.'

'Or in case my dad smashes it up when he's in one of his tempers and looking for some way of upsetting her.'

'Your dad sounds pretty horrible,' Ivy shuddered. 'No wonder you don't want to buy him a present.' She paused and looked thoughtful. 'You know, perhaps that's where you're wrong, perhaps you should buy him one. It might please him so much that he won't make trouble over Christmas.'

The two girls looked at each other and giggled. It was a joke that kept them laughing for the rest of their shopping spree, especially when Ivy picked out the most audacious items and suggested they might be suitable for Sam Jackson. In the end Trixie bought him a tin cigarette case with a picture of a boat painted on the front. 'He's always complaining that his ciggies get crushed when he has the packet in his pocket so this might please him,' she explained.

They were feeling tired by the time they'd finished their shopping, but they were both delighted with their purchases.

'We should have bought some fancy paper to wrap them up in, but I've only got three halfpence left and they are asking two pennies a sheet for it,' Trixie sighed.

'You can buy a whole roll for threepence,' Ivy pointed out, 'so why don't we buy one of those between us? We've got to go back to my place so that you can collect Cilla, so we can take all the presents up to my bedroom and wrap them up while you're there without anybody knowing what we've bought.'

'I hope Cilla has behaved and been a good girl for your mum,' Trixie said worriedly

'Of course she will have been. It's not the first time she's stayed with her and anyway, Mum knows how to keep her amused. There're the dolls for her to play with and when she gets tired of them there's always the jigsaw.'

Their plan worked well, and before Trixie took Cilla home she'd wrapped up the presents she'd bought, but agreed with Ivy that it was better to leave them there till the next day.

'Didn't you buy anything at all?' Maggie asked in surprise when Trixie arrived home very late in the afternoon.

'I've spent all my money and I've left the presents at Ivy's place till tomorrow,' she explained as she undressed Cilla and got her ready for bed. 'I thought they'd be safer there.'

After that Christmas Day couldn't come soon enough. Waiting was a mixture of frustration and torture as she went over in her mind what she'd bought and kept wondering if she'd chosen the right presents for everybody.

'That's the trouble with Christmas presents,' her mother smiled when she mentioned it to her. 'They look lovely in the shop or on the stall and then afterwards you wonder if you've done the right thing or not. It's even worse when people start opening them because you feel so anxious about whether or not they are going to like them. What have you bought for Cilla?'

Trixie hesitated. 'It's too late to take it back and change it so I think I'll just wait and see if she likes it.'

'You haven't told me what it is yet?' her mother persisted.

'I'd sooner wait till Christmas Day. You may think it's a daft waste of money.'

'Why would I do that? I'm sure that whatever it is you've picked it will be something she'll love. Have you bought anything for Ivy and Mrs O'Malley?'

The colour drained from Trixie's cheeks. 'Oh, Mam, I never gave it a thought. Mrs O'Malley has been so good to our little Cilla, I should have bought her something.'

'Well, it's not too late to do so. The shops will be open till midnight tonight.'

123

'But I haven't any money left!'

'Oh dear! Well, you tell me the sort of present you'd like to get for them and I'll see if I can jiggle the housekeeping and we can buy them something out of that. What about a box of nice chocolates or a big tin of biscuits that they can all enjoy?'

'If you do that then it's going to leave you short,' Trixie sighed. 'Why do we always have to scrimp and scrape like this, Mum? Wouldn't it be wonderful if we had enough money to buy whatever we needed and still have a few coppers left in our purse at the end of the week.'

'Perhaps I should try and get a full-time job,' Maggie sighed. 'I know your dad thinks I ought to, but who's going to look after Cilla if I do? I can't leave her here on her own all day; heaven knows what mischief she'd get into if I did that.'

'She is getting a lot better at entertaining herself when she's left for a short time in the mornings and evenings. In fact, she's getting brighter all the time,' Trixie mused. 'Do you think that perhaps she will be able to go to school one day?'

'She's still terribly backward, luv,' Maggie sighed. 'If she went to school she'd have to start in the infant's class and they'd probably tease her and make her life miserable.'

'Perhaps we ought to start teaching her at home. Look how quickly she picked up those rhymes that Ella and Jake taught her. If we helped Cilla to learn her letters, and perhaps her tables, then she might be able to go into a class where the other children were only a couple of years younger than her and it wouldn't matter so much.'

'I'm not too sure that I'm up to teaching her but perhaps between the pair of us we might manage something,' her mother agreed.

'I'll mention it to Mrs O'Malley as well. She's probably got some books that her little Nelly used when she was starting to read and I'm sure that she'd help teach her as well.'

'Is this going to be your New Year's resolution, getting little Cilla to be able to read and write?' Her mother smiled indulgently.

'It would be good for her if she could, and for all of us too.'

'That's true, but don't go saying anything about it in front of your dad. He'll only scoff, or else he'll start badgering and bullying Cilla and making her a nervous wreck.'

'Will he? He never speaks to her or has anything to do with her if he can help it,' Trixie said scornfully.

'Now don't start stirring things up by saying anything about it,' her mother warned. 'It's far better for things to stay the way they are than for him to be constantly taunting Cilla or shouting at her; you should know that.'

Trixie wanted to ask her mother again if she knew what her dad had meant when he kept saying that he had 'something planned for her' but she was afraid that if she did know it might spoil things over Christmas so she said nothing.

Christmas Day started off so well that Trixie felt that for once they were like a normal family. Sam Jackson went off to the pub in the morning for a drink with his cronies but he returned home in good time for them to sit down to their festive dinner.

Maggie had done them proud. She'd been scrimping and saving for months to make sure they had something special for Christmas Day. Along with the chicken she'd also roasted potatoes and parsnips as well as cooking Brussels sprouts. Even the gravy was so thick and tasty that Sam Jackson was unable to find fault with any of it and he tucked into it all with gusto.

Afterwards they had Christmas pudding and custard which Cilla enjoyed so much that she even had a second helping.

They waited till after they'd finished eating and Maggie and Trixie had cleared everything away, washed up and brought in a pot of freshly brewed tea, before they opened their presents.

'Sit down and open your present, Mum, while I pour the tea,' Trixie insisted.

Maggie gave a gasp of delight as she unwrapped her parcel and found the china cup and saucer that was prettily decorated with blue and pink flowers. 'It's lovely, Trixie, really beautiful,' she exclaimed with pleasure.

Sam was surprised to find he had a present at all, especially one from Trixie, but he spoiled the occasion by commenting, 'Trying to soft-soap me, are you? Well, you needn't bother. I've still got a surprise planned for you.'

Trixie tried to shut out his words as she helped Cilla unwrap her parcel. The delight on Cilla's face when she saw the Bonzo dog and began making little cries of excitement and happiness as she hugged it tight and ran to show it to her mother, brought tears to Trixie's own eyes and for the moment made her forget her father's threat, her disappointment over not seeing Andrew over Christmas and all the problems she'd encountered at work. She hoped that perhaps everything would be much better in the future.

Chapter Ten

When Trixie and Ivy returned to work after Christmas they were bubbling over with excitement not only about what they'd done over the holiday, the presents they'd exchanged and the food they'd enjoyed, but also about Ivy's suggestion that they should go out on New Year's Eve and celebrate in some way.

'I've never done anything like that before,' Trixie said doubtfully.

'There's a first time for everything,' Ivy giggled as she put on her overall.

'I'm not sure my dad would let me,' Trixie mused.

'Don't tell him. He'll probably be down the boozer so he need never know,' Ivy told her as she finished fastening the buttons.

'What if he gets home before I do? He'd kill my mum if he discovered that I was still out,' Trixie muttered as she pushed her hair up inside her cap.

'She's only got to let him think that you're home and in bed. He never checks up to see if you are, does he?'

'No, of course not! Mum would never dare tell him a lie, though, because if he

128

found out the truth he'd belt her one.'

'So you won't come, then?' Ivy said in a disappointed voice. 'It's a pity,' she sighed, 'because I thought we could go out with my brother and his friend...'

'Do you mean Andrew? Andrew Bacon?' Trixie gasped, her eyes widening in surprise.

'That's right. It's his suggestion, actually. He told Jake he thought it would be a good idea for him to bring us both along,' she added with a smile.

'What did Jake say to that?' Trixie asked as they made their way into the factory.

'He said he didn't mind although he didn't think it was going to be much fun for him having to take his sister along when he asked a girl out for the first time,' Ivy said as she followed her.

Trixie looked puzzled. 'Let me get this right. You mean they've only invited us because Andrew wants to go out with you?'

'No,' Ivy laughed. 'It's Andrew who wants to take you out; he's quite smitten. The trouble is, though, Jake has a bit of a crush on you as well and he thinks he's the one taking you.'

'Confusing, isn't it!' Trixie sighed, the blood rushing to her cheeks. 'I like your brother a lot, Ivy, I think he's very nice indeed but–'

'It's Andrew Bacon you're really interested in,' Ivy finished with a big grin.

The two girls looked at each other and shook their heads in bewilderment.

'So are you going to come out with us?' Ivy persisted.

'I'd love to, especially if Andrew is going to be there, but what about you? Are you sure you're not kidding me and that you really aren't interested in him?'

'I like him in much the same way as you like Jake. That's as a friend, but nothing more. Don't worry about it,' she went on quickly as she saw the doubt in Trixie's eyes, 'we'll be meeting up with Sid and Katy and heaps more chaps and girls before the evening's out. If you must know, I have my eye on another friend of Jake's,' she added with a winsome little smile, 'but I'm not even sure if he knows that I exist.'

Twice Fred Linacre spotted them talking and told them off. 'You can't do your job properly if you're gossiping,' he told them sharply.

'You want to remember that there're almost two million people unemployed in this country and you'll both be joining them if I catch you wasting any more time, Trixie Jackson,' he thundered the second time he caught them doing it.

'Miserable old sod, I thought he'd stopped picking on you, Trixie,' one of the older women commented when they stopped for their lunch break.

'It seems he hasn't,' Trixie sighed. 'I wasn't the only one talking.'

'Well, don't let it get you down, kiddo,' one of the others said, patting her on the shoulder.

'The trouble with Fred Linacre is he's got no one at home to nag so that's why he does it all the time when he's here,' another of them laughed.

'Who'd want to be married to him anyway, sour old devil; he'd be a pig to live with.'

There was raucous laughter as they all laughed and joked about it but Trixie and Ivy kept quiet. They didn't want to say anything that might be repeated back to Fred Linacre and cause even more trouble for either of them.

On their way home, Trixie confided in Ivy about her special resolution for 1923. 'I want to try and teach Cilla to read and write and perhaps even be able to do sums as well,' she told her. 'What do you think?'

'She should be able to; she loves looking at pictures and she can always name all the different animals and flowers and lots of other things such as all the little rhymes and songs my mum and Jake have taught her. How did she like her Bonzo dog?'

'She recognised him right away from the comics your mum has shown her. She's taken him to bed every night and she talks to him a lot during the day.'

'I expect my mum would help to teach her other things; that's if your mum is agreeable to her doing that,' Ivy suggested. 'She wouldn't want to poke her nose in where it wasn't wanted, of course,' she added hastily.

'There's no fear of that because Mum is always going on about how much your mum and Jake have helped Cilla. Anyway, I think it's time our mums met. I'm sure they'd get on well.'

'They might even know each other already by sight,' Ivy commented.

'You mean because they must use the same shops in Great Homer Street from time to time?'

'That's right, so why don't you ask her if she'd like to come round next Saturday afternoon; you can bring her when you come round with Cilla,' Ivy suggested. 'If it's a nice day we could take Cilla out and give the two of them a chance to talk and get to know each other.'

'That sounds like a lovely idea,' Trixie agreed. 'It will be safer than asking your mum to come to our place, because if my dad came home he might turn nasty.'

'You mean if he knew who it was and that she was Irish,' Ivy laughed. 'Remember the time he found me there and said I was never to put a foot over his threshold ever again?'

'I'll see if I can persuade Mum to come round to your place on Saturday, then,'

Trixie agreed. 'The trouble is she never goes anywhere except to the shops. She used to take Cilla to the park but now she says she feels embarrassed if people stop and speak to her and ask why a big girl like Cilla isn't walking.'

'That's daft! Lots of big kids ride in prams.'

'Not seven-year-olds! You wouldn't expect your sister to be in a pram if she was still alive now, would you?'

Trixie felt guilty the moment she'd spoken. 'I'm sorry,' she muttered as she saw Ivy's mouth tighten and her eyes fill with tears. 'That was a thoughtless thing to say.'

'It's all right. I understand what you mean and how your mum must feel.' Quickly she turned the conversation back to their own plans for the New Year; in particular, what they were going to do to welcome in 1923.

New Year's Eve was a night that Trixie knew she would never forget. She and Ivy had talked about it every moment they could, discussing every detail from the time they'd be meeting, to planning what each of them would be wearing.

At the very last minute they went along to Paddy's Market and searched through the rails of the second-hand clothes stalls to see if they could find a bargain.

'I suppose we could wear the same dresses

we wore to that birthday dance,' Ivy mused when they found they couldn't afford any of the dresses hanging on the rails and resorted to looking through the jumble boxes.

'I'd like to have a dress of my own, not borrow your Hazel's,' Trixie protested. 'Let's go on looking for a bit longer; you never know what we might find.'

Eventually, when they had almost given up hope, they had a stroke of luck. One of the stall-holders who was packing up for the night agreed to let them each have a dress from her stock at a knock-down price when they told her they wanted something to wear on New Year's Eve.

'It's only because I'm big-hearted and I was young once myself,' she cackled.

'They're both going to need a bit of alteration, but my mum will help,' Ivy said after they'd counted out their pennies and handed them over to the stallholder, thanking her and wishing her a Happy New Year.

As soon as they got home Ivy had told Jake that they'd definitely be going with him and Andrew to the Dorrington Dance Hall.

'That's good! Ivy and me will call for you around eight o'clock,' he told Trixie.

'No, you mustn't do that!' Trixie exclaimed in alarm. 'My dad might still be at home and he wouldn't let me go dancing,' she said uneasily. She looked across to Ivy for support.

'You come round to our place just before eight, then,' Ivy said.

'Where are we meeting Andrew?' Trixie asked before Jake could try and change the arrangement.

'At the Dorrington. That's why I said we'd call for you. It makes sense because we can go along Virgil Street to get there.'

'I'll leave home before eight and meet you on the corner of Virgil Street and Great Homer Street,' Trixie compromised.

'What about if your dad's off to the pub about then and spots us all?' Ivy asked.

'Well, if that happens, then I'll have to pretend I'm not with you, won't I?'

The subterfuge seemed to make it all the more exciting and Trixie spent Sunday in a dream. The only thing that worried her was that having only ever been to one dance before she still wasn't much of a dancer.

'Could you or Jake give me some help to improve what few steps I do know?' she begged.

'I wouldn't worry too much; the place will be so crowded that probably the most you'll be able to do is shuffle around the floor,' Ivy laughed.

The thought of doing that in Andrew's arms was bliss to Trixie and she counted the hours and even the minutes till it could come true.

'You're taking an awful risk planning to go

135

to this dance, you know,' Maggie said when Trixie told her what they were planning to do. 'If your dad should find out, he's going to be terribly annoyed.'

'Why should he be, Mum? Surely he can't expect me to sit at home for ever and not have any friends or go out and have some fun, now can he?'

'You know how he feels about Ivy and if he ever finds out that you've not only gone out with her but that the pair of you have gone out with boys—'

'Mum! Jake is Ivy's brother so we're not likely to get into any trouble with him.'

'What about this other boy you're talking about; this Andrew Bacon?'

'He's a friend of Jake's and I've told you all about him. I'm sure that even Dad would think that he was highly respectable.'

'Yes, I know, luv.' Maggie reached out and stroked Trixie's hair. 'I know you're growing up fast, but you're younger than Ivy so I can't help worrying about you even though I want you to have a good time.'

'You might, but I don't think Dad does.' Trixie smiled ruefully.

'He will if he finds you're still out gallivanting when he comes home from the pub. Do you know what time you will you be coming home?'

'Probably well before one o'clock. Ivy says we'll see the New Year in and then once all the hooters and sirens from the docks have stopped sounding we'll head for home. Please, Mum, agree I can go because I really want to,' Trixie begged.

New Year's Eve proved to be an even more momentous occasion than the party. Jake and Andrew were both wearing smart suits and Trixie and Ivy were wearing the dresses that they'd bought in Paddy's Market.

Ivy's dress was in a red shiny material trimmed with black lace around the bodice and at the bottom of the full skirt; Trixie's was in a shimmering blue fabric that clung to her willowy figure like a second skin.

'It's a pity we'll have to wear our ordinary coats over them because it spoils the effect,' Ivy sighed as they tried them on in Ivy's bedroom a couple of days before the big night.

'We could always cadge a black shawl from our mums,' Trixie giggled, 'except that would make us look right tatty and we might get mistaken for a couple of Mary Ellens from the back.'

'When I've tarted them up we'll look more like Lady Muck,' Ivy laughed. 'Ask your mum if we can borrow her shawl and bring it round to my place and I'll see what I can do to jazz it up. I've got quite a lot of ideas!'

Ivy was as good as her word; she transformed the two shawls. She threaded bands of bright red wool through her own mother's black shawl so that it matched her dress and she used some strips of white cloth that had once been a petticoat, to brighten up the shawl Trixie was going to wear.

'Now, instead of wearing our coats, we sling these round our shoulders and then we'll look like a couple of film stars,' Ivy explained.

The evening was even better than Trixie had dreamed it would be. The dance floor at the Dorrington seemed immense. There were huge mirrors on the walls, glittering overhead lights and the band was on a raised dais at one end of the room. The highly polished dance floor was so crowded that, as Ivy had said, all they could do was shuffle in time to the music. The fact that she didn't know the steps didn't matter at all – whether she was trying to dance with Andrew or Jake.

The moment midnight sounded Jake kissed her and wished her a Happy New Year and then Andrew did the same. Unlike Jake, when he took her in his arms, he didn't give her a resounding, friendly kiss on the cheek but a deep, tender kiss on the lips which left her so breathless and happy she felt as if she was in heaven.

'My New Year resolution is to see a great deal more of you,' he whispered as he released her and they exchanged greetings with Jake and Ivy and the rest of their crowd of friends.

The ships' hooters and sirens as well as horns and other noises were still sounding as they left the Dorrington and took to the brightly lit streets. There were fireworks going off on both sides of the Mersey, sending a rainbow of colour up into the night sky. To Trixie it seemed like fairyland, especially as Andrew had tucked her arm into the crook of his and was holding her hand.

When they finally decided it was time to go home Trixie paused when they reached the corner of Virgil Street.

'I really will be all right, it's not very far from here,' she protested when Andrew insisted that he didn't want to leave her there, but intended seeing her right to her door.

Feeling rather embarrassed, she explained that her dad didn't know she was out so she was hoping to slip in without him finding out. 'If he isn't in bed and he sees us together then he'll raise the roof,' she said ruefully.

'I am going to see you again though, aren't I?' Andrew insisted. 'You will come out with me, won't you, perhaps next week? We could go to the pictures or even go dancing again if you'd prefer that.'

'I'd love to,' Trixie sighed, 'but I can't promise because I'm not sure.'

'You don't have to tell him that you're going out with me,' Andrew said a trifle impatiently. 'Say you're going to the pictures with one of your friends.'

She shook her head, biting her lip uneasily. 'I don't think he'd believe me because he doesn't give me enough pocket money for me to be able to go out to the pictures with anyone,' she explained, the blood rushing to her cheeks in embarrassment.

He looked at her in astonishment. 'But you're working, so you're entitled to go out now and again.'

'I'll see what I can do and let you know,' she told him nervously. 'If I can come out with you, I'll arrange through Ivy and Jake for us to meet up. I do want to see you again, Andrew, because I really have enjoyed myself this evening,' she added, anxious that he wouldn't think she was putting him off.

'So have I,' he breathed softly, pulling her into his arms for a final kiss.

His words were still singing in her ears as she crept indoors and upstairs to bed and even when she fell asleep.

Chapter Eleven

The following Saturday was cold, wet and miserable and as they left work Ivy and Trixie agreed that it was as good a time as any for their mothers to meet.

'I must be mad letting you talk me into going out on a day like this,' Maggie groaned.

'You won't say that once you get there, and it's only a hop, skip and a jump away. It isn't as though you have to stand around waiting for a tram or a bus. It will do you good to get out; you never go anywhere except to the shops.'

'It's little Cilla I'm thinking about. I don't want her catching a cold.'

'It will probably have cleared up by this afternoon,' Trixie told her optimistically, 'and I really want you to meet the O'Malleys.'

The rain had stopped by two o'clock and even though her dad hadn't come in from the pub Trixie insisted that they went out.

'Your dad's not going to be too pleased when he comes home and finds me out,' Maggie said worriedly as she put on her hat and coat, 'and what about his dinner?'

'Leave it on a plate over a saucepan of hot water; that'll keep it warm for him.'

Reluctantly Maggie did as Trixie suggested and made sure that not only was there plenty of water in the saucepan but that the edge of it was over the hot coals so that the water in it would keep hot.

When they reached Horatio Street, Maggie seemed to be nervous and on edge when Ella opened the door to them and Trixie wondered if perhaps she was doing the wrong thing.

Her mother looked at her in dismay when they went into the O'Malleys' living room and, even before she'd sat down, Cilla ran over to a cupboard, opened it, and began taking things out. She immediately tried to stop her, but Ella waved her away.

'That's Cilla's cupboard; it's where we keep the books and toys she plays with when Trixie brings her round here. She knows she's allowed to get them without asking.' Ella smiled indulgently. 'She never touches anything else; she's a real little darlin', so she is, and not that much older than my little Nelly was when she died after the accident. Perhaps that's why I'm so fond of her.'

'Your little one didn't have our Cilla's problems, though,' Maggie sighed.

'No, that's true. She was as bright as a button, that's why I miss her so much. I grieve for her something dreadful,' Ella admitted sadly. 'That's why I love seeing Cilla and look forward to Trixie bringing her around.'

'What would you have done if she had been like Cilla?' Maggie asked hesitantly.

'I'd go to church and pray, so I would,' Ella said immediately. 'That's what I always do when I have something bothering me and it nearly always works.'

'You mean the answer comes to you out of the blue?' Maggie sighed enviously. 'I do know what you mean,' she went on quickly. 'I may not be a Cat'lic like you are, but I often used to pop into your church when Cilla was very little and, if I had a penny to spare, light a candle to see if it would help in some way'

'Did it?' Ella asked, looking at her sideways as if not sure what Maggie's answer was going to be.

'I think so. Look at her now; she's getting brighter and stronger all the time. Mind you,' she added with a wry smile, 'you've had a lot to do with that; you and your son and Ivy. She's really taken to all of you and you're so good with her.'

While they were talking, Ivy and Trixie brought in tea for all of them and as she sipped hers, Maggie looked round appreciatively at the cosy room and began to relax.

'I'm going to take Trixie upstairs so that I can show her my Christmas presents again,' Ivy told Maggie and her mother. 'Do you want me to take Cilla with us as well?'

'No, there's no need,' her mother told her.

'Just look at her, she's as happy as a sandboy doing that little wooden jigsaw. If she can't manage to do it on her own then we'll help her.'

'That was one of the pleasantest afternoons I've known in a long time,' Maggie told Trixie as they made their way home. 'What a nice woman Ella O'Malley is and how lovely she is with our Cilla. You know she wants to help teach Cilla to learn her letters? Well, we've talked it all over and she thinks that Cilla will master them in next to no time. Won't it be lovely if she does.'

Sam Jackson was already at home when they arrived back and he was far from pleased at having found the place completely empty.

'What's the idea of leaving me to get my own bloody dinner,' he ranted, the moment they stepped into the room. 'I'm slaving my guts out in all weathers down at the docks and when I get home I expect to have a hot meal ready and waiting.'

'It *was* ready and waiting for you, Dad; all you had to do was lift the plate off the saucepan and put it on the table,' Trixie told him. 'Even your knife and fork was put there ready for you.'

She ducked as his hand came up aiming for her face. He missed her mouth, but the back of his fist caught her a stinging blow across one eye. It was delivered with such force that it made her scream out with pain.

'Speak when you're spoken to! I was talking to your mother, not to you. The pair of you are sodding useless. As for you, you've got too much to say for yourself; you need bloody taming. I'll make sure you will be before long; mark my words.'

'I'll put the kettle on,' Maggie said quietly. 'I expect we could all do with a cup of tea.'

'A cuppa char,' Sam mimicked in a derisory voice. 'That's your bloody answer to everything. Anyway, where've you both been all dressed up like a pair of fo'penny rabbits?'

'We're not dressed up, we've nothing to dress up in,' Trixie muttered.

'You're looking for another smack round the gob, my girl.' Sam scowled. 'Go and brew that char your mother's on about and make sure it's not like gnats' piss. And don't forget to put three sugars in mine. Take her with you,' he went on, nodding towards Cilla who was standing by the door sucking her thumb.

'I'd like to put arsenic in it, not sugar,' Trixie muttered under her breath as she picked Cilla up in her arms and went to do as she'd been told.

She carried two cups of tea through to the living room, but took her own and a drink for Cilla into the bedroom. Her face felt sore and her head was aching and when she looked in the mirror she could see that her eye was cut at one corner.

It was not as bad as she'd feared, she decided as she smeared some Vaseline on to soothe it; with any luck, apart from the fact that it might look bruised, it probably wouldn't be too noticeable when she went to work on Monday, she thought hopefully.

As it happened, the state of her eye was the least of her worries on Monday. A few minutes before their midday break, Fred Linacre told them that he had a special announcement to make. They all waited expectantly, whispering between themselves.

'Perhaps they're going to give us all a bonus because we've worked so hard,' someone said hopefully.

'No, we're getting a half-day holiday because it's his birthday,' another joked.

'Perhaps he's going to start another savings scheme so that we can all have a day out in the summer.'

'More likely he's going to tell us off about something we're not doing right.'

As it was, none of them were anywhere near correct about what Fred Linacre had to say. He waited for complete silence, cleared his throat and squared his shoulders and then looked round at them all sternly.

'It's been decided to cut down on the number of girls working on this assembly line,' he stated. 'One of you has lost her job and will be leaving at the end of the week.'

There was a moment's silence, then a babble of voices began protesting and demanding to know who it was going to be. There was a note of fear in many of the voices. Many of the older women who depended on their wages to eke out a living were very apprehensive. They knew only too well that with the ever-rising unemployment on Merseyside they were unlikely to be able to find another job.

Fred let them get it out of their system and then he once more demanded silence so that he could announce who it was to be.

'The management have worked on the fairest system they can,' he stated pompously. 'That means the last in first out principle, so Trixie Jackson will be the one who's sacked. She'll be given her cards at the end of the week.'

There were expressions of relief till Ivy stated at the top of her voice, 'That's not fair. I was taken on at the same time as Trixie Jackson, so why pick on her?'

'Shush!' Trixie grabbed her arm and shook her head. 'You need your job, Ivy.'

'Of course I do, so do you; we all do, otherwise we wouldn't be here.'

There was a murmur of agreement and all

eyes rested on Fred, waiting for his explanation.

'We took that factor into consideration,' Fred told them. 'Ivy is an experienced worker and older than Trixie and that's how we made our decision.'

Some nodded in agreement, others continued to shake their heads and mutter about it not being fair. Trixie was too stunned to say anything. Even though she was grateful to Ivy for her loyalty it was the thought of what her father would say when she went home and told him she was out of work that was worrying Trixie the most.

Her mum would be upset but at least she'd be sympathetic. Her dad, though, would be furious. She wondered if there was any way she could keep the news from him for a while. If she could delay telling him till she'd found another job, then perhaps he mightn't be quite so mad at her.

Even as the idea came into her head she knew it was impossible. Unless she took time off she couldn't look for another one. If she walked out of the biscuit factory right now and couldn't find a job before the weekend, then she'd have no wage packet to hand over on Friday and he'd probably give her a hiding for not telling him. In addition, because he drank at the same boozer as Fred Linacre, he would probably hear about her losing her job and he'd be furious because she hadn't told him herself.

During what was left of their break some of the women tried to consol her. She smiled and nodded as they kept telling her that at her age she'd get another job in next to no time but she was pretty sure it wasn't going to be as easy as that.

A thousand and one ways of breaking the news to her dad went round and round in her head for the rest of the day till she thought she was going mad.

She talked some of them over with Ivy as they headed for home, but although it made her feel better it didn't solve the problem. She still had to face him and she could only pray that she had a chance to tell him before he heard it from Fred Linacre.

Her mother was beside herself with worry when she told her. 'He'll be so mad with you, my luv. Perhaps you should go out before he gets in. He's bound to know because he's so late that it looks as if he's called in at the pub on his way home; he's probably heard it from Fred, and you know what he can be like when he's had a few beers.'

'You mean if I'm not here then it'll give him a chance to cool down?'

'That's right, luv. Take Cilla out for a walk.'

'At this time of night when it's almost dark! He'll know I've done it to avoid him.'

'That doesn't matter; better for him to be cross about that than over you losing your job. Don't forget he said he was the one who persuaded this Fred Linacre to take you on in the first place so he's bound to think you've let him down.'

'It's not like that, Mum. They're cutting back and it was a case of my being the last one to be taken on.'

'You know that and so do I but can we convince him of that fact? No, it's too big a risk. You clear off for an hour or so with Cilla and I'll see if I can calm him down before you get back.'

'Going out somewhere?'

Trixie was just putting her coat on when her father arrived home.

She hesitated, not knowing quite what to say. He looked quite calm and he seemed to be in a surprisingly good mood.

'Well, go on, then, if you're going,' he said giving her a push. 'The sooner you go the sooner you'll be back and then I'll tell you the news I have for you.'

'The news?' She looked at him questioningly, fear making her voice tremble.

'That's right.'

'What news is that?' Maggie intervened, coming out of the kitchen carrying a plate piled high with steaming food. 'Come on; get your dinner while it's hot.'

Trixie hesitated as her father pulled out a chair and sat down at the table. Then, plucking up every vestige of courage she could muster, she faced him. 'Do you mean you've heard that I've lost my job?' she asked.

He stared back at her. 'Oh yes, I know all about that. You finish there at the end of the week, don't you?' he said with a humourless smile.

She nodded, nervously waiting for him to say or do something. She couldn't understand why he was taking it so calmly. She'd been expecting him to rant and rave, to give her a hiding, even, but to sit there holding his knife and fork with what was almost a smile on his face was so inexplicable and out of character that it completely bewildered her.

'Was that the news?' she gulped. She felt so frightened that she wanted to get the matter over with. Waiting to find out what he was going to do about it was almost as bad as the punishment he so often dished out.

'Losing your job's not all that important,' he said brusquely.

Trixie couldn't believe she was hearing correctly. 'So ... so what is the other news?' she asked in a puzzled voice.

He shrugged his broad shoulders but didn't answer as he concentrated on cutting up the meat on his plate.

'Please, Dad...' she persisted.

His mood changed. 'For God's sake, shut up. You can take your coat off and put her to bed,' he said nodding towards Cilla, 'because you're not going anywhere till you've heard what I've got to say.' He put a forkful of food into his mouth and chewed noisily. 'That won't be till I've finished this lot,' he added as he loaded his fork again.

Sam kept her waiting till he'd finished his meal and wiped round his plate with a piece of bread.

'Now,' he said, belching loudly, pushing his chair back from the table and going to sit in his armchair, 'you can go and get me a cup of tea.'

'I'll do it,' Maggie said, whisking his plate away from the table and heading for the kitchen.

'Well then, Dad? Are you going to tell me what this news is that you have for me?'

Trixie waited with increasing dread as her father picked a piece of meat from between his teeth with a fingernail. She could feel the goose bumps rising on her arms as she waited for him to speak. Why did he have to torture her like this? she wondered.

'It'll keep,' he said cryptically. 'For God's sake, get that one off to bed like I told you and let's have a bit of peace,' he added, nodding his head towards Cilla who was sitting on the floor in the corner, singing the same nursery rhyme over and over in a monotonous singsong voice.

As she put Cilla to bed, Trixie couldn't

stop worrying about what news her father could possibly have that affected her. It was strange that he hadn't seemed concerned about her losing her job and this made her all the more fearful about what he was going to tell her.

Chapter Twelve

Trixie waited all week for her father to make known whatever it was he had to tell her. She kept asking her mother if she knew what it was, but Maggie was as much in the dark as she was.

'Try and stop thinking about it all the time,' she advised. 'It's probably nothing very important; he's just having you on and trying to make you jumpy.'

'It's not like Dad to tease; he's usually far too grumpy to do anything like that,' Trixie said worriedly.

'It's probably some gossip that he's heard about you losing your job,' her mother reasoned.

'No.' Trixie shook her head. 'He mentioned something a bit odd before Christmas so I don't think it's got anything to do with losing my job. In fact, he acted almost as if it didn't matter.'

'Yes, I must admit that struck me as odd,' her mother agreed. 'I'd expected him to go off the deep end. Well, don't worry about it, luv. Whatever it was, he seems to have forgotten all about it, so let sleeping dogs lie, I always say.'

The revelation came on Saturday when Trixie arrived home with her final pay packet and handed it over to her father. He sat for a moment, turning it over and over in his hand and saying nothing, but he had a sly smile on his face that made Trixie cringe and her stomach churn as she watched him.

'So this is your final pay packet from the biscuit factory, is it?' he said ominously.

'Well, yes, but I'll soon get another job. I'll start looking first thing on Monday morning,' she said quickly.

'I don't think so.'

His curt tone sent a chill shuddering right through her. 'You mean you don't think I will find one?' she asked nervously.

He toyed with the pay packet like a cat would with a mouse, tipping it from one hand to the other, rattling the money inside it. 'I have other plans for you. I told you so before Christmas,' he reminded her. 'You haven't forgotten, have you?'

'No, of course not, but you never said what sort of plans they were,' she said tremulously.

'That was because it wasn't the right time to talk to you about them,' he said, his eyes

154

narrowing as he stared at her fixedly.

Trixie held her breath, waiting for him to go on, to explain what it was he had in mind. When he stayed silent she decided after a few minutes that he still wasn't going to tell her what he was on about – not yet, anyway.

'I'm going to take you out in a minute, so you'd better hurry up and clear your plate if you want to come with me,' she whispered to Cilla who was sitting at the table pushing food around on her plate instead of eating it.

'Oh no you're not!' Sam Jackson thumped his fist down on the table, making the dishes rattle and causing Cilla to burst into tears. 'You're not taking her round to mix with that Irish trash in Horatio Street any more. Go and smarten yourself up, girl, because you're coming with me,' he ordered.

'Out with you?' Trixie looked startled, wondering if she had heard him correctly. She couldn't remember going anywhere with her father for years; not since before he'd gone into the army, in fact. She looked at her mother for confirmation, but Maggie looked even more surprised than she was.

'Where are we going, Dad? If it's for a walk, then can Cilla come as well?'

'No, she bloody well can't. We're not going for a walk and you won't be seeing her again for a while so you may as well say goodbye to her now,' he added moving his chair away from the table.

'What on earth do you mean by that?' Maggie frowned. 'Trixie always takes Cilla out on a Saturday afternoon. Why are you telling her to say goodbye to Cilla; what's going on?'

Her father scowled angrily at Trixie. 'Do as you're bloody well told for once without the two of you asking so many damned questions.'

'I will, when you tell me what I'm supposed to be doing,' she said balefully.

'I'm waiting, so get yourself ready and stop giving me lip. Pack your clothes and anything else you want to take with you into a bag because you won't be coming back here again,' he bellowed.

'What on earth is he on about, Mum?' Trixie asked, really worried now. She didn't like the tone of her dad's voice and her heart was thumping, she felt so frightened. She could tell from the look on her mother's face that she was scared as well. Why couldn't he tell them what he was planning, and not keep torturing them like this? she thought resentfully.

'I really don't know, luv,' Maggie said quietly, putting an arm round her shoulders and giving her a reassuring hug. 'What are you on about, Sam? Why in heaven's name does she have to pack her bags?' she demanded.

'I would have thought it was obvious. She's lost her job so I've fixed up for her to do some other sort of work.'

'If you mean you want her to live in somewhere, then that's one thing I won't stand for,' Maggie railed.

'Shut your bloody mouth and don't make things more difficult than they have to be,' Sam told her furiously. 'She's lost her job and we can't afford to keep her if she isn't earning any money, now can we? We've got one useless little baggage to provide for so we don't want another.'

'Sam! That's a terrible thing to say,' Maggie exclaimed. There was a tremor in her voice and an ashen look on her face as she picked Cilla up and hugged her close.

'Cilla isn't useless,' Trixie defended heatedly. 'She's learning her letters and already she can read a few words. She might even be able to go to school quite soon.'

'Pigs might fly. She's as thick as a plank and always will be, so don't try to pull the wool over my eyes,' he exploded.

'No, Trixie is right. She really is telling you the truth, Sam. Little Cilla has turned the corner and is coming along by leaps and bounds,' Maggie said placatingly.

'I doubt it! If she is, then in future she'll have to do it without Trixie there to help because I've other plans for her.'

Maggie took a deep breath and faced him

challengingly. 'You'd better tell me what these plans are, then,' she insisted. 'I'm well aware that she needs to get another job because I certainly can't manage on the pittance I earn and the miserable amount you give me each week. I won't have her going into service, though,' she told him boldly. 'I've always said that no child of mine will ever become a skivvy for other people.'

'Watch your mouth,' he snarled. 'I don't take any lip from you or her. She's going to do as I say; I've set it all up for her.'

'So you keep on saying, but why does she need to take her clothes with her if she isn't going into service?'

'Stop asking so many bloody questions,' he bellowed angrily. 'You've five minutes,' he told Trixie as he stood up and rammed his cap on his head.

'She's not moving from this room till you tell me where she's going,' Maggie told him, standing between him and the door. Her arms were akimbo and there was a dangerous light in her grey eyes. 'Come on, let's hear it. I want the truth, mind.'

Trixie looked from one to the other of them in astonishment, She'd never heard her mother speak like that to her father before and she was surprised; not that it seemed to be doing any good, though, she thought miserably.

'Give over and stop making such a bloody

fuss. I've found her a place to work where she'll live in. You'll get your money each week; I've arranged that already.' He grinned. 'Her wages have been paid in advance for the next three months.'

'I've already told you, no child of mind is going to be a skivvy, so what is this job and where is it? She isn't old enough to be taken on as a nurse in a hospital; not even as a trainee.'

'She's going to work as a housekeeper for a bloke I know. He's taking her on a three-month trial and after that, if he finds she suits him, then he might marry her.'

Maggie stared at him open-mouthed. 'I don't believe I'm hearing this,' she exploded. There was red-hot fury in her eyes and in her voice. 'Paid in advance, did he?' she added contemptuously. 'What you really mean is that you've sold our daughter to some fella like she was a bloody slave!'

'It's not going to be like that at all,' Sam shouted. 'She'll be living in a better place than this, let me tell you. He's a middle-aged bachelor with a nice home, and he earns damn good money; he's not only highly thought of but is also very respectable.'

'A paragon of virtue as well, I suppose, who wouldn't dream of taking advantage of an innocent young girl,' Maggie said acidly. 'Where did you meet him, down at the boozer?' she went on, her voice full of disdain. 'What sort of services did you promise she'd supply him with, or would it be better if I didn't ask that?'

'Shut your foul mouth and mind your own bloody business,' Sam Jackson snarled. 'The deal's done. She's going there today, so don't let's have any more argy-bargy. One more word out of you and you'll feel the weight of my fist.'

'Don't talk about me as if I'm not here,' Trixie choked, tears streaming down her face. 'You can't do this, Dad. I won't go and you can't make me. This is my home and I want to stay here,' she sobbed. 'Mum needs me, and so does Cilla.'

'You'll do as I tell you. In the eyes of the law you're still a child till you're eighteen, so you have no bloody say in the matter. In fact, in a lot of things you have to do as I tell you till you're twenty-one, so don't you forget it.'

'I've done nothing wrong, so you can't send me away from home,' Trixie gulped. She brushed away her tears with the back of her hand and went over to Cilla and hugged her. 'Mum needs me to help her with Cilla, you know she does, Dad,' she pleaded, looking at him hopefully.

Her father turned away. 'I've said all I'm going to say, now stop blathering and get yourself ready.'

'Please tell us who this man is and where

he lives before I go anywhere,' Trixie begged, her eyes filling up with tears again. 'Please don't make me do it, Dad.' She caught at his arm. 'You can't expect me to move in with some stranger and have to put up with whatever he wants,' she sobbed.

'She's right, Sam. You must tell us more about him. I need to know as well. Surely you can tell us both a bit more about what you have arranged and set our minds at rest. I'll be worried silly if I don't know where you're taking her. Is she going to be safe with him?'

'Stop building it up into such a disaster; you make it sound like a fate worse than death.'

'It might as well be, since you insist that she has to live in,' Maggie pointed out. 'Some men, even so-called respectable ones, have horrible habits.'

Sam glowered at her and his face grew a dull red. 'I'm not bloody well asking her to move in with a complete stranger; I've known him, and spoken to him almost every day, for months.'

'You've only seen him in the pub; you've no idea what he might be like when he's at home in his own house. If he's a bachelor then he's used to being on his own so he might resent having someone living there with him.'

'Why the hell should he? He wants

someone to clean his house, do his washing and have his food on the table when he comes home at night and that's the only time she'll see him.'

'What about letting me go with you to meet him first and have a chat with him. I'd be a lot easier in my mind if you'd let me do that,' Maggie pleaded.

'Talk sense, woman! What's he going to think if I do a thing like that?'

'That we both think the world of our daughter and that we want to make sure she isn't going to come to any harm,' she told him boldly.

'For Christ's sake, give up and let your tongue have a rest. I've told him she'll be there by three o'clock this afternoon and I intend to keep my word. If we don't get a move on then we're going to be late and that will be a bad start.'

'I don't like it, Sam. She's only a kid and–'

As his hand went up to silence her with a blow, Trixie grabbed at his arm, diverting it. 'That's one of the reasons why I don't want to leave home,' she railed. 'Mum needs me here to protect her from your bullying as well as to help with Cilla.'

For a moment she thought she was in for a hiding but she didn't care. If he punched her in the face, or even walloped her with his belt, she'd be bound to have a mass of bruises and he wouldn't be able to make her leave home and go and live with a stranger in case he spotted them.

Sam Jackson was too clever to fall into that trap. Although his face was puce with rage and his fists were clenched into tight balls, he managed to keep them at his side.

He grabbed Trixie by the hair and began pushing her towards the bedroom. 'Get your coat and whatever you want to take with you and let's get going,' he muttered.

She still had an arm around Cilla and the child immediately started to scream as if she was the one being hurt, not Trixie. Snatching Cilla from Trixie, Sam almost threw the child at Maggie.

All three of them were crying and his voice was rising with increasing anger as he yelled at them all to shut up.

'You're going, and that's all there is to it,' he shouted at Trixie. 'Wipe your face and comb your hair; you look like some gutter urchin,' he growled.

'Well, that's all right because that's what you're trying to turn me into, isn't it!' she retaliated, now confident that under no circumstances was he going to hit her.

'At least tell us where she'll be living,' Maggie begged. 'Is it far away, will she be able to come and see us regularly?'

'She won't be coming visiting and you won't be going out looking for her. Is that understood? This is a clean break. Perhaps later on, when she's settled in, then she can come and see us if she behaves herself.'

'You make it sound as if she's going to be a prisoner. Will you be seeing her?'

'No, I bloody well won't. She's going to make a new life for herself. Like I told you, if she proves satisfactory then the bloke says he'll marry her.'

'I'm far too young to get married,' Trixie protested, looking at her mother for support. 'You said yourself I'm only a kid,' she taunted. 'Anyway,' she went on, 'what happens if I don't like him? I might already have made plans to marry someone else.'

Even as she spoke the words her heart sank. If she had no freedom then she wouldn't be able to see Andrew and he was the only man in the world she would ever want to marry.

'If it seems a good set up to me and I agree that he can marry you, then I've only to sign the right papers and you've no say in the matter,' he told her with sneer. 'Now have you got your things together, because I'm ready for off.'

'I haven't packed anything at all yet,' Trixie prevaricated. 'It's going to take me a while...'

Sam didn't wait for her to finish. 'You had your chance,' he told her. 'I'll give you five minutes, so make it sharp.'

Hastily she grabbed what she could find and stuffed it into a battered old fibre

164

suitcase that her mother brought out from the back of the cupboard.

'I'm not waiting any longer,' Sam said, grabbing hold of the suitcase and fastening it shut. He began to push Trixie towards the door, not even giving her time to kiss her mother or Cilla goodbye.

'Wait, Sam, let her put her coat and hat on, it's absolutely freezing out there,' Maggie protested as she held out Trixie's coat so that she could put her arms into it.

Sam grabbed it and her hat but didn't pause. 'She can put them on out in the street if she's cold,' he muttered as he pushed her through the door. He ignored the fact that Maggie was struggling to hold back her tears despite the fact that Trixie's distress was breaking her heart, and the pleading look Trixie was giving her mother.

He refused to let go of Trixie's arm as she struggled to get her coat on and to fasten it up.

'Where are we going?' she panted as he propelled her along Virgil Street and into Scotland Road.

She felt scared stiff but she was doing her best not to show it. His threats that she wouldn't be able to come back and see her mother and Cilla were still ringing in her ears and they, together with the uncertainty of what was going to happen, were all frightening.

It was at times like this that she wished he'd never come back from the war; if he hadn't, none of them would have had to put up with his bullying.

As they turned into Scotland Road she wondered if she could make a run for it but, although her dad was carrying the suitcase in one hand, he was holding her arm so tightly that there was no chance of her twisting free.

If only she could find a way of letting Ivy and Ella know what was happening but even her mother didn't even know where she was being taken.

Whatever would Andrew think when she didn't contact him as she'd promised to do? He might even think it was because she didn't want to see him again, she thought desperately, yet there was nothing she wanted more.

'Look for number twenty,' her father ordered, his grip on her arm tightening as they turned into Cavendish Road.

Trixie's heart thudded. She'd never even been down any of the roads this far from Scotland Road before and now, or so it seemed, number twenty Cavendish Road was where she was going to live and with a middle-aged man who was a complete stranger. How could her father do something like this to her? she wondered.

They paused as he spotted the number

painted in white on a black door between two shops. 'This must be the place,' he said, pushing her towards it.

She was so petrified that her legs wouldn't move. Her father nudged her forward and she stumbled. She would have fallen if her father hadn't still been holding her arm so tightly.

She was shaking so much that when the door opened she could only stare at the man who stood there, more convinced than ever that it wasn't just a bad dream but a terrible nightmare.

Chapter Thirteen

Trixie could hear her father talking, hear the welcome being extended to both of them to come inside, but the shock of seeing who'd opened the door and was standing there was so intense that her mind refused to function.

As her father, who was still holding her arm in a tight grip, propelled her over the stone step into the passageway beyond, Trixie blinked hard, not to dispel tears, but to try and clear her mind. She didn't want to believe it but the man whose home they were in was none other than Fred Linacre.

It couldn't be, she told herself over and over again. He certainly looked like Fred but there was difference. This man was wearing slippers and a dark brown knitted cardigan, and had a pipe stuck in the corner of his mouth. The Fred she knew always wore a pristine white coat-style overall. His white shirt and navy and red tie were the same, though, and so, too, was his voice.

'You've brought her, then,' the man greeted them, and it was his tone more than the words that sent a shiver through Trixie as they followed him along the stone passage where he opened another door on their right.

Again they followed him as he climbed up a staircase to a small landing where a door led into a living room. She could hear her father carrying on a conversation and laughing heartily at something one of them had said but she was feeling so confused that she couldn't take in what they were saying.

As she stood in the living room looking around the bleakness of the bare walls and sparse furnishings filled her with dismay. There was a dark brown leather armchair pulled up in front of the open fire, and a dining table covered with a dark brown chenille cloth and two upright chairs with seats of brown leather. There were no pictures or ornaments, no rug on the well-worn brown lino that covered the floor; nothing at all that

168

turned the bleakness of the room into a home. Even the mantelpiece was bare apart from a clock in a dark wood case that stood in the middle of it.

'Here's the rest of your money,' Fred said, pulling a small rolled-up bundle of notes out of his back pocket.'

'You don't need to check it; it's all there,' he stated as Sam Jackson started to flatten out the bank notes.

'Right; that's it, then. I hope I can count on you to keep to your part of the bargain,' her father challenged as he stood up and put his cap back on.

'Everything as we agreed. No meetings of any sort till the three months are up.'

'That's Easter time, then. Trixie'll still only be sixteen till–'

Fred Linacre hurriedly moved towards the door as if to show Sam Jackson out. 'We'll discuss all that another time, when we're on our own.'

'You promised–'

'I know what I said and I'll keep my word so you've nothing at all to worry about. Three months and I'll have made up my mind and be ready to tell you if she suits and whether I'm going to take her on permanently or not.'

'And in all that time you won't touch her; you swear that you won't try anything on,' Sam emphasised. 'I don't want her returned

169

as damaged goods. Perhaps I should have a look at what arrangements you've made about where she's going to sleep?'

'Are you doubting my intentions?' Fred asked angrily. 'We made a deal and I'll keep to my side of the bargain as long as you and your missus do the same. If I catch any of you lot coming around here trying to see her, then the deal's off and the promises I've made mean nothing. Stick to our arrangement or you most certainly will be getting damaged goods returned; you can count on that.'

'All right, all right.' Sam Jackson held up both hands and took a step backwards. 'Hold on, Fred, she's my daughter! Be fair now, whacker, I got to make sure she's going to be safe; you can't blame me for that.'

'Say your goodbyes to her and get out,' Fred snapped. 'You have told her, haven't you, that she's here for three months and that she won't be allowed to see anyone or to go out at all?'

Sam didn't answer as he headed for the door. He didn't wait for Fred Linacre to show him out and or even stop to say anything at all to Trixie who was standing there with a look of terror on her face at the thought of being left alone with Fred Linacre; the very thought that he might try to be familiar with her made her feel sick.

'Do you know why you're here, Trixie Jackson, and what arrangements have been made?' Fred Linacre demanded, in the domineering voice he used when he was at the factory, the moment the front door slammed behind Sam Jackson.

Trixie shook her head. What she had understood of the exchange between the two men frightened her. Her dad had said something about 'having something in mind for her in the new year', but surely this hadn't been what he meant.

He knew perfectly well how much she hated Fred Linacre. Having to work for him at the biscuit factory had been bad enough, but to have to live with him in his own home was going to be the worst sort of nightmare imaginable.

'I'll show you where you'll be sleeping; come along.'

She followed him out on to the landing, where she noticed that there were two doors side by side, facing the living room. He walked across and opened one of the doors and indicated with his head for her to follow him.

It was a dark, narrow room with a single iron bedstead, dark grey slub curtains across the narrow window and an oblong of grey carpet on the scrubbed floorboards by the side of the bed. The white cotton counterpane and coarse white cotton pillowcase both looked clean but the whole room looked dreary and uninviting. There were no pictures or ornaments; not even a piece of mirror or a cupboard to put things in, only a row of metal hooks fixed along one wall.

'This will be your room,' he pronounced. 'This one,' he pushed past her and went out on to the landing to open the other door, 'is my room.'

She peered in and saw that although it was larger it was equally Spartan. There was a double bed with white bedding, bare floor boards and dark green curtains. In this room, however, there was a dark oak chest of drawers at one side of the bed and a matching oak wardrobe that practically filled one entire wall.

'Come through here and I'll show you the kitchen and the rest of the place,' he ordered as he shut the door to his room and moved a few paces along the landing.

The kitchen was bigger than she had expected. As well as a range and a cooking stove there were shelves with white crockery laid out on them and cupboards for the pots and pans and for storing food in. There was also a small scrubbed table with a wooden chair where Fred obviously ate his meals. The window looked on to a yard that had a high brick wall all around it.

'There you are, then. Now, is there anything else you need to know?'

Trixie shook her head as she followed him

172

back into the living room. There was plenty she wanted to know but she was afraid to ask. She couldn't believe that she was going to have to stay here till Easter, but that was what she'd heard her father agree and, worst of all, she'd heard Fred say something about her mum not being able to come and see her.

She looked around her with a feeling of panic. She didn't even know what she was supposed to do. If it was to keep his house clean and get his meals ready, well, that wouldn't take her very long because there'd be precious little to do because the place was so bare.

She thought about her own shabby home in Virgil Street. It was only three poky rooms but it was more welcoming than this place. Fred's house was like a barn; she'd never seen anything so uninviting. It was hardly any better than the factory.

Her mum had prettied their place up with a couple of pictures and one or two ornaments and some cushions. She'd made a colourful rug out of their worn-out clothes; ones that were past mending but could still be cut into strips and stitched on to a piece of sacking to make a rug to go down in front of the fireplace.

She knew Fred was waiting for her to say something. Screwing her hands into fists to summon up her courage she asked, 'Where do I wash myself and ... and things like that? You haven't told me where the lavvy is, is it down the yard?'

'No! It's out here.' He led her through to another, smaller room off the kitchen. In one corner was a brick built-in wash boiler and a brown stone sink alongside it. Next to that was a boxed-in lavatory.

'There you are; there's the bog and you wash yourself and do all the washing out here, so you've no need to go out into the yard at all. In fact, you won't be able to, because I'll keep the door locked and take the key with me.'

'What about when I have to hang the clothes outside to dry?'

'You'll dry them indoors. There's a pulley rack in the kitchen. You lower that down, spread them out on it, and haul it back up to the ceiling. They're out of the way and they only take a couple of days to dry.'

Suddenly the enormity of what was happening struck home. 'Does that mean I'm not going to be allowed to go out at all?' she demanded.

'You mean your dad didn't explain it all to you?'

She shook her head, afraid to speak because she knew she was on the verge of crying and she didn't intend to let him see how upset and dismayed she was.

'You're not going out of this house till

174

Easter. I don't intend letting any of your family come round here either, and certainly not that Ivy O'Malley or any other friends you might have. Three months while you learn to run my home as I like it to be done, and then I'll decide if I'm going to marry you or not.'

'Marry me! I don't want to marry you; you're as old as my dad!' Trixie shouted angrily.

'Temper, temper,' he laughed in the tone he had used when taunting her at work. 'Mind, I was expecting that and I'll enjoy bringing you to heel.'

'I don't intend staying here,' Trixie told him furiously. 'You sacked me on purpose from the biscuit factory, didn't you, and then you told my dad that you'd offer me a job as your housekeeper. You've even paid him my wages already to make sure he forced me to come here. You're a wicked, scheming pig; both of you are.'

She stared at him with loathing, inwardly scared that he might hit her, but determined not to let him see how frightened she was.

'Well, I'm not staying here another minute so don't think that you can make me,' Trixie stated indignantly, pushing past him when he made no reply. She grabbed hold of her hat and coat and began putting them on.

'You're wasting your time, doing that,' he told her. 'There's only one door and that's locked and I have the key. You're staying right here for the next three months. By then I'll have tamed you, my girl, and if I like the results then I might make an honest woman of you. If I don't, then I'll send you packing.'

Ignoring him, Trixie went out on to the landing and ran down the stairs to the front door. Fred didn't even bother following her. She turned the handle, tugged and pulled, but nothing happened. The door was as solid as a rock and securely locked.

'I'm still not staying here,' she fumed as, slowly, she came back upstairs. She ran across to the window and tried to open it but that was as securely locked as the front door.

'All the doors in this place are locked and so are all the windows,' Fred told her with an amused smile on his face. 'What's more, it's a good twenty-foot drop to the pavement because there's a shop down below this flat. You're a prisoner, my girl, and you'll stay that way till the three months are up. What's more, you'll do exactly as I say.'

Trixie took a deep breath and tried to calm down. If she couldn't escape in the normal way then she'd have to think of some cleverer ruse. She might have to stay here for a few days but, sooner or later, she was determined to get free.

Surely someone would miss her, she

reasoned. Cilla would soon start fretting for her and her mother would eventually find out where she was and come looking for her for Cilla's sake.

Even though Trixie had lost her job at the factory, Ivy would wonder why she hadn't been to see them. She was bound to go round to Virgil Street to find out why Cilla hadn't been taken round to see them and then her mother would explain what had happened. Only, of course, her mum didn't know where she was, she thought unhappily.

Andrew would wonder why she hadn't been in touch with him to arrange to go to the pictures like he'd asked her to do. She sighed. Would he talk to Jake about it? she wondered. Or would he simply think she didn't want to go? She hoped he wouldn't think that, because she really liked him and after the dance at the Dorrington, she was pretty certain that he liked her quite a lot as well.

Although she felt both frustrated and scared, she was determined not to let Fred know this. Shrugging her shoulders she said in as nonchalant a voice as she could, 'Well, that's it, then, I suppose. If you won't let me out to go home, then I'll have to stay here whether I want to or not.'

'That's about it,' he said smugly, 'so the sooner you find out how I like things to be done the better.'

'I'll try and do my best,' she agreed. 'You tell me what you like to eat and which shops you want me to use and I'll make sure that everything I buy is of the very best and your meal will be cooked and on the table for you when you get home at night.'

'You won't need to go to those lengths,' he smirked, 'because you won't be going out to any shops.'

Trixie tried not to let him see how dismayed she was because she realised that he was blocking her one hope of escape. 'So how are we going to have any food, then, if I can't go out to buy it?' She frowned.

'Don't try and get smart with me,' he snapped. 'I know you're trying to pull a fast one, but I'm not that daft. I'll be doing the shopping, the same as I've always done,' he told her. 'Your job will be to have the stuff cooked and on the table.'

She knew from the tone of his voice that she was probably asking for trouble by goading him, but she couldn't help herself. It was the only weapon she had.

'So what do I do when the milkman calls for his money at the end of the week, or the postman knocks on the door because he's got a parcel that's too big to go through the letter box? Do I just make faces at them from the front-room window?'

'No one will call. I don't owe anybody a penny piece; I never get any letters or parcels, and I settle up with the milkman when I'm down at the boozer.'

'Well, what happens if one of my friends finds out that this is where I am and comes to see me?'

'If you're thinking of that Ivy O'Malley, she doesn't know where I live and I'll make damn sure she doesn't start looking for you.'

'You mean you'll threaten her, do you?' Trixie's eyes blazed with anger.

'I'll do better than that; I'll warn her not to look for you and remind her that if she ever does then I'll have her sacked.'

Trixie could tell that he meant it and she suspected that, much as Ivy would probably want to come and see her, she most probably dared not risk losing her job.

'Surely you're not going to stop me from seeing my little sister Cilla,' Trixie pleaded in a tearful whisper, hoping that this might have more affect on him than standing up to him seemed to do. 'She's backward, she's not like other children of her age, and my mum depends on me to help with her. She can't even go for a walk unless someone is holding her hand–'

'I know all about your sister,' he interrupted. 'Your old man's filled me in on that score and it makes no difference, so you can stop your snivelling. You'll be seeing no one till I say so and that won't be for at least three months.'

Chapter Fourteen

Trixie spent the first few days feeling scared and sorry for herself. She was so lonely. Even at the factory, although they weren't supposed to talk, there were plenty of other people there and they could exchange smiles.

The narrow little bedroom with its bare walls was like a cell, and even though she'd hung up the spare skirt and blouse she'd brought with her on the hooks on the wall, the place still seemed alien. She wished she had a picture of Cilla and her mum and she worried because she knew Cilla would be missing her.

She'd wanted to put her few items of underwear somewhere where Fred couldn't see them. There was no cupboard, and there were no drawers, so she left them in the suitcase she'd brought them in and pushed that underneath the iron bedstead.

The first night she cried herself to sleep, sobbing into the rock-hard pillow till it was so damp she had to turn it over. The bed was hard and lumpy and she tossed and turned so much that it was almost morning before she finally fell asleep.

She was wakened by Fred banging on her bedroom door and shouting for her to get up. She felt so frightened that she was too petrified to move. For a moment she couldn't think where she was or who was shouting at her to get his breakfast.

Then, as she slowly regained her senses, she burrowed down under the covers, pulling them up over her ears to shut out his angry voice. Perhaps if she defied him, then he'd get fed up of having her there and send her home.

Fred wasn't prepared to stand any nonsense. He hammered on her door again. This time he didn't mince his words about what would happen if she wasn't up, dressed and had his breakfast on the table right away.

Remembering the hidings she'd received from her father when she didn't obey him, her common sense prevailed. The sensible thing to do was to respond to his demands and make the excuse that she'd overslept. For the moment it was important not to antagonise him but as soon as he'd gone to work she'd try to find some means of escape, she promised herself.

She knew the door on to the stairway was locked and that Fred carried the key with him, but she was hoping that perha was a window she could open a shout to some passer by or ever through, and somehow or othe climb down to the ground.

The windows were not only securely locked but also, when she looked closer, she discovered to her dismay that all of them had metal bars outside. It meant that even if she could open them there wouldn't be enough room to crawl out, and the drop to the ground was far greater than she'd thought.

She could still shout out to someone, she reasoned, but she didn't think they'd take any notice. She'd already tried hammering on the glass whenever people walked by to try and attract their attention, but even if they could hear her they never bothered to look up.

There was only one window that mightn't be locked, she decided, but that was the one in Fred's bedroom. He'd told her not to go in there and that he'd clean the room himself for the present, so she didn't dare try it.

On the third day of her imprisonment, however, Trixie decided it was the only chance left, so she risked it.

The room smelled of cigarettes and old socks as she gingerly pushed open the door and tiptoed in. She stood just inside the door, laughing at herself for being so secretive. Fred was at work; there was no one else in the house, so why was she creeping about as though she was afraid she might be ught breaking his rules at any moment?

Squaring her shoulders, she walked boldly over to the window. The curtains were drawn as they were in the rest of the house, but she parted them enough to take a look at the window. Like all the others it was a heavy sash window and there were protective bars outside it which meant it was pointless trying to make an escape that way. Nevertheless, she made an attempt to open it, but, again like all the windows in the flat, it was securely locked.

Resigned and disappointed, Trixie closed the curtains again, making sure they were overlapped in exactly the same way as they'd been when she came in. Now she was in here she might as well see if there was anything of interest she decided as she gazed round the rest of the room.

She wondered what he kept in the chest of drawers and the massive wardrobe. She felt guilty about invading his privacy by opening the drawers but, she told herself, he was keeping her there against her will so she was entitled to do so.

There was nothing of any real interest in any of them. In the top one there were socks, ties, handkerchiefs and a couple of belts; in the second one there were some vests and underpants - all clean, and stored away neat and tidy. In the bottom one there were some big brown envelopes full of papers and tied up with string, but although she was full of curiosity, she felt she didn't dare open them to see what they were about.

She walked over to the wardrobe and opened the doors of that instead. There were several shirts hanging there, a dark grey suit and a black one, both on shiny brown wooden hangers. There were also half a dozen hangers all bunched together and whatever was on them was hidden by a sheet that had been wrapped round them.

This time she couldn't contain her curiosity. Very carefully she opened the sheet back and gasped when she saw that it was a collection of women's frocks and jackets.

A thousand and one questions buzzed in her head; who on earth had they belonged to? she wondered. Had Fred been married? If so, where was his wife now? Had she died? Or had she gone off and left him? Was that why he was such a grumpy old devil?

She took another look at the clothes and felt even more puzzled. They were an old woman's clothes; the sort of thing that was worn well before the war, probably at the turn of the century. The skirts were all ankle-length and the bodices had high necks and were heavily embroidered with lace and black jet beads. They were like the mourning clothes old Queen Victoria used to wear, she reflected.

Carefully she covered them over again and made sure they were hanging in exactly the same place as when she'd opened the wardrobe. She also made sure that Fred's suits were in place.

For the rest of the day she tried to work out what sort of woman might have owned the dresses and short jackets with their nipped-in waists and eventually she decided that it couldn't have been his wife because she wouldn't be that old, so the clothes must have belonged to his mother.

What she couldn't understand was why he had kept her clothes when there was no sign of a woman's hand anywhere else in the house. If he'd thought so much of her that he couldn't bear to part with her dresses, then why was there no picture of her anywhere in the house, or any ornaments and all the other bits and pieces that most women liked to have on show?

She toyed with the idea of asking him, but if she did that then he'd know she'd been rooting around in his bedroom and she wasn't too sure how he might react. So far, apart from taunting her when she'd begged to be allowed to go and see her mother and Cilla, he'd said very little. Each evening when he came home from work he'd brought in fresh meat and vegetables ready for the next day. He'd told her how she was to cook it all and then had left her to get on with it.

He'd neither praised nor criticised what she put on the table, nor had he asked her how she'd spent her day or if there was anything she needed.

She wasn't exactly miserable because Fred wasn't violent like her father, but she was frustrated by having so little to do. There seemed to be no books in the place and although Fred brought the *Liverpool Evening Echo* home with him each night, he never shared it with her. He sat reading it while he ate his meal and then he took it with him when he moved into his armchair, and he went on looking at it for the rest of the evening.

Sometimes he even stuffed it into his coat pocket last thing at night and took it to work with him the next day before she could have a look at it.

The flat was so bare that there was not very much work entailed in keeping it clean and tidy and Fred never told her of anything that he wanted done. He didn't even make any comment when she cleaned the windows.

The only thing he really seemed to be interested in was what she put on the table for him to eat at night and because he cleared his plate she assumed he'd enjoyed it.

For the greater part of the day after he'd gone off to work and she'd washed up the few dishes they'd used for breakfast, she sat by the window in the front room, staring out, wondering who the people were that passed up and down Cavendish Road. From time to time she'd stand up and even bang on the window to see if she could attract their attention but it never did any good at all. No one ever seemed to look up.

She could see people crossing the road and her heart would still thud hopefully, even though she knew they were only going into one of the shops underneath. She knew there was one on either side of the doorway to the flat and now she watched the people going in and out of them and tried to work out what it was they sold.

She even asked Fred what sort of shops they were but he'd stared at her as if he didn't understand what she was getting at, then grunted and turned back to his newspaper again.

On the Thursday she wondered if Ivy was missing her and whether she'd seen Andrew and if he'd asked why she hadn't made any arrangements to go to the pictures with him. Surely he'd say something to Jake, even if it was only to ask him if he could find out from Ivy if she was still interested in going out with him.

Once Andrew learned that she was missing and found that Ivy had no way of getting in touch with her then surely he'd suggest they ought to do something about it. He was bright and intelligent, so he wouldn't just dismiss it; he'd realise that there was something very strange about her disappearing like she had. He might suggest going around to her home to ask where she was or even that they should tell the police.

She was disappointed that her mother hadn't at least come round to see if she was all right. Even if she knew that it might be impossible to come in they could still have waved to each other and she would have made her understand by making signs at the window that she was being kept a prisoner here. Or she'd have written it down on a piece of paper and held it up to the glass.

The idea that she could write a notice asking for help and stick it on the front window gave her a fresh surge of hope. Surely there was a possibility that someone would look up and see it as they walked down the street.

She began looking for a pencil and some paper to write with and mentally composing her message. She couldn't find either in the kitchen or in any of the drawers. There wasn't even an old copy of the *Liverpool Echo* lying around, or she could have used one of the white areas that often surrounded an advertisement to write on. She went through to the wash-house where there were squares of old newspaper hanging on a nail by the lavvy to see if she could find one with a white space.

When she finally found one that would do she had a fresh problem; she still had nothing to write with, not even a stub of pencil.

She hunted through the kitchen drawers again but there was nothing, not even a piece of chalk in any of them. She went round and round the flat searching to no avail. Then she remembered the bottom drawer of Fred's chest of drawers, where all the brown paper packages were, and wondered if she dared look to see if there was a pen or pencil in there.

This time she lifted the packages out, feeling even more curious to know what was in them because they were quite heavy, but afraid to look. There was nothing at all that she could use to write out her notice.

Determined not to be thwarted, she went back into the living room and stared at the blank walls wondering if there was somewhere she still hadn't looked. The only place left was the very top cupboards in the kitchen but she thought it was highly unlikely that she'd find anything up there.

Now that the idea was in her mind, though, she felt compelled to look and make sure. She couldn't reach the cupboard doors without standing on a chair so she fetched one from the living room because the one in the kitchen was so rickety that she was pretty sure it wouldn't take her weight. If Fred came home from work and found her sprawled on the floor then he'd know she'd been prying.

Climbing up on the chair was easy enough but balancing and prising open the cupboard door was tricky. It wasn't locked but because of the heat and steam in the kitchen the wood had swelled up and it was difficult to pull the door back.

When she did manage to get it open she couldn't believe her eyes. The cupboard was crammed with all manner of vases, ornaments and bits and pieces which, in most homes, would have been out on display. They were piled in there so haphazardly, one on top of the other, that she began to panic in case any of them fell out and got broken so she quickly shut the door again.

This was even more difficult than opening it had been. She was unable to put as much pressure on it as she wanted because the chair she was standing on kept swaying and she was afraid she might fall off it. She was reluctant to slam the door too hard in case she broke something inside.

Her other worry was that Fred would be home any time now so she eventually slammed it shut and started getting his meal ready. If he found her rummaging up there he'd want to know why and if she said she'd been looking for a pencil he was bound not to believe her, it sounded such a feeble excuse.

What was more, he'd want to know what she needed a pencil for and she couldn't think of a reason because he did the shopping so she didn't have to write out a list.

He'd probably think she'd been planning to write a letter to her mother and that would give him something to think about. He'd know that she knew quite well that he wouldn't post it for her so how was she going to send it?

She couldn't sleep that night for thinking about all the things that had been up in the kitchen cupboard. She wondered if they'd all belonged to his mother and, if so, why he had put them away out of sight. Was it because he didn't like them, or because he didn't like having things like that on display?

If she could think of a way of talking to him about them, then perhaps she could persuade him to lift them down and let her see what was there. If she went about it the right way then he might even allow her to put some of the bits and pieces out on display around the place to make it look more cosy.

After all, she told herself resignedly, if she had to stay there for three months then she might as well try and make the place look as nice as possible.

Chapter Fifteen

Maggie Jackson was beside herself with worry. She couldn't eat, sleep or even sit still, knowing that Sam had made Trixie go off somewhere with him. He said it was a new job but from what little he'd told them she didn't like the sound of it. Worst of all, he wouldn't say where it was; only that she wouldn't be coming home again.

Maggie knew there was a man involved and no matter how hard she tried she couldn't help imagining the worst. Even though she told herself repeatedly that Sam wasn't a bad man at heart, and that he would surely never do anything that would put his daughter in danger, she was worried about what might be happening to Trixie.

Added to that, Cilla missed Trixie and was terribly upset and difficult to manage. It was heartbreaking to hear her sobbing and calling out her sister's name over and over again. Several times when she'd tried to cuddle her, Cilla had thrown a tantrum, kicking and struggling and pushing her away. She'd refused to have anything to do with her, screaming out Trixie's name and sobbing and banging her head against the wall in her frustration.

'Leave the stupid little brat alone,' Sam shouted when she tried to reason with her and explain why Trixie wasn't there. 'She's too bloody stupid to understand what you're telling her.'

'Then you try and explain where Trixie is; see if you can do any better,' she'd retorted exasperatedly.

'Talk to that idiot?' he scoffed. 'I wouldn't waste my breath. It's high time she was in a home or the madhouse.'

His constant rejection of Cilla upset Maggie and frightened her. She made sure that the child was never out of her sight when he was around because she had a sneaking suspicion that he would take her to one of those places if he ever got the chance and tell them that she was unmanageable and needed proper care.

She'd never understand the change in him, she told herself sadly. Before the war he'd been such a warm and loving man; now he barely gave her a civil word. It was as if all the goodness inside him had been destroyed while he'd been overseas in the trenches, leaving behind only evil and ill will.

When Trixie had been missing for a whole week and there had been no word at all from her, Maggie was missing her dreadfully and was so concerned that she decided to go round to the O'Malleys and see if they knew anything. She'd thought that Ivy would have been round long before now to ask where Trixie was and to see if she'd managed to find herself another job. The fact that there hadn't been a word from her made Maggie wonder if they knew something she didn't.

As she dressed Cilla ready to go out she kept telling her where they were going, knowing that Cilla was very fond of both Ella and Ivy.

'Trixie! Trixie!' Cilla repeated over and over again, smiling happily.

Maggie was tempted to try and explain that Trixie wouldn't be there but couldn't bring herself to spoil Cilla's obvious delight.

It was enough that the prospect pacified her. When Cilla even began singing nursery rhymes as they set out Maggie felt so relieved by the change in her that she almost had a smile on her own face when she knocked on the O'Malleys' door.

Ella, an apron around her middle and her hands covered in flour, answered it. She looked surprised when she saw who it was.

'Trixie not with you?' she asked, as she wiped the flour from her hands before reaching down to hug Cilla.

'No.' Maggie shook her head, trying to blink back the tears that threatened at the mention of Trixie's name.

'Why's that? Has she found herself another job?'

Maggie hesitated, not knowing quite what to say. 'I'm not sure...' she began, too choked to go on.

'What do you mean, you don't know?' Ella looked puzzled. 'Do you mean you don't want to tell me?'

'No, no, of course not,' Maggie said quickly. 'In fact, I've come to ask if you can tell me where Trixie is. I was hoping Ivy might know something, or that she might have heard from her.'

Ella looked bewildered. 'Are you telling me that Trixie's left home and you have no inkling where she might be?' she persisted.

'That's right. Sam says he's found her a job as a housekeeper to a middle-aged man. He made her pack a bag and I haven't seen her since. I'm worried stiff,' she confided.

'Oh dear, that's a terrible situation to be in,' Ella murmured as she straightened up. 'Come on in, take your coat off, sit yourself down, and I'll make a pot of tea and we'll talk about it.'

Cilla had already gone over to her special cupboard and was pulling out toys and spreading them around the floor. As she sat down and began playing happily with them Maggie breathed a sigh of relief.

'Poor little luv, she's been in a terrible state and crying her eyes out all week for Trixie,' she told Ella.

'Missing her, is she?' Ella said, smoothing

Cilla's hair.

'She's driving us mad with her tantrums. The trouble is she doesn't understand when I try to tell her that Trixie's gone.'

'What do you mean by gone? Don't you know where she's working?' Ella's voice was unusually sharp, as well as curious.

Maggie shook her head and gave a deep sigh. 'No,' she confessed. 'As I said, I came round to see you in the hope that Ivy might be able to tell me something. I don't know. I thought that she might have heard some news from her. I'm half out of my mind with worry and I can't get a word of sense out of Sam.'

'I'd better make that cuppa, it sounds as though you need it,' Ella said sympathetically. 'Make yourself comfortable; Ivy's popped out to get a loaf of bread but she won't be long. In fact, she should be back any minute.'

The moment they heard the door opening, Cilla looked up expectantly, calling out Trixie's name. Her face fell when she saw it was Ivy coming in and immediately she burst into noisy tears.

'Hey, come on, chuck, what's all this noise about?' Ivy asked, gathering Cilla into her arms and hugging her.

Cilla struggled to get free. 'Trixie ... Trixie ... I want Trixie, where's Trixie?' she howled, her tear-streaked face going red and creased up with crying.

Ivy looked questioningly at Maggie. 'Have you come to tell us what's happened and where Trixie's gone?'

'No, luv.' Maggie shook her head. 'I was hoping you'd be able to tell *me* something. I haven't heard a word from her since she went out of the house with her dad a week ago.'

'Where did they go? What has he got to say about it?' Ivy asked looking puzzled.

'He won't say. He told her to pack a bag and that he'd found a job for her and that she'd be staying there wherever it was and not coming home again. He wasn't gone all that long so it can't be too far away,' she added.

Maggie looked beseechingly at Ivy. 'Did she say anything to you? Have you any idea where she might be? If you know anything at all, then for God's sake tell me because I'm going half out of my mind with the worry of it all.'

Ivy shook her head. 'I haven't heard a word from her, not since I walked home with her the day she lost her job. I thought she must be scouring Liverpool looking for work and that was why she hadn't had time to pop round. I did think it odd, though, because she'd promised to meet Andrew Bacon to arrange to go to the pictures with him, and I haven't heard anything more

197

about it since; nor has Jake.'

'Who did you say... Andrew Bacon?' Maggie asked in a bewildered voice.

'Yes, you know, he's the chap who works at the bank; the one who helped her with the Christmas money,' Ivy reminded her. 'She must have mentioned him; we all went out together on New Year's Eve.'

'Oh yes, I know now who you're talking about. She's told me all about him...' Maggie's voice trailed off. 'Do you think he might know something?' she added.

'I doubt it, or he would have said something to Jake,' Ivy said.

Maggie groaned. 'Something terrible must have happened to her.'

'Ivy, tell Maggie what Fred Linacre said to you on Monday morning,' Ella prompted, 'while I go and get you a cup.'

'Oh yes.' Ivy frowned. 'He announced that a new girl was starting, Betty something or other, and that she'd be taking Trixie's place. Then he took me aside and said that if he heard me gossiping about Trixie or even mentioning her name then he'd see I was booted out and would make sure I didn't get another job anywhere in Liverpool.'

Maggie looked shocked. 'Oh dear, Ivy, what a terrible thing for him to say to you; how upsetting. Why on earth was he threatening you like that, do you think?'

'I've no idea.' Ivy shrugged. 'I told Mum

about it when I came home and she said the best thing I could do if I didn't want to lose my job was to say nothing.'

'Yes, of course, I can understand that. Jobs aren't two a penny at the moment – not on Merseyside, anyway.'

'I don't think they are anywhere else either,' Ella commented as she came back into the room. 'Most companies seem to be cutting back.'

'That's right. Wasn't that the reason my Trixie got the sack? When she came home and told us she'd lost her job she said that it was case of first in, last out, or something like that.'

'Yes, that's what Fred said when he announced she was getting the sack; which makes it all the more strange that another girl was taken on right away. I think he deliberately sacked Trixie for some reason, though I can't work out what it was.'

'This makes it more worrying than ever,' Maggie sighed. 'My Sam told Trixie before Christmas that there were going to be some changes in the coming year and he hinted that he had something lined up for her. Do you think he could be in cahoots with Fred Linacre and got him to deliberately sack Trixie?'

Ivy looked thoughtful as she took the cup of tea her mother had poured for her. 'Well, he did persuade Fred to take her on in the first place, didn't he?' she pointed out.

'You're right, luv,' Maggie agreed. 'So why ask Fred to sack her a couple of years later and why did Fred have to go and threaten you like he did?'

'Obviously the pair of them have cooked something up between them. Perhaps he didn't want me speculating about it to any of the other women, but we'll never know the real story till we can ask Trixie herself,' Ivy said philosophically.

'How can we do that when none of us have any idea where she is? I've a good mind to go round to this Fred Linacre's place and ask him outright if he knows anything about it,' Maggie said angrily. 'Do you know where he lives, Ivy?'

'No, but it's bound to be somewhere around here. All I know is that he's a bachelor and the women on the assembly line say that's what makes him such a misery guts.'

As they talked, the more Maggie became convinced that Trixie's disappearance was somehow linked with Fred Linacre and she resolved that she'd tackle Sam about it the moment he came home. Everything he'd said to Trixie before he'd taken her away the previous Saturday pointed to some sort of collusion between him and Fred.

He hadn't even shown any surprise when Trixie had come home and said she'd been sacked. Under normal circumstances he would have hit the roof and probably have given her a good hiding. Now she even wondered if he'd known before Trixie did what was going to happen. It did seem that she'd been sacked from the factory on purpose, Maggie thought as she sipped her second cup of tea.

'Ivy, are you sure you don't know where this fellow Fred Linacre lives?' she asked again as she put her cup back on the table, a worried frown creasing her forehead. 'Haven't you any idea at all?'

'No, I haven't. I can ask when I go into work on Monday, but I've never heard anyone mention it,' she added with a wry smile.

'This chap Andrew Bacon who works at the bank might know,' Maggie persisted.

Ivy shook her head. 'I shouldn't think he's ever met Fred Linacre,' she said.

'Well, he might have done at some time. If Fred Linacre is careful with his money then he might have an account at the bank where this chap is working.'

'Even if he does know, Andrew wouldn't be able to tell you,' Ella chimed in. 'Bank employees have to swear to secrecy when they're taken on, I remember him telling Jake that it's more than their job's worth to talk about any of their customers affairs.'

'Well, I'll have to see if I can get Sam to tell me; he must know because they drink at the same pub. Trixie might even be at Fred's place.'

'I'm sure you're wrong if you think that Trixie could be at Fred Linacre's place,' Ivy said in astonishment. 'She hated him! He was always taunting her about something or other.'

'I'm not saying she went to his place willingly,' Maggie said hastily. 'She didn't want to go with Sam last Saturday but he insisted, and what's more he made her take her clothes and stuff with her.'

Ivy and her mother said nothing. As Ella began gathering up the cups Maggie stood up and announced that she must be getting back.

'I can't wait to talk to Sam and find out what he knows,' she stated. 'I'll make him tell me; I'll get the truth out of him somehow or other,' she vowed.

'You be careful,' Ella warned her. 'Your Sam can be violent, you've said so yourself. He's knocked you about before and he's given Trixie a hiding. Without her there to take your part, or look after you if he thumps you about, then what's going to happen? You've got little Cilla to consider, you know.'

'I'm aware of that,' Maggie said worriedly, 'but I've got to get to the bottom of this one way or another. Trixie may be in some awful danger and even if she isn't, this fellow must be keeping her somewhere against her will and she'll be breaking her heart to come home.'

'Well, that's true enough,' Ella agreed as she helped Cilla to put her coat on.

'If either of you do hear anything at all about Trixie, then you will come and tell me, won't you? Promise me you'll do that,' Maggie pleaded, looking from one to the other.

'Of course we will. We'll be doing all we can to find out what's happened to her,' Ella promised. 'Neither of us had any idea that she was missing like this. Ivy thought she was so busy looking for a new job that she hadn't had time to get in touch.'

'Have a word with that Andrew and see if he knows anything. If he was as fond of Trixie as you say, then he might manage to find a way to let you know where this Fred Linacre lives, if he knows it, without breaking any of the promises he's made to the bank,' Maggie added hopefully.

Chapter Sixteen

Sam Jackson felt slightly uneasy as he walked into the pub at midday on Saturday and ordered a beer. Fred Linacre was already standing at the bar. It was a week since he'd taken Trixie along to his house and since then neither of them had spoken a word about it.

'Another pint?' Sam's voice was terse, a clear sign that he was on edge.

Fred Linacre turned and nodded, picked up his tankard, drained it, and held it out.

Sam pushed it across the counter towards the waiting barmaid who had put his beer in front of him. 'Fill that up again,' he ordered and counted out the additional money to pay for it.

'Shall we go and sit over in the corner, Fred?' he suggested when she'd pulled another pint and passed it across the counter. 'There're one or two things I want to ask you.'

'I thought there might be,' Fred answered laconically as he led the way.

'Well?' Sam asked as he set his glass on the table and sat down. 'What's the news? Has she settled in without causing any trouble?'

Fred took a long noisy swig of his beer, put his tankard down, and wiped the back of his hand across his mouth to remove the froth. 'It takes time,' he prevaricated.

'You mean she hasn't taken to living there with you?' Sam muttered. 'I was afraid of that.'

'I'll tame her; you leave things well alone. I don't want you or your missus sneaking round trying to see her or even speak to her.

Is that understood?'

'Clear as mud,' Sam said tersely. He took another drink of his beer, then thumped the glass down hard. 'I need to know that she's all right, though. I don't want you hurting her in any way. The odd cuff over the ear or around the gob is one thing if she answers you back, but I don't hold with you giving her a hiding.'

'Want to keep that sort of thing to yourself, do you?' Fred mocked sarcastically.

'Children are like animals; you've got to show 'em who's master,' Sam agreed. 'It's their parents' job to do that, though, not some bloody stranger.'

'Hardly a stranger, seeing as how she's living with me,' Fred countered with a smirk. He drained his glass and stood up ready to leave. 'I've got to get back because my meal will be on the table waiting and your Trixie's not too bad a cook,' he taunted. 'I won't be telling her that I've seen you, so don't worry.'

'Hold on!' Sam stood up, grabbing the other man by the arm. 'Set my mind at rest; tell me she's doing all right.'

'What would you do if I tell you she isn't?' He shook Sam's hand from his arm. 'We made a deal, remember?'

'I know we made a bloody deal but I still want to know she's all right,' he persisted. 'My missus is worried about her and the little one's never stopped screaming and crying for her since the day she left. Driving me mad, it is.'

'You should have thought about all that.' Fred shrugged and began pushing his way towards the door. 'Show 'em who's master, I'm sure you know how to do that.'

Sam drained his beer glass and followed Fred out of the pub, intending to try and persuade him to say more, but when he got outside Fred was way ahead of him. Annoyed, he shouted out to him to wait but Fred ignored him. He felt so angry that he decided to follow him back to Cavendish Road.

Fred had already disappeared into the passageway and no amount of hammering on the locked door of number twenty or shouting up at the windows seemed to do any good.

He was on the point of turning away when he spotted Trixie with her face pressed against an upstairs window. She looked scared stiff and she was mouthing something at him but he was too far away to make out what she was saying.

As he stared up, wondering what she was trying to tell him, he saw Fred appear there as well and roughly push her to one side and then look down and shake a fist at him.

Furiously, he hammered on the door again but nothing happened, no one came to answer it. He thought of going into the shop underneath to see if they could tell him anything about Trixie. Then he decided that would be futile and they probably wouldn't even know what he was talking about. He took another look up at the window but there was no one there; the drab grey curtains had been closed. For a minute or two he couldn't put Trixie's face out of his mind; she'd looked so unhappy.

Realising that Fred had got the better of him and that there was nothing he could do about it, he dismissed it from his mind, turned up the collar of his jacket, and set off for home.

The sound of Cilla sobbing and her repeating Trixie's name over and over again in a high-pitched monotonous wail as he reached his own home and let himself in, added to his irritation.

'Can't you keep that drippy idiot quiet?' he thundered the moment he walked into the room. He glared at Maggie as he shrugged off his jacket and settled down in his arm-chair, loosening the laces of his boots and kicking them off.

'She's missing our Trixie and so am I,' Maggie retorted. 'I think it's about time you told me what's happened to her. I don't like the rumours I've been hearing,' she added darkly.

'Bloody gossip, you mean, don't you?' he muttered. 'Women with nothing better to do but stand jangling to each other instead of minding their own business.'

'Is it gossip, though, or is it the truth what people are saying about our Trixie?' Maggie said, her voice shaking as she confronted him nervously.

'How should I bloody well know?' he sneered. 'I'm too busy grafting to put food on the table to listen to such tales.'

'What about when you go to the pub? What are the men in there saying, or haven't you dared tell any of them that you've sold your daughter into slavery?'

'What the hell are you on about?' Sam snarled. His face was red and his eyes hard and menacing. Maggie knew that any minute now he might lash out and she was bracing herself for the impact of his fist when it landed.

Sensitive to the tense atmosphere, Cilla began banging with her fists against the door and crying uncontrollably. Before Maggie could do anything to stop him, Sam was out of his chair and across the room and had picked up the child by the scruff of her neck and thrown her out of the room on to the landing.

As he slammed the door shut, leaving her out there in the darkness, her screams became so ear-piercing that other people living in the house started shouting out to them to do something to shut her up before they called the scuffers.

As Maggie rushed to rescue her, Sam's hand went out to grab hold of her and stop her.

'Leave me be,' she hissed. 'You know Cilla's terrified of the dark; she'll go demented shut out there on her own,' she said opening the door for Cilla to come back into the room. Cilla ran to the corner of the room and sat there, clutching Bonzo and rocking back and forth.

'She's barmy already,' he guffawed. 'Wonder who the hell it is she takes after?'

Maggie paused and looked at him with real hatred. 'She's your child,' she commented quietly. 'Before you went off to war you were a loving father, always taking our Trixie on your knee and making a fuss of her. It might help if you did that with Cilla instead of spurning her and bawling and shouting at her, like you do the rest of us.'

'The less I see of her the better I like it,' he stated coldly. 'When I went into the army I left behind a comfortable home and a wife and daughter I could be proud of, and after fighting in mud and muck for the sake of my country I come back to a shambles. Living here is not much better than being over there in the trenches. We scrimp and scrape to make ends meet and when you're not moaning about things I have to put up with you nagging me about something or other.'

'If you didn't spend half your wages down at the boozer then we wouldn't have to scrimp and scrape,' she rejoined pointedly. 'Without my share of Trixie's wages coming in each week I'm going to be worse off than ever.'

'How the hell do you make that out?' he demanded, staring at her angrily. 'You'll have one less mouth to feed, so you don't need as much money, you daft ha'porth.'

'And one less pair of hands to help me look after little Cilla. Do you ever stop and think how much of my time she takes up? I have to wash and dress her, cut up her food for her and keep an eye on her every minute of the day.'

'You fuss over her far too much. She's big enough to start doing things for herself. The more you wait on her, washing her and combing her hair, the less likely she is to try and do it for herself. She'll soon find out how to get the grub inside her when she's hungry enough. Stop treating her like a two-year-old. She's turned seven and she ought to be at school like other kids.'

'In her state! She can barely walk more than a few yards unless someone is holding her hand.'

'No, and that's because you push her everywhere in that damn pram. Make her use her legs.'

'Perhaps if you showed more interest and

took her out for a little walk now and again it would help–'

Maggie's words were cut short by a slap across her face that brought tears to her eyes but in no way stopped her diatribe.

'God only knows what you've done with our Trixie but, believe me, I will find out. If she's come to any harm then heaven help you, Sam Jackson, I'll get my revenge.'

He stared at her in surprise; disconcerted that she dared to answer him back. 'What the hell do you think you can do to hurt me, you silly bitch?' he asked scornfully.

'I'll go to the police and when they hear about the way you're always knocking us about then if Trixie doesn't turn up safe and sound or something terrible happens to her, you'll get strung up for murder,' Maggie threatened.

Sam didn't answer. As he made to walk away Maggie once again grabbed hold of his arm and stopped him. 'Is she with that fellow Fred Linacre? If she is, then I want to know where he lives; I'm going round to see if she's all right and–'

He shook himself free, pushing her away so hard that she lost her balance and crashed backwards into the wall. By the time she'd recovered her breath and managed to pull herself together he'd left and slammed the door.

Andrew Bacon compared the time on the bank's wall clock with his own pocket watch, and then once more checked the ledger in front of him to make sure every detail was correct. Satisfied, he carried it over to the big iron safe that dominated one corner of the office and carefully locked it away.

Returning to his seat at the counter he made sure that all his pens and pencils, date stamp, roller and ink pad were neatly aligned before he left for the day.

It had been a strange few weeks. He had started the new year off in good spirits after one of the most enjoyable weekends he'd had for a long time. He usually went out with Jake and one or two of their friends, chaps who'd been at school with them, but this had been different.

For a start it had been New Year's Eve and he'd gone with Jake and his sister and Trixie to a dance and he was certainly glad that he had. Afterwards they'd gone down to the Pier Head as the ships all sounded their hooters and sirens and they had joined in all the revelry.

He'd never had much to do with girls, but Trixie was different. She was pretty, for a start, and she was so easy to talk to, not like the prim, prissy girls who came to the night-school classes he attended, or the loud-mouthed girls he'd known at school. He'd enjoyed the evening. So much so that he'd asked her if he could take her to the pictures.

She'd agreed to think about it and to see if she could get out to meet him. Then they'd made an arrangement through Ivy and Jake to meet up on Wednesday so that they could finalise the arrangement.

When Trixie hadn't turned up on Wednesday night, though, he'd felt peeved. He was sure she liked him and he wondered why she was being quite so reticent.

He hadn't said anything about it to Jake because he'd felt such a fool at being stood up, but he wondered if he should mention it to him when they met tonight in order to satisfy his curiosity about why she'd done it.

Trixie and Jake's sister were such good friends that she was bound to have said something to Ivy about it and that was probably the only way he'd ever find out.

To his surprise, he found Jake waiting outside, lolling up against the bank wall smoking a cigarette.

'Talk of the devil.' He grinned as he went up to him. 'I was just thinking of you; there's something I want to ask you,' Andrew said.

'Something I want to ask you as well, mate. Have you time for a quick jar?'

'This time of day! All right, I'll have a half,' he conceded when he saw the look of impatience on Jake's face.

Once they'd got to the pub and ordered their beer, they carried their drinks across to a quiet corner. 'You first,' Jake said.

'No, mine is not all that important; let's hear what's worrying you?'

'Ivy asked me to have a word with you; it's about Trixie. I believe she was supposed to be meeting you or going to the pictures with you last Wednesday.'

Andrew looked startled. 'It was about Trixie that I wanted to talk to you,' he said, picking up his beer and taking a drink.

'Go on, then, what've you got to say? Trixie's mum is going out of her head worrying about her, what happened?'

'Happened?' Andrew looked puzzled. 'Nothing happened; she never turned up. I was wondering why and I thought she might have said something about it to Ivy.'

It was Jake's turn to look mystified. 'Ivy hasn't seen her and her mam's been round to our place to see if we know what's happened to her. It seems that last Saturday her old man took her somewhere and didn't bring her back—'

'And you're saying that she hasn't been home since?' Andrew interrupted.

'No. There's a bit more to it. Her old man insisted on her taking her clothes with her...'

'You mean he chucked her out? Why?' Andrew felt uneasy as he recalled Trixie telling him that her father probably wouldn't let her go to the pictures, particularly if he knew it was with a boy, and he wondered if it had anything to do with that. He was brought back to the present as Jake went on. 'He didn't exactly chuck her out, but last Saturday Trixie was sacked from the biscuit factory where she worked with our Ivy, and instead of flying off the handle as they thought he'd do, her dad told her that he had another job lined up for her. He ordered her to pack her things and said he'd take her there. The trouble is he won't even tell Trixie's mum where it is.'

Jake held up his hand as Andrew was about to speak. 'Hold on, hear me out. The foreman at the factory told Trixie she was getting the push because they were cutting back; "last in, first out", you know the drill. Ivy says that a new girl started there on Monday to replace her, so that was a cock and bull story.'

'What's that got to do with Trixie disappearing?'

'The foreman, Fred Linacre, is a boozing pal of Trixie's dad. He lives on his own and Trixie's mum thinks she's been taken to his place. What's more, she's convinced that she's being held prisoner there.'

'Bit far fetched and over the top, isn't it? I mean, who'd do a thing like that?'

'Trixie's dad, seemingly. He'd been given money to make sure she went wherever he's taken her or so her mum claims.'

'Why doesn't her mother do something

about it, like tell the police or go and fetch her home?'

'That's the problem. None of us know where this Fred Linacre lives but we thought you might. It's quite probable that he puts his money in your bank and, if he does, then his name and address will be on the bank's records.'

'Giving out that sort of information is more than my job's worth,' Andrew said quickly, fingering his collar uneasily at the thought of the implications involved.

'That's what I told Ivy, but she said that if you thought anything at all of Trixie then you'd want to help. It seems to be the only option open to us, mate; her mum really does think she might be in grave danger.'

Chapter Seventeen

Andrew couldn't stop thinking about how Trixie might be in real danger. It seemed all very strange to him that there was a possibility that her father was making her live with this Fred Linacre like Ivy claimed, but then there were some odd people living around Scotland Road.

Finding out the address where this man lived and then passing it on to Jake or Ivy

216

was out of the question. If it was ever found out that he'd done something like that then he'd be in serious trouble. He'd not been making an excuse when he'd told them that he really could lose his job.

There must be some other way that wouldn't jeopardise his career, he reasoned. Perhaps finding out the address and then going there himself might be the answer. That was risky, but if he acted sensibly, simply walked along the street and took stock of the house, it might give him a better idea of the situation.

It took him most of the day to gain access to the file he needed because even to do that he had to be very discreet so as not to arouse anyone's suspicion.

He didn't know Cavendish Road except by name – although, since it was off Scotland Road, he'd probably been down it many times. He resolved he would check it out when he finished work that night and casually walk past number twenty. If the house looked suspicious or run down and scruffy, and he thought there was a possibility that Trixie was in danger, then somehow he'd find a way to let Jake know.

To his surprise, the number he'd memorised wasn't a house at all; it was a door wedged in between two shops; one an ironmonger's and the other a furniture shop. He presumed the door must lead into a passageway or else a staircase which would give access to the living quarters above the ironmonger's shop. It was obvious from the lighted windows that the furniture shop used their upstairs as a part of their sales area.

Although he walked past several times, it didn't help at all because he couldn't really tell what was up above the ironmonger's. To get a better view, he crossed over the road a little further down and then turned and walked back.

He noticed that the windows above the shop had iron bars across them but it was impossible to see into the room beyond so he was unable to tell if anyone actually lived there.

If one of the shops had been a news-agent's, then he would have gone in and bought an evening paper and perhaps had an opportunity to ask if they'd seen a girl answering to Trixie's description around there recently. As it was, even if she was living in the vicinity, neither of the shops were the sort she was likely to visit.

He walked past on the other side of the road twice more, straining his eyes to see if he could see anyone in the room. Once he thought he caught the shadow of someone by the window and that they were waving, but when he looked again there was nothing and so he put it down to his imagination working overtime.

He didn't know what to tell Jake. He knew that both he and Ivy were relying on him to find out something but his strict adherence to banking rules stopped him from actually giving them Fred Linacre's address.

After he'd eaten his evening meal he told his mother he was going out for a while.

'Whatever for? You haven't got night school on a Monday evening, have you?' she asked in surprise.

For a moment he was tempted to lie. 'No,' he admitted, 'but I do need to see Jake about something.'

'Isn't it time you broke off seeing him? You're not school boys now; it's time you found some better-class friends, chaps you work with, not someone who wears greasy overalls and grafts down at the docks,' she said disparagingly.

'Most of the chaps I work with live out at Walton, Crosby or Maghull, or over in Wallasey,' he told her. 'Once they finish work they can't wait to get away from Scotland Road and the docks.'

'I know, I know. We'll move away from here the minute your father gets on his feet again,' she said irritably.

'Yes, I know that is what you want to do, but not everyone around the Scotland Road area is a slummy, you know.' He felt really angry about his mother's remarks about

219

Jake. 'Countless other families would move away, you know, Mum; only, like us, they've fallen on hard times and either lost all their money or their jobs and been forced to move into this area.'

He'd always known that his mother was a snob, ever since his first day at school when she had warned him not to play with any scruffy-looking little boys.

He still laughed to himself whenever he thought about it because, apart from him, they'd all been scruffy. He'd been the only one in trim grey shorts, a jumper without holes in the elbows, and grey socks and polished shoes. Several of them had poked fun at him, started pushing him about and asking him if he was one of the mannequins from Lewis's window. The only one who'd stuck up for him had been Jake and they'd been friends ever since.

Even so he'd never really fitted in. The other boys teased him and called him a swot because he preferred reading to fighting, and he was never allowed to stay out in the street at night playing tag or swinging from the lamp-posts.

The girls had laughed at him because his hair was always neatly cut and he always looked well scrubbed. Some of them even called him a 'Wallasey boy'. At first, before Jake had shocked him by telling him the real meaning of those words, he'd taken it as a compliment because they'd lived over the other side of the Mersey in a posh house at Egremont before his father's troubles had left them penniless. He'd rarely spoken to any girls, except Jake's sister Ivy, till she'd introduced him to Trixie.

Trixie was different from Ivy, not only in looks but also in so many other ways. For that matter she was different from any of the other girls around Scotland Road. He really liked her and it worried him to think that she could be in some sort of trouble.

He really did want to tell Jake where Fred Linacre lived but loyalty to the bank made it seem impossible. Then he hit on an idea; he could point out the house without actually telling him that it was the place they were looking for. That was why he was nipping round to see Jake on a Monday evening.

Jake was almost as surprised to see him on the doorstep as his own mother had been when he'd said he was going out.

'Coming for a jar?' Andrew invited.

'On a Monday, you mad, whacker? I've no ackers from now till payday. I thought you had some news for me.'

'Come on, don't stand arguing or your mum and Ivy will want to know what's going on. Get your coat and cap and catch me up.'

Andrew had only gone a few hundred yards along Horatio Street when Jake joined him.

'Where we going, then?' Jake asked as they turned in the direction of Scotland Road.

'Cavendish Road. It's a few turnings along on the right. Do you know it?'

'Is this something to do with Trixie?'

Andrew shrugged. 'It could be. I want to point out a house to you, or rather a flat up over a shop. Come on, you'll see what I mean; it's only round the corner.' As they turned into Cavendish Road he deliberately walked on the opposite side of the road to number twenty.

'See that ironmonger's over on the other side of the road?' he said casually. 'Look up at the windows above it, do you think there's anyone living there?'

'It's a job to tell with those bars across the window. Somebody seems to be up there because you can see a light. It's not very bright, probably only a candle or an oil lamp, but there's definitely a light on up there. It could be a storeroom, of course...' Jake's voice trailed off. 'Are you saying that's where Fred Linacre lives?'

Trixie felt desperate. She'd been confined to the rooms that Fred called home for over a week and she was no nearer finding a way of getting away than she had been when her dad had first brought her up there.

She was sure her mother must be beside herself with worry by now and she couldn't bear to think what sort of a state Cilla must be in. Even if her mum did try and explain things to her she'd never be able to make her understand.

She wondered what her dad was saying; was he telling the truth about where she was? He couldn't be, she reasoned, otherwise her mother would have tried to see her.

Each day she'd spent hours and hours sitting by the window watching to see if her mother walked down the road. Even if she couldn't let her in she could have waved to her and made her understand that she couldn't even open the window.

Being on her own for so much of the time was a torture in itself. She had no one to share her worries with or even to talk to. There was no way that she could think of that she could get a message to her mum or even to Ivy.

By now her mum must have gone round to the O'Malleys and told them what had happened and she wondered if Ivy had said something to Andrew so that at least he'd know that she hadn't deliberately stood him up.

She'd hated Fred when she'd worked in the factory but now she positively loathed him. He not only taunted her about being his prisoner, but he also kept hinting at what was going to happen to her in the future. From time to time he made it quite clear that he'd paid her father good money for her so that she was tied to him for life and that there was no question of her ever getting away from him.

That was a fate she definitely couldn't endure and she tried desperately to think of some way of forcing him to change his plans and let her go.

She turned over in her mind all the possible ways she could do this and then reluctantly abandoned them because she knew they wouldn't work, and that Fred was clever enough to spot what she was doing. She'd already tried to break the glass in the windows but it was too tough and, anyway, she knew that the iron bars outside were so close together that they would prevent her escaping.

The best way would be to attract someone's attention to the fact that she was imprisoned up there and it had to be in such a way that Fred would be forced to admit she was in his flat. Banging on the windows had proved to be absolutely useless so she knew she had to find some other method.

Finally, she decided the only way to escape was to harm herself in some way so that Fred had to call for help or she had to go to hospital.

It was the perfect answer, she told herself, and wondered why she hadn't thought of it before. All she had to do was decide what sort of an accident she was going to have.

Even that was not as easy as she'd thought. She couldn't get out on to the stairs so she couldn't fall down them. She tried jumping off a chair but apart from twisting her ankle slightly and making it painful to walk around, that was no good.

She took a sheet from the bed with the idea of making it into a rope and hanging herself. It seemed dramatic but it would be all right as long as she did it a few minutes before Fred came in so that he could cut her down before she actually came to any real harm, but she couldn't find anywhere to suspend the sheet from that would raise her high enough off the ground.

The only other way was to do something drastic like cutting herself so badly that there was blood all over the place. The idea scared her because it would probably be painful. She'd cut her finger once and she could still remember that it had hurt for days afterwards and yet there hadn't been very much blood. She'd have to cut herself pretty badly to make it necessary for her to have to go to hospital. But would he take her there? She wasn't sure. Supposing he just let her lie there and suffer or bleed to death and not do a thing about it?

The more she thought about it the more she was sure that if she was severely hurt then he would get help because if she did bleed to death he'd have a body on his hands. What was more, he'd have her father at his throat wanting his money back.

Bringing herself to inflict an injury serious enough to need hospital attention wasn't going to be easy. She wasn't frightened of blood, not even her own, but she was scared of pain. Making a cut with a knife long enough and deep enough to do some real damage would take a lot of courage.

The sooner she did it the better, she decided. She knew what time Fred would be home because she had to have his meal ready. If she did it about five minutes before he was due to arrive, then she'd be able to convince him that she'd cut herself while carving the meat.

She toyed with the big sharp carver, testing it lightly on the fleshy part of her arm to see how sharp it really was before deciding on the best place to make the cut. She did it so lightly that all it did was make a red mark that soon faded and didn't even draw blood. She tried to stick the very point of the knife into one of the veins on the back of her hand but, apart from making an indentation surrounded by a white area where the blood had momentarily been cut off, she couldn't bring herself to stab hard enough to break through the flesh. Anyway, there wasn't much point in opening a vein; it ought to be an artery so that the blood would pump out and go everywhere and he'd be so concerned about her that he'd rush to get help.

She was on the verge of abandoning her plan because she knew she hadn't the will-power to slash or stab herself with sufficient force to do any damage because the thought of the pain scared her, when she remembered the cut-throat razor Fred used when he shaved every morning. Now that would be sharp, she told herself. He kept it so by stropping it on a special strip of leather every time he used it and afterwards he had to be extremely careful when he cleaned it because it would slice through the towel if he held it at the wrong angle.

That would do exactly what she wanted and it would be so quick and easy to use that she would be able to cut herself before she knew she'd done it, she told herself.

She was standing in the living room, holding the razor in her hand, shaking so much that her teeth were chattering as she contemplated how she would use it and where it would be best to inflict the wound, when she heard the noise on the stairs that signalled Fred was home. The sound startled her so much that, before she could control it, her hand, which was still holding the razor, had gone to her mouth to stop herself screaming and the razor had slashed across her throat.

She felt a sharp, but not unpleasant sensation, as blood spurted like a miniature fountain, splashing on to her face, soaking the front of her blouse, and dripping down her skirt.

It gushed so quickly that she felt faint; almost as if the life was draining out of her.

As Fred pushed open the door and saw her swaying backwards and forwards, holding the back of a chair for support, his mouth gaped open in shock.

'Christ! What have you gone and done?'

She tried to speak but the words wouldn't come, and there was a mist in front of her eyes and a rushing sound in her ears. She felt as though she was floating. Before Fred could reach her she slid to the floor in a blood-soaked heap.

Chapter Eighteen

Maggie was shaking like a leaf and her mouth felt dry as the nurse escorted her to a bed that had curtains drawn around it to screen it off from the rest of the ward.

Her hand flew to her lips to stop herself from screaming as the nurse pulled the curtain aside and she saw Trixie lying there looking like a waxen doll. Her neck was swathed in bandages and there were so many tubes and wires attached to her body that she was filled with concern.

'Trixie.' Maggie's voice was a shaky whisper, but the nurse shook her head and shushed her to silence.

'Mrs Jackson, your daughter's been sedated, so it's pointless speaking to her because she won't hear you,' she said authoritatively. 'You may sit with her for a few minutes if you wish, but it would be better if you came back tomorrow.'

The nurse bustled away, closing the curtains before she left. Maggie sat there in a trance staring at Trixie. Trixie's arms were at her sides, stiff and straight, but Maggie was afraid to even hold her hand, in case it was the wrong thing to do.

The happenings of the last hours came flooding back into her mind. There'd been a loud knock on the door at home and the fright of finding a uniformed policeman standing there, telling her that her daughter was in hospital.

She'd been so upset that she hadn't known what to do. Sam wasn't home from work and she was unsure whether they would let Cilla into the hospital or not. She wished she'd asked the policeman but she hadn't thought about it till after he'd left.

In desperation she'd decided not to risk it because it would be terrible to arrive at the hospital and then find they wouldn't let her in, so she'd taken her round to the O'Malleys' place. When she told Ella what had happened she had said at once that she'd look after Cilla.

They'd been almost as shocked as she was by the news. Ivy had offered to come with her but Maggie had thought it was better for her to stay and help look after Cilla.

'She knows you so well, luv, and she'll usually do anything you ask her,' she pointed out. 'I'll be as quick as I can and I'll let you know how Trixie is when I get back. Perhaps you can go and visit her tomorrow; that's if she will still be there. I've no idea what has happened. The policeman said something about an accident but I was too stunned to ask him for details.'

Now, sitting at Trixie's bedside, Maggie was desperate to know how her daughter had come to be lying there unconscious and why her throat was so heavily bandaged.

She wondered if someone had tried to strangle her. She wished that she had let Ivy come with her after all. She would have asked the nurse all the right questions. Her own mind was in such a fuzzy state that she was afraid she was about to break down and cry if she didn't keep a hold on herself.

The nurse was back again so quickly that Maggie hadn't had time to pull herself together.

'I'm afraid you must leave now,' the nurse insisted.

Trembling and dazed, her eyes misty with tears, Maggie preceded the nurse from the ward, feeling distraught because she'd asked none of the questions going round and round in her mind.

As she walked away from the hospital all she could think about was how lifeless Trixie had looked and that the nurse had said the police would want to talk to her. She wasn't even sure if they meant her or Trixie, but it must be her since they couldn't talk to Trixie at the moment.

She wondered if she ought to tell them about Sam taking Trixie away just over a week ago. She couldn't help wondering, though, if this accident might have something to do with Sam in some way, or else with the unknown man. If she told the police that, it might land Sam in trouble.

Perhaps if she had plucked up courage earlier and gone to the police and told them that Trixie was missing then Trixie wouldn't be lying in a hospital bed now.

When she arrived back at Horatio Street she was so upset that Ella insisted she sat down and had a cup of tea before she said anything at all.

They were full of concern when she told them about the state Trixie was in and agreed that it was certainly a possibility that whatever had happened to her must surely have something to do with Fred Linacre.

'Andrew's been very helpful,' Ella told Maggie as she plied her with a second cup of tea. 'Poor lad, he was so anxious to help because he's taken a real shine to Trixie. It's more than his job's worth, though, to say outright where this Fred lives but he took our Jake to Cavendish Road and pointed out some rooms up over a shop there and, let's face it, a nod's as good as a wink now, isn't it!'

'So where is it in Cavendish Road?' Maggie asked. 'I won't go there,' she added quickly, 'but it might be useful to know so that if the police mention it I'll be able to put two and two together.'

They told her all they knew and begged her to come back and let them know exactly what was happening as soon as she could.

It certainly gave Maggie plenty to think about as she took Cilla home. She tried to work out what she would say to Sam. She knew she had to be careful because if she got his back up then he'd clam up and tell her nothing.

She was still taking her coat off when there was a sharp rap at the door and her heart pounded because she guessed that it was the police.

There were two of them, a burly sergeant and a youngish policeman. She asked them

232

to sit down, knowing she'd feel less intimidated if they were on eye level instead of towering over her. Cilla started to cry and it took Maggie several minutes to pacify her before she could give them her full attention.

By then Sam was home. He'd walked in without realising that the police were there and the minute he saw them he turned as if to go out again, but the sergeant stopped him.

'Sam Jackson? We need to ask you some questions in connection with an incident involving your daughter earlier today. Now what can you tell us?'

'Incident?' He looked mystified. 'What incident?'

He sounded and looked so surprised that Maggie didn't know whether to believe him or not when he claimed that he knew nothing about it.

'Do you mind telling us where you've been since you finished work?' the sergeant persisted.

Sam pushed back his cap and scratched his head. 'What the hell for? I've been in the boozer, if you must know, whetting my whistle after a hard day's work.'

'So who were you drinking with? Can you tell us the name of anyone who can vouch for the fact that you were there?' The sergeant remained firm. Sam merely shrugged his shoulders.

'One of the regulars; the foreman from the biscuit factory. He was drinking with me for half an hour or so,' he said evasively.

'What time did he leave?' the constable questioned, taking out his notebook ready to record the answer.

'I don't know, I didn't look at my watch. He left quite a while before me. I finished my pint and then I had a couple more before coming home.'

The sergeant checked the time on his own watch. 'Just how long were you there for?'

'Bloody hell, I don't know. It may have been two or three hours. It's thirsty work slugging your guts out down on the dockside. A man needs a pint or two to help him unwind.'

'Did you go to Cavendish Road, by any chance?'

'Where the hell's that?' Sam scowled, removing his cap and muffler and making for his armchair.

'It's off on the right higher up Scotland Road, as I think you know. Isn't that where this drinking companion of yours lives?'

'Fred Linacre, you mean?'

'Yes, that's the name of the foreman at the biscuit factory you said you were drinking with after work.'

'I think he does live somewhere around there,' Sam prevaricated. 'I never go to his place, though, because we always meet up in the boozer.'

Maggie looked startled; so it did seem as if it had something to do with Fred Linacre after all. He must have been who Sam had meant when he'd said she was working as a housekeeper for some bachelor. Surely, though, he wouldn't have sent her there knowing how much she hated the man.

'Are you also saying that you didn't know that there was a young girl living with him?'

'How the hell would I know something like that?' Sam muttered, looking uncomfortable.

'I thought he might have mentioned something about her while the two of you were having a pint since I understand that the young girl in question is your daughter,' the sergeant said blandly

Dark colour flooded into Sam Jackson's face and he cleared his throat awkwardly. Maggie was about to speak but the sergeant held up his hand to silence her.

'Are you categorically stating that you had no idea that earlier today your daughter Trixie Jackson was involved in a very serious incident of some kind?' the sergeant asked formally.

'Incident? What do you mean? I don't know anything about any sodding incident,' Sam blustered.

'Perhaps I should have called it an

accident, then?' The sergeant frowned and looked enquiringly at the constable. 'Would you say it was an incident or an accident?'

'It could have been an attempted murder,' the policeman answered quietly.

'What the hell are you two going on about?' Sam demanded looking more and more worried as the policemen continued their questions and suggestions.

'We're talking about the young girl, whom your wife was visiting in hospital a short time ago, and who was admitted earlier drenched in her own blood and with her throat cut,' the sergeant said sternly. 'Are you saying you know nothing at all about it?'

Sam passed his hand over his head in a gesture of dismay. 'I know nothing about that!' He turned to face Maggie. 'What do you know about this?' he demanded hoarsely. 'What the hell have you been telling them?'

'I haven't told them anything and all I know is that I've been to the hospital and that our Trixie's lying there unconscious and looking like a corpse. Her throat's all bandaged up as they've just told you and there are all kinds of tubes and wires attached to her,' she told him in an anguished voice. 'They told me to come home and go back tomorrow and she might be awake and able to talk to me by then.'

'Who on earth would do a thing like that to her?' Sam asked in disbelief.

'That's what we want to know, Mr Jackson, and you seem to be the most likely person to be able to tell us. We understand you took your daughter along to Cavendish Road just over a week ago and left her there in the care of Mr Frederick Linacre.'

'You mean Fred Linacre has done this to her?' Sam exclaimed.

'We don't know about that; in fact, for the moment, we're keeping a completely open mind about what happened. It could have been you who injured her,' he mused speculatively. 'Or it could even be that she tried to commit suicide. We think you'd better come along to the station and make a full statement. We shall be asking Mr Linacre to do the same.'

'He'll tell you the same as I've told you. We had a drink together in the boozer like we often do and then he went home alone. I haven't been near his place today'

'But you did hand our Trixie over to him,' Maggie accused, her voice rising in anger. 'You took money from him for her; you sold her to him like she was a slave.'

Her raised voice upset Cilla who up till now had been placidly looking at them all and sucking her thumb, but now she burst into tears and began screaming.

The sergeant nodded towards the young constable to indicate that he was to make a note of what Maggie had said.

'Is there anything else you wish to tell us about your daughter, Mrs Jackson?' the sergeant queried, raising his voice so as to be heard above Cilla's crying. 'Is there anything else you think we ought to know?'

'No, not really,' she murmured as she cradled Cilla in her arms, trying to soothe her. 'I don't think there's anything else I can tell you, except that Trixie didn't like this Fred Linacre. She didn't get on with him when he was her boss at the biscuit factory,' she explained.

'Is that why she stopped working there?'

'Oh no, it was because this Fred Linacre sacked her! He told her that they were cutting back and as she was the last one taken on then she'd be the one who'd have to go.'

'And after that you say your husband found a job for her?'

'That's right.' She glared at Sam. 'He wouldn't say what it was or even where it was. He told her she was to pack a bag and go with him. I haven't seen her or spoken to her since because he wouldn't tell me where she was.'

'And you say that was over a week ago?'

'Yes, and I've been worried out of my mind about her, wondering where she is and what might be happening to her. She's only sixteen, you know.'

'I'm sure you have been concerned. Well, you needn't wonder about where your husband is for the next day or two, Mrs Jackson. He'll be with us,' the sergeant said dryly.

'What do you mean? You can't lock me up, I haven't done anything,' Sam protested.

'I'm afraid we will be taking you in and detaining you till you've made a statement and helped us with our inquiries,' the sergeant told him.

'You can't do this.' Sam struggled violently as the constable took him by the arm and began to walk him towards the door. 'Maggie, say something,' he shouted, looking back over his shoulder. 'Tell them I had nothing to do with it. You know I wouldn't hurt our Trixie.'

Maggie shook her head. 'I don't know anything of the sort,' she muttered. 'I didn't even know for certain where our Trixie was, not till this minute, because you wouldn't tell me where you'd taken her. If you had, then I could have gone to see her, made sure she was all right and then none of this would have happened.'

Chapter Nineteen

Trixie was kept in hospital for almost a week. Maggie went to see her every day but she could only stay for a very short time because she had to leave Cilla with Ella.

Cilla seemed to sense that there was something wrong and she cried incessantly for Trixie; nothing any of them said or did would pacify her.

Ivy also went to see Trixie several times and even Andrew and Jake went to visit her towards the end of the week. Their visits proved to be the best tonic possible; they lifted Trixie's spirits and she replayed them over and over in her mind.

Andrew only stayed for about ten minutes but he brought her some red grapes. She'd never tasted them before and wasn't even sure about how to eat them. When he picked one of them off the stem and popped it into her mouth she was afraid to bite into it in case she mightn't like it.

When she did, and the sweet juice flooded into her mouth it was so startling and refreshing that she'd gasped with pleasure, making Andrew laugh.

Having visitors was wonderful but Trixie

also found that, in spite of the pain and dis-comfort, when she moved her head she was enjoying the luxury of lying there between the crisp white sheets simply listening and watching everything that went on around her in the ward. She experienced a wonder-ful feeling of peace knowing that she had to do nothing but lie there and relax.

She also had plenty of time to think and there were moments when she wasn't sure whether lying there in a hospital bed was a dream or not.

The police had asked her so many ques-tions that by the time they'd left she was in a state of utter confusion herself about what had actually taken place. She'd assured them, though, that no one had deliberately tried to hurt her, nor had she attempted to commit suicide as the sergeant suggested. She'd insisted, though, that she'd been kept a prisoner at Cavendish Road by Fred Linacre and begged them to make sure that she didn't have to go back there.

They'd assured her that they would have to look further into it when she told them that she'd been taken there by her father. However, when they told her that they'd be interviewing both Fred Linacre and her father she felt rather scared because she didn't want any more trouble.

'We have to interview them before we can complete our investigations,' the sergeant explained. 'Don't you worry about it, we'll get it all sorted out before you leave hospital.'

When she'd asked, 'Does that mean I can go home soon?' they'd not given her a definite answer and now the fear that perhaps she would have to go back to Cavendish Road and she'd injured herself for nothing kept floating in and out of her mind.

The other thing that concerned her was not being allowed to see Cilla. If only she could see her, then she could reassure her and tell her that she'd be home again soon so as to stop her fretting.

The nurse said they didn't allow children into the ward and even when she'd tried to explain that Cilla wasn't like other children and why she really did need to see her, even if it was only for a few minutes so that she could reassure her, the nurse still refused.

'You'll be home again by the end of the week,' she told her briskly, 'you can see her all you want to then.'

Maggie tried her very best to comfort Cilla but it was impossible to calm her down. Cilla wanted Trixie and nothing Maggie said or did made any difference. Maggie had begged them at the hospital to be allowed to bring Cilla in but they were adamant. Rules were rules, or so it seemed, and couldn't be bent for anyone.

Sam was feeling equally hard done by. He was shocked that Trixie had done such a stupid thing just to draw attention to herself. Although the police had let him come home after he'd made a statement he suspected that they were still on his case. He knew that both Maggie and Fred Linacre had blown the gaffe about him taking money from Fred in return for sending Trixie to live with him.

He couldn't see what was wrong with what he'd done. As he told the police, she was there as a housekeeper, doing the cleaning and cooking, so naturally he expected Fred to pay her some wages. He was only looking after it for her, making sure she didn't squander it.

As for her being kept a prisoner and not being allowed out of the place, Sam steadfastedly lied, insisting that he knew nothing at all about that, so they'd have to ask her or Fred about it.

He was trying to convince them that he was being a good father but even so he'd jibbed at the idea of going round to Cavendish Road and collecting Trixie's things. Maggie had stood up to him, though, and insisted that he should do it. 'She'll never be going back there again and we can't afford to lose all her clothes,' she'd argued.

Much as he'd have liked to give Maggie a bloody good hiding for answering him back as well as for jabbering to the police about him, he thought it was better to wait till it all blew over. Once Trixie was out of hospital he'd sort the pair of them out.

Trying to control his temper wasn't easy. At the boozer he discovered that Fred had put himself in the clear by spinning a yarn about what had happened that made it look as if he was the one who'd been misled. As a result, Sam found he was regarded as the villain and everyone was giving him the cold shoulder.

He didn't like drinking on his own at home. Anyway, there was no peace to be found there. Cilla was forever hollering and her crying and high-pitched screaming made his head ache. Maggie said there was precious little she could do to stop her because she was missing Trixie so much.

She'd even had the nerve to ask him if he would look after Cilla the day she went to bring Trixie home.

'Take her along with you. If *you* can't shut her up, then how the hell do you think I'm going to be able to?'

'They won't let kids into the ward, as you know,' Maggie told him.

'Then leave her with someone the same as you've been doing when you go to visit at the hospital.'

'That means the O'Malleys, since they're the only ones she'll go to and you keep telling us not to have anything to do with them because they're Catholics.'

'You have, though; neither of you take a damn bit of notice of what I say.' Sam scowled.

'I don't like to be bothering Ella and Ivy all the time.' Maggie frowned. 'They've been very good but I know it puts them out and since it's a Saturday afternoon they'll have Jake home from work. It will only be for about an hour so surely you can manage to take care of her for that length of time.'

Maggie had nagged away so much that in the end he agreed that he would look after Cilla.

'Stick her in her cot, then, and I'll sit in the other room and read the paper till you come home,' he promised. 'With any luck she'll go to sleep, but leave a biscuit or something that I can give her to shut her up if she starts yelling.'

As luck would have it, Cilla was sound asleep by the time Maggie was ready to leave. Sam made himself comfortable stretched out in his armchair with a bottle of his favourite beer and the newspaper. Before he knew it, he was also asleep.

When he woke up Maggie and Trixie were home. Trixie looked washed out and as thin as a rake and her throat was still bandaged. Maggie helped her in and made her sit down. Then she began fussing round her like an old hen, telling Sam to get off his backside and put the kettle on because Trixie was still so weak that she needed a cup of tea to get over the journey home from the hospital.

'Now you sit down here in your dad's chair and take it easy,' she told Trixie, 'and I'll go and see if Cilla is awake, although I think she must be still asleep she's so quiet.' She smiled. 'Wait till she sees you're home! She's missed you so much, she's never stopped asking for you.'

The next minute it was as if all hell had been let loose. Maggie was screaming her head off at him 'Where's Cilla?'

For a minute he hadn't known what she was on about. 'In her cot where you put her before you went off out, of course. Where else would she be?'

'She's not in her cot; so what have you done with her, Sam?' Maggie advanced menacingly towards him, her eyes wide, her face contorted with fear and rage.

'I haven't touched her,' Sam said, backing away from her as far as he could in the cramped kitchen.

'You wicked old devil, you've never cared about her, never even liked her. If you've done her any kind of harm...' she gulped as he pushed passed her and went into the bedroom to see for himself.

He couldn't believe his eyes when he saw that Cilla's cot was empty. 'How the hell did she manage to get out of there?' he asked, passing his hand over his head in a gesture of bewilderment.

'You tell me; you were the one supposed to be looking after her,' Maggie retorted accusingly, remembering all his threats about putting her away in some sort of mental home.

He raised his hand to slap her one for answering him back, and then he let it drop to his side. He knew that at the moment he was the one who was in the wrong and it was best not to antagonise Maggie any more.

'She can't have got far,' he muttered. 'She must be here somewhere, hiding under the bed or in one of the cupboards.'

'Why on earth would she do a thing like that?' Maggie questioned. 'Not unless you've been threatening her while I've been out,' she added suspiciously.

'I never set eyes on her. I was in the other room reading my paper the whole time you were out.'

'You mean you didn't look in on her even once to see if she was all right,' Maggie said accusingly.

'What on earth for? She was quiet, for a change, so I stayed where I was.'

'Drinking beer, studying the horses and snoring your head off like you were when we came in.'

As they continued to bandy words, levelling accusations at each other, Trixie began looking in the kitchen and then the bedroom to see if she could find Cilla.

'You come and sit down before you collapse,' Maggie scolded. 'We'll find her; she must be here somewhere because I wouldn't have thought she could open the door. She never goes outside on her own so she'd be too frightened to try and do that but, if she has, then she can't have gone very far.'

Their search was fruitless; she was nowhere to be found. Maggie went and knocked on the doors of the other people living in the house but none of them had seen her.

'It's no good, we must go to the police,' Maggie said in alarm as she pulled her coat back on.

'Hold your horses, we don't want the scuffers sniffing round here again,' Sam protested.

'It looks as though we've no alternative. We've no idea where she is or where to start looking.'

'The speed she walks at she won't be far away,' Sam argued stubbornly. 'Ask around. People will be bound to have noticed her if she's out in the street on her own.'

They searched for half an hour but without any success. Maggie wasted no more time. 'Are you going to go along to Hope Street and tell them that she's been missing, possibly for the past couple of hours, or shall I?' she demanded.

Sam hesitated, trying to think of a way out of it. He'd had more than enough of being interrogated by the police. 'Are you sure we've looked everywhere?' he prevaricated.

'We've even looked inside the wardrobe and under the beds,' she reminded him, 'so where else is there to look?'

'What about round at the O'Malleys? Do you think she might have gone there?' Trixie suggested.

'Don't talk so silly, luv,' Maggie said in an exasperated tone, shaking her head. 'You know she could never find her way from here to Horatio Street on her own.'

'Why not? She's a lot brighter than you think. When she woke up and you weren't here and she found herself all alone she might have thought that was where you were and decided to look for you.'

'She wasn't left here on her own, your dad was here,' Maggie said sharply.

'Yes, I know that, but if he was fast asleep and snoring his head off and not taking any notice of her when she called out then...' Trixie's voice trailed off as there was a knock on the door.

'Who the hell is that?' Sam growled. 'It doesn't sound like the police.' He pushed past them and opened the door and the next moment they heard a man's voice, one that set Trixie's pulse racing.

'Who the devil are you and what do you want?' she heard her father demand.

'It's all right, Sam; he's a friend of Trixie's, so ask him to come in,' Maggie called out, rushing over to the door. 'Come on in, Andrew.'

'This is my friend, Andrew,' Trixie told her father who was still regarding the stranger hostilely.

'Friend? How long has this chap been your friend?' Sam asked suspiciously.

'I helped Trixie when she was put in charge of the Christmas money,' Andrew explained.

'Oh, you're the one who did that, are you!' Sam scowled angrily remembering the frustration he'd felt because he couldn't get his own hands on it.

Realising that his reaction to Andrew was far from friendly and how annoyed he'd been because she had refused to let him look after the money, Trixie tried to change the subject before he said anything to upset Andrew.

'It's good to be home. I'm still feeling a bit weak, but I'll be fine in a couple of days,' she said quickly.

'Whatever happened to you? The police wouldn't tell me any of the details when I asked them. There wasn't time to ask you when I came to see you in hospital and neither Jake nor Ivy seemed to be very sure.'

''Course they wouldn't bloody tell you, you're not family,' Sam interposed quickly. 'Anyway, I think you'd better go, whacker; we've other things on our mind at the moment,' he muttered.

'Dad!' Trixie frowned in annoyance at his rudeness. 'I'm sorry, Andrew, but we are all rather upset at the moment because Cilla is missing. She's wandered off and we've no idea where she may have gone,' she explained.

Andrew looked bemused. 'Is she safe out on her own?' he asked frowning.

'Of course she sodding well isn't, she's bloody barmy,' Sam bellowed. 'Why the hell do you think we're all so worried?'

'Mum left her in her cot while she came to bring me home from hospital,' Trixie said with an awkward little smile. 'Mum thought she was still asleep but we've just this minute looked and she's not there, and we can't think where she might be.'

'She must have gone outside so I'm off to see if I can find her,' Maggie said. 'You can help look as well, Sam. You stay here, Trixie, in case someone brings her back home.'

'Will you be all right on your own, Trixie, if I go and help search?' Andrew asked.

'Of course I will. You'll probably only be gone a few minutes. She's not much of a walker. I think she might well have gone to

251

the O'Malleys' place.'

'Come on, Mrs Jackson, we'll go that way and Mr Jackson, you go in another direction,' Andrew stated.

Sam looked furious. 'Who do you think you are, giving out orders?' he grumbled, but nevertheless he pulled on his coat, rammed his cap on his head, and followed them out of the door.

Chapter Twenty

As Andrew and Maggie reached Scotland Road they spotted Cilla on the other side of the road. She was sitting on the edge of the kerb looking grubby and dishevelled. One minute she was poking around with something in the gutter and the next looking up and down the road as if not knowing what to do.

As Andrew called out her name and waved, Cilla looked up as if wondering where the voice was coming from. Then she saw them and excitedly struggled to her feet and tried to run across the road towards them.

The scream died in Maggie's voice as she watched in horror and disbelief as she saw a tram heading towards the small figure. Fear gave her speed as she ran across the road towards the child, in a desperate bid to get her out of the way of the tram. As she gathered Cilla up in her arms and turned to make for safety, the heel of Maggie's shoe caught in the metal lines.

She stumbled wildly, then lost her balance and fell heavily to the ground with Cilla still clasped in her arms. The last thing she remembered later was the wild clanging of the tram's warning bell then the terrible impact as it hit her.

Pandemonium reigned as people dashed into the road to help, then stood there, staring down at the two inert bodies that lay entwined across the gleaming metal rails, not sure what to do next.

Andrew elbowed his way to the front but even as he bent down he knew they were both injured and that it was better not to try and move them. Instead, he shouted over his shoulder for someone to send for an ambulance.

Two policemen appeared on the scene and they immediately took charge. They made the crowd move back in order to clear a way for the ambulance before taking a statement from the tram driver and several of the bystanders.

'You coming with us, mister?' the ambulance driver called out as Andrew remained standing there listening to the babble of voices all around him as people told each other what they had seen.

'No,' he shook his head, 'I'm only a friend and it might be best if I go with the police and let their family know what has happened.'

When they arrived at Virgil Street he left the two policemen to explain to Sam Jackson, who had arrived back before him, what had happened while he did his best to comfort Trixie.

'Can you stay here, whacker, while I go along to the hospital and see how they both are?' Sam asked in a subdued voice.

'Please, Andrew, I don't want to be on my own,' Trixie begged when she saw him hesitate.

'Trixie, wouldn't it be better if I went round and asked Ivy to come and sit with you?' he suggested as soon as the door closed behind her father.

Trixie shook her head, brushing away her tears with the back of her hand. 'I don't want to be on my own, I feel so scared. Perhaps we should go along to the hospital as well.'

'Nonsense! You're not well enough to do that. I'll go and fetch Ivy. I'll only be gone a few minutes.'

Trixie smiled wanly. 'Promise that you'll come back as well; please, Andrew,' she begged.

'I'll only be five minutes,' he promised.

The five minutes seemed like an eternity to Trixie as she sat there watching the clock and worrying about what had happened. She felt it was all her fault; if she hadn't been taken to hospital then her mother wouldn't have had to come and bring her home and so she would never have had to leave Cilla.

Her dad had never had any time for Cilla, she thought sadly. He didn't even seem to like her being near him which was probably why he hadn't bothered to check and see if she was all right.

She had to admit that he'd looked upset, though, when he'd gone off to the hospital with the two policemen. She wasn't sure whether that was because he was feeling guilty or whether he was worried about how badly hurt Cilla and her mother were.

When she heard the tap of the door and Ivy calling out to her she struggled across the room to open it, holding on to pieces of furniture because she felt so weak and unsteady on her feet.

She was relieved to see Ivy but disappointed that Andrew hadn't come back as she'd hoped he would.

'He was really shaken up by what happened,' Ivy explained, 'so Jake took him for a bevvy because he said he needed a drink to steady his nerves.'

'Did he tell you exactly what happened?'

Trixie questioned. 'All I know is that they were knocked down.'

'Well, he said that he and your mum were out looking for Cilla and spotted her on the other side of Scotland Road. When he called out to her she started to try and cross the road regardless of the fact that there was a tram coming. Your mum ran to grab hold of her and her heel caught in the tramlines.'

'And the tram mowed them down?' Trixie gasped, holding her hand to her mouth.

'The tram driver tried to stop and the warning bell was clanging like mad. I'm sure the driver thought your mum and Cilla would be able to get out of the way in time.'

Trixie nodded. 'Andrew said it was all over in seconds,' she said in a toneless voice.

'Look, would you like a cup of tea?' Ivy said briskly, avoiding her eyes. 'I think we should stop talking about it till your dad comes home from the hospital. You know what it's like when there's an accident, it can look worse than it actually is. There may not be very much wrong with either of them,' she said in a shaky, unconvincing voice and Trixie guessed she must be remembering what had happened to her own mother and little Nelly.

Time dragged; Ella came round and stayed for half an hour and had a cup of tea with them. Then she said she'd go along to the hospital and see if there was any news.

Andrew and Jake accompanied her but they became restless after a few minutes. Jake was prepared to stay longer and even suggested that if Ivy and Andrew wanted a break then he'd stay there with Trixie but Andrew said he must get home.

'You can stay here with us if you want to,' Ivy told her brother, 'or else cut along to the hospital and see if you can get any information about what's going on.'

It was almost an hour before Jake returned and Ella was with him when he did.

'We left your dad at the hospital,' Ella told Trixie. 'Your mum has been pretty badly hurt, luv, and he thought it best if he stayed with her. Now what do you want to do, come back to our place till he comes home or wait here?' she asked patting Trixie's arm.

Trixie stiffened and her face grew tight. 'Where's Cilla?' she asked in a strained voice.

The question floated on the air as Ella and Jake exchanged hesitant glances; neither of them seemed to be willing to tell her what they knew about her little sister.

She repeated the question; her voice rising hysterically as she looked from one to the other as she did so.

'Cilla wasn't very badly hurt,' Ella told her gently, 'but they're keeping her in hospital overnight just to make sure.'

Trixie looked so distressed that Jake put his arm round her shoulder. 'The doctor said that your mum holding Cilla like she did protected her,' he said consolingly.

Trixie shook her head as if unable to understand clearly. 'Does Mum know that Cilla's still in hospital?' she asked in a bewildered voice.

'No, I don't think so; not yet, because your mum hasn't regained consciousness,' Ella told her gently.

'I must go to Cilla.' Trixie pulled herself out of the chair. 'Ivy, can you help me into my coat, please.'

'I don't think that's a good idea, luv,' Ella protested. 'You're still very weak, you know. If you go out in this weather then you may get a chill and then what good will you be to help look after them both when they come home?'

Trixie stared at her as if she didn't understand what she was talking about.

'My mum's right, Trixie. I'll stay here with you till your dad gets home, unless you want to come back to our place.'

'I must stay here; they might bring Cilla back and I'll be the one who'll have to look after her till Mum is better.'

'No, luv, they won't be bringing her back tonight,' Ella said shaking her head, 'so why don't you come with us?'

'No, they won't, will they?' Trixie admitted in a tiny voice. Suddenly her face crumpled and her whole body shook as she gave way

258

to great gulping sobs.

Jake gathered her into his arms, holding her close and stroking her hair and murmuring words of comfort, his own eyes bright with tears as he tried to console her.

Ella, Ivy and Jake were all still there when Sam Jackson returned. One look at his ashen face conveyed all they needed to know even before he told them that Maggie was so seriously injured that it might be weeks before she was well enough to come home. He made no mention at all of Cilla till they questioned him about her.

'Cuts and bruises that's all,' he said dismissively. 'They said she can come home tomorrow.'

Ivy wanted to stay on but Trixie sensed that her father wanted to be on his own and she could understand this so she assured them that she could manage well enough.

'I'll look in and see how you both are in the morning,' Ella promised after she'd made a fresh pot of tea for Trixie and Sam. 'Make out a list if there is anything you need and I'll get it for you while I'm doing my own shopping.'

When they'd gone, Trixie poured out the tea and tried to persuade her father to have something to eat but he shook his head and said he had no appetite.

'Your mother's in a pretty bad way,' he said in a low voice as he sat staring into the fire. 'Never seen her like that before. She opened her eyes but she didn't know me; she kept asking for you and Cilla.'

Trixie leaned forward and stretched out a hand towards him. 'What did you tell her?'

'Nothing to tell her. I left it for the nurses to talk to her and tell her whatever they felt she should know.'

'Poor little Cilla, she's probably bewildered and unhappy being with so many strangers,' Trixie said dejectedly. 'I hope they will let her come home tomorrow.'

'She's been trouble since the day she was born,' her father said bitterly, running his hand through his hair. 'Why the hell did your mum have to be the one so badly hurt? It wouldn't have mattered so much if it had been Cilla,' he added callously.

'It's not been her fault,' Trixie defended. 'And she is improving. She's started to learn her letters and she can count.'

'She'll never be normal,' he said disparagingly. 'She'll be a burden to someone for the rest of her days.'

'That's a terrible thing to say,' Trixie bristled.

'It's the bloody truth! Time you faced up to things as well. You're going to have to from now on, because the doctors say your mother's not going to be much good for months to come so you'll have to care for both of them. Your mother's going to need a lot of looking after, make no mistake about that.'

'She is going to get better in time, though?'

'You'll find that out when she comes home,' he muttered. 'I'm going for a pint,' he added getting up and reaching for his cap.

'You can't do that, Dad!' Trixie gasped. 'What on earth will people think? Your child and your wife both lying in hospital and you're out boozing.'

'Don't you try and tell me what I can and can't do, my girl,' he told her, his eyes blazing. 'I said I was going for a pint, not a bloody bevvy, but if I decide to have a skinful when I get there then that's what I'll do. You get yourself off to bed and I'll see you in the morning.'

Trixie did go to bed but she couldn't sleep. She felt weak and despondent and she would have given anything to have her mother there fussing over her. Or even to have Cilla there in bed beside her with her little arms hugging her tight; to have Cilla kissing her and telling her how much she loved her.

Her pillow was wet with tears by the time she finally fell asleep and then she was wakened abruptly by the sound of her father coming home. He'd obviously had far more than a pint. He was stumbling around, and cursing under his breath as he bumped into the furniture.

261

She lay perfectly still, wondering if she ought to get up and make sure that he was all right, but common sense warned her that if he'd had a skinful then he would probably be in an aggressive mood. If that was the case, then if she said a word out of place he would as likely as not hit out at her and she didn't feel strong enough to stand up to one of his backhanders.

She now felt really tired and as he stopped lumbering about and she heard the bed-springs in the next room groan under his weight, she knew he had managed to make it on to the bed. With a sigh of relief she relaxed and drifted off to sleep, lulled by his rhythmic snores.

When she woke next morning she lay for a while thinking back over the events of the previous few days and wondering what was going to happen next.

Cilla and her mother being in hospital made her own accident seem less important, even though she knew it was bound to bring about big changes in her life.

The only good thing she could see coming out of all this was that since her mother was going to need nursing there would be no question of her having to return to Fred Linacre's place.

How long her dad would let her stay at home and take care of things with him having to pay for everything out of his wages remained to be seen. Sooner or later he was going to insist that she found herself another job. This time, though, she'd try and make sure that it was something she wanted to do. Never again would she let him browbeat her into working for someone like Fred Linacre or into having to live away from home.

She also thought about Andrew. He really must like her to come and visit her in hospital, she thought, dreamily. She would never forget the wonderful grapes he'd brought or the way he'd sat there and fed them to her.

Jake had been kind as well, of course, but it was Andrew she was attracted to and wanted as a boyfriend. She liked Jake a great deal; not only because he was Ivy's brother but also because he had proved to be such a wonderful friend. She always felt so comfortable with him and never felt shy with him or that she had to try and impress him; in fact, he was the sort of brother she would have liked to have had.

Her feelings for Andrew were on a very different level, probably because he was so very different from anyone else she knew. He was always so well groomed and smartly dressed, always so polite and he spoke so nicely.

Trixie couldn't understand why Ivy didn't seem to be all that impressed by Andrew. Occasionally she even pulled a face or made some joke or other about his impeccable appearance and polished manners. That was probably because he'd been Jake's friend since school-days and so they had almost grown up together, she decided.

She didn't think her dad had taken to him either, but then they'd all been in a bit of a state because of Cilla being missing

With a sigh, she flung back the bedcovers and eased herself out of bed. Her throat was still hurting and she still felt weak, but she knew she had too many problems ahead to indulge in self-pity. For a start, she must get to the hospital to visit her mum, if they would let her, and then collect Cilla and bring her home.

She hoped her dad would come with her because she wasn't sure if she could manage it all on her own. She'd have to take the pram because Cilla would be too weak to walk, and since she couldn't take the big pram on the tram then it would mean pushing it all the way there and back.

If only she could persuade her dad to carry Cilla then they could go by tram, but she was pretty sure he wouldn't agree to do that.

The only other way was to ask Ella or Ivy if they would come with her and then they could take the pushchair and that would be a great deal easier to manage than the big pram, but she wondered if they would want

264

to do that because she knew her mum's accident had upset them both and stirred up old memories.

Chapter Twenty-One

Trixie decided in the end that she would call round to the O'Malleys to ask them if she could borrow the pushchair, and was very relieved when Jake offered to go along to the hospital with her to help bring Cilla home.

Even so, she couldn't help feeling a little disappointed that it was Jake and not Andrew who was accompanying her.

Cilla held out her arms to Trixie and their tears mingled as they hugged and kissed. The nurse assured her that apart from a few bruises and minor cuts Cilla was completely unhurt and Trixie was pleased that she looked so well and seemed not only to have accepted her stay in hospital quite happily, but also to have forgotten that they'd been parted for quite a while.

She'd brought some clean clothes for Cilla and as soon as she was dressed Jake picked her up ready to leave and she gave him a big kiss and wrapped her arms around his neck.

'I shouldn't talk to her about what happened,' the nurse advised as they left the ward. 'I think she has already forgotten about it. The only people she has asked for have been you, Trixie, and someone called Bonzo.'

'That's her favourite toy.' Trixie smiled. 'She usually takes it everywhere with her, even to bed. It's surprising that she wasn't carrying it when she ran out of the house.'

They went back to the O'Malleys' house where Ella and Ivy had a special meal of all Cilla's favourite treats waiting for her and then Jake carried her back to Virgil Street.

Sam Jackson was out so Jake waited till Trixie had settled Cilla into bed. Worn out by all the events of the day, she was fast asleep in minutes.

'It's been an upsetting time for her,' Trixie murmured as they tiptoed out of the room. 'Would you like a cup of tea?' she invited.

'Only if you go and sit down and let me make it; it's been a trying time for you as well and you're still recovering yourself.'

Cilla was more than content when she found that Trixie was going to be at home with her all the time. Trixie tried to make the most of their time together by sitting down with her after breakfast each morning and helping her to read and write, and because there was no other distraction she made incredible progress.

Achievement also seemed to give Cilla confidence in other ways. Under Trixie's patient guidance she at last managed to wash and dress herself. They were both delighted about this and Trixie even encouraged her to help around the place by doing some dusting, laying the table and other easy chores.

When they went to the shops in Scotland Road or Great Homer Street Trixie encouraged her to walk rather than taking her in the pram. Once again, the results surprised Ella and Ivy; they could hardly believe how much progress Cilla had made when Trixie took her round to see them or left her there while she went to visit her mother in hospital.

Maggie was in hospital for three weeks and when they eventually discharged her she looked gaunt and weary They warned Trixie that she would be extremely weak for quite a while and would need a great deal of bed rest.

'I think it might be better if I slept with Mum,' Trixie told her father. 'She's bound to need attention during the night for a while and she'll probably be very restless and you need a good night's sleep.'

'Since I'm the only bugger working I'll probably be so dog tired that I won't notice if she's restless or not,' he grumbled, but he agreed to swap beds with Trixie nevertheless.

It was two months before Maggie felt well

enough to try doing things around the home and then it was only small tasks that didn't take too much effort. Often she gave up after a few minutes and sat down, rocking backwards and forwards with the tears running down her cheeks because she felt too exhausted to carry on.

Trixie watched over her like a mother hen. She made sure she had light, tempting food to try and build up her strength. She worried if she became overtired and was constantly warning her not to lift things or to stand for too long.

'If you do, then you'll have another restless night because you'll be in pain again and then I won't get any sleep either,' Trixie would scold but with a smile on her face that softened her words.

Maggie would nod submissively and obediently sit down, but often there was such a look of frustration in her eyes that Trixie wished she'd said nothing.

Sam hated everything to do with Maggie's illness. He came home, ate his meal, and then went off out again as speedily as possible. When Trixie remonstrated with him for wasting money on drink when they needed it to buy nourishing food for her mother he often turned on her and told her to mind her own business and that it was time she found herself a job because he was fed up of keeping her in idleness.

Whenever this happened and Maggie overheard him saying it she would always brush it to one side.

'Take no notice of him, luv, he doesn't really mean it. He knows he couldn't do one half of the things that you do for me. What's more, you're looking after Cilla as well as me and she can be quite a handful. Mind you, she does seem to be taking more notice of what's said to her these days and she's better behaved than she's ever been and seldom has any of her tantrums.'

'Cilla is making tremendous progress,' Trixie agreed. 'Ella and Ivy have noticed it too. She can read and write now and has even learned her tables, well up to the five times table, anyway. She really seems to enjoy helping me to do things in the house as well.'

'Yes, I know, luv. And she's been a little dear the way she's fetched and carried for me.'

'I was thinking that since she's so much better we might even manage to get her into school,' Trixie said hopefully

'Oh no, she's not ready for that,' Maggie protested. 'She's still very backward and if you send her to school she's bound to get teased and bullied.'

This was the least of their problems for the moment; what was far more worrying was making ends meet. Whenever Trixie spoke to her dad about it he only turned the tables by grumbling that he was the only one earning any money and it was time she found a job instead of sitting around at home.

'You know perfectly well that it's impossible for me to go out to work and look after Mam and Cilla as well,' she pointed out.

Sam knew that this was true but he still maintained that he couldn't afford to give her any more money for housekeeping. 'You could always get a job in the evenings,' he told her.

'If you want me to do that, then you'll have to stay at home and look after them when you come in from work instead of clearing off out the minute you've had your meal.'

He scowled at her but made no response. In desperation Trixie began cutting down on what she served up for his evening meal and this infuriated him.

'You lot are eating three square meals a day while all I get for slogging my guts out is my dinner when I get in at night and that's hardly enough to keep a boy let alone a hardworking man,' he exploded, his face mottled with fury.

'You have far more to eat than we do,' Trixie pointed out. 'We live on a slice of bread and dripping for our midday meal; I pack you sandwiches with either cheese or egg or bully beef in them. You get the biggest plateful at night and it always has most of the meat on it; all Cilla gets is the gravy and a few vegetables.'

'That's all she needs; she doesn't need feeding up because she doesn't do anything.'

'That's as maybe, but you know perfectly well that you are still not giving me enough to feed us all properly. If you cut back on your fags and boozing then we might be able to manage.'

Sam didn't answer; He picked up his cap and slammed out of the house. Trixie knew quite well where he was going and she also knew that in all probability he'd come back drunk.

The best thing would be for her mother and Cilla to be safely tucked up in bed before that happened, she decided.

To her surprise he was back within less than an hour. He wasn't alone. He had a brassy-faced buxom blonde woman of about thirty or thirty-five with him. She was wearing a grey coat that had a fur collar. It was open to show off her low-necked, bright red pleated dress and her silk stockings and high-heeled black shoes.

'This is Daisy,' he announced. 'She's looking for a room so I've told, her she can move into our big bedroom so you'd better show it to her, Trixie,' he ordered.

Trixie stared at him in astonishment. 'What on earth are you on about, Dad? That bedroom is yours and Mum's. You'll be moving back in there again any day soon now that Mum's so much better.'

'No.' Sam shook his head. 'I'm going to use the small bedroom so you can move Cilla out of there and in with you and your mum. That leaves the big front bedroom empty so we're letting it out. You're always saying you need more housekeeping money; well, this is how you can get it.'

'Are you going to show me this room or shall I go and look for a place somewhere else?' Daisy rasped. 'I can rent a room in much better places than Virgil Street and without all this damned arguing. I thought it was all cut and dried, Sam.'

'It is. I'm the one who says what's what around here so don't you worry about it, Daisy. I said you could have a room here and that's settled,' he stated forcibly.

'That's all very well but by the sound of things your daughter doesn't want me here, Sam.'

'I've just told you, I'm the one who makes the decision. I said you could have a room so it's yours if you want it.'

'Dad, it's untidy at the moment, there're all my things in there.' Trixie turned to Daisy. 'You won't want to see it like that. Give me a chance to clear it up first.'

'Now!' Sam's voice rose to an angry roar that startled Cilla so much that she burst

272

into tears, rushing to Trixie for comfort.

Gently Trixie disengaged the clutching little hands and lifted Cilla on to her mother's lap. 'Stay there, pet,' she whispered. 'I'll be back in a minute.'

Daisy had a self-satisfied smirk on her face as she followed Trixie. She gave a disparaging glance round the big bedroom. 'Yeah, I suppose it'll do,' she said grudgingly.

'Well?' Sam had followed them and now he was standing in the doorway waiting for Daisy's approval.

'Not exactly the Adelphi, is it?' she smirked. 'Give us a fag while I make up my mind if I'm going to take it or not.'

Sam brought out his packet of cigarettes and held it out to her. She selected one and stuck it between her brightly painted lips and waited for him to light it for her.

'How much did you say you wanted a week?' she asked as she exhaled a cloud of smoke.

'You'd better get back and see to your mother,' he told Trixie. 'Put the pot on and make Daisy a cuppa; we'll be joining you in a couple of minutes.'

Trixie felt a surge of hot anger as she did as she was told. Her dad had never mentioned that he was thinking about letting out one of their rooms.

It was one way of finding extra money, she

could see that, but if they'd talked it over first then she would have suggested a working man and that they should put him in the small bedroom that was Cilla's, not the main bedroom.

She and her mam had only been saying a couple of days ago that because she felt so much better it was time they went back to their normal sleeping arrangements. Now it looked as though that was going to be out of the question.

As she made the tea Trixie wondered what else her dad had promised this Daisy person. Was he going to expect her to cook for Daisy and do her washing and clean her room, or was she going to do all that for herself?

She didn't know which would be worse. Giving a complete stranger the run of their home, especially the kitchen, was going to take a lot of getting used to. Her mum wouldn't like having to do that, she thought as she placed the cups, teapot, milk and sugar on a tray and took it through into the living room.

They waited for ten minutes and still Daisy and her father hadn't come out of the bedroom so she poured out a cup for herself and her mother before it went cold.

They'd finished drinking it before her father put his head round the door and said that Daisy was leaving and that he was going with her to help her to pack her things and bring them back.

'Get your stuff out of that room and clean it up and make it look decent, Trixie,' he ordered and then slammed the door before she could voice a protest.

'What's going on?' Maggie asked in a bewildered voice. 'Who was that woman? Was it someone from the hospital to see if I was all right?'

When Trixie tried to explain her mother looked at her in disbelief. 'We don't want anyone moving in here with us,' she protested. 'There isn't room, for one thing.'

'We both know that, Mum, but it's what Dad wants. He sees it as a way of making some money.'

'Yes, but she's a complete stranger. We don't know her or anything about her; she could be anybody,' Maggie complained, shaking her head. 'We mightn't like each other or even get on.'

'Well, it looks as though we'll have to try and do so because Dad's made up his mind and it seems it's going to happen whether we like it or not.'

'What's put a daft idea like this into his mind?' Maggie said worriedly. 'All I want to do is to get things back to normal as soon as possible.'

'That's what we both want, Mum.' Trixie smiled. 'I suppose it is partly my fault because I keep saying that we need more housekeeping money.'

'I know things are tight, luv, but we always manage somehow, now don't we?'

'Yes, but I've been telling him that if he spent less on fags and beer he could turn up more housekeeping.'

'Oh, Trixie! Your dad doesn't take kindly to nagging, you should know that saying something like that would rile him,' Maggie sighed.

'He should have talked to you or me first, though, before he told this woman that she could definitely have a room here,' Trixie defended, her cheeks burning.

'I'm quite sure your dad doesn't know what he's talking about when he says he's going to sleep in that little room of Cilla's,' Maggie agreed. 'It's all right for her because she's only a child. So where is she going to sleep now?'

'We'll have to have her bed in our room, I suppose, although how we'll manage to do that I don't know.'

'Leave things be and I'll talk to him when he comes home,' Maggie promised.

'It's too late, Mum,' Trixie said wearily. 'He's already made all the arrangements and he's the told this woman that she can move in right away. He's gone with her to help her bring her things back here.'

Chapter Twenty-Two

There was another shock in store for Trixie and Maggie when, some two hours later, Sam returned with Daisy. They were not alone. Sam was carrying a dark haired little boy with vivid blue eyes and a cheeky little face.

'This is Daisy's kid; he's called Jimmy,' Sam told them as he put the child down on the floor and held on to his hand to steady him till he found his feet.

'You never told us that you had a little boy,' Trixie exclaimed, her voice registering annoyance as she stared angrily at Daisy.

'You never asked, luv. Sam knew, of course,' she added, grinning up at him as if it was a big joke.

Trixie bit her lip, knowing she'd been wrong-footed and unsure of what to say next.

'He's nearly two years old and he's already a right little devil,' Daisy said proudly. 'He takes after his old man, doesn't he, Sam?' Daisy went on as she ruffled the child's mop of thick hair.

'Stop all this chuntering and let's get your stuff inside,' Sam told her gruffly. 'Here,' he held out the child's hand to Trixie, 'you and your mother keep an eye on him while I help Daisy take her stuff into the bedroom. You *have* cleaned it out and made it ready like I told you to do?' he asked suspiciously.

'Yes, of course I have, but there's no cot in there. Neither of you said there was going to be a child,' Trixie added tartly.

She felt furious with her father. It wasn't fair on her mother to have a child of that age running around the place and probably crying and screaming when he didn't get his own way. With the state her health was in she still needed plenty of rest, peace and quiet. Even Cilla's chatter was sometimes more than she could stand.

'Don't worry your head about it, chooks, young Jimmy can sleep in my bed with me,' Daisy told her dismissively. 'After all, I've no one else to help keep my bed warm – leastways not for the moment,' she added with a raucous laugh.

'Right, well, let's start getting all your stuff upstairs. We should have made that taxicab driver do it, not just pile it all in the passage; not after what he charged.'

Trixie wondered who had paid the driver. Surely not her dad, he'd never paid for anything like that in his life. He hadn't even been willing to fork out for a taxicab to bring her mum home from hospital.

She bit her lip, there was not much point in her saying anything because he'd either tell her that it was none of her business or would give her a backhander for being cheeky. He'd also remind her that he was master in his own home and that she had to do whatever he said. Nevertheless, she was very surprised that he would take in someone who had a young child. He had no time for Cilla and he was quick to fly off the handle if she started crying or even made a noise when he wanted to sleep, so what would it be like with a two-year-old living there?

Time would prove what a mistake he was making and when he couldn't stand the noise and disruption any longer then he'd no doubt throw Daisy and her little boy out. In the meantime, for her mother's sake, she'd have to go along with his decision.

'I'll give you a hand with your stuff, Daisy,' she said with a resigned smile.

'No, you keep an eye on Jimmy and make us a cuppa. I'll help Daisy to settle in,' her father told her.

It was over an hour before Sam and Daisy finally finished carrying everything upstairs. Cilla seemed to be delighted with her new companion and she and Jimmy were playing together quite happily. Trixie spread a crust with margarine and a scrape of conny-onny milk on it for both them. Jimmy ate his as if he was starving and Trixie wondered when he'd last had a proper meal.

When Daisy finally came out of the bedroom she was wearing her outdoor clothes. 'Can you look after little Jimmy for a bit longer? He's no trouble, is he?' she said airily. 'I'm taking your dad for a bevvy to repay him for all his help.'

Trixie felt so annoyed that for a moment she couldn't think what to say. Then she caught her mother's eye and saw Maggie shake her head in warning.

'Mum, whatever is going on?' she burst out the moment the door closed behind her father and Daisy. 'Who does she think she is? She's just a lodger yet she acts as if she owns the place. And to turn up with a little kid without a word of warning! She didn't even ask us if we'd mind her bringing him here.'

'Well, if he's her child then she can hardly leave him behind,' Maggie sighed. 'Your dad obviously knew she was bringing him. Do you know how much rent he's charging her?'

'Of course I don't! He's never breathed a word about that and I don't suppose we'll see a penny piece of it.' She pushed her hair back behind her ears in an agitated movement. 'I can't manage now on the money he's giving me for housekeeping and if he expects me to feed her and her kid as well on what I get now, then there's going to be one almighty row, I can tell you.'

'Shush, shush,' Maggie tried to calm her.

'Don't take on so. I'll have a word with him tonight when we go to bed.'

'You won't get the chance, Mum, now will you? He's sleeping in the boxroom and you're sleeping with Cilla and me in my old room,' Trixie reminded her.

'Then I'll wait till everyone else has gone to bed and have a quiet word in here with him,' Maggie assured her.

Although it was quite late and past her bedtime, Cilla refused to go to bed because it meant being parted from Jimmy

'What am I to do?' Trixie groaned. 'Poor little thing, he's tired out but I can't see him settling down all on his own. Anyway, I can hardly put him in a big double bed, he's too little and we've no idea what time Daisy is coming home.'

'Probably not till chucking-out time,' Maggie sighed. 'You know how your dad hates to leave before they shout time. He says the last pint is the best pint.'

'Yes, and that's the one that sends him over the top,' Trixie said bitterly.

'Since you've moved Cilla's bed into our room why not put them in that together. It might make her go to bed if she knows he's going as well. Push the bed tight up against the wall and put Jimmy in that side and he can't come to much harm.'

'Her little bed is tight up against the wall as it is; there's hardly space to move around

281

in the room,' Trixie grumbled.

'Well, there you are, then. It seems to be the answer. When Daisy gets back, if with any luck he's asleep, she can simply lift him into her bed without waking him.'

When Trixie told Cilla what she was going to do Cilla was so excited by the idea that she couldn't get to bed quickly enough. For the first time since she'd been very small she didn't even bother to take Bonzo to bed but was happy to cuddle little Jimmy instead.

Sam and Daisy didn't come home till almost midnight and when they did they were both so drunk that they could hardly get up the stairs. There was no question of Daisy transferring Jimmy into her bed because she was incapable of doing so. Trixie was afraid to put him in there herself because Daisy might roll over on him during the night and suffocate him, or else push him out of bed.

There was also no question of Maggie having the quiet talk she'd hoped to have with Sam. He'd lurched off into the small bedroom in a complete drunken stupor and in a matter of minutes was snoring his head off. Maggie and Trixie both knew he'd be like a bear with a sore head the next morning and they probably wouldn't be able to get a civil word out of him.

'Never mind, luv,' Maggie murmured as she and Trixie prepared for bed themselves, 'there's always tomorrow. I'll have a quiet talk with him as soon as I can. In the meantime, we'll just have to put up with this Daisy and her little boy. You never know, we may be able to find out something from her if she's in a talkative mood when she sobers up again.'

'Yes, and till she does sober up we're going to have to look after her little boy, I suppose,' Trixie said dryly.

'He's not all that much trouble though, is he?' Maggie said placatingly. 'Poor little chap; I think he's probably used to being dumped on strangers.'

'It's a good job that Cilla has taken to him the way she has and that she isn't jealous of him, otherwise we would have trouble on our hands,' Trixie commented as she stood looking down at the pair of them curled up together and sound asleep.

In the weeks that followed it became the pattern of their lives. Daisy didn't usually put in an appearance till around mid-morning and by then Trixie had Jimmy already washed and dressed and had given him some breakfast.

Daisy would appear with her face all made up and with her outdoor clothes on, claiming that she was going to work so would they mind looking after Jimmy till she came home.

'They get on so well together that it must make life easier for you knowing that your

Cilla has a little playmate at last and that you don't have to bother with her so much,' Daisy commented as she nodded to where Jimmy and Cilla were sitting on the floor playing together quite happily.

'Yes, the two of them do get on quite well most of the time,' Trixie admitted, 'but it's not so easy coping with both of them when I have to go out shopping.'

'You've got a big pram, so pop Jimmy in that and he'll probably fall asleep before you get home. Unless, of course, Cilla still needs it. If she does, then I'm sure there's room for you to put them in together,' Daisy told her.

'Trixie takes the pram to put the heavy shopping in,' Maggie said quickly when Trixie didn't answer. 'She's encouraging Cilla to walk when they go to the shops.'

Daisy gave a supercilious smile. 'Another couple of years, mind, and my little Jimmy will be streets ahead of your poor little Cilla. It's a shame she's so backward,' she smirked.

Maggie and Trixie resented her remarks but neither of them said anything. They both disliked having her there so they regarded it as something of a blessing that she cleared off out and, as Daisy said, Jimmy was really no trouble at all.

They had no idea what her job was and she was always evasive when they tried to find out. It was obvious she was earning money and paying for her room so they kept their suspicions to themselves.

They still hadn't found out how much she was paying Sam and it took a great deal of nagging on Trixie's part before she managed to convince her father that he must give her more housekeeping because she most certainly couldn't manage to feed them all otherwise.

Daisy was a surprising ally when it came to this. She liked her food as well as her drink and she was highly critical about the sort of meals Trixie was putting on the table.

'Call this scouse! Can't you cook any better than this?' she'd asked scornfully as she sat down with them for their first meal together the evening after she arrived. 'There's no bloody meat at all in it and it tastes like dishwater.'

'Give me the money to buy decent meat instead of having to make do with scrag end or scraps and I'll cook you the best scouse you've ever tasted,' Trixie had told her with some asperity, looking across at her dad and hoping he would take some notice of what was being said.

The following week her dad almost doubled the housekeeping. Trixie was so surprised that she almost told him it was too much.

'That's for extra food now that there's another two mouths to feed and Daisy asked me to give you a couple of bob for yourself for looking after little Jimmy,' he told her gruffly

'Thanks.' She tried to sound grateful and nonchalant at the same time but it was difficult. She was tempted to point out that there was a lot more work now, what with feeding Jimmy and doing all the extra washing and housework so that it meant she never had any time to herself.

When she talked it over with her mother, Maggie pointed out that it might be better to say nothing and accept things as they were rather than have Daisy meddling in the kitchen or interfering with the way she did things.

'As I said before, Jimmy seems to be easy enough to deal with and Cilla certainly seems to enjoy his company. I'm feeling stronger every day too, so I'll be able to do a bit more and help you out, luv. Anyway,' she added thoughtfully, 'it means that your dad can't expect you to find a job, not if you have little Jimmy to look after and all the cooking and cleaning to do.'

'Yes, I suppose that's true enough,' Trixie agreed as she moved the fireguard away and began putting more coal on the fire, 'but I think we'll need to come to some arrangement with Daisy about looking after Jimmy herself a bit more so that I can go out.'

'You always seem happy enough to take

him with you, the same as you do Cilla,'
Maggie said, looking perplexed.

'I hardly ever see Andrew these days
because he doesn't like it if I have to take
them with us if we want to go out on Saturday afternoons,' Trixie explained as she
replaced the fireguard. 'Now and again I
leave them with Ella but only if Ivy is there
because I think she finds that looking after
the two of them is too much for her if she is
on her own. Anyway, why should she look
after Jimmy when she hardly knows him?'

'Well, now that I am so much stronger,
perhaps we could go back to our old
arrangement of me going round to Ella's on
a Saturday afternoon and then I could give
her a hand with the children and you could
go out with Ivy and Jake and Andrew.'

'I'll see what she says,' Trixie agreed. 'It's
not really the answer, though, is it, Mum?
It's not right that Daisy goes off out to the
pub every night of the week. If Andrew asks
me to go to the pictures with him I can't
very well leave you to look after two little
ones all evening on your own, now can I?'

Although Daisy promised that she would
always stay home if Trixie had a date, it
never happened. Each time Trixie asked her
to do so she claimed she'd either had to
work late or else she came home late and
said that she'd forgotten all about it and
Trixie found that at the very last minute she

had to call off the arrangements she'd made.

She hated letting Andrew down because it made him cross and each time it happened she worried that perhaps he wouldn't ask her out again.

Ivy had found herself a steady boyfriend, Hadyn Hill, and so she was able to understand the dilemma Trixie found herself in.

'I know my mum finds it too much to cope with the two children on her own when we want to go out together on a Saturday,' she said. 'The trouble is, she isn't feeling too well these days and she doesn't like going out at nights so it's no use asking her to go round to Virgil Street to be with your mum and the children.'

'I know that's not the answer and I wouldn't dream of asking her,' Trixie agreed.

She felt angry that Daisy was causing so much disruption in their lives. There were days when she felt so trapped that it was almost as bad as when she'd been living with Fred and times when she despaired of ever having a life of her own.

'Why don't you ask Jake if he'll look after Jimmy and Cilla? He could come round to your place and stay with your mother and give her a hand with them,' Ivy suggested.

'That's not fair, though, is it?' Trixie exclaimed, blushing because she felt embarrassed at the thought of asking him.

'Well, he hasn't got a girlfriend and he

can't go out with Andrew if you're going with him, now can he? Ask him, and see what he says. I'm sure he won't mind. You know he'll do anything for you. Look how he insisted on coming with you to bring Cilla home when she came out of hospital.'

Ivy was right. Jake didn't hesitate for a minute when Trixie asked him the next time she had a date with Andrew to go to the pictures and Daisy let her down.

Both children loved it when Jake came to look after them because he always played games and had a rough and tumble with them before it was time for them to get ready for bed.

After he'd helped Maggie give them some supper and tucked them into bed he'd sit there telling them a story till they fell asleep.

Maggie also liked Jake coming around and she was constantly singing his praises. 'He's so helpful and he brightens the whole place up,' she'd enthused as she recounted what he'd said or done while he'd been there. 'I like him far better than I do Andrew.'

'You hardly know Andrew, Mum. You've only met him a couple of times.'

'That's because he never comes here for you when he takes you to the pictures; he always meets you there. In fact, he's not been here again since the day he helped look for Cilla when she went missing.'

'So you don't really know him.'

'Just as well; he's too posh for my liking. I never feel comfortable with him.'

'And you do with Jake?'

'Oh yes,' Maggie smiled, 'he's one of us; there's no side on him and he thinks the world of you, you know, Trixie.'

Chapter Twenty-Three

Maggie's relapse came as a tremendous shock to Trixie. Her mother had been making such splendid progress. Now that the weather was so lovely and much warmer she was planning to resume her Saturday visits to see Ella.

One minute, or so it seemed, she was her usual self, sitting there singing nursery rhymes to Jimmy and Cilla while Trixie got them ready before Ivy came round to collect them and the next she was suddenly taken ill and was struggling for breath.

Trixie thought she might have swallowed something and it had gone down the wrong way, but when she tried to pat her mother on the back Maggie pushed her away.

'Don't ... don't do that,' she gasped. 'I'm not choking; it's just that I can't breathe.'

Trixie wasn't sure what to do so she fetched a glass of water and encouraged her mother to take a sip of it, but it did no good at all; Maggie was still gasping for breath.

Jimmy and Cilla, upset by all the commotion, both started to cry and although she didn't actually panic, Trixie felt her concern mounting and was very relieved when Ivy arrived.

Not for the first time she wondered how she would manage if she didn't have the O'Malleys to help her. It was not only Ivy and Ella; Jake was always ready to give her a hand. In fact, there were times when she felt guilty about accepting his help so much since she could offer him nothing in return.

'In my opinion you should send for the doctor,' Ivy told her. 'Do you want me to go for you?'

'I think you're right, so would you mind?' Trixie agreed. 'She does seem to be in a pretty bad way, doesn't she?'

'Shall I take Jimmy in the pram? I'm sure your mam would be better off without all his noise,' Ivy suggested.

'That would help. He has his coat and stuff on because we were all ready to go out,' Trixie said as she grabbed hold of him.

'Cilla can come as well, if you like.'

'No, leave her here with me. She doesn't like going in the pram with him and she'll hold you up because she walks so slowly.'

Ivy was back within a few minutes and assured Trixie that the doctor was on his way. 'Look, I'll take Cilla and Jimmy round to my mam's out of the way. If you can't come and let us know what is happening, don't worry because I'll get Jake to pop round and find out when he gets home from work.'

The doctor was extremely concerned by Maggie's condition and insisted it was essential that she must go straight into hospital for observation.

'Have you any idea what's wrong?' Trixie asked worriedly.

'I think she probably has a collapsed lung and that is why she is having so much trouble with her breathing. She was involved in a serious accident, remember, and I'm afraid this might well be one of the after effects,' he said sternly.

'Can it be cured?' Trixie asked hesitantly.

'Well,' he pursed his lips, 'I think we'll have to wait and see what the doctors at the hospital think they can do for her. She is a very sick woman, you know. Now, you get her things together and I'll arrange for an ambulance.'

By the time the ambulance arrived at Virgil Street Maggie was barely conscious of what was happening. Trixie went in the ambulance with her but once they arrived at the hospital she was told there was nothing she could do and that she must stay in the waiting room or else come back later.

She was torn between waiting or going to let Ivy and Ella know what was happening. By now her dad would be home and she'd not left a note for him and he'd be wondering where they all were, so she decided it might be best if she let them all know.

'Back in hospital is she?' Sam frowned. 'It's time she pulled herself together and got out of the house. Daisy says it's probably lack of fresh air that's wrong with her, that's all.'

'No, Dad, it's far more serious than that,' Trixie explained. 'The local doctor thinks that she has a collapsed lung. You should have seen her, Dad; she was gasping for breath almost as if she was choking.'

'Yeah,' he said dismissively, 'well, I'll be choking as well if you don't hurry up and put some grub on the table. Where's young Jimmy, has Daisy taken him out?'

'When does she ever look after him or take him anywhere or do anything for him?' Trixie asked bitterly. 'I had to ask Ivy to do it and take him and Cilla round to her place while I went in the ambulance with Mum and they're still there now.'

'When are you going back to see how she is?' he grunted as Trixie slapped a plate of food down on to the table in front of him.

'When I've finished waiting on you and our lodger,' she told him sharply.

'Cut along there any time you like. I'll tell

Daisy what's happened and I'm sure she'll understand,' he muttered.

'And what about Cilla and Jimmy? Am I to go and bring them back here first?'

'Might be best to leave them where they are till you know if your mum's coming home tonight or not. If she is, then you'll want to get her settled first.'

'If they say that Mum is well enough to come home, do I take a taxicab, like Daisy had when she moved here, or do we have to come home on the tram?' she asked sarcastically.

'Bugger off to the hospital and find out how your mum is and stop asking such damn fool questions,' her father growled.

The news was not good. They allowed her to see her mother but Maggie barely acknowledged that she was there. Her face was as white as the pillows she was propped up against and her breathing was so laboured that Trixie could see that every breath was painful.

She sat holding her mother's hand, talking to her quietly and willing her to get better. She'd only been there about ten minutes when a middle-aged nurse tapped her on the shoulder and told her that she should leave and let her mother rest. She tried to protest but the nurse was insistent. 'There's no point in sitting here because she's only semi-conscious and doesn't know what you are saying to her.'

'Can I come back again later tonight to see how she is?' Trixie begged.

'It would be best if you left it till the morning. There may be a change for the better by then.'

When she left the hospital Trixie didn't go straight home, even though she knew her father probably expected her to do so. Instead, she went round to Horatio Street to let Ella know the news and to collect Cilla and Jimmy.

Ivy had already gone out to meet Hadyn but Ella persuaded Trixie to sit down and have a cup of tea and something to eat before she went home.

When she stood up to leave Jake insisted on coming back to Virgil Street with her.

'You look all in yourself,' he told her, 'you need someone to help you get these two off to bed and I don't suppose Jimmy's mother will be around at this time of night to help you to do it,' he added as he helped to put Jimmy's coat on.

Trixie didn't attempt to stop him or even thank him, because she was sure that he could tell from the expression on her face how grateful she was. When he put an arm around her shoulders and gave her a big hug she instinctively kissed him on the cheek, grateful that she had such a wonderful friend who was always so ready to help her.

Both children were overtired and somewhat subdued. Trixie helped Cilla to get ready for bed while Jake put Jimmy into his pyjamas. There was no rough and tumble or games and both children settled down straight away and didn't even ask for a story.

'Poor little devil, he looks lost in that big bed all on his own,' Jake remarked when he came back downstairs.

'I know, but Daisy can't be bothered to get a cot for him. She says they've managed all this time without one and that he's too big for one now.'

'You don't like Daisy, do you?' Jake smiled. 'I can understand why; she looks a right floozy with her bright red lips and the black around her eyes and that brassy-looking blond hair. Anyone can see it's artificial, so why does she bother?'

'You'd better ask her,' Trixie laughed. 'And while you're at it ask her why a woman of her age tries to dress like a flapper with her short skirts and high heels.'

'No fear!' Jake exclaimed in pretended horror. 'She might clock me one. Or if your dad was around and heard me asking questions like that then he might do it for her.'

'Fancy a cup of tea?' Trixie asked as she cleared away the dishes her dad had been using for his meal when she'd gone out. 'I'm afraid there's nothing stronger.'

'Tea and a chat will be fine.' He smiled.

'I've been wondering if you've started making any plans for the future?' he said as he drank his tea.

'Not yet, but I did intend to do so. I brought home an instruction book from the library to try and learn typing and short-hand, but I didn't get very far with them. Practising typing on a paper keyboard wasn't very easy and I couldn't make head nor tail of those funny little squiggles in the shorthand book. I suppose you need to have some proper lessons to start you off.'

'Can't you manage to go to night school?' Jake frowned. 'That's the best way to learn.'

'I did think about it but then Daisy moved in and that put paid to the idea because there was the problem of needing someone to be here to give Jimmy some supper and put him to bed...'

'That's Daisy's responsibility, not yours.'

'Yes, I know, but Dad seems to expect me to do it, and to keep the peace I just went along with it. I didn't want any shouting or fights because it upset my mum so much.'

'That's all very well, but it's your future that's at stake. You hated it in the factory.'

'Well, I don't suppose I'll be going back there again in a hurry not now that Mum's taken a turn for the worse. I'll be needed here to look after her and Cilla, won't I?'

'And to continue to look after Daisy's kid as well, by the sound of it,' Jake said angrily.

After Jake had gone home Trixie thought a lot about what he'd said and she knew he was right. Unless she stood up to her father and Daisy and told them she couldn't look after Jimmy, she was going to find herself responsible for him for ever.

She wouldn't waste any more time thinking about it, she told herself, she'd wait up and tackle them both when they came in from the pub. They probably wouldn't be late tonight because her dad would be worried and want to know how her mum was.

it was well after midnight when Daisy and Sam came home, and both of them were unsteady on their feet. Daisy was laughing so much that she was crying and her make-up was streaked all down her face. Trixie took one look at them both and knew it was pointless trying to discuss anything with them while they were in that state.

She felt so angry that her dad had gone out and got so drunk while her mother was lying desperately ill that she went off to bed without a word and left them to sort themselves out.

Next day when she went to the hospital the news was not good and when her dad came home that night all thought of night school went out of her mind.

Maggie hovered in a semi-conscious state for almost a week before dying in her sleep. Trixie was heartbroken and Cilla utterly bewildered by it all. If it hadn't been for the support she received from the O'Malleys, especially from Jake, who seemed to be constantly helping her, she didn't know how she would have got through the next couple of weeks.

Her dad made arrangements for the funeral and for a few evenings even managed to stay away from the pub, but once it was all over he returned to his normal ways.

Every evening, the moment they'd finished their meal, Daisy tarted herself up and she and Sam went out for a bevvy. It was often almost midnight before they returned home and they were usually so tipsy they could barely stand up.

Trixie felt devastated by his behaviour because it was callous even for him, but she decided to leave it till the weekend and then she would tackle them about the situation and point out that she needed some free time to go out.

She rehearsed what she was going to say over and over in front of her mirror and kept reminding herself that no matter what her dad said, or what interference there was from Daisy, she would remain calm and not lose her temper.

As it happened her father forestalled her. When he didn't come home on Saturday when the pubs closed after their midday opening Trixie wondered if he'd had an accident of some sort.

It was a lovely summer day and she'd planned to take the two children to St John's Gardens to play but had felt too anxious to do so.

It was almost six o'clock before he finally turned up. Daisy was with him. As usual she was dressed up to the nines, only this time she'd gone even further than usual and was wearing a new bright blue dress and a matching straw clothe hat which was trimmed with a mass of pink roses at one side. Trixie noticed that her dad also had an enormous rose in his buttonhole.

'Sit down, Trixie,' he told her, and she could smell that he'd been drinking. 'Me and Daisy have something important to tell you. We've been along and got spliced.'

He started laughing, a big belly laugh, a sound that Trixie hadn't heard from him since she'd been a small girl. It was as if he was extremely amused about something. Daisy joined in, screeching noisily in unison with him, as if sharing some huge joke.

'I'm your bleeding stepmother now,' she chortled. 'You'll be doing things my way from now on, not any old how like you did when Maggie was alive.'

Trixie was shocked into silence as she stared from Daisy's highly painted face to her father's bleary eyes. She tried to tell herself that this couldn't be happening, that her dad couldn't mean it.

'You can't have done, Dad. It's only a month since Mam's funeral,' she gasped, the colour draining from her face with shock.

'It's been long enough for us to give notice at the Register Office, hasn't it, Sam?' Daisy defended boastfully, looking up at him with a knowing smile.

'What can you be thinking of, Dad?' Trixie persisted. 'What on earth will people say?'

'I don't give a bugger what people think or what any of them say and that includes you as well, my girl. Daisy and me are shacking up together and if you don't like it, then you know what to do; get out and take your sister with you.'

Trixie stared at him dumbly, her eyes filling with tears and her throat constricting as she tried to hold back her sobs; her heart ached she missed her mother so much. It was hard enough to come to terms with her loss, let alone accept this new development.

She stared at Daisy with loathing, wondering how her father could possibly let this raddled harpy take her mother's place in their home and in their lives.

She looked across the room to where Cilla and Jimmy were playing together, oblivious of what was happening, and wondered how she was going to explain this to Cilla.

If only she could find a way to do so she'd like nothing better than to do as he said and get out, take little Cilla with her, and start a new life for them both somewhere else, but how could she when she had no money, no job and nowhere to go?

Her father and Daisy both knew this and that she had no option but to knuckle down and accept the situation whether she wanted to or not. From the smug smile on Daisy's face Trixie knew that from now on she would be at her beck and call and that it wasn't going to be easy because Daisy would be hard to please.

Chapter Twenty-Four

Trixie soon found her life becoming almost unbearable as Daisy revelled in her new role as Mrs Jackson. She made it obvious right from the start that she regarded Trixie as nothing more than a skivvy; someone there to do her bidding.

Usually Daisy and Sam wanted nothing to do with looking after Jimmy but now they both undermined Trixie's authority by spoiling him a great deal and because of this he was often naughty and disruptive. They were forever bringing home little presents for him or Sam would take him on his knee and feed him titbits from his own plate.

Both of them completely ignored Cilla. Daisy made it quite plain that she couldn't stand the sight of her. If Cilla went up to her she pushed her away and it upset Trixie to see the look of bewilderment on the child's pretty face.

The first change Daisy instigated was to move Jimmy into the small room that Sam had been using, which was no more than Trixie had expected. What she hadn't counted on, though, was that Daisy insisted that Cilla's little single bed should be moved in there for Jimmy to sleep in. This meant that whether Trixie liked it or not she was forced to have Cilla sleeping in her bed.

Jimmy didn't like being in a room on his own. He would try and creep into Trixie's room and into bed with Cilla but this meant that the two of them caused ructions and neither of them managed to get to sleep even when they were very tired indeed.

Whenever Trixie tried to put a stop to it by taking Jimmy back to his own room it usually resulted in Jimmy howling and crying so loudly that none of them could get any rest.

The other big change that both saddened Trixie and, at the same time made her blood boil, was that Daisy immediately began disposing of anything that had belonged to Maggie. It wasn't simply her clothes; Trixie could have understood that, but all her mother's favourite ornaments and even some pieces of furniture that had been part of their family home for as long as she could remember.

Daisy's taste was not what Trixie was used to. The garish colours and ornate bits and pieces that Daisy either bought new or picked up from Paddy's Market or second-hand shops jarred on her eyes and nerves. To her surprise her father seemed to like them and was forever saying how much brighter and more cheerful their home was since Daisy had moved in with them.

Trixie noticed that the only thing he did object to was when Daisy threw out the old but very comfortable black leather armchair that he'd always considered to be his special chair.

Daisy replaced it with a smart sofa that was upholstered in bright blue plush. It was reserved for her and Sam and no one else. Not even little Jimmy was allowed on it and if he so much as dared to touch one of the brightly covered, blue and black striped cushions with their ornate gold tassels which were piled up on it then he was shouted at or even smacked by his mother.

Daisy had also replaced the sturdy repp living-room curtains with floral cretonne ones which were in a jazzy pattern of blue, gold, black and white. In the bedroom that she now shared with Sam there was a rose-pink gaudily patterned artificial silk counterpane and matching frilled pillowcases.

Trixie wondered where all the money was coming from, but she knew better than to ask any questions, even when a tallyman started calling regularly each week. It was no longer any of her concern since Daisy had taken control of the purse strings.

Daisy was the one who now did all the shopping. She didn't go to the market, or wait till late on Saturday in the hopes of buying meat that the butcher knew wouldn't keep over the weekend at a bargain price. Daisy only bought the freshest meat and vegetables and seemed to be prepared to pay top price for them.

Trixie found that she was expected to make appetising meals for Daisy and Sam from whatever cuts of meat and assorted vegetables Daisy decided to buy.

They no longer sat down to eat as a family. Trixie was told to use up the previous day's leftovers to make a meal for her and the children. Then she was expected to cook something quite different for Sam and Daisy and serve them separately.

Their nightly excursions to the pub still went on and Trixie found that she was no longer able to go out in the evenings. The only time she ever managed to see Andrew was on Saturday afternoons or occasionally on a Sunday when she was taking Cilla and Jimmy for a walk to St John's Gardens.

He seemed to be pleased to see her but he always looked slightly annoyed when she turned down his invitations to go to the pictures with him during the week. Lately, she noticed, he hadn't even asked her.

'Surely Jimmy's mother would keep an eye on him and Cilla for one night down the week,' Jake suggested when she asked him if he would explain things to Andrew.

'Of course she could, but she won't. I even asked Dad if he would keep an eye on them so that I can go out now and again on my own, but he simply scoffed at the idea.'

'Well, you didn't really expect him to agree to do something like that, did you?' Jake said in surprise.

'Oh, I don't know; it's amazing how much he's changed in the last few months. If Daisy asks him, he does things about the place; things that he'd never have dreamed of doing for my mum when she was alive,' Trixie sighed.

'Does he still go out boozing as much as ever, though?' Jake probed.

'Oh, yes! They both go to the pub every night as well as at the weekends; he's well and truly under Daisy's thumb,' she admitted resignedly.

'And you are under hers,' Jake commented despairingly.

Trixie looked worried. 'Andrew probably hasn't asked me out lately because he thinks that I can't be bothered to make the effort to go out with him and that's not true,' Trixie said quickly, her cheeks flushing.

'It's also probably because he has a lot of new friends these days. He knocks around with chaps and girls from work so I don't see as much of him as I used to either.'

Trixie nodded unhappily. 'I like Andrew, though, so next time you see him, Jake, do you think you can try and find a way of letting him know that?'

Andrew didn't take it at all well. When she saw him leaving the bank the following Saturday as she was on her way to the park he looked quite annoyed.

'Jake explained the situation and made your excuses,' he greeted her abruptly. 'It would have been much better if you'd told me yourself instead of using him as a messenger. I really think you should try and speak up for yourself, Trixie, and not be so self-effacing,' he added in a disparaging tone.

Trixie hated it when Andrew criticised her. It always made her feel so inferior when all she wanted to do was please him and not have him look down on her.

She still loved him with all her heart, but recently he seemed to have changed. He was so smartly dressed, even when he wasn't at work, that it made her feel shabbier than ever. She always made sure that her clothes were pristine clean and well pressed but she wished she could afford something new occasionally. It was quite impossible to buy anything out of the couple of shillings she was given as pocket money each week.

'Surely it's time you left home and found yourself a decent job,' he commented sharply as if reading her mind.

'I did try but I needed to go to night school and there was no one to look after Cilla–'

'Or Jimmy!' he interrupted. 'Jake said that his mother would have looked after Cilla, she has a soft spot for her, but she can't cope with Jimmy as well because he's such a little devil and into everything and won't do as he's told.'

'It's because Daisy spoils him all the time. She's so wrapped up in her new life and re-organising everything at home that she gives in to him completely and lets him do whatever he wants.'

'She couldn't do that if you didn't let her. I keep telling you that you've got to stand up for yourself. Don't ask if you can go out, simply tell her you're going. Heaven's above, Trixie, you're eighteen and it's time you grew up and stopped being so timid and letting people push you around,' he said vehemently.

He sounded so cross with her that she found her heart pumping like a sledge hammer. She was so afraid he was going to say that he wasn't going to waste time trying to see her any more.

Jake had said he didn't see very much of Andrew these days so she suspected that, like Jake, she wasn't really all that important in Andrew's life any more. Yet he did still seem to be fond of her, she reflected, even if it wasn't the same overpowering love that she felt for him.

'How about coming to the pictures with me next Saturday night?' he asked suddenly.

From the tone of his voice she was sure he was testing her to see if she had the strength to stand up to Daisy and she was determined to let him see that she could.

'All right.' She took a deep breath because she wasn't at all sure what sort of reaction she would get when she asked at home if she could go out. Saturday night was their favourite night for the pub. 'What time shall we meet?'

'Half past seven, outside the Rotunda. Don't be late and don't you dare make any excuses for not turning up. You've got a week to tell Daisy that you'll be going out next Saturday night, plenty of time for her to make arrangements for someone else to take care of Jimmy if she doesn't want to do so herself.'

The week went by in a haze. One minute the days seem to be flying because she was desperately trying to find a way of telling Daisy she was going out. The next, every minute was dragging because she couldn't wait to be with Andrew and on their own.

When Saturday came she knew she'd have to say something, otherwise it would mean that Andrew would be stood up and that really would be the end of their friendship.

She waited till after Daisy and her dad came home from their midday session at the pub and had eaten their meal. She'd made sure that it was cooked to perfection and that the children were playing happily in Jimmy's bedroom so that there would be no distraction when she broke the news to her dad and Daisy.

'What do you mean, you're going out tonight? Who's going to look after the kids?' Daisy demanded.

'I thought perhaps you and Dad would like to have a night in for once,' Trixie said tentatively. She hated herself for being so timorous but she was anxious not to provoke them in any way.

'What the hell makes you think that?' Daisy asked derisively. 'We always go to the boozer on a Saturday night; it's the best night of the week, isn't it, Sam? There's usually a sing-song or sometimes even a knees up,' she added with a suggestive laugh.

'Surely you wouldn't mind, just this once,' Trixie said disgusted by the wheedling tone of her own voice.

'That's where you're bloody well wrong,' her father announced with a humourless smile. 'You can't just spring something like this on us at the last minute and expect us to take any notice. Not that we would stay in no matter when you told us,' he added scathingly.

'Looking after the kids is your job,' Daisy pointed out. 'It's not much to ask. After all, you don't have to go out to work. We provide the ackers and you live in the lap of luxury. All you have to do is make sure the place is tidy, keep an eye on the kids and cook some food for us.'

'I need to go out with my friends now and again,' Trixie pointed out stubbornly.

'Then do it during the day,' Daisy shrieked, her mouth screwed up petulantly. 'You do as you like all day so you've plenty of time to meet them then.'

'I've arranged to go out with Andrew and he works all week,' Trixie stated as she cleared away their dirty dishes.

'Andrew? You mean that cocky young upstart who works at the bank?' her father said in a derisory tone. 'You want to watch your step with him, my girl. He thinks himself a cut above us so he's only going out with you for one thing.'

'And we don't want any more unwanted brats around the place, there're enough problems with that half-wit sister of yours,' Daisy said nastily, lighting up a cigarette.

'Cilla is no trouble at all, but I can't say the same for Jimmy,' Trixie flared, stung by Daisy's comments. 'He's a right little terror and it's because of the way you both spoil him.'

'If he is, then it's more likely because of the way you're looking after him. He was as quiet as a mouse and barely said a word when I first brought him here,' she stated, blowing a cloud of smoke in Trixie's direction.

'That's only because he hadn't started talking,' Trixie reminded her. 'I don't suppose you noticed, though, because you spent so little time with him. Pity you didn't leave him with his father; that's if you know who he is...'

Before she had finished speaking her father's hand had caught Trixie across the side of her face sending her toppling backwards. 'Don't you ever let me hear you say anything like that again,' he said angrily. 'In case you're unaware of the fact, Jimmy is my kid! I'm his dad and that means he's your brother.'

Trixie stared at him, wide-eyed with shock. 'He can't be,' she argued. 'He was almost two when you brought him here. Anyway, it's only been a few months since Mam died and you've only been living with

Daisy since then, so how can he be yours?'

'It's high time someone told you the facts of life,' Daisy sniggered. 'Anyway, your dad and me are old friends and we were having an affair a long time before he brought me back here to live,' Daisy added triumphantly, stubbing out her cigarette.

'You're lying,' Trixie exclaimed in a shocked whisper. She turned to look at her father. 'Tell me it's not true, Dad?' she begged in an anguished voice.

'What the hell does it matter whether it is or not?' Sam blustered, 'Jimmy's my kid and they're both living here now and if you can't stomach it then you know what to do, otherwise we've all got to get on with one another.'

'And I've got to have a life of my own,' Trixie insisted.

'We'll think about that; we all need a bit of time to simmer down,' her father told her truculently.

'I've already told Andrew that I'll meet him tonight and I can't let him down,' Trixie persisted.

As she saw the scowl that darkened her dad's face she thought for a moment it was all going to blow up into a full-scale row, and then to her surprise he simply shrugged his shoulders.

'In that case, then you'd better go. We'll manage somehow, won't we?' he said turn-

313

ing to Daisy.

Trixie could see that Daisy was on the point of arguing, but a warning shake of his head from her father stopped her. She didn't look pleased but she made no attempt to say any more. Instead, she patted her blond hair, shrugged and averted her eyes.

As she began to get ready Trixie felt full of gratitude to Andrew. He'd been so right. The only way for her to handle the situation was to stand up to them both.

She made mugs of hot sweet cocoa for Cilla and Jimmy and gave it to them with a couple of biscuits. She explained that she was going out and they seemed to accept the situation quite happily.

Before she left she made sure they were undressed and in bed and as she tucked them both in she told them that they must be good for Daisy. They were both so tired that she felt sure they would be asleep in next to no time.

'I'm off, then,' she said, going into the living room where her dad and Daisy were sitting close together on the new settee. 'They're both almost asleep and I won't be very late.'

'We won't be waiting up for you,' Daisy told her tartly. 'The door will be on the latch so just make sure you come in quietly and don't disturb us.'

'I'll remember,' Trixie agreed with a smile.

314

'I promise I'll be as quiet as a mouse.'

Inwardly she was laughing to herself, thinking of the noise the pair of them usually made banging into the furniture, falling up the stairs, laughing and shouting when they came in after being out on one of their late-night drinking sprees.

She still felt both uneasy and shocked by her father saying that Jimmy was his. She wondered if it was really true or whether he had been saying that to please Daisy.

Once again she thought back to the day he had brought Daisy home. Jimmy hadn't been with her – well, not till later on. Surely if he was Sam's child, then her father would have said something to them before he and Daisy went to collect him and her belongings.

Yet how could he have said anything at the time? she reminded herself. If he'd claimed Jimmy was his then it would have broken her mother's heart and she certainly would have objected to Daisy moving into their home.

Still, for the moment, none of that really mattered, she told herself as she hurried to the Rotunda.

She was free and going out with Andrew on her own for the first time in more months than she cared to remember. He was taking her to the pictures, so what more could she want from life?

Chapter Twenty-Five

The visit to the pictures was everything Trixie had dreamed it would be. It was magical from the second she arrived and found Andrew waiting outside the Rotunda for her, looking so handsome in his smart grey flannels and navy blue sports jacket, to the moment when he took her in his arms and kissed her goodnight.

The film was so very romantic; it was *The Sheik* and starred Rudolph Valentino and Wilma Banks. The Pathe newsreel was also romantic because it was all about Lady Elizabeth Bowes-Lyon who had married the Duke of York – one of the Royal Princes – in 1923.

There was also an item about the Charleston, the fast and furious new dance which was becoming hugely popular even though some people considered it to be immoral. Trixie thought about the time when she had gone dancing with Andrew and wished that she could be in his arms, dancing with such crazy abandon.

For the moment, though, it was sheer bliss to be sitting next to him in the cinema, his arm around her, his handsome face so close to hers that she could feel his breath fanning her cheek.

She felt almost cheated when the picture ended and the lights came on; the organ rose out of the pit and music streamed forth as people stood up as the 'National Anthem' played and they prepared to leave.

They made a detour of St John's Gardens as they walked home and Andrew drew her towards a bench so that they could sit down. For a moment she felt so nervous that when he put his arm around her she pulled away from him.

'What's the matter?'

'I ... I don't know,' she whispered uncomfortably. 'It ... it doesn't seem right.'

'You are a little goose!' He pulled her into his arms, nuzzling her neck, uttering tender sentiments of love, while all he time his hands roamed so suggestively over her body that she was unable to resist his embraces.

His passion alarmed her but she felt thrilled that his feelings for her were so intense. She became aware of every movement, every nuance; his touch sent ripples down her spine. Even so she was frightened that he might go too far, but thankfully he seemed to sense this and managed to restrain himself.

She was both relieved and disappointed when he pulled away and began straightening his clothes.

'We must go. It's time I took you home or

317

else you won't be allowed out again,' he said, kissing her briefly as he pulled her to her feet.

When they parted at the top of Virgil Street she vowed to herself that she would insist on going out more often. Andrew was right, she was eighteen, and no longer a school child. It was time she had a proper life and time to go out with her friends or on her own, as she would have done if she had been going out to work.

Ivy certainly did; she and her new boy-friend Hadyn Hill went out at least twice a week. They usually went to the pictures on Saturday night or else went dancing. Re-membering how exciting the Charleston had looked when she'd seen it on the screen made her long to go dancing with Andrew.

When she went indoors she was careful not to make a sound. All she wanted to do was to creep into bed and relive every moment of her wonderful night out. She drifted into sleep, imagining that Andrew's arms were still wrapped around her, holding her close and whispering sweet words of love.

They hadn't made any definite plans about when they would next see each other but the following week when she took Cilla and Jimmy round to see Ella and Ivy they were both excited that Jake had finally finished his apprenticeship at Cammell Laird's.

'It's going to make a tremendous difference because they've offered him a job there and he'll be getting a man's pay from now on,' Ella enthused.

'The really exciting thing is that we're going to have a party to celebrate,' Ivy burbled, her eyes shining. 'We're having it here on Saturday night and you're invited.'

'Well...' Trixie hesitated. She wanted to accept because she realised it meant a lot to Jake and he'd done so much for her, but she was hoping that Andrew might invite her out on Saturday night and in some ways that would be even more important than Jake's party.

Ivy took her hesitation to mean she wasn't sure if she could get free. 'You can bring Cilla with you,' she added quickly. 'Surely Daisy can look after Jimmy for once?'

'Jake is insistent about you coming,' Ella added. 'It's going to be such a really special occasion for him. He's invited Andrew and several of their friends from school.'

'I'd love to come,' she said quickly, her face flushing at the mention of Andrew's name. 'I'll try and persuade Daisy and my dad to have a night in and to look after Cilla and Jimmy.'

She waited all week for some word from Andrew about the party and kept telling herself that he knew either Jake or Ivy would be inviting her and that was why he hadn't bothered to say anything.

Daisy and her dad didn't seem to be too pleased about having to stay in again but when she explained why it was so important her dad agreed that finishing your apprenticeship was a real milestone in any bloke's life, so he said they'd do it.

The first person Trixie looked for when she arrived at Horatio Street was Andrew, but he was nowhere to be seen. Ivy introduced her to her new boyfriend, Hadyn, and then left her to talk to Jake while she and Hadyn went into the kitchen to help Ella.

Jake gave her a big hug and thanked her for coming. He seemed to be very pleased about his achievement and talked at length about what a difference his new status would mean to him.

'I'll have money in my pocket for the first time in my life,' he said happily. 'I've never been able to afford to go out and spend like Andrew and the others from school. Now, I'll be able to see that Mum has more money for housekeeping and still have plenty left for myself. I'll even be able to take you to the pictures and perhaps we can go dancing again. I enjoyed dancing with you,' he said hopefully.

Although she was smiling and nodding in agreement with what Jake was saying, Trixie knew she shouldn't be building up his hopes because she was far more interested in Andrew. She was wondering when he would

320

arrive and worried in case he didn't.

Finally, when she could stand it no longer, she asked, 'Did you invite Andrew?'

'Of course I did. My oldest mate, isn't he? He's supposed to be picking up Maria Perks on his way. Do you know her? She was in our class at school and she works at the same bank as Andrew.'

Trixie shook her head. 'Not really.' She knew the girl he was talking about; she was very glamorous with short blond hair and dressed in the latest flapper styles with knee-length dresses and high-heeled strappy shoes. She hadn't realised that Maria worked at the same place as Andrew.

When Andrew arrived about half an hour later, Maria was clinging to his arm and laughing up at him as they shared some private joke and Trixie felt a pang of jealousy because she knew that she was absolutely no match for Maria.

It seemed ages before he managed to disentangle himself from Maria and come over to her and even when he did, he was still chuckling over something that had been said between them.

As the evening drew to a close Trixie was dismayed when Jake came over and put an arm around her waist and said, 'Andrew has promised to see Maria home since he brought her, so I said I would make sure you got home safely.'

'Thanks, Jake.' She tried to smile but she felt bitterly hurt.

'He lives almost next door to her,' he added by way of explanation, as though sensing her disappointment.

It had been an enjoyable evening and at least she'd spent some time in Andrew's company, she told herself. Nevertheless, she felt cheated that it wasn't Andrew who was seeing her home and that it meant that she would probably have to wait a whole week before they could go out together again.

The following weekend made up for everything. They went to the pictures and all her fears that he might like Maria better than her vanished as they sat in the back row and Andrew was more amorous than ever.

His kisses were eager, almost hungry, and when he suggested they left before the big picture ended because he wanted to be alone with her she readily agreed. He could make her do anything he wanted, she reflected.

As they found a sheltered seat and he unbuttoned her coat and pulled her into his arms she felt an unbearable excitement that filled her with longing and alarm.

As his love-making became more and more intimate and demanding she felt flustered and tried to push him away but he was stronger than her and very insistent.

As she looked up at the night sky, a star-splattered canopy above their heads, she knew they had something special and that it was a night she would remember for ever.

When she got home, she was so caught up with her plans and dreams about what the future could bring that it wasn't till she was about to go into her bedroom that she realised how quiet it was. She smiled to herself; Daisy and her dad must have decided to have an early night. With any luck, she thought optimistically, they might even start to like staying at home one or two nights a week.

As she placed the candle on the chest of drawers and started to undress, she realised that Cilla wasn't in bed. Frowning, because she knew that meant that she was in Jimmy's room, even though Daisy had forbidden it, she pulled her dress back on, picked up the candle, and went along to collect her.

As she'd thought, they were curled up together, but even as she moved towards the bed she felt a sense of unease. They weren't lying side by side. Cilla was lying on top of Jimmy and the pillow which was under her head was completely covering his face.

She placed the candle down safely before she lifted Cilla up to take her back to her own bed. As she did so, it dislodged the pillow and it fell on to the floor but Jimmy didn't stir; he didn't move at all. Very gently she touched his face hoping it wouldn't disturb him. When she found that it was cold and moist she recoiled, gripped by a feeling of fear.

She took Cilla to their room and put her into bed, then went back to check again on Jimmy.

She held the candle and held it so that she could see his face more clearly; his lips were almost white and tinged with blue. She lifted one of his hands and it felt cold and lifeless. When she lifted his arm and then let go it dropped back on to the bedcovers. She tried to pick him up but his arms and head dropped lifelessly and she knew it was too late to try and revive him.

For a moment Trixie didn't know what to do, her brain seemed to stop functioning. Moving Cilla had wakened her and she had come back into Jimmy's room and was standing against the side of the bed yawning and sleepily rubbing her eyes but saying nothing.

Telling her not to move, Trixie took the candle with her as she rushed across the landing and banged on her father and Daisy's bedroom door. When there was no answer she pushed it open. Holding the candle high she could not only see that they were not there, but also that the bed hadn't been slept in.

Immediately she suspected what had happened and she felt angry and frightened. They'd gone to the pub as usual leaving

Cilla and Jimmy on their own. Jimmy had probably heard them leave and started crying and Cilla had gone in to him and tried to get him off to sleep.

She looked down at Cilla who was sucking her thumb. 'What happened, to Jimmy, luv?' she asked gently.

Cilla shivered convulsively. 'I'm cold,' she complained, avoiding Trixie's eyes.

'Were you trying to stop Jimmy from crying?' Trixie said softly. Cilla nodded.

'Shall we go and sit by the fire?' Trixie said, putting an arm round her sister's shoulders. 'Come on, it will be lovely and warm and you can tell me all about what happened,' she said as she guided the trembling little figure out of the bedroom.

They'd only just been in the living room a short while when there was a noise on the stairs and the door burst open and Daisy and Sam almost fell across the threshold as they stumbled inside. Daisy was in a merry mood, singing and laughing, but Sam was belching and cursing.

'It's all your fault; you went out and left them,' Trixie accosted them accusingly.

The anger in her voice momentarily silenced them as they stared back at her. 'What the hell are you talking about, what's happened?' Sam's voice rose angrily. 'What's she doing up?' he asked, nodding in Cilla's direction.

'What have the pair of them been up to, now, the little devils?' Daisy chortled. 'We left them both sound asleep when we nipped out for a quick bevvy.'

'Yes, and as you left you slammed the door behind you,' Trixie said accusingly.

'What's that supposed to mean? Of course we bloody well shut the door,' her father answered.

'So loudly that it must have woken Jimmy up. He was probably crying and that was why Cilla must have gone into his bedroom to try and console him...'

'And?' her father prompted, his face mottled with rage when she hesitated, shaking her head and biting her lip as if at a loss for words to explain what must have happened after that.

Daisy pushed past them and made her way into Jimmy's bedroom. Her shriek when she found his lifeless body sent shudders through Trixie and scared Cilla so much that she burst into noisy sobs.

'Sam, Sam,' Daisy screamed. 'Get in here, there's something dreadfully wrong with little Jimmy.'

When Sam reached the bedroom he found Daisy standing at the side of Jimmy's bed sobbing uncontrollably. She had picked up the pillow and was clutching it between her two hands and swaying unsteadily as she stared down at the child.

'What the hell have you gone and done?' Sam gasped as he snatched the pillow away from her.

'I haven't done nothing,' she screamed back at him, 'but I'm pretty sure that someone has. That pillow has been pushed down over his face, I'm sure it has, he ... he ... he's been smothered.'

After that it was pandemonium. Sam shouted and cursed; Daisy screamed and sobbed; Cilla clung to Trixie almost as if she knew they were going to blame her and needed protection. Trixie's mind was in a whirl although she was perfectly sure that she was right about what she thought had happened.

They all knew it was too late to do anything to save Jimmy but they didn't know what they were supposed to do. They hesitated about sending for a doctor so late at night because they knew it would be futile and he could do nothing to help them.

'I don't suppose it's any good taking him into hospital, either,' Sam said, suddenly sober, and running his hands through his hair in despair.

'We should send for the police,' Daisy insisted. 'They'll know what we ought to do, and what to do about her, the murdering little bitch,' she added glaring at Cilla.

'That's not fair, trying to put the blame on Cilla,' Trixie defended. 'The real culprits are you two going off out and leaving the two of them on their own.'

'Huh! Don't you try all that mightier-than-thou-stuff with me,' Daisy said furiously. 'She was the only one here and someone smothered my little baby with that pillow,' she sobbed hysterically. 'That's unless you did it.' She pointed an accusing finger at Trixie. 'You got home before us, you could be the culprit. You were the one who should have been here looking after them, that's what we keep you to do.'

'Bickering between ourselves isn't getting us anywhere,' Sam said wearily.

'Then do something.' Daisy was trembling and sobbing hysterically, her face raddled with tears. 'Go and fetch a policeman or a doctor or else take little Jimmy along to the hospital and see what they have to say,' she gulped noisily, clutching at Sam's sleeve.

'I'll go and find a scuffer; there's bound to be one patrolling in Scotland Road. There's nothing anyone can do for the kid now, but at least we can tell him that the poor kid died in his sleep before anyone gets the wrong idea.'

'What do you mean by that?' Daisy screeched, her face mottled with rage. 'That's not what happened to our little Jimmy and you know it as well as I do; that little bitch did it on purpose,' she added, pointing an accusing finger at Cilla.

'Shut your mouth!' Sam Jackson muttered. 'You don't want to let anyone outside these four walls hear you say a thing like that because you'll be stirring up trouble for all of us.'

'It's the truth and you damn well know it,' Daisy reiterated. 'She wants putting away. What is she, nine years old, and she talks and acts like a kid of three. She's not normal, I tell you. She's always been jealous of our little Jimmy and this was her way of getting rid of him.'

'You're talking bloody rubbish, Daisy,' Sam told her roughly.

'I think you may be right when you say Cilla put the pillow over his face but she was trying to quieten him because he was crying so much after you'd both gone off out and left him,' Trixie explained.

'How do you know that if you weren't here?' Daisy retorted belligerently.

'It's what Cilla told me happened,' Trixie admitted. 'She was only trying to do her best to get him off to sleep.'

'She was trying to kill him, to get rid of him,' Daisy sobbed. 'I shall tell the police when they get here and tell them to take her away and lock her up.'

'That won't bring Jimmy back. If you're set on doing that then it's probably better not to call them at all,' Sam said exasperatedly.

'You will have to report it, Dad,' Trixie pointed out. 'It's all part of the law, isn't it, when someone dies?'

'When someone's killed, you mean. Murdered in their bed by a lunatic,' Daisy shrieked.

'That'll do, luv.' Sam put an arm around Daisy's shoulders to try and comfort her. 'Try and calm yourself. Make her a cuppa, Trixie, while I go and find a scuffer.'

Dawn was breaking before the police had finally finished interrogating them all. There had been so many questions that Trixie felt in a complete daze. Her father looked grey and drawn and she wished there was something she could say to comfort him but the words stuck in her throat.

Daisy was lying on the sofa with a wet flannel over her eyes and clutching a bottle of smelling salts in one hand. She was weeping noisily and moaning that she wished she was dead, the same as her dear little boy, because her life would never be the same ever again.

Daisy and her dad certainly shouldn't have left the two children all on their own but Trixie couldn't help feeling sorry for Daisy; after all, Jimmy was her little boy.

It had been a dreadful thing to happen. She'd grown to like little Jimmy herself and she knew Cilla was very fond of him.

330

Chapter Twenty-Six

The next few days were such a nightmare that Trixie could hardly think straight.

Daisy was adamant they ought to tell the police that Cilla had smothered little Jimmy. Trixie was convinced that this was only because she hoped that it would result in Cilla being sent away and she was determined that this wasn't going to happen.

It was hard work defending her but eventually Trixie managed to convince her father that it was in all their interests if they agreed that no one knew how Jimmy had died.

'If you put the blame on Cilla then you'll probably find yourself being prosecuted because you should never have gone out and left a girl as irresponsible as Cilla in charge of a young child,' she argued, although she hated drawing attention to Cilla's shortcomings. 'When the police or any of the authorities realise that you two were out boozing then it won't go down at all well and as I've already said, you'll probably end up before a judge yourselves and it could result in prison for both of you.'

Although Daisy maintained she didn't care Sam was more pragmatic.

'There's no sense in putting our necks in a noose,' he pointed out; 'it won't bring our little Jimmy back. I know you're upset, Daisy, but it might be better to let it pass. Given time we can always have another kid if you want one but if one of us, or both of us, gets put inside then we won't even be able to do that.'

In the end, after a heated discussion, Daisy insisted that Sam recalled the doctor who had confirmed that Jimmy was dead and she begged him to give her a strong sedative because she was so upset. She then refused to make a statement to the police, claiming that she was too distraught to be interviewed, but stated that Jimmy had severe breathing difficulties whenever he had a heavy cold.

The doctor was prepared to say that in his opinion it was an unfortunate accident but one which could easily occur when the child concerned had weak lungs and pulled a heavy feather pillow on to his face while asleep.

He did add, however, that in spite of what the child's mother said, he had never been called in to attend him, nor had the child been brought to his surgery.

Trixie confirmed that she was out and that when she left that evening Cilla was already in her own bed and asleep and that normally she slept right through the night so it was unlikely that she would be able to tell them anything.

After spending five minutes with Cilla the police decided that they were wasting their time and that she was incapable of giving them any useful information, so they decided to dismiss her from any further inquiries.

Eventually, to Trixie's relief, it was finally resolved that Jimmy's death was one of misadventure. Daisy and Sam were strongly reprimanded for leaving the children on their own, even though they claimed that they were out of the house for only a little over half an hour.

Trixie breathed a huge sigh of relief when she heard this but she knew the matter was nowhere near over. The police might be prepared to ignore any part Cilla might have played in Jimmy's death, but Daisy certainly wasn't.

Even after Jimmy's funeral, Daisy was still alluding to the fact that Cilla had been the only one in the house when Jimmy had died. She did everything possible to make life difficult for the little girl and constantly asked her veiled questions about what happened that night after she and Jimmy had been left on their own.

Cilla didn't understand what she had done wrong or even why Jimmy was no longer there. She looked for him constantly, searching everywhere, pining because she'd lost her playmate.

Trixie did her best to explain to Cilla that Jimmy wouldn't be there any more, but it was impossible to make her understand. Cilla continued asking for him and stared blankly at Daisy when she accused her of killing him.

This annoyed Daisy intensely and she went out of her way to let them all know how much she hated the girl. Whenever Cilla came near her she pushed her away so roughly that the child frequently fell over, or banged into a piece of furniture or a wall. She shouted at her and scolded her constantly, even if she had done nothing wrong. She even tormented her by snatching her toys away and telling her that they weren't hers but belonged to Jimmy. She even took her food away from her whenever she had the opportunity to do so.

It all became so disrupting that Trixie was really worried and knew that things could not go on as they were for very much longer. The sympathy she'd felt for Daisy over losing little Jimmy ebbed away and she felt that she must get away from Virgil Street as soon as possible or at least get Cilla away before Daisy did her some actual harm.

Daisy and Sam were drinking from the time they woke up in the morning till they went to bed. Sam dragged himself out off bed and down to the docks each morning but if he was fortunate enough to find work then the minute he finished and returned home he had a short snooze, ate his meal, and then he and Daisy went off to the pub and it was late evening before they came home.

Although Daisy no longer appeared to go out to work and Sam's wages fluctuated depending on how often he worked, there still seemed to be money to spend on drink as well as on food.

It was all a mystery to Trixie and her tactful probing met with either a snigger or a blank look from Daisy, or an outright snarl to mind her own business from her father.

In return, Daisy turned the tables on Trixie by complaining frequently and openly about how much it cost them to keep her and Cilla. It was usually followed by exhortations that it was time she found herself a job.

When Trixie tried to point out that it was impossible to do that because of looking after Cilla, Daisy was quick to tell her to find a job where she could take Cilla along with her.

'I'm not looking after the murdering little bitch,' she ranted. 'I can't bear to even look at her, not after what she did.'

'I wouldn't dare trust her with you; you'd probably go out and leave her on her own,' Trixie retorted, stung to tears.

335

'Then get yourself a job where you can take her along with you; that's if you can find one where they don't mind having an idiot about the place.'

Trixie knew that finding a private school that would take someone like Cilla was out of the question because with whatever job she could get herself she wouldn't be able to earn enough to send her there.

Paying someone to look after Cilla, a kind capable neighbour who could be trusted to treat her right, would be the answer, but she wasn't sure that she could earn enough even to do that.

In desperation she even toyed with the idea of asking Ella to help but Ivy had said that her mother was far from well and so she felt it would be unfair to suggest it. Apart from health reasons, why should Ella put herself out for them when her father had forbidden her to ask any of the O'Malleys to either her mother's funeral or Jimmy's?

'We don't want that popish lot lighting their candles and waving their incense all over the place,' Sam sneered when she'd suggested it.

If only she could find some work, and keep it secret from Daisy, she thought wistfully. If she could do that and then save up enough to find a room somewhere else for herself and Cilla, as well as pay someone to look after Cilla, then she could build a new life for the two of them.

She wished she could talk about it to Andrew and see if he had any clever solutions to her problem. The trouble was that he was away on a training course; one that was very important for the advancement of his career, he'd told her.

At one time she would have confided in Ivy but these days she was so engrossed with her new boyfriend that she hardly saw anything at all of her.

Ella seemed to be very wrapped up in what was happening with Ivy and Hadyn. They were planning to get married and there were long discussions about whether they should move in and share Ella's home in Horatio Street or find somewhere of their own.

Jake became Trixie's mainstay. He was so supportive and encouraging that she sometimes wondered how on earth she would manage without him.

He was always ready to listen and to offer advice. He took her and Cilla for walks and he told Trixie that if he wasn't at work then he was even willing to look after Cilla.

She was grateful but she knew that it was impossible because he worked all week. It was thanks to Jake, though, that she did eventually manage to find some work. It was part time, working on a Saturday and Sunday serving tea, coffee, sandwiches and buns from a snack-bar stall down by the

Pier Head.

'I'm a regular there,' he told her, 'and the chap who runs it was moaning that it was difficult to get someone to work at the weekend and he likes to provide a seven-day service. He does hot food during the week but at the weekends people out for the day usually only want a cuppa and a quick snack especially while they're waiting for their boat if they're going over on the ferry to New Brighton or Egremont, and he wants someone to help out then.'

Trixie's eyes shone with excitement. 'That sounds absolutely wonderful, Jake.'

'So I'll tell him you'll do it. I don't know what the money will be like because I didn't think to ask. You can settle all that with him when you start.'

Trixie hesitated, her face suddenly clouding over. 'I'd forgotten about Cilla,' she confessed.

'That's no problem,' he told her cheerfully. 'I explained that you would probably have your little sister with you for part of the time and he said that it was all right.'

'What happens when he finds out that she is there all the time?' Trixie frowned.

'She won't be. On Saturday, as soon as I've finished work, I'll take her for a walk and I'll come down on Sunday morning and take her to the park or somewhere.'

Trixie stared at him wide-eyed with astonishment. 'I can't let you do that, Jake,' she protested with a smile. 'That will be your entire weekend wasted.'

'Wasted? What do you mean, wasted? I enjoy taking Cilla out.'

'And she likes being with you,' Trixie assured him. 'It's just that I feel it's asking too much of you.'

'I offered; you didn't ask,' he corrected her. 'Are you going to take this job or not?'

She nodded, smiling, tears of gratitude shining in her eyes.

'Good, well, I'll let Steve Sinclair know – that's his name, by the way. Steve's Snacks, he calls his place. It's not very grand, just a small shed with a long counter facing the dockside, with a canopy over it, but it's clean and well run. He and his wife manage it between them so one of them will be there to help and tell you what to do.'

Trixie felt rather nervous about starting work there the following Saturday, especially since she had to take Cilla along with her. Steve greeted her like an old friend, however, and she felt at ease the moment she arrived.

Steve was a heavily built, square man with a receding hairline and an infectious smile. His wife, Sylvia, who arrived about an hour later, was thin and birdlike with sharp blue eyes that darted everywhere, taking in all that was going on and making sure that everything was in its place and that things were being done as they should be.

Sylvia was never still for a moment. She liked everything to be meticulously clean, from the huge urns from which they dispensed the tea to the state of the counter.

When she wasn't serving then she was washing dishes, drying them, polishing the cutlery, or else wiping down the top of the counter and rearranging the salt and pepper shakers, the bottles of sauce and the bowl of sugar that were permanently kept there.

Steve did all the food preparation. He'd been a ship's cook and his training stood him in good stead. He could work efficiently and quickly and he never became flustered. No matter how many orders were piled up waiting for his attention he carried them out at an amazing speed.

Although they were both highly efficient, they were also both warm and friendly. In between preparing food, or sometimes even at the same time, Steve greeted customers in a hearty manner, took their orders and never seemed to make a mistake.

They both accepted Cilla without any fuss. Steve made her a milky drink and put a straw in it which delighted her; Sylvia let her pick her own cake from a tray of iced buns. They sat her on a little stool in a corner where she happily tucked into her little feast while they explained to Trixie what her duties would be.

Swathed in a white coat, Trixie buckled down and mucked in, serving customers, washing up or doing whatever else she was asked to do. All the time she was keeping an eye on Cilla who seemed to be quite happy sitting on the stool and watching what was going on.

From time to time, Sylvia or Steve would stop and speak to her, pass her something to eat or say something that made her chuckle. In fact, the morning passed so quickly that Jake was there to take her out before Trixie realised that it was past midday.

He stopped for about twenty minutes, having something to eat and a hot drink, then put Cilla's coat on and took her for a walk.

By the time they returned Trixie had almost finished for the day so he waited and walked home with them.

'Well? Do you think you can stand the pace?' he asked as they walked up Water Street on their way home.

'I've enjoyed every minute of it,' Trixie assured him.

'I'll come down to the stall in the morning at about ten o'clock and take Cilla off your hands,' he promised.

'You can make it later if you like. Surely you'll want the chance of having a lie-in on a Sunday morning?'

He grinned. 'Who's been telling you about my bad habits? Was it Ivy?'

'No one told me, I simply guessed. After all, you have to be up very early all through the week so it's only natural that you'd want a lie-in on Sunday.'

'True. So if you think you can manage with Cilla for an hour or so I'll come down mid-morning.'

'I can probably manage all day if I have to.' She smiled. 'Steve and Sylvia are so nice to us, I've never enjoyed work so much in my life; it's certainly different to being in a factory.'

'She's behaved well today because it's all been new to her but the novelty of watching you work will wear off and she might like to go for a walk tomorrow,' he told her firmly.

Trixie enjoyed the new routine. It was something to look forward to all week. Daisy saw Jake walking home with them once or twice and she assumed that Trixie had taken Cilla round to see Ella, and Trixie saw no reason to tell her anything different.

'If that's what she wants to think then that's fine,' she told Jake. 'It means that as long as she doesn't know I have a job I have no need to tell her and I can save all the money I earn towards getting a room of my own and then Cilla and me can move out.'

She'd thought he would think that was a good idea and she was surprised when he started to speak and then suddenly stopped and said nothing.

When she pressed him to find out if he agreed it was the best thing to do he was somewhat evasive and changed the subject. Instead of talking about her problems he began telling her about the arrangements Ivy and Hadyn were making for their wedding and how his mother was hoping that they would decide to live there.

'How do you feel about that?' she asked.

He shrugged. 'I don't suppose it will make a lot of difference to me and if it's what Mum wants, then I hope they do. I think she's afraid that if they move away she won't see very much of them.'

'Or if you decide to get married and leave home then she will be on her own,' Trixie said thoughtfully.

'I don't think there's a lot of chance of that happening, do you?' he said with a bitter note in his voice.

Trixie looked at him, startled. 'Why ever not? I'm sure you'll meet someone one day and want to get married and have a home of your own,' she told him.

'Maybe I've already met her,' he said quietly.

'You dark horse!' she teased. 'I've never heard you mention any girl that you were sweet on.'

He didn't answer and from the look on his face she decided that it was a subject he didn't want to talk about, so she said no

343

more. Nevertheless, she wondered what had happened to make him look so uncomfortable when she'd mentioned the subject.

She kept thinking about it after they'd parted and hoped things would turn out all right for him because he was such a kind and helpful person that he deserved to be happy. She even found herself feeling a little jealous that he had found someone who obviously meant so much to him while she was still not sure about Andrew's feelings for her.

Chapter Twenty-Seven

Trixie thoroughly enjoyed working at Steve's Snacks and a real friendship developed between Steve, Sylvia and herself. The new routine soon became so well established that Trixie and Cilla both looked forward to the weekends because it took them away from the flat and Daisy.

Trixie also enjoyed being able to talk to the customers; in some ways it compensated for the fact that Andrew was away and most of the time, if it hadn't been for Jake, she would have been very lonely.

Cilla soon understood that that while Trixie was busy serving customers she must stay quiet. She would sit on her special little stool watching everything that was going on in wide-eyed wonder or else playing with her doll or looking at a picture book.

On one or two occasions when Jake needed to go somewhere on his own, Steve and Sylvia accepted that Cilla would be staying the entire day with Trixie. They made no fuss about it but even went out of their way to keep Cilla entertained.

Cilla didn't seem to mind. She would chatter away happily to either of them. Lately Trixie noticed Cilla had become much more observant and now that she was older she was beginning to understand a great deal about what went on around her, and some of the things she said troubled Trixie.

When she was with Sylvia she seemed to open up and confide a great many things about what happened when she was at home; many of which seemed to either shock or worry Sylvia.

Afterwards Sylvia often tactfully worked the conversation round to talking about some of the things Cilla had told her and this embarrassed Trixie. Whenever possible she merely smiled in a non-committal way and tried to change the subject. Sylvia could be persistent, though, especially when Cilla appeared with bruises on her arms or weals on her legs where Daisy had hit her, and she would deliberately question Cilla to find out how she had come by them.

'For poor little Cilla's sake, you ought to get away from this Daisy,' Sylvia admonished Trixie, her sharp blue eyes full of concern as she placed a cup of tea in front of her.

'I know, and that's what I'm trying to do. That's why I'm working at weekends, to try and save up enough to rent a room for us well away from her and my dad.'

'You'll never be able to afford to support yourself independently on what you earn here.' Sylvia frowned, wiping down the counter so vigorously that everything on it rattled.

'No,' Trixie sighed. 'I'm beginning to realise that. I've tried to save every penny I earn, and I have, except for a few things that I've had to buy for Cilla, but it doesn't add up to much.'

'Of course it doesn't! Why don't you find yourself some other work during the week?'

'It's not easy. I dare not leave Cilla at home on her own because of Daisy, and no one's willing to employ you if you have a young child with you all the time, especially one like Cilla. You and Steve have been the exception to the rule,' she added gratefully.

Sylvia smiled. 'She's no trouble at all and extremely obedient. I'm sure you could take her with you absolutely anywhere.'

'Would you have taken me on if I'd said I

had to bring Cilla with me if Jake hadn't put in a good word for me?' Trixie asked bluntly as she tidied the counter.

Sylvia looked thoughtful. 'Probably not,' she agreed. 'I understand what you're saying, so I think the answer is for you to find another job where someone can recommend you and explain to your new employer about Cilla.'

'That's not going to be easy,' Trixie sighed. 'I was very lucky over this job because you knew Jake well enough to trust what he said about me.'

'What's worked successfully once can happen again,' Sylvia told her optimistically as she folded up the cleaning cloths and tidied them away.

It was almost a month later when Sylvia told Trixie that she had found the perfect job for her.

'It's a cleaning job, but you wouldn't mind that, would you?' she said forcefully. 'It's every evening from six o'clock till about eight. It's at the chiropodist's in Cazneau Street. That's not all that far from where you live, but you must be on time because he would want to let you in before he left and then when you leave you slam the door behind you and it will lock itself.'

'You've explained that I will have to take Cilla with me?' Trixie asked tentatively. It sounded perfect, but she didn't want to get her hopes up too quickly.

'Of course! He said that will be no problem as there will be no one else there. You must make sure that she doesn't touch anything, of course,' Sylvia warned.

'She won't, I'll make sure of that,' Trixie promised earnestly.

'That's exactly what I said to Mr Browning.' Sylvia nodded. 'I also told him how good she is when she comes here at the weekends and he seemed to be quite impressed. I've said you will go along on Monday afternoon so that he can explain everything to you. He's hoping you will be able to start right away.'

'It sounds ideal,' Trixie told her. 'I'll be there on time, don't worry, and I'll let you know next Saturday how I've got on.'

Mr Browning was a tall, thin man, meticulously dressed in a dark suit under a knee-length white coat. He wore glasses and his sparse black hair was receding rapidly from his high forehead. He had a nervous habit of rubbing his hands together while he talked. His fingers were so long that Trixie felt mesmerised by them.

Her list of duties was very explicit; he showed her where all the cleaning materials were kept and asked her to make sure they were stored away in precisely the same order when she'd finished using them and to lock the cupboard door.

'I like order in my consulting room so I must ask you to make sure that when you do the cleaning you return every item to precisely the same place where you found it. When I am attending to my clients I want to be able to put my hand on instruments, lotions and everything else I use instantaneously. Do you understand?'

Trixie assured him she did and they agreed she would start work right away.

'You will be bringing this little girl with you each time?' he questioned.

'Yes, Mr Browning. I have to bring my sister; I have no one I can leave her with, I'm afraid.'

He studied Cilla from over the top of his glasses. 'Doesn't she go to school?'

'No.' Trixie shook her head. 'She can read and write her own name, though. I've taught her to do that at home. And she can count and add up,' she added proudly.

'Can you make her understand that she mustn't touch anything here?' he asked, frowning.

'Don't worry, she's very well behaved,' Trixie assured him. 'I'll bring some books with me and she'll sit and look at those while I'm working like she does at the snack bar,' she added.

'I see!' He pursed his thin lips thoughtfully.

Trixie felt her heart thumping as he rubbed a hand over his chin. She desperately wanted him to give her the job, especially after Sylvia had seemed so certain that it was right for her. She wondered if she ought to say something to try and convince him or whether it was better to stay silent and let him think it through on his own.

'Well, I think we'd better agree to a week's trial and see how things work out,' he agreed at length. 'You'll be here at six o'clock this evening, right?'

'Yes, and thank you, Mr Browning. I'll do my best to give complete satisfaction.'

Trixie went home feeling elated. The wages were not very much but they would be regular. If she saved every penny and added it to what she earned at Steve's place then, in about three months' time, she was confident she would be able to afford to finally leave Virgil Street and rent a place for herself and Cilla.

She wondered how long it would be before Daisy found out that she was working. So far her weekends at the snack bar seemed to have passed unnoticed.

Fortunately, whenever Daisy asked Cilla where they'd been she never answered. Her behaviour annoyed Daisy and often resulted in her calling Cilla a 'daft little idiot' but, as a result, so far she'd never found out the truth about what they were doing.

Leaving the house at half past five every evening and not coming home again till after eight o'clock, was another matter, though, and Trixie realised that sooner or later Daisy was bound to notice and start asking questions.

Furthermore, Trixie mused, she'd have to give Cilla her tea before they went out and the fact that she was doing this earlier than usual would arouse Daisy's curiosity if she was at home.

It also meant that although she left Sam and Daisy's meal ready Daisy would have to take it out of the oven, and if they still weren't back when Daisy and Sam went off to the pub that was going to make her suspicious when it happened every night of the week.

She wondered whether it was best to wait till Daisy or her father said something or whether to be up front and tell them that she had an evening cleaning job, but if she did tell them about it, then they would expect her to hand over whatever she earned towards the housekeeping and that would defeat her plans.

The first couple of weeks went well. Mr Browning confirmed at the end of the first week that he was very satisfied with her work and that he wanted her to continue. Sylvia was delighted that it had all turned out so successfully and Trixie felt that at long last she was getting control of her life and could start to plan for the future.

Now that Andrew had finished his course and was home again they could plan things together and she hoped he would be as enthusiastic and encouraging as Jake was when she talked to him about her hopes of leaving Virgil Street.

As the days began to get shorter and it was almost dark by teatime Daisy started asking pointed questions about where they were going, especially when it was cold or raining.

Trixie shrugged and tried to make light of it but she was afraid to openly lie and say she was going round to see Ivy in case Cilla might say something to the contrary. Also, she knew it would look strange if she went to see Ivy every night.

For a time she managed to fend off Daisy's prying with one excuse or other, but how long she would manage to go on doing so she wasn't sure. She narrowly avoided everything coming out into the open when Cilla had an accident.

The normal routine was that each evening, the moment they arrived at the chiropodist's, Cilla climbed up into the big leather chair in which Mr Browning's clients sat while he attended to their feet, and sat there till Trixie had finished her work and they were ready to go home.

Usually she sat perfectly still but on this particular evening she had started playing with the lever which raised, lowered and tilted the chair to the angle Mr Browning wanted. Somehow she managed to get her arm pinioned between the mechanism and the main body of the chair.

For a long time she sat there with her arm trapped, but not saying a word. When Trixie was ready to leave she held out a hand to her, but Cilla remained where she was.

'Come on, time for us to go home,' Trixie called as she walked towards the door.

When there was no response she turned round and was surprised to see that Cilla was still sitting in the chair.

'Hurry up,' Trixie urged. 'My feet are killing me and all I want to do is get home and take my shoes off.'

Cilla still didn't move so she went back and took her by the hand to pull her from the chair. Then and only then did Cilla let out a sharp cry of pain and Trixie realised that her arm was stuck.

Trixie tried everything she could to free it but it was stuck fast. She was afraid to put too much pressure on it, or to move the lever at all, in case she made matters worse or even broke Cilla's arm.

After a moment of panic she tried to reason out the best thing to do. She needed to get help but who could help in such a matter? she asked herself. The only person she could think of was Jake but it would take too long to go all the way to Horatio Street to fetch him and she couldn't be sure he'd even be there.

If she left Cilla trapped in the chair and on her own then she would probably become distressed and frightened because she might think Trixie had gone away and left her. She tried to think of some other way of getting help. In the end it seemed that the only thing she could do was to go down into the street and see if she could find a policeman.

She tried to explain to Cilla what she was about to do and although she nodded her head and seemed to understand, Trixie could see the scared look in her eyes when she went towards the door.

She propped the door open so that it wouldn't lock behind her, and was lucky in that the moment she went out into Cazneau Street she found a patrolling policeman. He listened to her story and agreed to come with her to see what he could do.

As he walked into the room with Trixie he removed his helmet and then knelt down by the side of the chair and talked to Cilla. In a quiet, reassuring voice he tried to find out how she had managed to trap her arm.

Cilla was unable to tell him. She was now sobbing noisily and Trixie tried her best to calm her down and explained that she wasn't in any trouble and that the police- man was only trying to help her to get free from the chair.

Even with his help it was impossible to free Cilla's arm. 'It's been trapped so long that it's become very swollen and that is making things more complicated,' he said as he stood up and replaced his helmet. 'Try and quieten her and I'll fetch some more help.'

He was away for about ten minutes and Trixie was beginning to get very worried. When he returned there were two other uniformed men with him but they were firemen, not policemen.

Once again Trixie tried to explain what she thought must have happened. When she saw the tools they'd brought with them she was also rather concerned that they might cause some damage to Mr Browning's chair.

'We'll do our best not to do any damage, Miss,' the one in charge assured her, 'but our main concern is to free this child's arm.'

Trixie hovered, keeping a watchful eye on what was happening and at the same time trying to comfort Cilla.

Almost a quarter of an hour elapsed before they finally managed to free Cilla, who by this time was screaming with pain.

'Her arm is crushed and needs medical attention,' the senior fire officer insisted as he carried her out to where an ambulance was already waiting to take them to the hospital.

Cilla became almost hysterical as they attended to her arm and her terrified screams upset Trixie who was unable to calm her. They all did their best to try and explain to Cilla what was happening but it seemed to be impossible to make her understand.

When they'd finished dressing her arm the staff nurse said that they would be keeping her in overnight and told Trixie to come back in the morning. 'By then we'll be able to decide if she's well enough to be discharged.'

Trixie begged to be allowed to stay with her.

'That's not necessary,' the staff nurse told her firmly. 'She will be in good hands, there's no need for you to worry.'

'She's not like other children, she doesn't always understand what is happening,' Trixie pleaded. 'If I walk out and leave her—'

'Yes, I understand what you are saying.' The staff nurse frowned. 'She has already disrupted the entire ward with her screaming. In fact, she can be heard all over the hospital.'

'Perhaps I could take her home and bring her back in again in the morning so that you can see if her arm is all right,' Trixie suggested hesitantly.

'Wait here and I'll see what Sister thinks about it.'

'We wouldn't normally permit you to do this,' the sister told her severely, 'but since the only alternative will be to sedate her–'

'No, please, that's not necessary,' Trixie protested. Cilla was already tense with fear and exhausted by all she'd been through and Trixie knew that what she needed more than anything else was the reassurance of her own bed and familiar surroundings. Once they were home she was sure she would calm down.

'If you take her home then you must bring her back tomorrow so that we can look at her arm again after the swelling has gone down and make sure that there's no hidden damage. Whatever you do, don't unwrap the bandages or let them get wet. The desk clerk will tell you what time we will want to see you, so make sure you're punctual, understand?'

Chapter Twenty-Eight

It was almost ten o'clock by the time Trixie and Cilla reached Virgil Street. Trixie was hoping there would be time to make something to eat and get Cilla off to bed before Daisy and her father came in so that they wouldn't see her heavily bandaged arm and start asking questions.

She felt utterly exhausted and wanted to

get to bed herself. She also wanted to be on her own to try and work out what she was going to tell Mr Browning. She decided she'd have to go along there first thing in the morning and explain to him what had happened before he heard it from someone else.

Cilla was restless and kept Trixie awake for most of the night. The following day it was still quite dark when she pulled herself out of bed and started to dress. As she peeped out of the window at the miserable grey October morning she shivered not only with the cold but also with the thought of the meeting with Mr Browning that lay ahead.

She waited till she heard her father leave for work before she roused Cilla. She wanted to get her dressed so that they could be on their way before Daisy was up and started asking questions about Cilla's bandaged arm.

After a hurried breakfast, Trixie cleared away their dishes as quickly as possible. She was anxious to be at Mr Browning's before he saw his first client.

By the time they were ready to leave it had started to rain and there was such a high wind that she didn't think it was any good taking an umbrella. Yet, if she didn't do so then Cilla would get wet and if she arrived at the hospital with her bandages all wet they were bound to be told off by the sister.

As she had foreseen, they were turning the

corner into Cazneau Street when a sudden gust caught the umbrella and swept it from her hand and she knew it was useless to try and recover it.

If only Jake was there he would have chased after it and he would probably have offered to carry Cilla as far as Cazneau Street, she thought mutinously.

Why did she always think of Jake whenever she had a problem when she ought to think of Andrew? she wondered. It was probably because Andrew was never there to help her like Jake was and he didn't have much time for Cilla either. How on earth would she manage without the O'Malleys – especially Jake, who was always so kind and understanding to Cilla as well as to her?

They were both soaked through by the time they reached Mr Browning's. His response when Trixie told him what had happened the evening before was not very understanding.

'I thought you said that your sister would sit quietly while you got on with your work?'

'She was sitting quietly in the chair; it was where she always sat,' Trixie explained.

Mr Browning frowned heavily. 'You should never have let her sit there in the first place. If it is damaged in any way then I shall hold you responsible.'

'The fireman was very careful to make sure that it wasn't. Only my sister's arm came to harm,' Trixie defended. 'She had to be taken to hospital and I am on my way to take her back there so that they can make sure that there is nothing broken. It was so swollen last night that they were unable to examine it properly.'

'I see!' He took off his spectacles and polished them vigorously with a large white handkerchief which he took from his top pocket. 'Does this mean you won't be able to work this evening?'

Trixie looked rather taken aback. 'I had every intention of doing so,' she said stiffly.

He nodded, biting his lips and frowning. 'What about your sister? Under the circumstances, I trust you are not thinking of bringing her with you again?'

'Of course I will be bringing her! I told you there's no one she can stay with and I certainly can't leave her on her own.'

'So this sort of thing can happen again, can it?'

Trixie flushed angrily. 'Accidents do happen, Mr Browning. I'm very sorry about it and I can assure you it won't occur again.'

He ran one of his bony hands over his chin as he stared back at her and she thought for a moment that he was going to sack her. Then he gave an imperceptible shrug of his thin shoulders. 'Very well, make sure there's no repetition of anything like this.'

Although it meant she still had her job, his attitude rankled with Trixie. He seemed to be barely concerned about how badly hurt Cilla was. His only worry was that his precious chair might have been damaged, she thought rebelliously as she took Cilla's hand and they went out into the cold, wet street again.

Her reception at the hospital was not much better. She was five minutes late arriving which brought a sharp reprimand from the sister. It was followed by an acid comment that both of them were so wet that they were making puddles on the polished floor as the water dripped from them.

'You'd better not sit down; other people won't want wet chairs,' the sister said sharply, her well-starched dark blue dress and crisp white apron crackling as she led Cilla away into a curtained-off cubicle.

'Please stay out in the waiting room,' she ordered sharply as Trixie made to follow her.

The iciness of her tone and her officious manner upset Cilla who became frightened and began to cry and shout for Trixie. After a few minutes, when it became obvious that they were not going to be able to remove the dressing unless they used force to hold her down, the sister told Trixie she'd better join them.

It was left to Trixie to take off Cilla's soaking wet outdoor clothes and then to begin to unwind the bandages and remove them from her arm. By then Cilla had calmed down and the nurse who was also in attendance was able to take over.

Although her arm was still swollen and very badly bruised they ascertained that there were no bones broken and after a fresh dressing had been put on it she was discharged.

The rain had stopped by the time they left the hospital. It was still cold and miserable, though, and on the spur of the moment Trixie decided to go and see Ella. She felt in need of a friendly face and the opportunity to tell someone about the accident, someone who would understand and be sympathetic.

Although Ella welcomed her and made a great fuss of Cilla as she made them a hot drink and listened to what had happened, she was much more concerned with all the changes that were happening in her own family.

'Ivy and Hadyn are planning to get married next Easter,' she told Trixie excitedly.

'Have they found somewhere to live?' Trixie asked as she sipped her tea.

'They'll move in here, of course. It's the only way we can all manage,' Ella pointed out. 'If Ivy leaves I'm going to find it hard to manage on the little I earn with my sewing and what Jake gives me each week. Although he's had a good pay rise and has a steady job, what he hands over only pays the rent and keeps us in food. There's nothing left spare for all the other things we need. If he should ever decide to leave home then I'd be in a right pickle. If Ivy and Hadyn move in here then we'll all be better off,' she said with a contented smile.

Trixie couldn't help wondering why, if things were as tight as Ella said, she didn't get a full-time job herself since she was an experienced alteration hand. Working at one of the better-class dress shops would have brought in a lot more than she made working from home, but she didn't like to voice her thoughts aloud.

She supposed it was because of her arm that Ella preferred to work from home fitting in her sewing jobs between cooking and looking after her family, and as long as it suited them all, it probably was the best way to live. She wished Daisy was at home more, then she wouldn't have to do so much.

Daisy still kept a tight hold of the purse strings and she had also started going out at regular times of the day once again. Where she went or what she did, Trixie never managed to find out. It was some means of earning money, she was sure about that, because, despite the fact that her father and Daisy still went to the pub every night, Daisy always seemed to have enough to buy new clothes and little treats for herself.

Trixie felt anxious about going into work that evening. She was afraid that once he'd had time to think things over Mr Browning might decide that having Cilla around the place was too great a risk to take any more.

There was no way she could avoid him because he waited for her to arrive to let her in.

His greeting was cool, almost frosty, but he did enquire about what had happened that morning at the hospital and seemed relieved to know that Cilla's arm was only badly bruised.

'You will make quite sure she doesn't sit in that chair ever again,' he said forcefully as he shrugged on his overcoat and picked up his trilby ready to leave. 'It was very fortunate that it wasn't damaged in any way.'

'Indeed it was, Mr Browning.'

'So where is she going to sit?' he demanded.

'Well, on the floor, in the corner,' Trixie told him.

'I see!' He stood there frowning for such a long time that Trixie's heart started thumping and she wondered yet again if she was going to lose her job.

To her surprise he went to the other side of the room and picked up a padded stool and placed it in one corner of the room. 'There, she can use that,' he told her. 'Let her sit on it; she can't get caught up in any mechanism and it's more comfortable than the floor.'

Before Trixie could thank him he'd gone.

Much to Trixie's surprise and relief Daisy and her father appeared not to notice the bandage so she didn't bother telling them about the accident.

Cilla's arm was still bandaged when Trixie took her to Steve's Snacks the following Saturday morning and she had to tell Steve and Sylvia what had happened. Sylvia was so sympathetic and made such a fuss of Cilla that for the first time Cilla started talking about what had happened.

When Jake came to collect her to take her for a walk she told him about the accident while Trixie merely listened and nodded from time to time.

Although the swelling soon settled it was several weeks before the bruising had gone but Cilla seemed to have forgotten all about the incident, except that she kept well clear of the chair.

It was almost Christmas before Daisy found out that Trixie was working and when she did she was furious that she hadn't been told. There was a heated row and Sam was involved as well. He took Daisy's side and said that Trixie was deceitful and underhand to be earning money and not giving any of it to them.

'I buy all my own clothes and anything else I need and I also do the same for Cilla,'

Trixie protested.

'Yes, and we keep you both and feed you,' Daisy stormed.

'In return for me doing all the housework, the cooking, the washing, the ironing and everything else that needs doing here, while you swan around,' Trixie retorted.

The slap across the face from her father made her teeth chatter and brought tears to her eyes, there was such force behind it. In the past she had always been on her guard, ready to dodge away or step back so that she didn't get the full force of his hand, but this time he'd caught her completely unprepared.

She said nothing, afraid that if she did it might only result in another blow, but she resolved that things couldn't go on as they were any longer and that the time had come to put her plan to leave Virgil Street into action.

She had saved hard and although she still hadn't anywhere near as much as she would have liked now that she had two jobs, she was sure that if she could find a really cheap room somewhere she would be able to manage.

For the rest of the week she could think of nothing else and she knew from the way Daisy was watching her every move that she had to do something as quickly as she could. For one thing, she was afraid that Daisy might find her little stash of savings and if she did manage to get her hands on it then that would be the end of all her plans.

Remembering how Andrew had helped her to look after the Christmas savings when she'd worked at the biscuit factory she wondered if she should ask him if he could open an account for her at the bank so that she'd know her money was safe.

She saw him so little these days, though, that she decided in the end that it would be better not to wait but to ask Jake to look after it for her. Andrew would probably tell her that it wasn't a large enough sum to merit opening a bank account.

Jake might think the same, of course, but at least he knew she was saving up to try and get away from her father and Daisy.

Her face was still bruised when she saw Jake at the weekend and he was so concerned that it was a simple matter to ask his advice and to look after her money for her.

'Of course I'll look after it, where is it now?' he asked, his voice full of concern.

'On me; I carry it in a purse around my waist.' She smiled. 'I daren't leave it anywhere in the house in case Daisy should find it.'

'Then give it to me and I'll take care of it for you. Would you like me to scout around and see if I can find you a room? I'll see what I can do if you tell me how much you can afford. Remember, though, they will probably expect at least two weeks' rent up front and you'll also have to have enough money left to buy food and heat and so on.'

'Yes, I know all that and it was why I didn't want to have to make a move yet. I was planning on doing it in the New Year,' she sighed. 'You know, a New Year and a new start. That was the goal I'd set myself.'

'Well, we're only a few weeks off Christmas and it's bound to take a couple of weeks to find somewhere so you are more or less on target then,' he told her.

Trixie found that his interest and promise of help boosted her confidence. She could do it and she would, she told herself. She might only be able to afford one small room but she'd make it a home for her and Cilla.

Chapter Twenty-Nine

Two weeks later, even with Jake's help, Trixie had still not managed to find anywhere to rent. She felt very frustrated; her only consolation was that she knew the money she had worked so hard to save was safely in Jake's keeping.

Now that she knew Trixie had an evening cleaning job Daisy made sure that Trixie never had a minute to spare during the day. There was always something or other extra that Daisy insisted needed doing in the house.

To add to Trixie's unhappiness, Daisy had once again started picking on Cilla, pushing her out of the way, slapping her or shouting at her for no reason at all. She constantly accused Cilla of killing Jimmy and threatening some form of retribution.

The only good thing that seemed to be happening in Trixie's life was when Jake told her that Andrew had now finished the course he'd been sent away on and would be having a party at the weekend to celebrate the fact that he had now been promoted.

She felt extremely hurt that Andrew hadn't let her know himself; but then, she thought sadly, he hadn't been in touch with her all the time he'd been away. She'd dreamed of receiving a letter from him telling her how much he was missing her and how he was longing to see her again; or even simply telling her about where he was staying and what the course was all about, but there hadn't even been a postcard from him. She wondered whether it was because he hadn't missed her as much as she missed him or because he'd been studying so hard.

Every time she remembered the last time they'd been together on the night before he was due to go away, she recalled his passionate kisses and intimate embraces. She loved him so much that her heart ached.

'The party is on Saturday night and he's asked me to make sure you are there,' Jake told her.

Trixie felt the blood rush to her cheeks. Even though he hadn't written, it seemed Andrew was as keen as ever to see her. Now that he was back in Liverpool everything would be all right again; she was sure of it.

Her elation immediately turned to dismay as she thought about Cilla.

'I can't leave her alone with Daisy, I don't even feel safe with Daisy myself,' she shuddered. 'She has such a wild look in her eyes when she talks about Jimmy that sometimes I think she's unhinged and I'm sure she's going to do one of us some harm as soon as she gets the chance, so it means I'll have to miss out on the party,' she explained to Jake.

'You must go,' Jake told her. 'Bring Cilla round to our place, I'm sure Ivy and my mum will keep an eye on her.'

'Ivy will be out with Hadyn, won't she?' Trixie frowned.

'I don't know. Now that they are so keen on saving up for their wedding next spring they tend to stay in quite a lot. Anyway, my mum will be there and Cilla is always happy enough to be with her. Or else I'll stay and look after Cilla.'

'You can't do that! It would mean you'd miss the party and Andrew would be very hurt because you're one of his best friends.'

'Not any longer,' Jake said dryly. 'Andrew's moved on. We haven't had a night out together for months.'

'That's because he's been away on this course,' Trixie pointed out. 'I haven't seen or heard from him for months either.'

'So he's been neglecting both of us,' Jake said wryly. 'Still, it's more important for you to see him than for me to, so I'll look after Cilla and you can go to the party.'

'If your mum doesn't mind looking after her, then promise me that you'll come as well?' Trixie begged, laying a hand on Jake's arm.

Jake shrugged. 'OK, if it will please you, but I really don't mind missing out,' he assured her.

For the rest of the week Trixie could think of nothing else except being with Andrew once again. He'd been away over two months and there had been times when she'd worried that he'd met someone else and that was why he hadn't bothered to write to her.

When she collected her wages from Mr Browning on Friday night she had the sudden impulse to dash up to St John's Market and see if she could find herself a new dress to wear on Saturday night.

'Come on,' she told Cilla as they left Cazneau Street, 'we're going shopping before we go home.'

The market was bustling as people

searched for Christmas bargains. Trixie headed for the second-hand dress stalls. She wished she could afford to go into one of the many big stores in the centre of Liverpool and buy the prettiest frock she could find but she knew that would be reckless.

Even so, she felt that she owed it to Andrew to look nice so she was justified in having something new for such a special occasion as his party. It also meant she'd have something new to wear at Christmas.

The dress was lovely; it was dark red, straight hanging, and had a belt of draped material at the waist that was trimmed with a large buckle. The square neckline had a wide beaded trim and a clasp at one side that was a smaller version of the buckle at the waistline.

Although she couldn't try it on, Trixie was sure it would fit her and even though it was a couple of shillings more than she had wanted to pay, she was so delighted with it that she decided she must have it.

Cilla was watching excitedly and then began touching the dresses hanging on the rail, stroking them and holding the skirts up to her face. Materials seemed to fascinate her and she would stand smoothing the soft or silky fabric whenever Ella was working on a dress, rubbing it against her face as if she enjoyed the feel of it.

Trixie was well aware that Cilla was at last

growing up and although she sometimes found it difficult to express her feelings or thoughts in words Trixie was often acutely aware of what she was thinking.

She'd also noticed that Cilla spent ages brushing her hair and looking in the mirror and also had begun to take quite an interest in what she was wearing and how she looked. She wished her mother was there to see this; it would be their first Christmas without her and so much had changed since she'd died.

Now, as Cilla smiled at her, making it quite clear that she was also hoping for a new dress, Trixie hated to disappoint her. Yet she knew that if she bought her one as well then it meant spending almost all her week's wages.

As she paid the stallholder and held out her hand to Cilla, ready to walk away, she saw tears fill the girl's eyes and there was such a look of disappointment on her face that Trixie hesitated.

As Cilla grabbed hold of her hand and pulled her back towards the rail Trixie gave in. Why shouldn't Cilla have a new dress as well? she asked herself. She doesn't have many pleasures in her little life. She has no friends of her own age, Daisy bullies her, Dad ignores her and she has to spend hours sitting in a corner while I work. It's almost Christmas and she's too old for toys so this could be her special treat.

Deep down Trixie knew that it would be far more sensible to buy her a warm winter coat because she had practically grown out of the one she had but that wouldn't have the same excitement attached to it as the new dress.

When she explained to Cilla that if she bought her a dress then it would be her Christmas present, Cilla clapped her hands enthusiastically. Together they sorted through what was on sale and finally found a blue wool dress with long sleeves and a reasonably high neckline that would be both pretty and sensible.

When Trixie handed the garment over, the stallholder studied Cilla with a kindly smile as she took the money and put the dress into a bag.

'Would you like this to wear with your new dress?' she asked as she held out a pretty blue hairband to Cilla.

'Sorry, it's lovely, but I haven't any more money to spare,' Trixie said quickly.

'I'm not asking you to pay for it, luv,' the woman told her. 'It's a little Christmas present. Isn't it, dear?' she said looking at Cilla who nodded and gave her a beaming smile.

When they reached home, Trixie smuggled the parcel into their bedroom and hid it underneath the bedclothes so that Daisy wouldn't find it. She put a finger on her lips to signal to Cilla that it was to be kept a secret.

The moment her father and Daisy went out to the pub she fetched the bag out of its hiding place and unfolded the two dresses. They were even nicer than she had thought when she'd chosen them.

Cilla was eager to try her dress on so Trixie helped her to change into it. When she saw the delight on her little sister's face as she put on the hairband and then admired herself in the mirror, Trixie felt it had been well worth sacrificing their savings for that week.

As she tried on her own new dress and discovered how well it fitted, Trixie hoped that Andrew would think it looked attractive when he saw her in it for the first time.

All day on Saturday she could think of nothing else. When she told Sylvia what was ahead Sylvia looked puzzled. 'I thought it was Jake you were keen on,' she said in surprise. 'All this talk of saving up to get a place of your own and Jake looking after the money and taking care of Cilla so that you can work and so on.'

'Jake's the best friend in the world, I don't know how I would manage without him, but I'm in love with his friend, Andrew Bacon,' Trixie told her dreamily. 'It's over two months since I last saw him and I can hardly wait for this evening.'

'So is Jake going to this party as well?'

'We hope so, if his mother will look after Cilla, otherwise Jake has will stay home with Cilla.'

Sylvia raised her eyebrows but said no more and for a moment Trixie wondered why she seemed to be so surprised by the arrangement. Did other people think that Jake was her boyfriend because they were always together and he did so much to help her? She pushed the matter to one side; all she wanted to think about was that she would soon be seeing Andrew again.

The party was in a restaurant in Great Homer Street and by the time Trixie and Jake arrived it was already very crowded with people neither of them knew.

The man on the door looked at them questioningly and explained that it was a private party. He didn't seem to be very convinced when Jake said they'd both been invited and insisted on calling over to Andrew to verify that this was true.

It took Andrew several minutes to extricate himself from the circle of back-slapping friends who surrounded him. As he began to make his way towards the door exchanging remarks with people as he did so, Jake raised a hand in greeting.

'They're friends,' Andrew called out to the doorman, 'you can let them in.'

Trixie waited expectantly for him to come

over to them but instead he went back to the group he'd been talking to. Disappointed, Trixie let Jake take her coat and hand it to the cloakroom girl. She barely noticed his admiring look when he saw her new dress as they went into the restaurant.

As she stood there beside Jake, slowly sipping a glass of wine and looking around, she suddenly felt very out of things. She'd thought her new dress was lovely but in comparison with some of the dresses the other girls were wearing it was plain almost to the point of dowdiness. It was the sort of dress they would wear perhaps on a Sunday for going to church or spending the day with their family. Their party dresses were much more flimsy and floaty, in delicate silks and chiffons, with low necks, puff sleeves and fancy flouncing.

She wished she could turn and run away before Andrew realised how out of place she was in such a gathering. Even Jake, she reflected, although he was wearing his best suit, didn't look anywhere near as smartly dressed as the other men there, even though he was the most handsome.

She stole a sideways glance at him, wondering if he felt as uncomfortable and out of place as she did. He certainly didn't look as though he was enjoying himself, she thought ruefully. She was very glad that he was there because Andrew was paying her no attention whatsoever and she would have felt dreadfully out of things if she'd come on her own.

The evening was almost over before Andrew came over to where she and Jake were standing in a corner; he'd had so many drinks that he was very exuberant.

'What's wrong with you two?' he greeted them. 'Why aren't you enjoying the party? Come on; enter into the spirit of things.' He flicked open his cigarette case and held it out to Jake. 'Your glass is almost empty and you're not even smoking!'

He turned to Trixie as if seeing her for the first time. 'I haven't had time to talk to you properly, have I?' he admitted with an apologetic smile.

'No, I'm still waiting to hear all about your course and if it was successful.'

'Of course it was! What on earth do you think I'm celebrating otherwise?'

'I hoped that perhaps it was because you were glad to be back in Liverpool again.'

He shrugged dismissively. 'Any excuse for a good party, what do you say, Jake?'

'I'll leave you two to catch up,' Jake said awkwardly.

'There's no need, I can't stop now because they want me over there,' he nodded in the direction of the crowd he'd been with, 'things will probably quieten down in about another hour so the three of us will have a chance to get together then.'

'That's if we're still here,' Jake said, looking at his watch.

'Why, where are you going?' Andrew frowned. 'The night's still young; it's not even midnight yet.'

'It had better not be,' Trixie said quickly. 'I've left Cilla with Ella and she likes to go to bed around eleven.'

'Cilla or Ella?' Andrew said with a sneering laugh.

'My mother,' Jake said quietly. 'She's not much of a one for late nights so we'll have to be off soon.'

'Well, perhaps I'll see you tomorrow afternoon, Trixie, when you take Cilla to the park,' Andrew said almost dismissively as someone caught hold of his arm and began to pull him back into the noisy crowd in the middle of the room.

'I don't go to the park on a Sunday any more. I work on a Sunday,' Trixie called after him.

He didn't even turn; he merely waved a hand in the air and she wasn't even sure if he'd heard what she'd said.

Trixie had been looking forward to seeing Andrew again so much that she felt very disheartened and let down as they left the restaurant. It should be Andrew, not Jake, walking her home, she thought disconsolately and then felt cross with herself for thinking that when Jake had gone to so much trouble to make sure she could go to the party.

Chapter Thirty

The first thing Sylvia wanted to know when Trixie went to work on the Sunday was how she had enjoyed the party and although Trixie told her that it had been good fun she knew in her heart that it had been a terrible disappointment.

To have been so near to Andrew, to see have seen him laughing and talking with all his close friends while she and Jake had been left almost isolated, left her feeling desolate and unloved.

She wasn't sure what Jake had felt but she had been very conscious that he hadn't gone out of his way to push into the crowd that was surrounding Andrew. Even when the two of them did eventually talk to each other there had been no real spark between them.

Jake seemed to be able to accept that Andrew had grown away from him and found new friends, but then it was different for him. They'd merely been school friends; she was in love with Andrew and she had thought he had deep feelings for her, but now she wasn't so sure.

Meeting up wasn't going to be easy now that she worked all day on a Saturday and Sunday. She could hardly expect Jake and Ella to look after Cilla in the evening as well as all day. There was no point in suggesting to Andrew that they went to the pictures one night in the week instead of on a Saturday night because she worked until eight o'clock every evening from Monday to Friday.

It was now so near to Christmas that by the look of things Andrew was going to be caught up in celebrations with his friends and family and have no time at all for her.

She'd had so many dreams for the new year but now 1927 looked as though it might turn out to be no better than any other year had been. She still hadn't found a room that she could afford and life at Virgil Street was getting worse by the day.

She'd resigned herself to not seeing Andrew till after Christmas so she was surprised when she bumped into him in Scotland Road one evening when she was on her way to her cleaning job in Cazneau Street.

He seemed taken aback when she told him that she couldn't stop to talk because she was on her way to work.

'Where is it? What time do you finish? I could come and meet you afterwards,' he suggested. 'I haven't seen anything of you except very briefly at my party since I got back.'

'I finish at eight. I work at the chiropodist's in Cazneau Street.'

'I'll be waiting for you,' he called after her.

All the time she polished and cleaned she kept thinking about Andrew, she was so elated that he still wanted to go on seeing her. Even so, she was almost afraid to believe that he would be there waiting for her when she finished work.

'At last,' he exclaimed, giving her a peck on the cheek and ignoring Cilla. 'Come on, let's go for a drink and I'll tell you all about what's been happening and you can tell me about your job?' he told her, putting his arm around her and hugging her close.

'That will be lovely, Andrew, but it will have to be a milk bar because Cilla is too young to go into a pub.'

'Let's take her home first, then.'

'I'm sorry, but I can't do that. I can't leave her there on her own.'

'Why not? Won't your father be there, or that woman who lives with him? Can't they keep an eye on her for an hour or two?'

'It's not safe to leave Cilla with them because–'

'Then in that case if we can't go for a drink I'll walk you home and see you some other time,' he said abruptly, cutting short her explanation.

Hurt and disappointed she still insisted on explaining what had happened to turn Daisy even more against Cilla.

'That's why I'm working every evening as well as at weekends. I'm trying to save up enough money to be able to rent a room and move out. Daisy is evil, and I'm scared she'll do us some real harm if she gets the chance. I really am frightened, Andrew.'

'Then perhaps you should leave there before she does,' he advised. He took out his cigarette case and selected one. 'Perhaps it's time you moved in with me?' he suggested, exhaling a cloud of smoke.

Trixie stared at him, her eyes shining with love and relief. 'Oh that would be wonderful, Andrew,' she gasped. 'Do you really mean it? It would be perfect. When ... when can we arrange it?'

'Soon.' He shrugged. 'I'll have to make some plans and arrange things first,' he told her.

'It can't be soon enough,' she told him fervently.

'I understand, sweetheart, but don't worry. We'll fix up something early in the New Year.'

'Oh that would be fantastic!' Stopping, she stood on tiptoe and kissed him on the cheek, all her fears about how much he cared for her gone.

He pulled her into his arms, nuzzling her neck and then kissing her passionately. 'You've no idea how much I want this, how much I want to make you mine completely and have you all to myself,' he whispered hotly. 'Look, I must go now,' he murmured. He turned on his heel and walked off in the other direction before she had the chance to ask him anything else; even when he was hoping they could be married.

Trixie found every minute of waiting was sheer hell. She was on edge, tense and suspicious of everything Daisy said or did. Knowing that she couldn't leave Cilla alone with Daisy, not even for a few minutes, was so worrying that in the end she could stand the strain no longer. She decided one afternoon to leave early for work and to see if she could meet Andrew as he left the bank to find out what plans he was making for them.

She left Cilla looking at a book while she went into the bedroom to get ready. Within minutes she could hear Cilla screaming and Daisy's raised voice. As she hurried back into the living room she was in time to grab Daisy's upraised arm as she was about to lash out at Cilla who was crouched on the floor at the side of the table, cowering as Daisy stood over her, threatening her with a rolling pin.

'What on earth do you think you are doing?' Trixie gasped as she wrenched the rolling pin from Daisy's hand. 'If you'd hit her with that you could have killed her.'

'Like she killed my Jimmy,' Daisy retaliated. 'And she's a thief. I found her in my bedroom looking in the cupboard; if I hadn't gone in at that moment then she'd have stolen something.'

'No, she wouldn't; she was looking for Jimmy,' Trixie said wearily. 'She still doesn't understand why he isn't here and that was his favourite place to hide when they used to play hide and seek.'

'He's not here because she killed him; that's why he isn't here,' Daisy retorted. 'Bloody little murderer, she ought to be locked up. She should be somewhere where there're bars on the windows and locks on all the doors so that she can't get out,' she added vindictively.

Trixie pulled the trembling child to her feet, trying to ignore the puddle on the floor, and hugged her close. 'It's all right,' she murmured gently. 'Come on, let's get you some dry clothes and find your coat; we'll go for a walk.'

'She's peed herself, has she?' Daisy said contemptuously. 'Dirty little madam!'

'Yes, she has,' Trixie agreed calmly. 'It shows the harm you can do by shouting at her.'

Ignoring Daisy who'd followed them into the bedroom she began to remove Cilla's wet dress and knickers and began rummaging in the chest of drawers for some clean dry clothes.

'You won't find any there,' Daisy said triumphantly, 'you haven't done any washing this week, have you?'

Trixie didn't bother to answer; instead, she fished out the bag with the dirty washing in it from underneath their bed and began sorting through to find something for Cilla to wear.

'You're as dirty a bitch as she is. I can see where she gets it from now,' Daisy sneered as Trixie shook out a crumpled dress and then tried to smooth out the creases before putting it on Cilla. 'Don't bother washing it, just shake it and wear it again,' she taunted.

When Trixie didn't answer and Daisy realised that she wasn't going to rise to her taunts she turned on her heel and went out of the room, banging the door behind her.

Once more feeling dry and comfortable, Cilla reached up and pulled Trixie's face down to her level and gave her a big slobbery kiss. Then she tried to help by pushing the bag of dirty clothes back underneath the bed, but Trixie stopped her.

'We'll take that with us when we go out,' she told Cilla. As she spoke she began emptying the few other bits and pieces of clothing that were in the rickety chest of drawers, as well as the two new dresses she'd bought at Christmas, into the same bag. Then she helped Cilla to put on her outdoor things, took her hand, picked up the bag, and left without a word to Daisy.

Cilla didn't even ask where they were going but trotted along obediently at Trixie's side, occasionally grabbing hold of her coat to steady herself, or when they crossed the road.

Trixie didn't want to embarrass Andrew by waiting right outside the bank for him so she stood on the corner of Scotland Road and Collingwood Street and hoped that she wouldn't miss him as he left for home.

She was so engrossed in watching for him that she didn't see Jake approaching from the opposite direction and was quite startled when he touched her on the shoulder.

'Oh Jake! You nearly made me jump out of my skin! I wasn't expecting to bump into you.'

'I didn't think you'd be waiting for me,' he stated, giving her a lopsided grin.

'No, I'm hoping to catch Andrew when he leaves the bank. He's said I can move in with him and I wanted to know if I could do so right away. It's sheer hell with Daisy. She's on the rampage again over Jimmy dying and today I caught her about to wallop Cilla with a rolling pin.'

Jake frowned. 'That's terrible!' He reached out and stroked Cilla's face. 'You all right now, luv? What about you and me going and buying some sweeties in a minute? You'd like that, wouldn't you?'

Cilla let go of her hold on Trixie's coat and stretched out her hand to take Jake's.

'You're not really thinking of moving in with Andrew, are you?' he asked worriedly. 'I'm surprised you are even contemplating it. People will talk; if you're living in sin you'll get yourself a bad name.'

'Jake!' Trixie gave him a furious look. 'Moving in right away won't matter because we're planning to get married quite soon,' Trixie said confidently.

Jake raised his eyebrows questioningly. 'So when were you going to tell me?'

'I was waiting to hear what arrangements Andrew has made first,' she said evasively.

'Well, make sure you know what you're doing; remember you can't always believe everything Andrew says.'

'Now you know, aren't you going to congratulate me and wish us well?'

Jake didn't answer; instead he turned his attention to Cilla who was still holding his hand and hopping from one foot to the other impatiently.

'Shall I take Cilla on home with me and then you can come and pick her up when you've spoken to Andrew? It might be easier to talk to him on your own.'

'Thank you, Jake, that really would be a

great help but I have to be at work by six o'clock and I won't have time to come round to your place and get to Cazneau Street by then and I mustn't be late.'

'Then I'll take her home with me and you can pick her up later when you finish work.'

'Would you! Thanks, Jake. What would I do without you?' she added with a grateful smile.

'I don't know, perhaps you'll tell me some time.' He grinned. 'Come on, then.' He moved off, holding Cilla's hand and listening to her chattering away about what sweets she liked best.

It was almost twenty minutes before Trixie spotted Andrew leaving the bank. He was so engrossed talking to some of his colleagues that he would have walked right past her if she hadn't called out his name. Then he stopped in surprise and, frowning, excused himself from the group and came over to her.

'Is something wrong?'

'Yes, in a way,' she said hesitantly. 'We talked about me moving in with you and...' she hesitated, feeling shy of actually asking him outright. Then a vivid picture of Daisy wielding the rolling pin at Cilla flooded her mind and she took a deep breath and rushed on, 'and I wondered if it was all right to do so right away.'

Andrew chewed his lower lip, avoiding her

eyes. 'This is a bit sudden. I thought we agreed that it would be after Christmas. I told you I needed time to make some arrangements.'

'I know, but I can't stay at Virgil Street with Daisy another minute because things there have got so bad.' She indicated the bag at her side. 'I thought it would be all right, so I've brought all my clothes and everything.'

'Well,' he gave a reluctant smile. 'In that case, then I suppose I'll have to say yes, but–'

'Great. Look, I have to go to work right now but tell me the address and I'll come there as soon as I finish at eight o'clock. I'll have to go and collect Cilla first; we bumped into Jake and he's taken her to buy some sweets and then he's said he'll take her home with him till I finish work.'

'Cilla! You're planning on bringing Cilla with you? You mean that if you move in with me she's coming as well?' Andrew frowned.

'Surely you knew that? I wouldn't dream of leaving Cilla behind, she's the main reason why I'm so anxious to get away from Daisy. She's still convinced that Cilla had something to do with Jimmy's death and she'll half kill her if she gets the chance. That's why it's so important for me to move out as soon as I can. Only today...' Trixie stopped as she realised Andrew wasn't listening to what she was saying. His whole demeanour had changed.

'What's wrong, Andrew? You must have realised I would have to bring her.'

'It's rather difficult,' he said stiffly. 'I was about to tell you that because of my promotion I will be moving away from Liverpool. It's a great career move and if it was just the two of us then you would be able to come with me but I couldn't take Cilla along as well... that would be impossible. The bank wouldn't like it.'

Trixie looked puzzled. 'Why on earth does the bank have to know?' she asked in a bewildered voice.

'For security purposes, of course,' he snapped. 'They have to know where I'm living.'

'I can understand that but they don't have to know who is living with you, surely.'

'I'm afraid they do, which is why it's not going to be possible to take Cilla, Trixie. I'm sorry and all that, but you must try and understand my position.'

He started to move away but Trixie grabbed hold of his arm and stopped him. 'Hold on, Andrew. A couple of minutes ago you were all prepared to let me move in with you, so how come everything's changed in a matter of minutes?'

Andrew looked uncomfortable. 'I was waiting to find out about my transfer; that's

391

what I meant when I said I had some arrangements to make first.'

'That's a load of nonsense,' she refuted. 'You only changed your mind when I said that Cilla would have to come as well. Admit it; you don't want her with us, do you?'

He hesitated for a minute, chewing on his bottom lip. 'If you really want the truth, then the answer is no, you're quite right and it is better if you realise that right from the start, Trixie. As I told you, I want you to come and live with me, that's fine, and–'

Trixie didn't wait for him to finish. Turning on her heel she walked away, half blinded with tears. She'd thought that Andrew's love for her was strong enough for him to accept how much her sister meant to her and to understand that she would always be responsible for her, but now she knew she had been under an illusion the entire time. He wanted her but he was not prepared to take Cilla as well.

As she walked towards the O'Malleys' house the other thought that came into her head not only stunned her but also made her feel ashamed; Andrew had never once mentioned anything about them getting married.

He probably had never intended that they should, she thought miserably. He was prepared to have her living with him, sleeping with him, probably cooking and cleaning for him, but he didn't want her as a wife, she thought bitterly.

Jake had been right when he'd warned her not to believe everything Andrew said, she thought grimly, and she wondered what he would say when she told him about what had happened now. He'd probably be as understanding as he usually was, she reflected gratefully.

What was she going to do now? she asked herself. By this time Daisy would probably have discovered that she'd taken everything she owned when she'd left the house with Cilla and so she probably wouldn't let her back into the house.

Not that she wanted to go back there, but where else was there for her to go? She would have to wait till Daisy and her dad were home, in bed and asleep, and then hope she could get in without waking them.

Chapter Thirty-One

Trixie breathed a sigh of relief when she arrived home and found everywhere was in darkness. She whispered to Cilla that they mustn't make a sound in case they disturbed Daisy or their father. As they crept into their own bedroom she hid the bag with their clothes in it under the bed. She'd sort that all out in the morning before Daisy was up and then no one would be any the wiser about what she'd been planning to do.

Cilla was almost too tired to even undress herself and Trixie had to help her. Within a few minutes, though, they were both in bed. Cilla fell asleep almost immediately but Trixie lay there going over and over in her mind the events of the evening.

She felt humiliated by Andrew's attitude and the way he had walked away from her. She felt embarrassed by the way she'd clung on to him all this time, hungry for every kind word or smile that came her way. Most of the time he'd probably been laughing at her, she thought bitterly.

She'd been so convinced that he had the same sort of feelings for her as she had for him, yet now, when she looked back, she realised what an utter idiot she had been. It was so obvious that his interest in her was centred on one thing only. He didn't want someone like her as a girlfriend, not when he had so many other really lovely girls all vying with each other for his attention.

She'd made it so obvious that she was ready to do anything at all he asked of her that she couldn't really blame him for taking advantage of the fact. She was the one at fault and she felt dismayed that she'd expressed her feelings so openly.

Perhaps if her mother had still been alive and she'd had someone close to confide in about such things then she would have realised the truth. She'd been so hungry for love and affection that she'd built Andrew up into something he wasn't.

Now, for the first time, she realised that he was selfish, egotistical and interested only in himself and his achievements at the bank. If she had gone to live with him she would have been little more than a live-in housekeeper. He'd probably still have gone off gallivanting with his friends and left her on her own most evenings.

He had certainly made it quite plain that he didn't want anything at all to do with Cilla and in that respect he was no better than Daisy.

She turned on her side and put an arm round Cilla, cuddling the thin little body close to her. What she felt for Cilla was more than mere affection, more than sisterly duty It was a deep, lasting bond and, whatever happened in the future, Cilla would always come first. If it meant that Trixie had to work for the rest of her life to look after her then that is what she'd do.

Cilla was growing up, she would never be normal, but already she was able to understand a great deal of what was going on in the world around her. She'd carry on helping her to read and write and teach her to do jobs around the home so that she could look after herself if she ever needed to do so. Soon, quite soon, Cilla would be old enough and sensible enough to be left on her own. Trixie was confident that once she was able to take on a full-time job she'd be able to support the pair of them.

She'd always promised herself that 1927 would be a turning point and the year when she'd make a break from Daisy and her dad. Even though they'd still have to stay with them for a while longer she fully intended moving into a room of her own as soon as she could do so.

It wouldn't be a very momentous Christmas, but they'd manage to get through it somehow and next year would be very different, Trixie vowed.

She was still scheming and planning for the future when she fell asleep. Next morning as she helped Cilla to dress her head was buzzing with good intentions but Daisy put paid to those. She had a list of all the extra cleaning she wanted doing before Christmas; unnecessary things such as taking the curtains down and polishing all the brass rings they hung on, as well as turning out all the kitchen cupboards and giving the range an extra polish.

There were so many jobs that Trixie couldn't see how she could fit them all in and do her two jobs as well. It would be

Christmas in less than a week's time and there was so much extra cooking to do as well as everything else.

With Christmas Day 1926 falling on a Saturday at least it meant that Steve would not be opening his snack bar that weekend. Trixie had been looking forward to being able to take things easy, but now with all the extra jobs Daisy had insisted must be done it looked as though she'd be working harder than ever over Christmas.

Still, she reflected glumly, there was precious little else to do. Daisy and her father spent more time at the pub and when they were at home they both had a hangover and they were either bickering noisily or else snoring their heads off.

Ella had invited her to come round there on Christmas Day, but in her present mood she felt it would be intruding and she also felt embarrassed because Jake knew what had gone on between her and Andrew.

He must think I'm a right idiot chasing after Andrew, she thought bitterly. Thinking back, she could see that Jake had several times tried to warn her that Andrew was more interested in all the new friends he'd made at the Bank than he was in either of them. She didn't think Jake would have gone to Andrew's party if she hadn't been so keen to go and had begged him to go with her.

Constantly chastising herself for being so foolish was getting her nowhere, she decided. Perhaps buckling down and doing all that Daisy wanted to have done was not such a bad idea; it would at least keep her from dwelling on what could never be. She'd let Cilla help. It would take longer but it was better than letting her sit in a corner and watch.

Christmas Day was as disappointing as Trixie had anticipated. Although she cooked a traditional meal of roast chicken with Christmas pudding to follow Daisy and Sam were too hung-over to fully enjoy it, although Daisy insisted it was what they must have.

I could have served up sausages and mash for all the appreciation I got, Trixie thought resentfully as she cleared everything away afterwards and listened to the pair of them snoring.

Once she'd finished the washing up and Cilla had helped to put the dishes away they went round to Horatio Street. She'd bought a pretty little shawl for Cilla to give Ella, one that she could wear indoors or wear as a scarf under her coat when she went out.

Ella was delighted with her gift and when Cilla opened the present that Ella gave her and found a lovely red jumper, she was equally pleased and hugged and kissed Ella enthusiastically.

'You need to thank Jake as well,' Ella told her.

With a beaming smile, Cilla bestowed a big kiss on Jake's cheek and received a bear hug in return.

Jake also had a present for Trixie but he waited till they were on their own before he gave it to her.

She gasped with pleasure when she saw the heart-shaped silver locket and then felt overcome with guilt because she hadn't bought him a present after all he'd done for her.

'I didn't expect one; you'll need all your money for when you set up home with Andrew,' he told her. 'I thought this might be the last chance I have to give you something,' he mumbled.

Trixie felt the hot blood rush to her cheeks. 'That won't be happening,' she confessed. 'You were right when you said he doesn't always mean what he says.'

'Really!' Jake looked at her questioningly.

'I'll tell you all about it some other time when we are on our own,' she promised, 'but will you continue looking for a room for me and Cilla?'

Ivy and Hadyn were there and as they all sat round drinking tea and eating mince pies Trixie listened enviously as they went into details about their forthcoming wedding and all their plans for the future.

Although she tried hard not to think about

Andrew, she couldn't help doing so. She wished that she was able to tell Ivy that she was also hoping to get married very soon but she knew that all the plans she'd once had were now mere figments of her imagination.

Instead of wasting time thinking about them she'd concentrate on encouraging Cilla to be more independent so that in time it would be quite safe to leave her on her own once they moved into their own place.

She'd enjoyed not having to work at Steve's place over Christmas although it did make a dent in her savings. She wished now that she hadn't spent out on new clothes for herself and Cilla, although she had to admit that Cilla had loved wearing her new dress and having it admired by Ella and Ivy.

The following Saturday was New Year's Day and she wondered if Steve would decide not to open then as well because he would have had such a late night on the Friday with it being New Year's Eve. He certainly looked very tired when she arrived.

'I'm going home as soon as Sylvia arrives,' he yawned. 'She went home just after midnight so she's hoping that the two of you can manage without my help here for a couple of hours while I catch up on my sleep,' he told her.

'If you want to go right now and not wait

for Sylvia, I'm sure I can cope,' Trixie told him.

He looked doubtful, and then shrugged. 'I'm pretty sure there won't be many people about first thing,' he agreed. 'They'll all want to sleep off the food and drink they indulged in at parties last night. You two are both looking very fresh,' he added, patting Cilla on the shoulder, 'didn't you stay up to see the New Year in?'

Trixie shook her head. 'No. I decided there was no point in doing so,' she admitted. 'Like Cilla, I was tucked up in bed well before midnight.' What she didn't add was that she had been woken in the early hours of the morning by her father and Daisy when they'd come home roaring drunk. They'd been singing at the top of their voices and crashing into every piece of furniture there was. When she'd heard Daisy yelling her name and shouting that they wanted her to make them a hot drink she'd cowered down under the bedclothes and hoped they'd go off to bed and not come banging on her bedroom door.

They'd still been sound asleep when she and Cilla had left that morning but the place had looked a shambles. All her hard work at cleaning and making it look nice over Christmas seemed to have been wasted.

The morning at Steve's Snacks was so uneventful that Trixie found herself telling

Sylvia all about what had happened between her and Andrew. She even told her how he had invited her to go and live with him then rescinded his offer when he knew it would have to include Cilla as well.

'I think you have had a lucky escape, my girl,' Sylvia told her severely. 'You are right when you say that all he wanted was someone to look after him without any obligation on his part. It's lucky for you that you discovered what he's really like before you left home.'

'I know that, but I still have to get away and find a place of my own. I'm more convinced than ever that Daisy is going to do Cilla some harm.'

'As long as she is with you all the time then I don't think she's going to have much success, do you?' Sylvia smiled. 'Keep saving and looking for a room you can afford. One will turn up, never fear. I'll ask around as well.'

'Jake says there wasn't much point in doing so over Christmas but that now the holiday is over he'll start looking again,' Trixie said hopefully. 'He really is a very good friend and I do appreciate the way he takes Cilla out and about while I'm working here.'

Sylvia nodded but before she had a chance to say anything they had a stream of customers and for the next couple of hours they were so busy serving mugs of steaming hot tea, coffee and cocoa that there was no time for talking. Very few people seemed to be hungry; they were all demanding hot drinks because it was such a cold day.

Even Cilla was complaining about being cold which was very unusual because normally she didn't seem to notice what the temperature was. By the time they were ready to go home she was shivering uncontrollably and when Sylvia put a hand on her forehead she found it was burning hot.

'Cilla's running a temperature,' she warned Trixie. 'The best thing you can do is get her home and to bed right away. Have you got a lemon? If so, give her some hot lemon and put a dash of whisky in it if you have any. Nip it in the bud before it turns into something serious.'

They spent a restless night, Cilla was tossing and turning and complaining that her throat hurt and so did her chest. Trixie was up several times making her drinks and trying to soothe her.

By the morning it was quite obvious that Cilla was far from well. She not only had a head cold but a sore throat and a cough as well and was feeling very sorry for herself. It was quite clear that she wasn't well enough to go out. What worried Trixie was that it meant leaving her at home when she went to do her cleaning job.

She wondered if she could manage to go

to work without Daisy knowing that Cilla was there on her own or whether it would be better to tell Daisy that Cilla was ill and warn her to stay away from her in case she caught whatever Cilla had.

When Trixie tried to explain to Cilla that she would have to leave her when she went to work Cilla didn't want her to go and became very upset and tearful about being left on her own with Daisy.

'She won't even know you are here if you keep quiet,' Trixie told her. 'I won't be gone all that long and I'll bring you back some nice sweets to make your throat feel better,' she promised.

Chapter Thirty-Two

The first thing Trixie heard when she got back was Cilla sobbing. They were deep, painful sobs that tore at her heart. She sensed it was not because Cilla had been left on her own but for some other reason; it sounded as if she was in terrible pain.

Without waiting to take off her outdoor clothes Trixie picked up a candle and rushed into the bedroom. Cilla, her face red and blotched, was not only sobbing but was also writhing in pain and clutching at her chest as if trying to pull something away from it.

'There, there,' Trixie placed the candle on top of the chest of drawers and then crouched down beside the bed, stroking her sister's hair back from her tear-stained face. 'Is your chest hurting because you've been coughing so much?'

'No, no, it's burning,' Cilla sobbed hysterically.

Gently Trixie pulled back the bedclothes and started to undo the front of Cilla's nightdress, and then she stopped in surprise. Strapped across Cilla's chest was a big wad of brown paper that looked like a parcel. As she loosened the string that was holding it down and pulled it away she saw that on the underside it was coated with something thick and sticky, some kind of paste that was yellow and evil smelling.

Taking the utmost care she peeled it away and then stared in horror. Underneath it Cilla's skin was covered in blisters and in places raised in red weals.

'Oh, my God! Whoever did this to you, my luv?' she whispered, her own eyes filling with tears.

She didn't need Cilla to answer. She knew there was only one person who could be so sadistic as to treat someone as helpless as Cilla in such a fashion.

Hearing a noise behind her she looked up to see Daisy standing in the doorway, her arms folded across her chest, watching her every movement.

'So you don't think much of my mustard plaster, then?' Daisy observed with a sour laugh.

'How could you do such a thing?' Trixie said angrily. 'How could you torment her like this?'

'My mum and dad always swore by a mustard plaster for a bad chest,' Daisy told her. 'I thought it would make her better more quickly. Do you think it's done the job?' she asked, moving closer and peering over Trixie's shoulder so that she could see better.

'No, I don't! She's in absolute agony. You must have made it far too strong and it's going to take weeks for her chest to heal,' Trixie exclaimed furiously

'It won't take long for her cough to improve, though,' Daisy observed. 'Mustard, treacle and brown paper; that or goose grease. My dad swore by them both and Sam seemed to think it was a good idea.'

Trixie didn't bother to answer. She was too concerned with wiping away the residue of the mustard plaster and trying to decide what she could put on the tender, broken skin to cool it down and at the same time help it to heal.

She couldn't think of anything in the house that would do that and she daren't risk leaving Cilla while she went to ask Ella in case Daisy hurt her further.

For the moment she resolved she would bathe it very gently with tepid water and then later on, after Daisy and her father had gone out to the pub, she'd have to go round and ask Ella for advice even though it meant leaving Cilla on her own.

Ella and Jake were shocked when Trixie told them what had happened. 'I think she needs to be seen by a doctor,' Ella told Trixie. 'If it is anywhere as bad as you say then you'll have to be careful that it doesn't become infected and turn sceptic. It could have been any old brown paper; goodness knows what was wrapped in it before Daisy used it.'

'I hadn't thought of that,' Trixie admitted. 'I wonder if I will be able to get a doctor to come out at this time of night?'

'You could take her to the hospital as an emergency,' Ella suggested. 'That might be the best thing to do because they'll not only know what ought to go on it but they'll also have everything to hand and be able to treat her then and there.'

'I agree,' Jake said firmly. 'Come on,' he stood up, pulling a muffler around his neck and putting on his cap, 'I'll come with you. We'll wrap her up warm in blankets and I'll carry her. We can get a taxicab so that she won't catch cold.'

Cilla was still in great pain but she trustingly let Jake envelop her in a blanket and carry her to the taxicab. She sobbed most of the way to the hospital and when they arrived there she clung on to Trixie's hand begging her not to leave her on her own whatever happened.

When Trixie was about to explain that she might have to do so because they could very well insist on keeping her in overnight, Jake signalled to her not to say anything.

'Don't let's upset Cilla more than we have to,' he whispered quietly. 'Let's see what they want to do first and perhaps they'll let you stay with her.'

Realising how much he cared and that he was just as anxious as she was, Trixie nodded in agreement. She was grateful to Jake for his concern and knew she was lucky to have such a good friend. No matter what happened it seemed he was there at her side offering support and help.

Remembering the last time she'd had to bring Cilla to the hospital she didn't hold out much hope that they would let her stay but she hoped they would, because she was fearful that Cilla might not pull through.

It was a long night. Trixie wanted Jake to go home and get some sleep because she knew he had to be up very early next morning but he refused to leave her there on her own.

'Let's wait and see what happens,' he said

firmly. 'I'm not going to be able to sleep till I know that Cilla is going to be all right and I certainly don't intend to leave you here on your own,' he told her, taking her hand and holding it gently in his own. 'Daisy is the wickedest woman I know,' he added bitterly.

'It's retaliation for what happened to her little Jimmy. She still blames Cilla for what happened to Jimmy.'

'That was an accident and it was Daisy's fault and no one else's,' Jake said firmly. 'She should never have gone out and left him.'

There was no question of Cilla being allowed to go home or of Trixie being allowed to stay at the hospital till morning.

'The risk of some form of infection is far too great for you to take her home,' the sister in charge told them, 'so she must stay here for the present. It may only be overnight but most likely it will be for two or three days. We need to make sure that the skin is healing after the blisters have dispersed. She also needs medication for her cough and to help clear up the congestion in her lungs.'

Trixie had thought Cilla would be very upset about her leaving, but the medicine they'd already given her seemed to have calmed her and made her very sleepy so she made no protest at all.

As they left the hospital, Jake was most insistent that Trixie should go back to his place for a hot drink but she demurred.

'Ella will be in bed by now and I have disturbed her enough for one evening,' she protested.

'I'm pretty sure she won't be in bed; she won't rest till she knows how Cilla is,' he assured her.

'You need to get some sleep,' she pointed out. 'If I come back with you, then we'll spend ages talking and it will be time for you to get up before you get to bed.'

'All right. I can see that I can't persuade you. You are sure now that you are going to be safe? I don't trust Daisy; she really is evil.'

'I'll be keeping out of her way, don't worry. The very sight of her makes me want to hit out and I know that won't do any good at all.'

'Let my mother know how Cilla is after you've been to the hospital to see her tomorrow and I'll be waiting for you when you finish work in the evening,' he promised as they parted.

'I'll do that and thank you for all you've done tonight. I'm always saying I don't know how I'd manage without all your help and I mean it,' she told him gratefully.

Cilla still had an exceptionally high temperature the next day and there was no question of her coming home. She was so ill that she didn't seem to recognise Trixie, even though she sat beside the bed, holding her hand and talking to her.

'Perhaps that's just as well,' Ella said consolingly. 'At least she isn't making herself worse by pining for you.'

'Give her a few days of their special care and she'll be as right as rain,' Jake assured her.

Trixie was so used to Cilla following her round, dogging her footsteps like a shadow and chanting her tables or singing nursery rhymes, that she felt desolate without her.

Daisy also noticed Cilla's absence but in a very different way. 'Done what you should have done years ago and put her somewhere out of the way, have you?' she smirked, taking out a packet of cigarettes from her pocket and lighting one up.

When Trixie went to walk past her she grabbed her by the arm and swung her round to face her. 'Don't you walk away from me when I'm talking to you,' she hissed, blowing a cloud of smoke into Trixie's face. 'This is my home and if you want to stay under this roof then find yourself a proper job and pay your way. You've no excuse now since you're not saddled with that little idiot.'

'As a result of what you did the other day, that little idiot, as you call her, is in hospital,' Trixie told her in an icy voice. 'She's so seriously ill that she has to stay there.'

'Hospital? Pull the other one,' Daisy blustered. 'All I did was stick a mustard plaster on her chest. It's the best cure there is for bronchitis, everyone knows that, even your dad.'

'Properly applied it might be, but not when it is so strong that it causes blisters and weals like that one did,' Trixie said in a withering tone.

It was over a week before Cilla was well enough to leave hospital. Her cough was gone but her chest was still covered in tiny scars where the blisters had either burst or dried up. She was prescribed some special cream which Trixie was instructed to apply night and morning. She was also told to bring Cilla back again in two weeks' time so that they could make sure it had cleared.

At first Cilla seemed weak and nervous but once Trixie started feeding her up with tempting nourishing meals she was back to her former self in next to no time.

She showed real fear of Daisy and even though the weather was atrocious and Trixie knew that Cilla shouldn't really go out she had no option but to wrap her up warm and take her when she went out to clean Mr Browning's surgery each evening.

At the weekend, Cilla went round to Horatio Street. Ella looked after her on Saturday morning. In the afternoon, and again on Sunday, Jake helped her with her reading and they played board games.

It began to rain in the middle of Sunday afternoon and it quickly turned to sleet and snow as icy winds swept in over the Mersey churning up the water so that it was lashing against the dockside. The scene was so wet and grey that Steve decided to close early.

'There won't be many people out and about in this just for the fun of it,' he said gloomily. 'You cut along home, Trixie, I'll finish up here and I can manage if anyone does drop in for a cuppa.'

By the time Trixie reached Horatio Street to collect Cilla it was already quite slippery underfoot. The snow had not only thickened but, because the ground was so cold, it was also settling on the roads and pavements and clogging every step she took.

'Come on in and have a hot drink; you look half frozen,' Ella greeted her as she opened the door. She helped Trixie out of her coat and gave it a good shake to free it of snow. 'Come on, come and sit close to the fire and get yourself thawed out; you look shrammed.'

'You mustn't take Cilla out in this,' Jake protested when half an hour later Trixie asked him to fetch Cilla's coat and said she'd better be getting home.

'Come over and take a look out of the window,' he urged, when he saw her hesitate.

The scene outside had a Christmas-card look about it. The ugly buildings and drab

surroundings were all magically transformed into a white fairyland.

'Pretty, pretty,' Cilla exclaimed, clapping
her hands excitedly as she stood at Trixie's
side looking out.

'It might be pretty, luv, but it's very very
cold,' Ella told her. 'Jake's right,' she said
turning to Trixie, 'it would be madness to
take Cilla out in this. She'd probably end up
straight back in hospital with a chill or
something worse.'

'Mum's right, the best thing you can do is
let her stay here overnight and pick her up
tomorrow,' Jake agreed, 'that's if the snow
isn't any deeper.'

'It will probably be a mass of grey slush by
the morning,' Ella said philosophically.

While they were talking Ivy and Hadyn
arrived home. Both of them were covered in
thick snow and shivering with the cold.
Hadyn didn't want to stop or even take his
coat off. 'I want to get home before it gets any
worse,' he told them. 'There's going to be
chaos in the morning if it goes on snowing all
night.'

'Can you see Trixie to her door, Hadyn?'
Ella asked as he made to leave. 'She's going
to leave Cilla here for the night rather than
take her out in this.'

'I can as long as she's ready to come right
now,' Hadyn said a trifle reluctantly.

Trixie hesitated; she was still very undecided about what to do for the best. She was afraid that Cilla might become confused about where she was or not settle. As if he could read her mind, Jake clinched the matter.

'Cilla's had so many upsets lately that it might be a good idea if you stayed the night as well,' he suggested.

'Are you sure about this?' Trixie said worriedly. 'Isn't it going to put you out finding us somewhere to sleep?'

'No, it won't be any problem at all,' he said quickly. 'You and Cilla can have my bed and I'll kip down here on the sofa. That's all right, Mum, isn't it?' He smiled confidently at Ella who nodded in agreement.

'If that's what you're going to do then I'm on my way,' Hadyn said pulling on his cap, wrapping a muffler around his neck, and turning his coat collar up around his ears.

'I'll come to the door and see you off,' Ivy told him, linking her arm through his then quickly withdrawing it because his coat was so wet and cold.

For a moment, Trixie thought that it might be better if she went home after all. She suspected that her staying overnight was going to disrupt things for all the O'Malleys. Then, because she knew that Cilla might do that anyway if she was left there on her own, she decided that perhaps staying there was the best thing to do after all.

Chapter Thirty-Three

It was still snowing heavily when they woke the next morning. Jake and Ivy had already left for work by the time Trixie and Cilla were up and dressed.

'I don't suppose you will be able to take Cilla out in this weather again today,' Ella said cautiously as she sat at the table with them drinking a cup of tea while they were eating a bowl of porridge for their breakfast.

'Well, I'm not sure,' Trixie said hesitantly. She wished Ella would say outright if she didn't want Cilla to stay there with her.

She stood up and went over to look out of the window. Although it was still snowing the flakes were much lighter and the sky brightening as though it would soon stop and perhaps the sun might even come out. As Ella had foretold the roadway was a dirty grey mush where carts and people had been travelling or crossing. The snow on the pavements was equally churned up but not quite so mushy.

'It will be very slippery underfoot, there're bound to be a lot of accidents,' Ella commented as she joined her at the window. 'I hate having to go out in it.'

'Then why don't I go and do your shopping for you and at the same time I can pop home and get some clean clothes for Cilla?' Trixie suggested quickly.

'Would you?' Ella said gratefully. 'You've no idea how scared I am about walking in it when it's like this. The moment I feel my feet start to slip then I stiffen up like a board and the next thing I know I'm on my back.'

'You tell me what you want, or write out a list while I wash up the breakfast things,' Trixie suggested.

'No, I'll see to those; you get your coat on and go and do the shopping. There'll be a run on things in the shops this morning; people will be stocking up in case we have some more snow and they mightn't be able to get out again for days. They'll all want meat and vegetables to make some hot stews.'

Ella was right on all counts. People were stocking up as though destined for a siege and the roads were even more slippery than Trixie had expected. Added to which she found her shoes were no protection at all against the cold and wet and in next to no time her feet were numb and she felt frozen right through.

Ella had given her such a long list that she knew it was going to take two trips so she decided to do the shopping first and take that back before she went home to collect some clean clothes for Cilla.

It was mid-morning by the time she arrived at Virgil Street and Daisy was waiting for her; she was scowling and in a vile temper.

'So where the hell do you think you've been all night?' she demanded as Trixie struggled out of her coat and shook the snow from it. 'Your dad wanted to know when you didn't come home.'

'I doubt that,' Trixie told her. 'He probably didn't even notice that I wasn't here.'

'He noticed all right. For a start, where was our meal last night? Selfish little cow; not a word and we sat here waiting, expecting you home at any moment.'

'Surely you could have made something,' Trixie told her. 'You're always telling me that this is your home.'

'Yes, and we let you stay here without asking you to hand over a penny piece in return for you doing the cooking–'

'And the cleaning and washing and ironing and shopping and anything else you want doing,' Trixie retorted as she took off her wet shoes.

'You've got a lot to say for yourself this morning,' Daisy sneered. 'Stayed out last night so that you could share a bed with some fancy man, did you?'

Trixie gave her a scathing look but made no reply. As she started to move towards her

418

bedroom Daisy stopped her.

'You may as well put your coat back on and go and get the shopping; it will save me having to get all wrapped up to go out,' she ordered, passing her the list and some money.

Trixie hesitated for a moment, wondering if she dared to refuse and remind Daisy that usually she always insisted on doing the shopping herself. Then common sense got the better of her and she thought it was wisest to say nothing.

'When's that sister of yours coming home, then?' Daisy asked as she stood watching Trixie put her damp coat and wet shoes back on again.

Trixie shrugged and bit her lip. She didn't want to tell her that Cilla was already out of hospital because if she did then she'd start asking questions about where she was and why she wasn't at home.

'Making a mountain out of a molehill, all this fuss and palaver over a poultice,' Daisy muttered. Trixie knew from her tone that she was worried and inwardly she couldn't help feeling that it was what Daisy deserved to be.

When she returned with the shopping Trixie insisted that she must go and change her clothes because she was wet through from the snow. At the same time she packed a shopping bag with some clean clothes for Cilla although she knew that she'd have to wait till she went to work that evening to smuggle them out.

For the rest of the day Daisy watched her closely constantly finding fresh jobs for her to do.

'Going rather early, aren't you?' Daisy grumbled when she got ready to leave. 'There's still plenty that needs doing around here, you know. And what's that you've got in there?' she asked, indicating the bag Trixie was carrying.

'Some clean rags to use as dusters,' Trixie said abruptly and headed for the door before Daisy could ask any more questions. She hoped she still had time to nip round and explain to Ella why she hadn't been back sooner.

She was only able to stay for a few minutes and this upset Cilla who clung on to her as she headed for the door.

'I'll come back later and collect you and take you home,' she promised.

'I think you should leave her here for another night,' Ella advised. 'It's so slippery out and we don't want her falling over. You can stay as well, if you like.'

Trixie thought about this while she was doing the cleaning and she had to admit it seemed like a good idea. Perhaps she ought to go home first and make sure that her dad had been given a decent meal. At the same time she could explain to him what was going on and that would make amends; that was if Daisy was telling the truth and he really was worrying about her and Cilla.

They were waiting for her, both of them looking angry and ready for a row when she walked in.

'Where's Cilla?' Sam demanded before she could say a word.

'You told us she was in hospital, but your dad's been there tonight and they say she's not there and that she was sent home days ago,' Daisy added.

'That's right, she was discharged yesterday. She's not properly better, though. I have to take her back so that they can make sure that the scarring you inflicted on her has healed,' she said looking straight at Daisy.

'So where is she? What have you done with her? Why haven't you brought her home?' her father bellowed, his face getting more red and angry by the minute.

'Do you think I'd bring her back here and leave her on her own to be ill-treated again?' Trixie questioned, her eyes blazing.

'I don't know what the hell you're on about.' Her father looked puzzled. He looked from her to Daisy and back again. 'As far as I know she was taken off to hospital because she had a bad cough and a touch of bronchitis.'

'So that's what she told you, is it, and you believed it?' Trixie said contemptuously. 'She didn't bother to tell you that she'd put a mustard plaster on Cilla's chest while I was out. Or that it was so hot that it blistered all the skin of her chest and brought it up in weals. It was so bad that she had to stay in hospital for almost a week...'

'Then where is she now?' Sam persisted, running his hand through his close-cropped hair in bewilderment.

'Somewhere safe,' Trixie told him defiantly. 'Somewhere where neither of you can hurt her.'

The blow felled her to the ground. Sam stood over her, and was about to kick her in the ribs, but Daisy restrained him.

'Don't do that or she'll end up in the bloody hospital and you'll be accused of ill-treating the silly little bitch and she'll make more trouble for the pair of us.'

'Get up and get out and take your things and your sister's with you and don't come back,' Sam snarled, nudging her with the toe of his boot in spite of what Daisy had warned.

Trixie pulled herself to her knees. Her jaw ached and she'd banged her side as she fell and there was such a sharp pain in her ribs that she wondered if she'd broken one.

She stumbled into the bedroom and lay down on the bed for a few minutes to try and get her breath back. Still in pain she tried to pull herself together and began stuffing as many of her clothes and Cilla's as she could into a pillowcase.

She knew that Daisy was standing in the doorway, arms folded across her chest and watching her.

'I'm just making sure you don't take anything that doesn't belong to you,' Daisy smirked. 'By rights you ought to hand over all that money you've been secretly squirrelling away all these weeks, but I suppose you're going to need it to live on now that you can't scrounge off your dad any longer,' she taunted.

'You're going to find things very different in the future after living here and having everything found for you,' she persisted when Trixie continued to ignore what she was saying.

'You're going to find things very different, too, because from now on you will have to do all your own housework and the cooking,' Trixie retaliated. 'My dad's never been much use around the house,' she added as a parting shot as she humped the pillowcase towards the door, anxious to get away before there was any more trouble.

Fortunately the snow had stopped but it was still very cold and the keen wind made her face ache. She pulled her coat collar higher to try and shield it but her jaw was so tender where she'd taken the blow that the pressure made her wince.

The pain in her side was also getting worse and when she picked up the pillowcase and tried to carry it in her arms she couldn't do so. In desperation she had to resort to dragging it along the ground even though the pavements were still wet and slushy.

By the time she reached Horatio Street she felt absolutely exhausted. Jake and Cilla were standing by the front window looking out for her and when Jake saw her staggering down the street he came hurrying out to help her.

'You'll catch your death of cold, Jake, you haven't even got a coat on,' Trixie admonished as he took the pillowcase from her. As he was about to put an arm around her waist to support her she pulled away and slipped her arm through his instead.

'We'd better get back indoors as quickly as possible,' he commented. 'What's happened to you, fallen over in the snow?' he asked as he helped her into the house.

Trixie was tempted to agree with him and say that was what had happened, but because she was so utterly weary and so in need of comfort, she told him exactly what had happened.

'How could any man do such a thing to a young woman? He might have broken your jaw and disfigured you for life,' he said shaking his head in disgust as he helped her out of her coat. 'You're going to have a dreadful bruise there in the morning,' he commented, gently examining the swelling along the lower edge of her jaw as he settled her near the fire.

Cilla crouched beside her chair clutching tight hold of her hand and trying to comfort her while Ella bustled around making her a hot drink.

The moment Trixie finished her drink and put down her empty cup Cilla tried to hug her. The pain that shot through her ribs was so intense that she screamed.

'I'm so sorry,' Trixie gasped as Jake and Ella looked alarmed and Cilla burst into hysterical tears. 'I caught my side against something as I fell and I seem to have hurt myself rather badly.'

With Jake and Ella giving her a helping hand she went into the bedroom where she and Cilla had slept the night before.

'You go and keep an eye on Cilla while I find out how badly hurt Trixie's ribs are,' Ella told Jake.

Very gently Ella felt along Trixie's ribcage and shook her head. 'I'm not sure if you've broken one or not, luv,' she admitted.

'So what do you think I should do? Ought I to go to the hospital?' Trixie asked uneasily.

'Why not wait and see how you feel in the morning and if it is still as painful tomorrow, then perhaps you should. They can't do a lot, mind you, not when it's your ribs. They might strap it up for you and that would possibly make it feel a little bit easier.'

Trixie lay awake most of the night, making sure that there was as much distance as possible between herself and Cilla. Her ribs were painful and her jaw was throbbing but it was what was going to happen to them both in the future that was worrying her the most.

She was so afraid of her father's outbursts that she never wanted to go back to Virgil Street ever again but what else was she going to do? she pondered. She still hadn't found a room anywhere that she could afford to rent.

She'd been turned down so often and told bluntly that they didn't want a woman with a kid who'd be around the place all day when they could let the rooms to a man working at the docks who'd be out from under their feet during the day and be prepared to pay extra if they provided him with a meal and did his washing.

She couldn't impose on Ella much longer, but if she would let her stay there for a couple more nights then Daisy would start to miss having an unpaid skivvy and be able to persuade her father to keep his fists to himself if she agreed to go back.

Even if that problem was solved there was also another worry: Daisy hated Cilla and might do her harm again, this time for good.

Chapter Thirty-Four

Ella said she was quite willing to let Trixie and Cilla stay with her till Trixie was able to find a room. She even cleaned out the tiny boxroom that was only used for storing her dressmaking things so that Jake would have a bedroom and not have to sleep on the sofa.

Cilla seemed very happy about the arrangement although whether she fully understood why they were living there Trixie wasn't too sure. The only person who seemed to be at all worried by what was happening was Ivy.

Trixie had seen very little of her since Ivy had been going out with Hadyn. They were not nearly such close friends as they'd been when they'd worked together and they no longer confided in each other as they used to do.

'When we're married we're moving in with my mum,' she reminded Trixie when she heard that she and Cilla were staying on.

'I'm quite sure I will have found a room by then,' Trixie assured her with a smile. 'Easter isn't till the middle of April this year so there's plenty of time.'

'Not really, there isn't,' Ivy argued. 'We're

planning to decorate before then and get our own furniture so that we have it just as we want it to be before our wedding day.'

'I do understand but as I said, Easter is well over two months away,' Trixie replied.

'That's not very long because Hadyn will have to do all the painting and everything in his spare time. He can't do it in the evenings because he'll be too tired, so that means it will have to be on Saturday afternoons and Sundays.'

'He can probably do the whole thing in one weekend – well, two at the most.'

'I want it to be done properly; I don't want it to be a rushed job, so we'll have to start on it by the beginning of March at the very latest,' Ivy persisted.

'Don't worry, I'll try my best to be gone before then,' Trixie agreed.

'I hope you will move as soon as possible, because my mum is going to need a rest to get over all the upset of having you both here,' Ivy told her forcibly. 'I don't want her laid up ill before the wedding because I will need her to give me plenty of help with making my dress and everything.'

Trixie felt rather hurt by Ivy's seeming in-difference to her problem and thought that there'd really been no need for her to be quite so outspoken but she put it down to the strain of the forthcoming wedding. She suspected that it was of such tremendous importance in Ivy's mind that it was taking precedence over everything else.

As soon as she had the opportunity to speak to Jake she begged him to try and help her find somewhere as soon as possible.

'Don't you like living with us?' he teased.

'You know I do and I am very grateful to you all,' she said quickly, 'but I also realise that it is putting you all out.'

'Has Mum said anything to make you think that?' He frowned.

'No, of course she hasn't!'

'Ivy has, though; that's it, isn't it? Well, take no notice of her. Ivy's head is full of plans about how she is going to change things here before she and Hadyn get married. I think Mum might regret ever agreeing that she could come and live with us.'

'Don't say that, Jake, and whatever you do don't let on that I have said anything to you because the last thing I want to do is cause any trouble.'

Although he promised not to mention it the whole episode worried Trixie and she went out of her way to make sure that they caused as little disruption as possible.

She carried on working, even though her ribs still felt bruised and sore, especially when she was polishing furniture or cleaning windows, but she daren't risk losing her job by asking for a few days off; she needed the money now more than ever.

As soon as Cilla was well enough to go out she offered to take her to work in the evenings so that Ella could have some time on her own but Ella assured her that she was quite happy for Cilla to stay with her.

'You've no idea what a help she is to me,' she told Trixie. 'She's showing so much interest in sewing. She sorts out my reels of cottons and takes out the pins and puts them back in the pincushion, and she picks up any threads on the floor. She's even trying to do some sewing herself.'

'Really?' Trixie shook her head in disbelief. 'You do surprise me. Are you sure you can trust her with a needle, though?'

'Of course I can, and with scissors too; it's as if she's done it all her little life.'

'I know she's always enjoyed touching the silks and velvets when you've been working but I never thought she'd be able to do any sewing.'

'She can do more than that,' Ella boasted proudly. 'She's helping me as I'm making Ivy's wedding dress and then we're going to make a rag rug out of the scraps I trim away. It's a secret, though, because she wants to give it to Ivy and Hadyn as a wedding present.'

Trixie felt pleased that Ella was helping Cilla so much but even so there were a good many times when she worried about what the future held for them both. Once or twice, when she had been feeling low and everything had seemed to be too much for her, she had even wondered if perhaps Daisy and her father had been right about Cilla. Perhaps she would be better off in a home where people understood her disabilities and would care for her instead of trying so hard to help her to lead a normal life.

When she voiced her worries aloud to Jake one Sunday afternoon when he came down to the snack bar to walk her home he looked at her in astonishment.

'I'm surprised at you even thinking that,' he admonished. 'Cilla needs love and affection and she'd never get those if she was in a home. Look at the way she rushes to kiss you when you've been apart, even when it's only been for a couple of hours. And the way she holds your hand whenever she gets the chance and struggles to do things to please you whenever she can. Love is something we all need from those we care about; you need her love as much as she needs yours,' he added.

She knew he was right but she was surprised to hear him say so with so much fervour. She gave him a sideways glance and saw that his mouth was set rigid, almost as if he was angry about something. The outburst was so unlike Jake that it made her wonder why he was so upset.

He really was the most important person in her life next to Cilla, and because she cared so much about him she wished she could say something to help. She hadn't seen Andrew since the day he'd told her that she could move in with him but that she couldn't bring Cilla, but now she had no regrets that it was all over between them. She now knew that his feelings for her had been lust, not love, and she was still ashamed of herself for the way she had let him dupe her.

What she wanted from life now, she decided, was somewhere where Cilla would be safe and to be able to earn enough to keep them both.

Staying with Ella was undemanding and she was so grateful for the opportunity to be there. Even so, although Ella said she liked them being there, and that Cilla was a help, not a hindrance, she was determined not to lose Ella's friendship, or upset Ivy, by being there any longer than was absolutely necessary.

When it came to almost the end of February and she still had nowhere to go she began to be really worried and once again pleaded with Jake to try and find somewhere for her because she was having no success whatsoever.

'It will be all right; I've been to see a place that I think will be fine,' he assured her. 'I'll be able to tell you a lot more about it in a few days' time.'

'Really! Oh, it will be wonderful for us to have our own place, won't it, Cilla?' Trixie said smiling down at her as she walked along between them.

Cilla smiled back at her and nodded and squeezed both their hands very tightly.

'It is more or less finalised; there are only one or two details to be sorted out but I didn't want to say anything till it was all settled,' he told her.

Excitedly, the moment they arrived home, Cilla told Ella that they were going to move.

'Oh yes, and when were you thinking of telling me, then?' Ella asked looking from Trixie to Jake enquiringly.

'There's nothing definite yet,' Trixie said quickly. 'Jake's only just told me that he has found somewhere that looks promising but there are still things to be settled. Cilla heard us talking about it and she seems to think it is going to happen right away; you know how easy it is for her to misunderstand things.'

'She hasn't, though, has she, Jake?' Ella said quietly. 'A chap called here while you were out and left a rent book for a place in Bostock Court. He said it was in your name, Jake, not in Trixie's, so what exactly is going on?'

Jake looked uncomfortable. 'I was going to explain it all to you, Mum, as soon as everything was signed and settled and I'd had time to ask Trixie...'

'Explain? What is there to explain,' Ella interrupted, 'except why you've rented rooms in your name instead of Trixie's?'

'He's probably only done it because I've had no luck in getting a place,' Trixie told her quickly. 'I've been telling him that landladies don't seem to like the idea of a young woman and a child moving in; they're probably afraid the rent won't get paid or something, I suppose,' she added with a rueful smile.

'Really!' Ella sounded unconvinced. 'I think there is far more to it than that!'

'If you want a better explanation as to why the rent book is in my name then it's because I'm moving as well,' Jake blustered. 'I thought it was going to be a bit overcrowded here with Ivy and Hadyn as well as both of us all living together. I've talked it over with Hadyn and he agrees with me. He and Ivy want to be here with you, Mum. Hadyn says he'll pay the rent and all the household bills, and if the three of you are living together then in a way you'll be better off. Ivy is delighted by the idea.'

'Did none of you think to ask me if that was what I wanted?' Ella questioned in a piqued voice.

'We were going to talk it through with you, though we were pretty sure that you'd see it made sense. As Trixie said, Cilla has rather jumped the gun.'

'I'm still not clear in my mind what you are planning to do, Jake. Do you mean you and Trixie are going to be living together?' she asked in what seemed to be a rather shocked voice.

'Hold on, I don't understand what's going on either,' Trixie questioned, looking from Ella to Jake in bewilderment.

'Not exactly,' he said hurriedly. 'I'm renting this place. It has three rooms and a kitchen. There are two bedrooms, one for Trixie and Cilla and one for me, and we can share the living room and the kitchen.'

'Sounds a pretty odd set up to me,' Ella told him. 'You didn't say what it was you were going to ask Trixie,' she added.

Jake looked uncomfortable and Trixie continued to stare at them both in confusion.

'I would have thought the best thing would have been for Ivy and Hadyn to take those rooms and for you two to be the ones to stay here,' Ella went on. 'That way you'd have someone to keep an eye on Cilla while you were both at work. I would expect you to get married, of course, but that shouldn't be any problem.'

'Mum!' Jake sounded shocked as he heard Trixie gasp. 'You've got to have someone in love with you before you ask them to marry you,' he mumbled going red in the face with embarrassment, 'and I don't think Trixie feels that way about me.'

'How do you know? Have you ever asked her? You've been dancing attendance on her long enough, so at least she'd know what she was getting,' Ella stated looking straight at Trixie. Although her voice was slightly accusing there was a twinkle in her eye and Trixie felt the colour rushing to her cheeks.

'Yes, yes, yes.' Cilla had been listening in silence to the exchange between them all, but now she was jumping up and down in glee, clapping her hands and hugging first Jake and then Trixie. 'We can all live together because we all love each other,' she told them solemnly. Then she ran across to Ella and hugged her. 'I love you too,' she said with a beaming smile, 'do you love me?'

'Of course I do and that's why I want Jake and Trixie to stay here. I don't want to lose my special little helper, now do I?'

She looked up at Jake, 'You'd better tell Ivy and Hadyn that you agree that they can move into Bostock Court and then arrange for the rent book to be changed to Hadyn's name.'

'I can't do that, it will upset all their plans,' Jake protested.

'It will upset them a great deal more if you don't agree to make the change,' Ella told them dryly. 'They were both here when the chap called and they really liked my idea that they should be the ones to move in there rather than in here.'

'They'll change their minds when they've had time to think about it,' Jake told her.

'Not a bit of it! In fact, if you leave Cilla with me and get yourself along to Bostock Court, you'll find that they're around there right now looking the place over. You know our Ivy, she'll already have all the rooms furnished in her mind by now and you can't go and spoil everything for them when it is so near to them getting married.'

Jake looking questioningly at Trixie. 'So what are we going to do?'

'Well, it has all rather taken my breath away,' she admitted, 'but we can hardly change all your mum's carefully made plans, now can we?'

'You mean...' Jake couldn't speak he was smiling so broadly.

'Ella's opened my eyes to something I should have known a long time ago. I really do love you, Jake,' she admitted shyly.

'And I feel the same way about you. I always have, so it looks as though we'd better do things the way Mum suggests,' he said as he pulled her into his arms and kissed her on the lips.

'Get along with you both, and have a good long heart-to-heart talk and sort things out and tell Hadyn and Ivy they can have the flat,' Ella told them. 'And fix the date for your own wedding; it's high time someone around here saw sense,' she added with a laugh.

'Come to think of it,' she went on when neither of them answered her, 'you could even make it a double wedding at Easter along with Hadyn and Ivy. Cilla could be bridesmaid, couldn't you, pet?' she added, giving Cilla a big hug.

'I think you want to stop trying to be a matchmaker and rushing things, Mother,' Jake told her sternly.

'Rushing things? I don't know what you're talking about; I'm sorting things out for you since you don't seem to be able to do it for yourselves. You two have been as close as peas in a pod for years so, as I've already said, it's high time the pair of you saw some sense.'

As they headed for the door Ella called after them, 'Why don't you bring some fish and chips back with you and a bottle of wine or some beers so that we can celebrate all the changes there are going to be?'

Chapter Thirty-Five

Trixie and Jake were married on the same day and at the same time as Ivy and Hadyn in the imposing St Anthony's Church on the corner of Dryden Street and Scotland Road. Ivy had magnanimously agreed to share her big day now that she and Haydn had the perfect flat to live in.

Her wedding was everything Trixie had dreamed it would be although she had to admit that she felt somewhat overawed by the splendour of St Anthony's with its intricately painted altar statues and marble lecterns.

She felt an overwhelming feeling of gratitude to Ella for pointing out that Jake was the man who really loved her with all his heart and making her aware that although she didn't realise it because she took his help for granted, she'd grown to love him deeply over the years.

Cilla was bridesmaid, walking sedately behind Trixie and Ivy as they made their way down the aisle to the strains of the powerful organ. When they passed their bouquets to her Trixie was afraid for one moment that Cilla was going to drop them but somehow she managed to clutch on to both of them, smiling hugely all the time.

Ella had worked extremely hard, Trixie reflected, not only making wedding dresses for her and Ivy but also a beautiful dress in pale blue satin for Cilla and a smart dress and matching coat for herself.

As they emerged from the church into the spring sunshine the street was packed with well-wishers. In addition to regular members of the congregation who'd known the family for years there was a crowd of Ella's neighbours who had seen both Ivy and Jake grow up. There was also a bevy of girls and women that she and Ivy had both known at the biscuit factory waiting to shower them with confetti.

At Ella's suggestion, and because it was the right thing to do, Trixie had invited both Daisy and Sam.

'You know what I think of Cat'lics and their popish carrying on,' her father said angrily. 'I told you not to have anything to do with that lot and if you defy me and go ahead and marry him then you're no longer a daughter of mine.'

Far from feeling upset because they had no intention of attending Trixie breathed a sigh of relief. That part of her life was over for good; she'd never go back to Virgil Street ever again and she wanted nothing else to do with either of them.

Her one regret was that her mother wasn't there to see her being married. Maggie had always liked Jake and they had got on so well together when he'd helped to look after Cilla and little Jimmy.

Trixie deplored the fact that she had let herself be so infatuated by Andrew that she had caused Jake so much heartache. She should have known, when he had done so much to help her, that it was more than mere friendship and that it was because he had deep feelings for her.

It had taken her a long time to grow up and realise how much she cared for him. There had been times in the past when she'd wondered how she could ever manage without him, but she had only thought of it in terms of him being such a wonderful friend, not that it was an expression of love for her. The feeling of happiness it had brought she'd attributed to the fact that he not only accepted Cilla but was also genuinely fond of her and always anxious to help her in any way he could.

Now she knew better; it had not just been the feeling of safety and security that had made her feel so relaxed and contented in his company but also the love between them that was growing more forceful every day.

She rarely thought about Andrew nowadays but whenever she did she mentally cringed at how stupid she had been to become so infatuated by him that their relationship had eclipsed her true feelings for Jake.

Andrew had never truly loved her and she'd been lucky that things had fizzled out when they had. Her mother had been so right, when she'd said that Jake was worth twenty of him. She'd been able to see right from the start that Jake's feelings were deep and genuine and always would be.

It had taken her a long time to find this out and to realise what a sweet and generous man he was. Now she looked forward to their future together, knowing that he would always be devoted and loving; always ready to shoulder her problems and do anything he could to make life easier for her. Most important of all, he accepted Cilla; she was almost as much family to him as Ivy or his mum.

Living with Ella would be an added bonus. They had always got on well and Ella had always had a special spot in her heart for Cilla. She'd done so much to help bring her on, to teach her things and make sure that she was able to understand and cope with the world around her.

Life with Jake would be very special. From the very first time he kissed her she wished she'd listened to her heart so much earlier. He had a wonderfully warm way of cradling her with his arm that made her feel safe and secure.

When they had a family of their own Ella would be there to help and advise her; just like her own mother would have done.

They'd grown so much closer in the last few weeks, ever since she'd been aware of the feelings she had for him and he had for her. It was as if all the shadows and sadness had gone from her life. The awakening of her sense that at last she'd found true love gave her a grand and glorious feeling, and she constantly found herself staring at him in silent joy.

It was as if she and Jake were in some wonderful magical world; every kiss and every embrace entwined them closer together. There were no secrets between them and she never had to struggle to get his attention because she never felt neglected; their laughter or even casual remarks took on a new meaning. He'd become the most important person in her life apart from Cilla.

As, one by one, the guests and well-wishers started to depart Trixie could feel the excitement mounting inside her. Quite soon now, when all the celebrating was over, when Hadyn and Ivy had said goodbye and gone home to their flat and Cilla and Ella were both tucked up in bed, she and Jake would finally be alone.

That was the moment when they could

both express their deepest feelings for each other and when, at long last, they would finally know the bliss of complete fulfilment.

This Large Print Book, for people
who cannot read normal print,
is published under the auspices of

THE ULVERSCROFT FOUNDATION